END OF THE LINE

SHIRLEY HUGHES

ABOUT THE AUTHOR

Shirley Hughes has 55 years of experience and knowledge of the opal industry under her belt.

Shirley was first employed in a small, end-of-the-line town in south-western Queensland.

In 1979 Shirley moved to Western Australia. She lives in Western Australia with her son, Russell.

This book is dedicated to my son, Russell

CONTENTS

PART I

BROLGA

TC and Sam sat on the old, paint-chipped bench stool on the Curloo Railway Station. They were hot and tired and dishevelled. Excited, in a way, with curious anticipations as to where they were going and what awaited them when they got there.

They were a strange pair to be such close friends. Sam, whose real name was Samantha, was tall and gangly. She rarely gave a thought to her appearance; couldn't care less. Her hair was all over the place like a mad woman's breakfast. She wore loose, daggy clothes, usually jeans and a man's shirt, often no shoes. On dress-up occasions, she would wear a pair of thongs.

Sam swore a lot and had all the confidence in the world. She would talk to anyone, black, brown, or brindle, young, old, or indifferent. She never feared rejection from anyone. On the rare occasions that her conversation or attention was rejected, she would simply shrug her shoulders and say, 'Oh, bugger off! Don't know why I bothered, anyway,' then walk off. Everyone said Sam should have been a male. She sure acted like one.

Without looking at TC, Sam said, 'Bloody hot, isn't it, TC?'

TC rolled her eyes. 'Please don't, Sam.'

'Oh, stuff it. You're such a prude,' muttered Sam as she stood up, stretched, and wandered off in the direction of an elderly, grey-haired, part-Aboriginal man who was sweeping red dust off the long, grey concrete railway platform.

'When's the bloody train to Brolga leaving?' enquired Sam of the old porter.

'You mean the Flying Flea, luv?' he replied.

'What's the Flying Flea? Look at me, will you. I'm too bloody big to ride on the back of a 'crawling' flea, let alone a flying one.'

'No, no, no, lovey, we call it the Flying Flea because it's so small. Only two carriages, and it travels so fast it literally flies over those old railway lines.'

'Thank God for that' said Sam. 'Wouldn't want to have a crash landing,' she laughed. 'You still didn't tell me when the FF is leaving.'

'Don't worry, luv. It'll go when the driver and guard recover from last night's hang-over. Big Two-Up game last night. Illegal; still, the coppers close their eyes. Just fun, luv. Just fun. A lot of men get together, drink a lot of grog, while they bet on heads or tails.'

'Bloody great. Thanks a lot.' She strolled back to TC, who had overheard the conversation and wore an expression of terrified disbelief.

'I want to go home, Sam.'

'Forget it, TC. Nothing back there for us.'

Sam slumped down on the bench. 'Hope those bastards' hangovers aren't too bad. I want to get moving. Brolga, here we come.'

As an afterthought, she added, 'We'll make it big one day, TC. If we don't, I'll bloody well kill both of us.'

'Speak for yourself, Sam. If I want to commit suicide, I'll do it myself.'

What seemed like an eternity later, the Flea crawled to a stop alongside the platform. Sam and TC were the first of the passengers to board. As they did, the old porter said softly to himself 'Good luck, kids.'

¶

As the girls settled themselves into the small passenger carriage of the Flea, Jake, along with three of his mates, were at the rear of the Curloo Hotel packing their gear into the trunk of Jake's car. They were all feeling lousy from too much booze and too many cigarettes. They also felt drained as a result of their sexual exploits with the barmaids they'd latched onto after the Two-Up game.

Jake, as usual, was in command. They always travelled in his car at his expense; so, that gave him rank.

'Come on, hurry up. Want to get home before the Flea. The Greeks said there was some new talent coming in tonight.'

One of the said, 'Don't know about you lot, but a woman's the last thing on my mind after that wildcat I scored last night.' They all laughed as they climbed into the car.

'Let's hit it,' said Jake. 'Gotta beat the Flea. Perhaps my dream girl is on it,' he laughed.

'Much bloody chance of that as there is of a donkey winning the Melbourne Cup,' quipped one of his mates.

'You're too particular, Jake. Anyway, you already have most Brolga belles lusting after you. Leave a few for your mates.'

'Never know,' said Jake as he pulled his Fairlane to a stop outside the hotel office. 'Let's pay the bill, grab a carton, and piss off.'

Jake Carmichael was the most eligible young man in Brolga. He was six-three, lean with thick, black, curly hair and sideburns. He wore his hair short with the front pulled down in a slight peak over his forehead. He was always immaculately dressed, thanks to the fact his family owned four businesses, including a fashionable drapery store, in Brolga. He had managed the businesses since his father had prematurely passed away when Jake was just nineteen. He loved Fords and traded in every time a new model Fairlane was produced.

His mother, Thelma, had never participated in the running of the business. It was a full-time job looking after her six children, the oldest of whom was Jake. Consequently, Jake had free reign over the business and spent money when and as he saw fit.

What can you expect from a kid his age, thought the people of Brolga. His father spoiled him rotten from the day he was born.

Jake had been a promising junior accountant with the Commonwealth Bank when his father died. His ability and speed with figures were uncanny. That, coupled with his personality, would have surely seen him reach high places within the banking business had it not been for his father's untimely death, after which he resigned and took on the running of the shop. This suited him fine because there were no restrictions whatsoever. He could do what and when he chose. Apart from everything else, he had his choice of the cream of the crop regarding young Brolgaite females.

Jake and his friends left Curloo for Brolga. Jake was driving, and the speedo hit a hundred before they left the paved road and hit the bulldust track just a few miles west of town. The car swerved, spun around, and faced Curloo again as he jammed on the brakes.

'Oh, shit,' his friends yelled. One of the boys had just bitten the cap off a beer bottle and was taking his first mouthful as the car hit the soft, red dirt and spun. 'Know the arrival of the Flea is the major attraction of the week, but this is ridiculous,' he muttered. He then proceeded to wipe the spilled beer off his shirt with his left hand. Still clutching the beer bottle with his right, he raised it to his mouth and took another swig.

¶

As Jake regained his sense of direction and righted the car towards Brolga, somewhere in Brisbane Vance and Delores Callahan were loading their sons, Jonathon and Andrew, into the family station wagon. Although Andrew was only a few months old, Delores was pregnant again.

'Are you drunk, Vance?' snapped Delores. 'Every time I leave, you always come after me. Why?'

'Why do you always come back to me when I come after you?' replied Vance.

'Forget it, Vance! Two things I do know is that you are not driving and that bottle of rum goes.'

'You forget it, Delores. You drive. The rum stays.'

'Vance, you make me so angry! Sometimes I hate you.'

'Good! Rack off, then.' Dolores ignored him and proceeded to make her children comfortable.

'Where to now?' she asked as she positioned herself behind the wheel of the car.

'West, Delores. No further than Curloo. If I'm not awake by then, wake me.' As Vance fell asleep, he was thinking. *Why would she drive further than Curloo? That's where we live, isn't it? Sometimes she asks stupid bloody questions.*

¶

Brolga, the end of the railway line into the west. Anything and everything arrived in Brolga by train, be it furniture, clothing, mail orders from big department stores in the cities, medicine, beer, hard liquor for the Greeks' pubs, fresh, canned, and frozen produce for the one grocery store. All came by train. Even Australia Post used the train as a means of transporting mail in and out of Brolga. On rare occasions when there was an emergency at Brolga's tiny hospital, the Flying Doctor was called in. Depending on his mood that day, he would sometimes bring the mail with him from Curloo.

Anything addressed to anyone west of Brolga was offloaded and carried by trucks to its final destination, often as far as Birdsville near the border of New South Wales, South Australia and Queensland. The trucks made a run twice a week and were always welcomed by the station people as their only regular means of receiving long-awaited goods and general news from the rest of the world.

Brolga boasted a sign just east of the town. The sign announced, "Welcome to Brolga—population of town and surrounding district 540."

Just two days after its erection a couple of months previously, local louts scratched on the bottom of the illustrious sign, "50 dogs, 75 cats, and the odd, stray brolga. ENTER AT YOUR OWN RISK". Brolgaites over the age of twenty-five ignored the boys' artistic genius and thought, *Silly, young pricks. They'll grow up one day, hopefully.*

The arrival of the Flea twice a week was the source of some excitement to most of the people of Brolga, especially the young. The only other distraction from the total boredom was the movies shown at the Brolga Theatre three times weekly. On Wednesday night, they would show two films. On Saturdays and Sundays, two different films would play on both nights. Often Brolga people, especially the young, would go to see the same movies two nights in a row just for something to do.

The Flea arrived Wednesdays and Saturdays; so, if it was late getting into Brolga, it meant the movies would start late. During rare flood times when the Flea couldn't get through due to flooding rivers and creeks, there were no movies at all. In fact, very little of anything.

The town centre was one block long. It consisted of three pubs, all owned by the Romeo brothers, the picture theatre and two cafes, also owned by Greeks, a small bank building and two drapery stores, one old and Carmichael's new one on the left. On the right, there was the bakery, a tiny dress shop, the older drapery store, Greek-owned modern newsagency, a vacant shop which adjoined the newsagency and had a leased sign in bright purple letters across the glass frontage, another small bank, and a couple of flats.

There was a median strip that ran the length of the block. Located on the strip, directly opposite the Empire Hotel, was a long, council-erected park bench. The locals referred to this as 'the Seat of Knowledge' because every night a half dozen or so of the male town elders would gather on the sacred seat. Most of them escaped to this location to avoid nagging wives, whinging kids, and after-dinner boredom. Apart from those factors, they wanted to keep up with what was going on in the Greeks' pubs, the town's youths' activities, and generally reminisce about days gone by. They were also always hoping to view some drama to recall in years to come. Brolga history in the making, so to say. After the pubs closed, they would make their way home, wake their wives if they were asleep, explicitly relay every detail of the evening's action in the hub of town, then go to bed conjuring up ways to embellish the true facts before they spread the news to anyone who would listen the next day.

¶

As the Flea approached Brolga, Sam stuck her head out the window and yelled into the wind, 'This is so dammed exciting!' She looked over her shoulder. 'We're almost there, kid. Life's bloody short, then we die.' TC grimaced and shook her head. Sam saw the look on TC's face and sat down again.

Jesus, we're an odd match, she thought. *Regular Laurel and Hardy. TC's five-two; I'm five-ten. She weighs a hundred and fifteen; I'm a hundred and sixty. She's got big tits; I've got none. I swear like a drunken sailor; she wouldn't say* shit *for a hundred quid. She's a dreamer, thinks she's going somewhere; I'm a realist, know I'm going nowhere. She likes pretty clothes; I couldn't care less. She curls her hair; hell, I hardly ever bother to brush mine. I'm not frightened of anything; TC's scared of the dark. She'd starve rather than steal a loaf of bread or ask anyone for a penny; I'd not only pinch the loaf of bread, I'd rip off a dozen or so pies to go with it; if some bastard was silly enough to give me money, I'd take it. Survival of the bloody fittest in this world. Wish I didn't worry about TC so much. She'll have to toughen up sooner or later. Life does that to people. Oh! Stuff it,* as she jumped up again and resumed looking out one of the Flea's windows.

TC sat silently and observed her friend's back, along with the other four passengers, none of whom appeared enthralled as Brolga came closer. In one corner was slumped a man who had obviously recently consumed an abundance of hard liquor. The carriage reeked of rum, which secreted from the pores of his skin. Whenever he stirred, he took a large swig from the almost-empty bottle he clutched tightly. Sam had commented, 'Poor bugger.' TC agreed with Sam and pondered as to what had occurred during his life to render him in his present condition.

Also in the tiny carriage was an extremely overweight Aboriginal woman with two small children. From the conversation the girls had overheard, it appeared that the woman was the grandmother of the little ones. She had made the trek to the city to rescue her grandchildren from the grasps of her alcoholic son and daughter-in-law. The smaller of the two children shook all the time as he cuddled closely to his grandmother.

'You with Granny now, Joey. Don't ya worry. No one to hurt ya anymore. Granny take care of all of ya.'

Joey's sister was asleep, covered with an old blanket, on the other side of Granny. She slept with her head on her grandmother's lap and hugged her knees.

The driver of the Flea activated the whistle as the tiny train approached Brolga Railway Station. Sam, with her head still out the window, yelled, 'Bloody hell, we're finally here. End of the bloody line. Look at all these people. Looks like Times-effing Square.'

Within seconds of the Flea's pulling to a stop, the Aboriginal woman and her grandchildren were on the platform and surrounded by a horde of Aboriginals in all shapes, sizes, and ages who were all apparently relatives, according to the loud conversation taking place amidst the laughter, hugs, and kisses.

'Shit,' said Sam. 'You'd think the old lady had climbed bloody Mt Everest to rescue the kids, the way that mob's carrying on.' The man smelling like the Bundaberg Rum distillery alighted from the train and quickly disappeared into the crowd. 'Geeze, that old lady's lot disappeared quickly,' remarked Sam, as the girls collected their meagre luggage. 'Faster than a bloody speeding bullet.' Sam had no idea how fast a speeding bullet travelled; she'd heard it somewhere, probably in a John Wayne movie, liked the way it sounded, so used the phrase whenever she could. 'Let's get the effing off this Flea, kid. You go first; you're better looking than me.'

TC rolled her eyes and sighed, 'Okay, Sam, let's go. As you said before, it's the end of the line. If we want to go any further, looks like we have to walk.'

The girls were both dressed in black pedal-pushers with matching pink blouses. The blouses were hand-embroidered all over in black silk thread with *Elvis Forever, Fats Domino, Jerry Lee, I love rock and roll, Elvis is King, Little Richard, Chuck Berry*, and *Rock, Rock, Rock*. Sam's cousins had embroidered her blouse for her. They had a huge argument when Sam had insisted on having *Life Sucks* in huge letters in the middle of her man's shirt, which she had pinched from her brother. It had been white, so Sam dyed it pink. She wore it hanging out over her pedal-pushers and had bare feet. TC wore her blouse tucked in with a gold belt and gold flat shoes with little gold bows on the front.

'These outfits might be shit hot in the city, TC, but I think we'll look a bit out of place amongst the local yokels.'

TC looked over her shoulder at Sam. 'Too late now.' They stepped down onto the platform. A sea of faces stared at them.

Sam nudged TC and whispered, 'Check my effing face, will you? Has the bastard turned green?' TC ignored Sam and looked straight ahead into the crowd without really looking at anyone or anything.

¶

Jake and his friends were there when the Flea arrived that night. 'Holy shit. There she is,' said Jake as TC and Sam walked towards them.

'I told you bastards I was going to meet my dream girl tonight. Here she is right in front of us.'

Jake had been engaged to the daughter of the Chairman of Brolga until he caught her having it off with his best friend. Wasn't just the fact that they were screwing. It had hurt a lot that they did it in the back seat of Jake's own car. He hadn't been to another dance since that night when he'd noticed them both missing from the hall, gone looking for them, and found them at it in his bloody car. He'd said nothing, returned inside, and mustered the help of a couple of his friends, who went back to his car with him. Jake then had a loud argument with his fiancée, who threw the two-carat diamond ring in his face as she fled his car. He picked it up, drove to the creek, where he sat in deep thought for a while. He got out of the car, walked to the creek bank, and mumbled to himself, 'Women suck,' as he threw the ring into the muddy water.

Often young Brolga people went to see the same movie two nights in a row just for something to do. The Seat of Knowledge regulars never attended the movies. They always met the Flea and then returned to their favourite haunt to observe the goings-on in the Empire pub.

The crowd on Brolga Railway Station dispersed, most following the Empire Theatre's projectionist, who had in his possession his precious reels of film. Jake and his mates headed straight for the pub. Jake's confidence motored on high, as usual. They swaggered jokingly, all looking forward to the rest of the night. As usual, they would drink until the pub closed. Then they would pick up the nurses coming off duty at the Brolga Hospital, and head for the creek, where they would party 'til dawn, sleep for a couple of hours, go home, kiss their mothers good morning (like saying 'Look, Mum, I'm still alive, aren't you lucky?'), take a shower, dress in their macho rugby-league football uniforms, and hopefully run onto the field appearing to the opposing visiting teams as if they'd been training forever, and slept like babies for weeks.

Comfortably ensconced on the Seat of Knowledge, the elders watched with interest as Jake's group entered the hotel bar. Old Jock, the most vocal of the select group, said, 'Wish I was that age again. Silly, young buggers don't know what life's about yet. Can't put old heads on young bloody shoulders. Shame, isn't it? World would be a bloody marvellous place if the young knew in advance what it's taken us all these years to learn.' All nodded in agreement.

¶

Sam and TC were still standing on the now-almost-deserted railway platform. They had been told someone would meet them. They could see some slow movement at the far end of the now dimly-lit station where a couple of figures appeared to be unloading from the goods car. In the background, they could also just make out the image on an old truck.

TC began crying. 'I'm terrified, Sam. I want to go home. Please, let's go home.'

'What the hell, TC. Get real. We're here and that is that.' Sam couldn't look at TC, whom she knew was on the verge of hysterics now that the reality of being stranded at the end of the line had hit home. Sam threw her shoulders back.

'We'll be alright, kid. I'm going to ask these assholes what the hell's going on.' Sam walked towards the men with an air of authority, even though for once she almost lacked any confidence whatsoever. 'Stuff it,' she mumbled to herself, 'I'm not frightened of any bastard.'

As she got closer, she could see that most of the cartons being offloaded were stamped "Romeos—Brolga" and were methodically being stacked on the back of the old, green, tray-backed truck. Sam looked back at TC, who was dragging their luggage towards her. TC didn't appear to be crying now. Sam said, 'Thank you, Lord, for that.' Then, 'Holy hell. TC's the bloody religious one, and here I am thanking the Lord. What a bloody mess. Wish I could be more like TC. Also wish I could stop saying *bloody*. TC never does. Feel like I'm lost in a bloody 'Sorry, Lord' desert. Got to stop saying *bloody*. Got to.'

TC was alongside Sam by now. Sam was rendered speechless when she heard TC demand of the man dressed in a green shirt and trousers with "Romeo Brothers" embroidered on his shirt pocket, 'Why the hell didn't you meet us? You wouldn't work for me. It's taken you an hour to do fifteen minutes of work. Slow motion, that's for sure. 'Bad enough for us to have to come to this place. We've come a long way. Been scared almost senseless by the trip on the Flying Flea, and you leave us standing around here like shags on a rock, without ever so much as a welcoming hello.' My name is TC and my friend is Sam. May I suggest we get going NOW.'

Bloody hell thought Sam. *Didn't think she had it in her.*

The last of the boxes labelled "Romeos—Brolga" were quickly loaded onto the truck. The man in green then threw the girls' bags on the top and ushered TC and Sam into the vehicle's cabin. He walked briskly around the truck, climbed into the driver's seat, turned the ignition key, pulled the gear lever, and the truck rattled into motion.

Sam and TC sat silently. The driver turned towards TC and said quietly, 'You're too bloody vocal, girl.' He had a smile on his face as he added, 'My name's Peter. Please don't tell the bosses I was slacking. It's just that life gets tedious hanging around the pub all the time. They work me from daylight to midnight and rage at me all the time. Only chance I get for some idle conversation and a break is twice a week when the Flea comes in.'

TC remained silent but felt sorry for the man if his story was true. Sam couldn't restrain herself, so asked, 'Why don't you leave if you're so bloody unhappy?'

'Jack and Bert are my cousins. They came to Australia many years ago when they were boys. They had nothing. Now they own most of Brolga. As a favour to my mother, their aunt, they brought me out here. I love

Australia and my cousins. I understand I have to work hard; otherwise, I will shame my mother. I have to earn money to send back to my mother and family in Crete. Please don't tell my cousins I was enjoying myself.'

The girls looked at him and chorused, 'Don't worry.'

As the old truck pulled to a stop at the rear of the Empire Hotel, Peter walked around and opened the door for them. Sam and TC stepped down from the truck. Both girls thought of Peter as their first friend in Brolga.

Sam said, 'Thanks for the lift, Pete.'

TC nodded as Jack and Bert Romeo emerged from the back verandah of the hotel. They were smiling profusely. Both were immaculately attired in expensive imported suites—Bert in grey, Jack in black. Both had silver hair and looked as if they were very well fed. Both were thinking, *Little one for the bar. Lot of money to be made there with all the young Brolga studs filling the bar every night to ogle and dream. Put the tall one in the house.*

Pia, Jack's wife, and Mara, Bert's wife, were waiting. They were both dressed in black. Both of them were childless, so they always wore black as a sign of grief for not having given their respective husbands a child to carry on the Romeo name and business empire. They both felt a great resentment towards the young girls who came to work in the Romeo Brothers' hotels.

Pia was thinking, *Bet Jack puts the short one in the bar and the tall one in the house.*

Mara was wondering as to which one of the girls had called about the jobs. She'd wager anything it had been the tall girl. The small one looked sad while the other one didn't appear to care.

'Good heavens, those clothes they are wearing are revolting.'

TC squeezed Sam's hand and wished she'd never agreed to Sam calling about the jobs they'd seen advertised in the Brisbane paper–

"Romeo's Brolga Hotels require one barmaid and one housemaid. Travel expenses paid if required. Will be deducted from first month's pay. Refunded after 12 months. Please phone."

Preceded by Pia and Mara, Jack instructed the girls to follow them to the office. Pia and Mara stepped into the small room and observed their husbands' backs as they entered the bar. TC and Sam, carrying their bags, brought up the rear. As they were about to pass the office door, Pia beckoned them in.

Jake was heading for the "gents", which was situated to the left of the office. He caught a glimpse of TC as she disappeared into Romeo's money-counting room. 'Obviously no loot in there now; otherwise, the door would be locked. Bet old Pia and Mara are about to give those poor buggers the third degree. Small one's a cutie, though. Dress her up. I bet she'd be something else.'

Brad Lester was also on his way to the men's ablution block, glanced into the Empire's office as he passed by, and was immediately in love with Sam. Brad had always felt a sense of insecurity and not belonging in Brolga. He was extremely handsome; and, although his mother was half Aboriginal and his father as black as the ace of spades, Brad was a white as any other non-Aboriginal in Brolga. Every time the elders on the Seat of Knowledge saw Brad, they would discuss the phenomenon.

'Pretty bloody incredible,' old Jock would say. 'Old Mrs Lester doesn't seem like the sort to play around, does she? That bloody Brad looks as white as us. Buggered if I can figure it out. Strange. Really strange. His brother's okay. Black, though, isn't he? Oh, well, nothin' surprises me anymore.' Jock's friends always nodded in agreement while keeping their eyes focused on the Empire, waiting for something newsworthy to occur.

Sam and TC stood listening to Pia Romeo. They saw her as the most elegantly dressed lady they had ever seen and felt somewhat in awe of her and totally out of place there in their "Elvis Forever" outfits. Pia appeared not to notice their attire as she directed them to fill out forms relevant to the terms of their employment.

'TC, you will work here at the Empire in the bar. Sam, you will work as a housemaid and alternate between our three hotels. You start at 6 am, Sam. You will be in the bar at 9.45, TC. Your regular work rosters will be available in the kitchen tomorrow morning. You are now dismissed.

Please wait until Peter comes to show you to the staff quarters, which I'm sure you'll find quite adequate.'

The girls left the office. TC was frantic. Sam placed her arm around her friend's shoulder.

'Luck of the draw, TC.'

'I don't want to be in this awful place, Sam. Mumma would kill me if she knew I was so much as thinking of working as a barmaid.'

'I know, I'm supposed to be the barmaid, you the housemaid. These effing Greeks aren't stupid, TC. You're prettier than me, so they'll display you in the bar and hide me in the house.' Sam was furious. TC sighed and dropped her shoulders in resignation to the situation.

'Here we go, TC. Looks like we're about to get our first glimpse of the "adequate" staff quarters.' Pete picked up their things and led them across the backyard.

⁋

Bert Romeo closed the doors of the Empire, everyone ordered one for the road, and the Seat of Knowledge patrons stood up and dispersed in different directions. 'Nothing exciting tonight,' said Jock. 'Bloody right there,' agreed his mates.

⁋

The staff quarters were located in the huge backyard of the hotel, about fifty yards to the left of the main building. The quarters were housed in a wooden building which was perched on very low, capped-concrete stumps. There was a door at either end of the dilapidated structure which had pushed-out, wooden-framed and cracked-glass windows, which, due to their warped condition, could not be properly closed. The two doors also did not close adequately. There was a narrow, splintered, wooden verandah about eight feet wide, off which six very small rooms ran side by side. At one end of the verandah were a tiny shower cubicle and a separate toilet. Each bedroom contained two narrow, collapsible iron-and-wire bunks with fire mattresses about four inches thick and one pillow for each bunk. Ripped and stained curtains hung over one small, push-out, wooden window. The linoleum on the floors was torn, exposing large sections of bare boards beneath. On either side of each room was a makeshift wardrobe ingeniously constructed of sawn tea chest lids perched atop two narrow strips of dowelling, which had been nailed to the walls, side and back. Pieces of elastic were strung across as hanging rails. Torn, threadbare curtains, with elastic threaded through the top, were stretched around the tea chest lids. Supposedly, these curtains were to keep the dust off the staff's clothing. Between the bunks and below the window was an old, chipped chest-of-drawers. Most of the drawers had no handles, just pieces of wire looped through the holes where the handles or knobs used to be.

There were two empty rooms in the quarters building. Sam and TC chose the one with the least number of tears and holes in the curtains, as the window in both rooms would not close properly.

'Well, colour us lucky, TC. This place isn't just adequate; it's effing paradise. Like to see those bloody, stuck-up Romeo bitches live in this sumptuous luxury.' Adequate, my ass. Not fit for pigs.'

TC was making her bed with the two thin sheets, pillowcase, and grey blanket, which had been on the end of each bunk.

'Looks as if we're worse than pigs, Sam. I'm going to unpack, have a shower, and try to get some sleep. The way I see it, we've got no options. Got no money to get out of this God-forsaken place. At least, they'll feed us here. For now, we'll just have to put up with things. Tell you what, though, Sam; when I get out of here, I am never going to live in a dump like this again!'

'Shit, tell me about it, TC. I'm only nineteen and feel as if I've effing hit skid row already. I'll take a shower while you unpack.' She grabbed the towel and soap from her bag and left the room. She was back in a couple of minutes.

'TC, the water smells like rotten eggs! Not only that; it's boiling bloody hot! Stuff it, TC! We've got to get out of here!' Sam yelled loudly.

'What's all this noise about?' snapped a voice from the doorway of

TC and Sam's newly acquired room. They both looked up to see a very small, very short woman of around sixty years of age. She had reddish hair, with grey at the front and sides, which hung halfway down her back. She wore a floral cotton dressing gown with frills around the sleeves, neck, and arms, and an angry look on her face.

'The water stinks!' replied Sam. 'It's also too hot.'

'What do you expect, girl; you're in bore-water country. The minerals in it make it smell, and it's hot because it comes straight out of the ground. If you want to take a shower, you have to turn on the cooled water tap outside first. Only way to get cold water here is to store it in a tank or put it in a fridge. Now stop making so much noise. Some people need sleep. My name's Jess. People say I've been here forever.'

'I'm Sam. Been here about two hours,' said Sam.

TC smiled at Jess. 'Sorry about the noise. I'm TC.'

¶

Brolgaites referred to the Empire Hotel's senior barmaid as "Old Jess". To them it did appear as if she'd been there forever. Jock and his elder friends often talked about the wild affair Jess and Jack Romeo had shared years before. One day while Pia Romeo was inspecting the staff quarters, she knocked on Jess' door and then opened it to find Jess and Jack in the throes of passionate love-making. There followed an incredible scene with Pia screaming in Greek, Jess cowering against a wall, attempting to cover her nakedness with a sheet with "Romeo Brothers Hotel" emblazoned in large print across one edge, and Jack slowly and methodically dressing himself. Pia was crying, Jess was crying, and, as Jack adjusted his fly buttons, he yelled at both of them, 'Shut up.' Pia picked a statue off Jess' dressing table and threw it at Jack. It hit him spot on in the middle of the forehead. Jack fell to the floor immediately. The two women fell into each other's arms. They thought he was dead. They hated each other; however, both loved Jack desperately. Pia and Jess began screaming, Pia in Greek and Jess in English.

People came from everywhere to see what the commotion was about.

A staff member pushed the door of Jess' room wide open. No one could believe the scene in front of them. Jack was out cold on the floor with a trickle of blood flowing slowly from his forehead and down his face. Pia, in her usual black, was clinging to Jess, who was only covered by a sheet. They were huddled in a corner, crying profusely and sharing the edges of the sheet to wipe their tears away. Pieces of shattered porcelain were scattered all over the room. Both women were hoping for even the slightest movement from Jack.

'Holy shit,' yelled someone, 'better get the bloody doctor.'

'Get real,' said one of the barmaids. 'He's in the pub, drunk as a bastard.'

'Better call the matron, then. At least, she'll keep her mouth closed.'

Jack opened his eyes, rolled them back, and slurred with as much authority as he could muster, 'Call no one. Everyone except Jess and my wife get the hell out of here. Not a word of this to anyone or I'll kill the lot of you.' Pia and Jess both fainted. Their beloved was alive. By the time the pub closed that night the story was the talk of the town.

Old Jock and his cronies discussed the incident a thousand times but never could solve the mystery as to how and why Jess got to keep her job and Pia and Jess seemed to get along so well for the past twenty-five years or so since the day Pia had hit Jack with the statue. Simple fact was, after Jack woke up, told everyone to go, and realised the women had fainted, he slowly pulled himself up from the floor and stumbled to the verandah of the quarters where he found a bucket filled with water from the cooling tank. He returned to Jess' room and threw the water over his wife and Jess. They both woke up immediately.

As they did, he roared, 'Jess, our affair is over. Pia, I will send you back to Greece if you ever from this moment on mention what happened here today. Jess, you have a job here for life. You will never have me again. You may hate each other. That's fine with me. Just don't let anyone, including me, be aware of it.' Neither woman nor Jack ever again spoke about what the locals referred to as 'the day Jack's dick died.'

¶

Sam was five minutes late on her first day on the job at the Empire.

Stuff'em, she thought. *Bastards won't sack me; I owe them ten quid for my train fare.*

TC, on the other hand, was ready one hour before she was due to start. She had dressed in one of her two black work skirts, her only white blouse, under the collar of which she had tied a pink satin ribbon with a discreet little bow at the front. Her hair fell in a long ponytail at the back with a ribbon the same colour as her flat shoes.

TC gingerly approached the door to the bar as Sam slid down the polished rail of the elegant, winding staircase to the upper level of the hotel.

'Lambs to the slaughter, eh, TC? Those lecherous bastards will love you. You look like bloody Sandra Dee. As for me, kid, way to go. Finished my work already. Think I'll sit in the kitchen for the rest of the morning and gossip with the old chef.'

'Good for you, Sam. My mother will kill me.'

'She doesn't have to know, TC.'

'I'm scared witless, Sam. By the way, my mother knows everything.'

'Oh, wake up, TC! You're such a bloody limp-wrist sometimes!' Sam swaggered off towards the kitchen, flicking the feather duster she carried here and there as she moved. TC knocked on the bar room door, which was quickly opened by Jess.

'Good girl, you're a bit early. Come in, then; don't just stand there. You done this work before?'

'No,' replied TC, who felt as if she was about to collapse.

'All right, you've got a damned lot to learn and not too much time to learn it in. This dump will be wall to wall with hung-over assholes within half an hour. Fill that bucket, grab that mop, and go over the floor. Peter's already done it once but the joint still smells like a brothel after Saturday night's trading.' TC wondered what a brothel was, but she didn't dare ask.

TC couldn't control her tears any longer. Jess, whose expression had been stern and her voice abrupt, put her hand on TC's shoulder and softly said, 'Don't worry, luv. I'll look after you; I'll teach you the ropes.'

TC took a handkerchief from the pocket of her skirt and dried her eyes. Somehow, she felt safe with Jess.

'Thank you, Jess you are very kind. I'll do my best. Now I'd best get this floor done.' Jesse thought to herself, *I like this kid. Have to look out for her. What with all the mongrels that come into this place, I'll have to have eyes in the back of my head. Poor little bugger, don't know how she ended up in this hole. Bet it's got something to do with that Sam. Got a gut feeling, if I'd had a daughter, she'd be a lot like this one.* From then on, Jess protected TC, and TC respected Jess.

At exactly 10 am, when the voice on the radio announced, "The time is ten o'clock, and the Commonwealth Bank is open for business", Bert Romeo opened the door of the Empire.

¶

On their arrival in Curloo, Vance and Delores Callahan had a loud and vocal argument orchestrated by Vance.

'Stop shouting, Vance, you'll wake the boys.'

'No wonder they're sleeping. Poor little buggers must have been terrified, the way you drive.'

'How the hell would you know? You were in a drunken stupor and, I might add, clutching that rum bottle like a man possessed.'

'Up yours, Delores,' yelled Vance. 'I'll drink if I want to when I want to.'

Delores was tired after driving so far. She had taken her time because of the children. What she had really wanted to do was plant her foot, fly off a bridge in the hope that her drunken, sleeping husband would drown. Miraculously, the children and she would escape. She would meet a billionaire who would fall desperately in love with her, accept her children as his own, and they would all live happily ever after in an idyllic booze-free environment. Delores loved Vance, but sometimes he was just too much.

'I'm tired, Vance. Are you capable of carrying Jonathon into the house? I'll take Andrew.'

'Of course, I'm capable. By the way, Delores, we're going to Brolga.'

Delores was about to pick up her baby. 'We're what?'

'Going to live in Brolga. I'm opening a new shop there.'

'I'm not going, Vance.'

'Oh, yes, you are.'

'You can't make me,' replied Delores as she carried Andrew and guided the now wide-awake Jonathon into the house.

'Oh, yes, I can.'

'How? Just tell me how you can make me go and live in a place like Brolga?' Vance put his face very close to hers and smiled.

'Because you love the money, Delores.'

'When are we leaving?' She settled her baby into his cot, then covered Jonathon, who was already on his bed and asleep again.

'I'm going tomorrow. You tidy things up here. I'll tell you when I want you and the boys to come.'

Vance collected a glass from the kitchen cupboard and poured a drink from the bottle of Bundaberg Rum he'd brought in from the car. As he did, he thought, *Knew the money bit would get her. If ever there's been a woman born to shop, it's been Delores. Anyway, she's pregnant again; that'll keep her off my back for a while. Don't know why I got married. I'm lousy husband material. Doesn't matter. Seemed like the right thing at the time.*

'Isn't it a bit early to be drinking that?'

'Probably; however, I'm thirsty. When I've finished this bottle, I'll go get another one, that is, if I'm still thirsty.'

'Sometimes you make me sick, Vance.'

'Sometimes you make me sick, too, Delores. Why don't you go to bed? Have a sleep.'

'All right, Vance, I can see there's no point in trying to talk to you when you're like this. I'll talk to you later.'

Don't like your chances, thought Vance, as he threw down the rest of his drink and immediately poured another one.

I'll be on my way to Brolga before you and the boys wake up. Got a feeling about Brolga. Think I'll make a lot of money there. Mind you, have to make a bloody lot of money to keep Delores happy. Doesn't worry me, though. She seems to close her eyes to my indiscretions, so I'll pretend to close my eyes to her spending habits. Long as I can afford it, that is.

Vance poured drink after drink until the bottle was empty, collected the car keys, staggered outside, spoke to the car as he seated himself and ignited the engine. 'Car,' he said, 'take me to the nearest pub, then point us in the direction of Brolga.' As he pulled into the driveway of the Curloo Hotel, he looked down at his crumpled clothes. *Oh, shit,* he thought, *I feel like crap. Appears to me, I look like crap also.*

'Bottle of Bundy, mate' he requested as he approached the small serving window at the rear of the Curloo.

'Sure, mate' replied the man behind the window. 'Want some ice as well?'

'Not bloody likely. Going to Brolga. Be warm water before I get half way. Give me some Coke, though. A swig of Bundy and a swig of Coke sounds like rum and Coke to me.'

'Sounds like rum and Coke to me, too, mate. Here ya go. Have a safe trip. Take it easy, mate. See ya next time.'

Wouldn't count on it, thought Vance, as his right foot hit the accelerator of the Holden. *Don't think I'll be back to Curloo for a while. Lucky if I make it to Brolga.*

§

Vance enjoyed his drinking. He didn't realise that it gave him an escape route from reality for the duration of his binge. He was finding of late that the binges were becoming more frequent, lasting longer, and the bottles were emptying faster. Vance's mind became sharper and sharper and his memory more vivid when he was drinking. On reaching a certain level of intake, he would undergo a distinct change of personality. The smart-talking, quick-witted, often-sarcastic, and on occasion foul-mouthed, Vance would appear. This Vance always had to be the centre of attention. He would at times become insulting and sometimes verbally cruel, if necessary, to achieve his goal. His drinking sprees usually lasted until Delores packed up and left him. Vance would yell 'Good bloody riddance' as she headed east with the children.

Oh, Anna, he thought, *So young and beautiful with your soft skin, eyes blue as the sky, gentle nature, and everything else about you. How will I live without you?*

Amongst other things Vance was a chain smoker. He realised he was almost out of cigarettes, so he wheeled into the service station on the outskirts of Curloo, stumbled from his car, and purchased three cartons of Craven A. Back in the car, he turned the key and was about to blast off when the gas boy said, 'Any fuel?'

Vance, with a look of sudden shock on his face replied, 'Shit, mate, forgot about that. Fill her up, will you?' Vance opened his bottle of rum; while juggling that between his knees, he bit the top off a small Coke bottle. He took a swallow of Coke with his left hand and a much heavier swig of rum with his right. He had repeated this three times when the young man said, 'That'll be fifteen quid.' Vance handed the Coke bottle through the window.

'Bin it, will you? Only trouble with those lids, you can't recap them.' He carefully re-corked his rum bottle, which he placed on the seat beside him, then fumbled in his pockets and came up with a twenty-pound note and said, 'Keep the change,' as he planted his foot and sped away, roadside gravel flying in his wake as he swerved from side to side.

The young man at the petrol bowser uttered a silent prayer of God-speed for Mr Callahan, whom he knew was a prominent businessman in Curloo. His mother had recently repeated to him some gossip about Mr Callahan, but Curloo was rife with gossip, most of which was untrue or at least exaggerated. Whenever Delores left Vance, he would stage wild parties for a couple of weeks, dry out for a few days, hire someone to clean the house, become Mr Quiet Respectable Businessman for a few days more, then start phoning Delores, convincing her to return. If the calls didn't work, he would cut off the money supply. He knew that one always worked.

As Vance's wagon hit the dirt road to Brolga, his mind was, indeed, working overtime. Memories were coming through faster than he could handle.

Slow down, mind, he thought. *Can't think of anything but Anna now. How did this happen?* He thought of his childhood, his doting mother and sisters, his wild, teenage years when he learned to gamble, smoke, and drink, about how, when, and where he met Delores, their marriage and children. Most of all, he was thinking of how unhappy he felt. Anna had simply disappeared without a word. Her mother phoned one morning a month ago with the news that Anna had gone away and wouldn't be able to work for him anymore.

'Where's she gone?' Vance enquired.

'I'm sorry, she asked me not to tell you. She said to tell you not to worry about her and one day you'll understand.' With that, Vance went on a binge. He was heartbroken. He didn't care about his business, spent every waking hour in one of the dozen or so Curloo bars. He would switch from one to the other, making it more difficult for Delores to find him. Delores left a little over a week later. *Who could blame her,* thought her friends. The only person in Curloo who knew the reason for Vance's condition was Vance. Anna's mother had strong suspicions that it had something to do with her daughter's sudden departure. She said nothing to anyone. Vance decided he had to get out of Curloo. He couldn't stand the thought of running his pharmacy without Anna being there, so he decided to sell. The local Flying Doctor base staff had told him about Brolga and the opportunity existing for a pharmacist with enough guts and foresight to open there. Vance hired a manager for his Curloo shop until he could find a buyer, took a lease on a new shop he heard was available in Brolga, called Delores until she agreed to come back, and here he was in a drunken stupor heading west.

Vance dropped his cigarette as he reached for the rum bottle.

'Oh, shit.' He slammed on the brakes. The car swerved off the road and stopped just a few inches short of a big gum tree. 'Must be the biggest bloody tree within a hundred miles,' he muttered as he fumbled for the handle of the car door. He finally manoeuvred his way out of the car and leant down in search of the burning cigarette, which was smouldering on a brown paper bag under the seat. He put the cigarette in his mouth and inhaled deeply as he rolled and squashed the almost alight paper bag between his hands.

'I need a drink. No. I need to take a leak first. Shit, I feel terrible.' His mouth was dry. He felt dizzy and had trouble focusing as he reached for his Craven A and matches. He lit the wrong end of his cigarette, which he threw aside in disgust before climbing back into the car, where he immediately passed out.

¶

Vance came to hours later as a truck hauling two stock carriers filled with sheep passed him at break-neck speed. He opened his eyes and gagged as he breathed in the thick, red dust stirred up by the passing truck. He blinked his eyes and put his hands to his throbbing head. It was morning. He slowly looked around.

'Where the bloody hell am I? Shit, look how close I am to that bloody great tree.' He lit his first cigarette of the day. It tasted foul, so he stubbed it out in the ashtray. Vance got out of the car and was urinating as another truck passed by. This time the driver sounded the horn loudly and waved. A few seconds later, Vance was encased in a cloud of dust so dense he couldn't see more than a couple of feet in front of him.

'God Almighty, why do I do it to myself?' Then he remembered. He took the bottle of the rum from the car, took a swig, rinsed his mouth, then spat it out.

Oh, Anna, he thought as he raised the bottle to his lips, swallowed hard, and threw the empty bottle into the bushes. He glanced at his watch. It was nine-fifteen. Forty-five minutes and the pubs would be open. He lit another cigarette. 'Hope this bloody car knows where it's going.' He slowly backed the car away from the tree. The sun was behind him, so he pointed the car in the opposite direction.

'West is this way. Man's lucky it's not mid-day. Wouldn't know which way to head.'

¶

Vance pulled up to the curb outside the Empire as Bert Romeo leisurely opened the doors for the long day's trading. Vance's throat was dry. He knew his body needed water. He also knew he would opt for rum and Coke.

Right on time. Couldn't have done better if I'd tried, he thought, as he left his car and walked into the bar. It never occurred to Vance to think of his appearance or the impression it projected to others. He was literally covered in red dust. The pocket of his wrinkled shirt was torn due to countless insertions and extractions of his packets of cigarettes, which he always carried there. His trousers looked as if he'd lived in them for six months. The front of them as well as the front of his shirt had masses of small burn holes caused by dropped lit cigarettes or matches.

He placed a ten-pound note on the bar in front of him, ordered a rum and Coke from an unsmiling Jess, lit a cigarette, and looked around the bar. TC was waxing the stained, solid-wooden doors of the refrigerators. Vance looked at her briefly.

She can't be more than fifteen, he thought. *Can't be legal to have someone that young working in a bar. Not even way out here.* In fact, TC was eighteen. The fact that she wore no make-up except pale pink lipstick, and the ponytail along with the pink ribbon bows created an illusion of her being much younger. Jess slammed Vance's drink down, took his money, and quickly returned with his change.

'Just passing through?' She hoped he'd say 'yes'.

'No. Staying. I'm the chemist. Opening soon.'

'Sure, and I'm the Queen of England. I reckon you're just another drunk. You certainly smell and look like one. Chemist, my foot.'

'I've had a few rough weeks. You'll see. I'll scrub up okay.'

'Yeah. Seen your kind before.'

'Who's the kid with the bows? What did you do, rob a kindergarten?'

'Smart mouthed, aren't you? Keep your eyes off her. She's special, that girl. Too good to be in this joint selling grog to the likes of you.' Vance placed his empty glass on the bar.

'Give me another one.'

'Only if I have to. You look like you need a bath more than you do another drink.'

'That's my business. Give me the drink.'

Jake and a couple of his cronies entered the bar and positioned themselves opposite Vance. Jake was gung-ho to get a good look at TC.

'Check out the ponytail,' Jake said loudly to his mates. 'Not bad at all.'

TC was embarrassed. She didn't know which way to look. Jess shrugged at the presence of Jake and the others. She knew the young buggers would be in this morning. Every time 'new meat,' as the locals referred to newly arrived barmaids, came to town, the so-called studs of Brolga hung about the bars like bad smells. Trying their luck, so to speak.

Don't like their chances with this one. She's too smart for this lot. At least, I hope she is, thought Jess as she gave TC the nod to serve them. TC put down her polishing cloth and gingerly approached them.

One of Jake's friends ordered in a loud voice, 'Middies all round, darls. By the way, Jake's got the hots for you.' TC didn't know what 'the hots' meant. She concentrated on selecting glasses from the refrigerator as she could feel their eyes scrutinizing her back. Jess helped TC with the beer-pulling. TC felt inadequate and embarrassed as she placed the beers on the counter.

'We're having a party down the creek tonight,' announced one of Jake's friends. 'Do you want to come?'

'No, thank you. I'm busy.' Beer splattered everywhere as everyone, including Jess and Vance, burst into laughter.

'Busy? In Brolga? Don't you know this is the arsehole of the world? Nobody and nothing are busy here, except if they're busy dying of boredom.'

'Three more middies down the track,' Jake said. 'What's your name?'

'TC.'

'I'm Jake. Why don't you come down to the creek tonight?'

'What for?' Everybody laughed loudly.

'Apart from the movies, that's all there is to do around here.'

'No, thanks. I've got things to do.' With that, Jake's friends, who were all council workers, decided they had better go to work. They had agreed on a reason for taking the morning off. They debated for a while over flu or diarrhoea.

'Diarrhoea sounds good. Got a bad piece of meat in Curloo.'

'Sure as hell, true for me,' acknowledged the young man who was still fagged out by sexual activity with the female he had encountered after the Two-Up game.

'Perhaps we all quit. Tell the truth. Had enough of this dead-end dump.'

'Get real. We've all got the runs. Agreed?'

'Fine. Let's get going. Leave Jake here with Jess, TC, and whoever the down-and-out, rum-and-Coke-drinking clown is across the way.'

Jess loathed Jake. He'd never done anything to her personally; always been polite, as a matter of fact. Just too damned sure of himself. Even when he'd been engaged, he'd gone on breaking hearts. All the girls loved him. He was the best catch in the area. Trouble was, he knew it. Jess decided she would have to keep an eye on him where TC was concerned and became upset when she noticed TC smiling at him as he walked to the other side of the bar, where he struck up a conversation with Vance.

¶

Jake and Vance talked and laughed with each other as the bar filled quickly with men, most of whom appeared in a trance.

'Why are they moving so slowly, Jess?' asked TC quietly as she observed every movement Jess made.

'They're all drunk or hung over. Most of them are never any other way. Drinking's not only the main means of passing time around here; it's also the disease that will bring the end to most of this desperate mob.'

As TC hustled around following Jess' instructions, she heard Jake say to Vance, 'Time I got going and taking care of business.'

'Me, too' replied Vance, who looked over his shoulder at the departing Jake.

Vance lost his balance and fell off his bar stool. After some groaning, moaning, stretching, and repositioning, he slumped into the corner, mumbling, 'Anna, Anna.' TC tried not to look at Vance. Jess was obviously disgusted.

'I told you, girl, the greatest mob of arseholes on earth are here in Brolga. Drunken shearers, drovers, and the like. Their dogs are better than most of them. Now be a good girl and fetch Bert or Jack. Can't have that so-called pharmacist sleeping it off in the corner all day. Should know better. If he is who he says he is, must be an educated man. No wonder he and that Jake got along so well. Two of a kind, that's for sure.'

TC mentally compared the dashing time-to-do-business Jake and the forlorn Anna-mumbling figure on the floor and could not see any similarity whatsoever. As she went off in search of the Romeo brothers, she knew she had to escape from this environment. Those men had hopelessness written all over them. She remembered that same look on her father's face many years before. It was the morning after he had beaten her mother black and blue. He'd been very drunk, and her mother had told TC and her sister and brothers to forget it because their father couldn't remember what he had done.

TC located Jack Romeo and told him about Vance. Within a little while, Bert and Jack successfully managed the relocation of Vance from the bar to an upstairs room, which they always used for drying out bad cases. Neither of the Romeo brothers wanted any of their clients to suffer death by obvious intoxication. Bad for business. Consequently, on occasions such as this, they would wean the poor soul off the drink and make certain he had a bed and food as they nursed him back to health. Jack looked at his brother with a heavy sigh.

'Better call the sergeant and get him to take charge of the man's car.' Bert Romeo nodded his head.

'We'll let him sleep it off for a while. Better tell Peter to check on him every half hour or so. Don't want him to wander.'

'No, he'll probably fall down the stairs like that last so-and-so. Come on, Bert. I'll talk to the sergeant about impounding the car.'

Jack called the sergeant and was advised by his wife that her husband was at the hospital where three people were fighting for their lives. They'd been driving from Curloo to Brolga, taken a bend in the road too fast; the car swerved and was a write-off. A young Brolga transport driver had come across their bodies strewn about the road ten miles east of Brolga. The Flying Surgeon had not yet arrived.

'Who are they?' asked Jack Romeo, with genuine concern in his voice.

'I don't know. I'll have my husband call you.'

Jack Romeo put down the telephone, looked at his brother as he said, 'Sarge's at the hospital. Three people are dying. Result of a car smash. Have Peter drive the pill-pusher's car around the back. Don't know who they are, but if they go, we'll be busy around here.'

'I understand,' nodded Bert.

Old Jordan Blake was a handyman-cum-carpenter, jack of all trades, who lived with his wife in a thrown-together, shack-type residence, at the front of which was a crudely painted sign saying,

"Carpenter, handyman, grave-digger, coffin-maker, and wakes a speciality. No time's the right time, but if you got to go, we'll send you off in style. Phone The Shack, Brolga 211."

Every time a resident of Brolga died, Old Jordan would hammer away all night, producing by next morning a coffin extraordinaire. He would drink beer after beer while he listened to Slim Dusty music. The more beers he drank, the more intricate was the detail on the unfortunate Brolgaite's eternal capsule.

If it was a poor Brolga resident who died, the wake at the Shack would only last one night and one day. Should he score a coffin for someone well healed, the wake could last up to a week. All and sundry were welcome at the Shack. Yarn after yarn would be recalled in drunken reminiscence, while the poor deceased was in the ground and unable to confirm or deny the multitudes of conflicting stories regarding his or her past life.

Just so happened, as Vance Callahan was in his *non compos mentis* state in the care of the Romeo brothers, that three Brolgaites died in two days. Old Jordan couldn't have believed his luck.

Poor bastards are dead he thought to himself, *But, shit, what a wake we'll have! We'll have to hire a couple of town drunks to dig the graves. Of course, I'll have to mark the holes out and check the lengths and breadths myself. Doesn't matter, better get going and tell the wife to get the Shack in order. The whole fucking town will be there. What a bloody fantastic, ripper party this one will be.*

The police sergeant—who was receiving call after call from Delores Callahan, rushing back and forth to the hospital, consoling grief-stricken relatives, ordering graves and coffins from Old Jordan, rounding up town drunks to dig the graves—was at the end of his tether. He thought to himself that he'd better get the bloody drunks to dig an extra grave in case that bloody chemist died, as well. 'Shit, what a week. Wish I could get a job in a normal town. Brolga sucks. Not even any regular-type arseholes to arrest here. Can't even get the bastards for drink driving. Place is so small they can stagger home after a night, sometimes days, on the piss at the Romeos' pubs. Still, old Bert and Jack are pretty good to me. Free grog whenever I want it, twenty-four hours a day. Shit, better get the drunks to dig two extra graves instead of one. The way this week is going, I'll probably drink myself senseless at the sure-to-be, month-long wake, crawl home after the last beer has gone, pull out my gun, and shoot my fucking brains out. Come to think of it, a man's brainless already for being in this god-forsaken dump. Now, I better go and see how Old Jordan's going with the coffins. Got to get these people in the ground before they start to stench up the hospital. Poor bastards.'

It was decided between the sergeant, Jordan, and the relatives of the deceased that, if Jordan could get the coffins done in time, the funerals would all be held at the same time. Old Jordon would carry the Catholic deceased in the back of his old ute; a brand-new ute was borrowed from the local Holden dealer to haul the Anglican's corpse to the Brolga cemetery.

Of course, the Holden dealer was an Anglican himself. *Those bloody Micks,* he thought to himself. *Think they own the fucking town. We'll show them. I can turn the speedo back later. Let's think of it as a test drive.*

Old Jordan sawed and hammered for thirty hours straight. To his neighbours it was obvious that with every beer he drank the Slim Dusty songs became louder. Jake, who lived opposite, stuffed cotton wool in his ears. He liked Slim's music himself, but, shit, thirty fucking hours!

Jake and his family were devout Catholics. His mother, Thel, was deeply upset that the Catholics were getting their ride to glory in the back of Old Jordan's battered ute, while the Anglican was going in style.

When Jordan had finished the third coffin, he called the police sergeant and said, 'Let's go.' The sergeant could tell that Jordan was plastered, but thought, *What the hell, the drunker he is the better the job.*

The Romeo brothers, rubbing their hands together, knew they would get lots of business as a result of these three deaths. Shit, the whole town was somehow involved. Better close the pubs and go to the funeral. Funerals are good for public relations. They were Greek Orthodox—more closely related to the Anglicans than the Micks, so decided that Jack would attend the Anglican's ceremony (since he was the senior brother) and Bert would go to the double Catholic deal.

'The pubs will all be full in a couple of hours. Also, Jordan will, as usual, be around for at least fifty cartons plus gin for the ladies, scotch for the men. That is, after all the beer is gone,' said Bert.

Jack replied, 'I don't mind when people die around here, Bert. Most of them are mongrels, anyway. Great for business.'

¶

Vance, still in his drunken stupor, felt that something was going on. Hadn't seen the Romeo brothers for a few hours. *Strange,* he thought. Anna was still running around in his cobwebbed brain. He hauled himself off the bed and manoeuvred himself out of the room. When he encountered the seemingly three hundred steps of the winding staircase before him, he went dizzy and started to tumble towards the bottom of the in fact fifty steps. As he was falling, he yelled, 'Oh, God!

'Bloody hell,' said Jack Romeo with a slightly Australian, but heavy Greek, accent. 'That maniac chemist has fallen down the bloody stairs.' Bert and Jack raced to the rescue of Vance. God only knew what they would find.

Vance was at the bottom of the staircase. His clothes in which he had been sleeping for days were in a dishevelled state. He was mumbling incoherently. Jack and Bert gave him water after screaming to Old Jess in the bar to fetch it.

Old Jess was thinking, *Why don't they let the drunken bastard die?*

'Where am I?' asked Vance.

'At the bottom of the bloody stairs,' replied Bert.

'Something's going on,' replied Vance.

'You better believe it,' replied Jack.

'About one percent of Brolga's population has died in the last two days. They are having a triple funeral. The whole bloody town will be thirsty after this deal.' Vance suddenly jumped to his feet. The Romeo brothers were amazed.

'I love parties. Better get cleaned up,' said Vance.

Old Jack replied 'Only way to clean you up by the looks of things is for you to strip and we'll hose you down.'

'Okay,' replied Vance with excitement in his voice. Vance was so far out of it he didn't care what happened as long as he could be a participant of the party. These Romeo people had limited his alcohol intake for days.

He thought, *Screw them. I need a real booze-up.*

Bert raced into the office and called Jake.

'Need some clothes for this bloody mad chemist. Looks like the crazy bastard wants to go to the funerals as well as the wake. He doesn't even know the poor buggers who have died.'

'I like him,' replied Jake, 'We'll have him dressed up like a prince.'

Prince of drunks, thought Bert.

After all, he and Jack had the hosing-down ceremony to attend to. They had been dressed in their best black suits to go to the funerals as well. Even though Brolga was but a pin-prick on the map of Australia, just about everyone except the appointed grave-diggers turned out in their Sunday best whenever there was a wedding, funeral, or christening (depending whether or not they were invited). Funerals, of course, were different. Almost always the grief-stricken relatives of the deceased were too distressed to worry about who attended the graveside of their loved, or often unloved, one.

Old Jordan would race around taking mental notes of the attendees so that he could figure how many were likely to show up at the Shack for the wake. His main priority was to know how much grog to order from the Romeo brothers. On credit, of course. Had to wait until he was paid for the graves and coffins before he could pay for it. Anyway, old Jack and Bert knew he was good for it. No wakes in Jordan's Shack ever cost, right down to the last beer, more than he was sure to receive for his services. Mind you, he always stashed a dozen or so for his missus and himself to drink after the crowd had cleared.

Jake arrived at the back of the pub, proudly hauling Vance's new wardrobe from his flashy Fairlane. He was surprised at the sight in front of him. There was Vance, naked, apart from a pub towel flung around his body, yelling at Bert and Jack that the water was boiling. Vance's soiled clothes were strewn all over the place, and his skin was red from the heat of the artesian bore water spurting from the hose.

'Thank God you're here with some gear,' screamed a relieved Vance. 'These bloody Greeks think I'm a turkey, and they're trying to parboil me. Give me those clothes, mate.' He desperately grabbed for the packages Jake was holding while holding the wet towel to his person.

'What'll I do with your old clothes?' said Jake.

'Throw them to the crapper,' replied Vance. 'Looks like they've already been there.'

'Yeah,' said Jake as he picked them up with the end of a broom and flung them one by one into the bin.

Vance made his way awkwardly to the shower room of the pub while Jake, immaculately dressed, as usual, took off for the funerals. Catholic side, of course, but better stroll, for business purposes, to the other side just once.

Jack and Bert hurried to their rooms to find their 'grieving' clothes laid out by their respective wives. Old Jess never attended funerals (or anything else for that matter) in Brolga. She had been peeking from an upstairs window of the pub. She was intrigued by the ridiculous scenario.

Can't believe this bloody, stupid town, she thought to herself. *Mob of maniacs, mongrels, and half-breeds, all drunks mostly. Jack and Bert should have drowned that idiot chemist. Wish his skin had peeled off. Perhaps the water wasn't quite hot enough. Better luck next time. I'm pretty sure there'll be one. Don't know what I'm still doing in this dump. Wasn't for Jack I would have been out of here forty years ago. Now I better go down to that kid TC and get this place ready for hell.'* As an afterthought, *'Hope those poor dead buggers don't go to hell. Not all three of them, anyway. They've already had hell here in Brolga. Oh, well, God bless them, wherever they go.*

As Jess moved away from the window, Vance emerged from the bathroom as Jack and Bert stepped off the verandah. Both Romeo brothers' wives, dressed, of course, appropriately in black, were ensconced in the rarely-used, often-polished, Romeo brothers' grey limousine. Very flash thirty years before, now outdated, it only had three hundred miles on the speedo, so, now an antique and beautifully maintained, it was the showpiece of Brolga and was only taken out on special occasions such as this.

The three miles to the Brolga cemetery was dirt road. Only the first two blocks of the main street (Brolga Street) were paved, and the Romeo wives discussed as they waited for their husbands that they must have Peter, the yardman, thoroughly clean and polish the car after the six-mile journey.

Pia said to Mara, 'Perhaps he won't have time tonight. The hotel will be a mess.'

Mara replied, 'No matter. I shall leave instructions. It must be attended to first thing in the morning.' She added, 'Naturally, after cleaning that cesspool of a bar and hosing down the footpaths. As the boys always say, 'Business comes first.' Keep the drunks of Brolga happy and spending their money. We can go to Greece every second year.'

Their conversation turned to silence as they observed Jack on one side, Vance in the centre, and Bert on the other side. Both husbands immaculately attired in their black suites, black bow ties, and crisply-starched, blazing-white shirts, with black socks and mirror-polished, black-leather shoes. To the horror of Pia and Mara, the creature their husbands hauled between them wore no shoes.

Thank the Lord, they both thought in unison, *he is at least wearing acceptable black socks.* He wore a white shirt, unironed, of course. It obviously had just been removed from its box. The shirt had a couple of straight pins with little fake pearl tops sticking out of the collar. There was also another one of these stuck in the tail of the shirt, and every time Vance took a step he would yelp. His black trousers were inches too long, so he had rolled them up like blue jeans.

Vance was, even at that age, almost bald on the top of his head, but Delores had forbidden him to go radical and have it shaved off, so he grew his hair extremely long on one side and, with the help of a comb or a brush and usually hair spray, he would smooth the long growth over the bald area. He would apply so much hair spray that his hair (what he had left of it) felt like a concrete slab. That hair was going nowhere. He wore an unknotted black tie flung around the open-necked shirt.

Vance had not had the luxuries such as a comb or brush, not to mention the essential hair spray, on this occasion, so his hair was strewn about in ridiculous array. Bits and pieces sticking out everywhere.

Mara Romeo thought, *Good God, he looks like a worn-out, blond bottlebrush.*

How embarrassing, thought Pia.

Vance kept mumbling, 'Where's the party? I want a party.'

Jack replied, 'Soon, soon. First, we have to see these people in their graves.'

'Shit, I hope I'm not one of them,' muttered Vance.

If only, thought Pia and Mara.

¶

As the prestige limousine of Brolga approached the cemetery, the passengers and driver could clearly see that, apart from the dogs, cats, and the occasional Brolga, their entire hotel staff, including TC, and the entire community, including the town drunks, shovels poised in hands under Jordan's instructions, were in attendance. It appeared to Vance in his incomprehensible condition that all the big, flash, white cars appeared to be parked to the right while to the left were parked old, beaten-up utes, station wagons, most of which had been beaten in, up, or out a little.

Smack in the middle where the Romeo's limo parked, the space was shared with Old Jordan's rusted-out ute, to the right, and this real fancy new ute to the left. Even in his oblivious state, as he alighted, stumbling, from the best car in town, Vance was still switched on enough to realise that something was wrong. Only as he hopped on his besocked feet from right to left, Catholic to Anglican, did it dawn on him.

'I want to go to the middle.' Eventually Vance would, he knew that. Right now, he wanted a party. The sooner this famous wake began, the better. The ground was hot with burrs entwining themselves within his socks.

Most Brolgaites attending the funerals, apart from Jake, the Romeos, and the police sergeant, were wondering, *'Who on earth is this prick? He's not a regular. Every time he moves, he screams. He wears no shoes. Looks ridiculous.'*

Never mind, some thought. *Some strange things happen here. Just about all of us came here to escape something. By the looks of this bugger, he's left quite a few horrors behind him. Hope they stay where he left them.*

In all fairness to the deceased, first the Catholic priest read burial rights for the one of his flock. The fact that the man had not attended church for thirty years meant nothing. Let's face it, the young priest had consciously justified to himself during many heart-wrenching hours that it was his duty to do this for this stray from the church. Secretly, he had it in his mind that action in Brolga was so minimal (only three or four of his denomination attended mass on some Sundays) that usually he sat or stood there and went through the motions of a mass without actually muttering an audible word. This was a big deal, two lost souls on their way in one day. Perhaps if he did his bit as well, he could look forward to having more faces to talk to occasionally. At least, hopefully, one every Sunday.

The Anglican minister came second. He was a very nice, young man. He also knew that, while Brolgaites did the best they could at living life to the best of their ability, the town should have been called 'Hopeless' instead of 'Brolga.' Often, he prayed that he and the Catholic priest could conduct Sunday masses together. At least they would both have something in common. Even though the words were different, at least they would have concurred on the meaning of the thing. After the Anglican minister had finished his duties, the Anglican community of Brolga started to head off. They wanted the best seats at the pub. The Anglican minister, feeling great sadness for his prospective community, very thoughtfully and consciously walked to the Catholic side of the Brolga cemetery to pay homage to the third lost soul.

The Romeo brothers and wives didn't know quite what to do. Vance was standing there in a haze. He kept looking at one grave of a long-lost Brolgaite. Somehow, the name became stencilled into his brain. He would always remember that tombstone and the name of the famous lady of Brolga who had been laid to rest there—Elmira Ferguson. Vance was impressed by the wonderful tombstone. He recalled that his dear mother had grown and sold chokos when in season, to get money to see him through pharmacy school. When she had died, he couldn't afford to provide anything so grand for her. At the moment, he was depressed and desperately needed a drink, preferably a rum.

The Romeo brothers didn't want to upset half their Brolga patrons by not waiting to hear the last words to be said for the second deceased Catholic, so Jack asked the police sergeant to get back to the pub and make his presence known. He whispered, 'Old Jess is there. They won't give her any trouble. Take this nuisance of a chemist with you, please, mate. Must be learned to do what he does. Shit of a drunk, though. Hate to ask you to do this, but if we leave, it wouldn't look too good for us, what with our wives here and all.'

'Okay,' said the sergeant. 'Grog still good?' he whispered.

'Anytime, boy,' said Bert and Jack in unison.

The police sergeant had been keeping his eye on Vance throughout the burials. He couldn't believe that this idiot, who had been jumping about without shoes for the past hour, was going to be filling prescriptions in a week or so. He certainly hoped that neither he nor any member of his family became ill enough to see the fly-in-fly-out doctor during what was left of his posting in Brolga. Even though the free grog, twenty-four hours a day, was a good deal, he couldn't wait to escape from this end-of-the-line dump. Vance's mind was still focused on the name 'Elmira Ferguson' as the sergeant took him by the arm and escorted him to the new Holden utility car, in which the keys dangled in the ignition.

'Need a rum,' mumbled Vance.

The police sergeant was surprised that the generous donor of the transportation for the deceased Anglican had apparently deserted the vehicle. He looked around, couldn't see him, so he and Vance got in the car and took off. Truth was, the Holden dealer was so keen to claim a stool at the pub that he had taken a lift to town with Old Jordan. The Anglican minister had driven the car to Brolga's cemetery with the enclosed coffin in the back.

Everyone in town knew, thought the Holden dealer. *Who the hell is going to buy the bloody thing now? Perhaps it is cursed now. Wouldn't drive it for quids,* he thought to himself. *Some damned expensive donation I made.* The ute became known to the locals as the 'death car.' After today, it was never driven again except for Anglican funerals and always by a man of God.

¶

The already-full bar of the Empire became more crowded as the Catholic funeral attendees straggled in one by one. Not only was the bar at the bursting-at-the-seams stage; the ladies' lounge and long verandah outside the bar were packed, as well.

Old Jess spat the dummy when one of the more affluent cow cockies ordered a half dozen fancy drinks and requested they be served to his wife and her friends in the ladies' lounge. She had listened stone-faced as he talked to her, slammed a beer in front of him, then turned away, mumbling to herself, 'Ladies? Bloody, stuck-up bitches forget I've been here forty long, hell-filled years. Forget I can remember when and why they came here. Nothing but jumped-up housemaids or so-called governesses. Came out here to work on the stations and find themselves a rich cockie's son. How could they fail with all those sex-starved young bucks as their captive audience? Not exactly overrun with movie stars or bathing beauties around this area. Now they sit in there like bloody queens ordering cocktails. Where do the bloody scrubbers think they are? The New York Plaza? Stuff them! They'll drink what I give them or nothing at all. Go drink at the bore head, for all I care.'

¶

Old Jordan was already in full flight. He'd forgotten about the grave-diggers stranded at the cemetery until Jack Romeo reminded him.

'Better take one of those cartons you ordered, boy, and drive out to pick up those poor buggers at the cemetery. Probably all dehydrated well and truly by now. They'll be hanging out for a cold beer.'

'Oh, shit, Jack. Thanks, mate. Hope I can drive. I've had a few.'

'You'll be right, Jordan. The copper's here. He won't leave as long as we feed him free beer. I'll keep him here till you get back.' Jordan lifted the carton of XXXX onto his shoulder and weaved his way to his battered ute parked in the backyard of the Empire. Before starting out, he extracted a bottle of beer from the carton, bit the lid off with his teeth, took a good swig, and drove off.

¶

The gravediggers had long since completed their mission. They sat under a tree, cursing Old Jordan. It was getting late, and they were all craving a drink.

'Just because we're Brolga's renowned drunks, I don't think it's fair we had to get this crappy, bloody job laid on us.'

'So, we could go to the best bloody wake in Brolga's history, that's why,' replied one of his mates.

'If Jordan doesn't come soon, I'm walking. Not staying out here amongst all these poor, dead bastards too much longer. Apart from that, don't want the fucking wake to be over before I get there.'

With that, the four of them stood up and began walking from the graveyard. They rarely wore shoes, usually got around Brolga barefooted or in 'Japanese riding boots' (rubber thongs). They hobbled along the dirt track with their feet in pain, cursing and swearing in their almost sober state, more than they did when they were blind drunk down the creek. The foursome had walked about half a mile when along came Jordan. The ute was weaving from one side of the track to the other. They scrambled into the gully at the side as Jordan wheeled past them before slamming on the brakes. Sore feet forgotten, the men ran to the ute.

'Silly bastard, could have killed us!' Old Jordan all but fell out of the car.

'Wouldn't have to take you too far to bury you if I had to,' he muttered.

'Smart bastard.'

'Where's the grog? Hope you bought some. A man's dying from thirst out here.'

'Some in the car.' Jordan turned his back to them and stood, wobbly on his feet, as he urinated.

'Was this a full carton?'

'Was when old Jack gave it to me.'

'No wonder you're pissing, you old bastard; there's only six left here.'

'Where are the shovels?'

'Fuck the shovels, Jordan. You get in the back where you belong. We'll draw sticks to see who drives and which one of us has the privilege of riding with you. All we need is a couple of mangy, blue cattle dogs and the picture would be complete. By the way, you promised us the wake of the century, so you better get some bloody sleep before the pubs close and the party begins at the Shack.'

Jordan did exactly as he'd been instructed. He jumped into the back of his ute, settled down amongst the grey blankets he'd used to protect the polish on the coffins. He fell into a deep sleep.

¶

Jack and Bert Romeo were tired by 11 pm. Bert had escorted the police sergeant across the street to his house behind the police station hours before. The sergeant's wife was obviously cheesed off as she said, 'Let the drunken mongrel sleep there on the couch.' Bert had made a hurried retreat back to the Empire, which was still bursting at the seams.

Have to help Jack count the money, he thought, as he knocked on the locked office door. After a few seconds, Jack looked through the peephole, saw it was Bert, and quickly opened the door just wide enough to allow Bert to enter.

'Bert, terrible thing to say, mate, but look at all this money. Pretty bloody good for us when we have multiple deaths here in Brolga. Thirty thousand quid plus on the table, and the bastards are still drinking in all three pubs.'

After rolling countless coins, folding notes, double-checking the tally, depositing the cash in the safe, which Jack Romeo key-locked in the rear office, securely closing the door, they made their way to the hotel kitchen, where the tireless Cheffie prepared them a snack.

'The women will expect a trip home to Greece,' remarked Jack.

'Good. Hope they go together, give us a break,' replied Bert. Jack nodded in agreement.

Jess hurried into the kitchen. She was furious.

'Jordan wants to collect the grog for the wake, Jack. Looks like he's been to hell and back. I've got news for him; hell's in that bloody bar. Give him what he wants, Jack, and for heaven's sake tell all those drunken bastards it's closing time. If they want to continue drinking, they should follow Jordan to his god-damned Shack. I need some bloody sleep.'

'All right, all right' snarled Jack. 'We'll get rid of them soon. Go back to work, girl.' Jess glared at the two men, who looked so relaxed as they ate.

'I'll clear the joint myself, Jack, if you don't. Surely, you've made enough money by now? Half of them, including the cockies, are asking for credit.'

'I'm coming, Jess; you call last drinks. I'll tell Peter to help Jordan load his order into the ute.'

¶

Louise Swagg had been a barrister's private secretary. She travelled to Brolga in her new BMW sports car (compliments of her barrister boss and lover) to visit her life-long friend, Vera, whose husband was Brolga and district's only building contractor. Any new houses, buildings, upgrading of same, renovations or such required by Brolga town dwellers or residents within a thousand-mile radius called Vera's husband, Vaughan, to do the job. Consequently, Vaughan and Vera were extremely well-off. Louise had left Brisbane in a hurry after her lover's wife had unexpectedly visited her husband's office one afternoon to find her beloved and Louise at it on his antique, office desk. All hell broke loose, and the show-down ended when Louise wished husband and wife the very best of boring lives together as she flung office keys and a diamond ring at the barrister. Louise had second thoughts and retrieved the ring from the floor.

'What about the car?' he asked.

'Get real, you gutless son-of-a-bitch,' replied Louise, as she jammed the ring on her finger. 'I earned that thing. I'm keeping it. You promised me everything, gave me nothing except this ring, the BMW, and lousy sex a few times. I'm out of here.'

Louise was well educated, her diction perfect, grooming immaculate. She had a perfect command of the English language with a broad vocabulary and a sense of humour beyond belief.

Vaughan and Vera had, of course, attended the funerals. Naturally, Louise went along with them. No point sitting at home alone. After only a couple of weeks with her friend, Louise realised that anything to do in Brolga was a big deal. Even if it meant attending funerals. Perhaps there'd be some excitement at the pub later. From what Vaughan and Vera had told her, the Empire was the hot spot in Brolga. Louise had become, in such a short time, so bloody bored listening to Vera whinging about Vaughan working all of the time and Vaughan skiting about his business monopoly, how much money he was making, how he'd like to screw this one and that one of the Brolga beauties. Louise, quite frankly, was at the end of her tether. Consequently, on the funeral day had dressed herself up to the nines in anticipation of having a great time.

Vaughan, Vera, and Louise made their way to Brolga's cemetery in the BMW, which drew great attention from the gathered Brolgaites. Louise parked her car as discretely as possible.

Shit, she thought. 'All these bastards are looking at me as if they know how I earned this fucking thing. Stuff them,' she muttered to herself as she saw the Romeos' car come to a halt. She was amused to see the elegantly-attired Romeo brothers and their wives accompanied by the blond Steve McQueen look-alike who wore no shoes.

'I love him,' mused Louise. 'A bloody renegade, just like me.'

'Perhaps there is some excitement in this place after all.'

Louise observed Vance's behaviour throughout the burial service, even when he appeared to be momentarily enthralled by some deceased woman's tombstone.

Got to get to know this outrageous creature better, thought Louise.

I think I love him. Sure, I love him. What a rat. Still, I've always fallen for losers. He's got that hopeless look about him, Louise thought, as she watched Vance dance from foot to foot.

¶

Louise zeroed in on Vance back at the Empire and, by the time Jess called last drinks, they were best friends, firing joke after joke off at each other. As Jess yelled, 'One for the road, you mob of drunks. Anymore grog tonight, find it at Jordan's,' Louise and Vance fell into each other's arms in laughter.

'Come on, roughly-rolled swagg,' said Vance.

'Looks like we hit the undertaker's joint. That is, unless you've got any better suggestions?'

Louise laughed, 'I haven't,' as she looked down at Vance's now bare feet. He had long since discarded the burr-ridden socks.

'Are you really a chemist?'

'I can be anything you want me to be,' replied Vance with an innocent look on his face.

'Let's try, lunatic?'

'Sure, I'm a lunatic. Let's go to the undertaker's party.'

'Why the hell not.'

¶

The wake at Jordan's Shack lasted seven days and became known as one of Brolga's legends. Seat of Knowledge gentry, even though cheesed off that they hadn't attended, until this day discuss the great wake.

During that seven days, Jordan's neighbours took to stuffing their ears with cotton wool at night as strains of Slim Dusty became louder and louder. No point in complaining to the police sergeant, as he, too, was attending the wake most of his waking hours.

Louise and Vance fell in love (during their time off from the wake hours) in her BMW, which she parked by the creek, out by the tiny airport, or in the bush—anywhere Vance suggested except the cemetery, with which he appeared to have an obsession as a parking spot. Whenever they retired briefly from Jordan's Shack, Louise would ask Vance, 'Where to, lover boy?'

Vance would reply in drunken oblivion, 'The cemetery, Roughly Rolled; want to screw you on the Ferguson grave.'

'Are you fucking crazy, Vance? No way.'

'Head this car for anywhere you like, then, Louise. I just want to jump on your bones.'

'No problem,' Louise would laugh loudly and head the BMW in any direction other than the Brolga burial grounds.

Vance and Louise were of equal intelligence and, under the influence of alcohol, shared sharp humour. They laughed incessantly, even when indulging in passionate love-making. Vance casually mentioned to Louise that he had a wife named Delores who was born to shop.

'So what?' replied Louise. 'You're here with me now. Must be some bloody thing wrong for her to let you loose.'

'I also have two sons.' Vance showed some remorse on his face as he announced this.

'Do they look like you, Vance?'

'One does. One doesn't.'

'Oh, shit, Vance, let's make love; worry about all that when we have to.'

Vance laughed loudly 'Come here, Roughly Rolled Swag,' as he began literally tearing her clothes off. 'Think I love you, Louise; you're my kind of woman.'

'Know I love you, maniacal chemist,' said Louise softly with a giggle in her voice. 'Come here, lover boy.' They kissed passionately and were carried away within the sea of desire, sex, and delusional dreams of impossible tomorrows.

By the third day of the legendary wake, the Romeo brothers decided to open their pubs with skeleton staff only. It was obvious to them that the drinkers of Brolga were either doing their drinking at Jordan's Shack or crashed on floors all over town. Probably in the Shack, on its roof, or in Jordan's yard, resting up for the next bout of fun and frolic.

'Holy shit,' said Jack Romeo to his brother. 'This bloody wake will send us bloody broke.'

'Not for long,' replied Bert. 'The grog at the Shack will run out sooner or later. Then they'll have to come for more supplies.'

'Mob of drunken losers,' sighed Jack.

'Carton sales are still good. Without those losers, my brother, we would be broke.'

'I agree, I agree.' Bert walked away, thinking to himself how wise his brother was.

¶

All other Brolga inhabitants, including the regular Seat of Knowledge patrons, were incessantly discussing the outrageous goings-on at Jordan's place. Jake, much to Thel's disgust, walked across the road to the Shack every night, armed with a carton of XXXX.

'The devil will get you, Jake,' Thel would say with a smile on her face.

'Think he already has, Mum.'

'Promise me you won't drink too much, Jake.'

'I already do, Mum.'

'I know,' Thel would reply as she watched her oldest son, carton on shoulder, head across the street to Jordan's.

¶

TC and Sam temporarily found themselves redundant.

'Last on, first off,' Jack Romeo had informed them. 'Still, you can have free board and lodging until the wake is over.' TC nodded at Mr Romeo as a sign of thanks.

Sam looked Jack Romeo directly in the eyes and replied, 'Yeah, wrapped in fucking luxury. Know homeless people who have more adequate accommodation than we do.' TC looked at Sam in surprise.

'Why the 'F' are you looking at me like that, TC?'

'Because, Sam, we've got no money. Nowhere to go.'

'Yes, we have, TC. Let's go to the fucking wake. Every other bastard is there. Why not us?' Jack Romeo observed TC's face as she looked at her friend with shocked, wide eyes.

'She's right, girl. Go. Let my brother and me know what's happening there.'

Sam was seething. 'What do you think she is, you tight, ding prick? The bloody CIA? Let's get the bloody hell out of here.' Sam virtually pulled TC from the office. Sam was mumbling 'Fucking tight, ding bastards.'

'What if they fire us forever, Sam? How will we get out of this place? No money.'

'TC, for God's sake, don't be bloody ridiculous. They're too smart for that. We're still fresh meat. Lambs for the slaughter, kid. Now let's get prettied up and hit the effing wake. Wish we had a camera. We could possibly endear ourselves to the Romeos forever by presenting them with proof of Brolga's debauched party animals. Pity those poor bastards had to die to get this place in party mode. That's life though, kid. Grin and bear it.'

¶

It was dusk as TC and Sam approached the front door of Jordan's Shack. They paused briefly outside to read the rudimentary sign, which said

"Come in if you're good-looking. Piss of if you're not (unless you're the carrier of a carton or two or three). No tears allowed within this compound. Wake celebration in progress—even the dead need a laugh. Cartons at the front door. Good-lookers enter there. Uglies through the back door. Good luck if you score."

The proverbial country-and-western music was blasting out. Slim was singing about how lonesome it was in a pub with no beer. TC and Sam both believed they possessed the attributes necessary to enter through the front door, around which there were stacked countless cartons of beer.

'No fucking wonder the pub's got no beers,' whispered Sam. 'It's all bloody there.' TC rolled her eyes backwards.

'Sam, for God's sake.'

'No, TC, those cartons aren't for the Lord's sake; they're for the Brolgas' drunks' sake. Let's have a good time. Hope they've got some Elvis or Jerry Lee music.'

The girls entered the Shack to find Jordan asleep on a tired mattress. He was holding a brown beer bottle upright. It was an almost full bottle. Vance and Louise were cuddled up together on an old, worn couch in the corner of the small room. On the floor in front of the couch was a half-empty bottle of Bundaberg rum, a couple of glasses, and a half-empty Coke bottle which lay on its side. The Shack was strewn with sleeping bodies, empty beer bottles, the occasional empty rum, gin, or vodka bottle, many glasses either empty or with remnants of half- or almost-finished drinks, several overflowing ash trays, and beer bottle tops everywhere.

Old Jordan's wife, Carmel, was in the Shack's tiny kitchen washing dishes. Her daughter, Lynette (everybody called her Lou), was making sandwiches and adding them to a huge, already over-stacked, platter.

'Can't pile too many more on here, Mum.'

'Get another plate, then.' Both mother and daughter appeared extremely tired.

Why wouldn't they, thought TC and Sam in unison.

Carmel looked up and acknowledged the two girls who were standing just inside the door, taking in not only the scene but also the incredible architecture of the building. The walls were constructed of corrugated iron with only two windows, one in the tiny, front room and one above the bench in the kitchen. The window frames were unpainted four-by-two pieces of timber with panels of tin nailed to them instead of inserted glass. They were pushed out and up with another piece of four-by-two two-feet long. The floor was swept hard-packed dirt. The entire place looked as if it had been thrown together in fits and starts with bits and pieces of this and that.

'Come on in, girls; pick up some of those empty bottles on the way. I'm Carmel; this is my daughter, Lou. Those empty cartons, put them in there.'

'I'm Sam; this is TC.'

'TC, you start on the plates and the other rubbish; I'll find the cartons for the bottles. Bloody millions of them, aren't there?' she whispered.

'Never seen anything like it.'

'Lou, hurry up with those *sangas* and help these kids get this joint cleaned up before this mob wake up and the next onslaught starts.'

TC and Lou liked each other instantly and chatted as they carted the dishes to the kitchen, retrieved the countless bottle tops and threw them into a plastic bucket into which they also emptied the ashtrays. They both hated the smell of the stale cigarette smoke lingering within the tiny abode, and both felt nauseous as they took the emptied ashtrays to the kitchen. Well, they were really cut-off jam tins. Still, they had to be washed after Carmel had finished the dishes. There was no sink in the Shack. Carmel's sink was a medium-size aluminium wash tub, which Lou helped her mother carry to the backyard to empty every night and back into the kitchen every morning before Carmel would bring in the hose and quarter-fill the tub. Dishes used during that day would be stacked in the tub, and last thing at night she would bring in the hose and add hot water to the then-cooled water so she could wash her dishes cleanly. Jordan had been promising to erect a cooling tank for years but never seemed to get around to it.

'Oh, well,' Carmel would think to herself. *At least our toilet and bath have running water, even if it is always hot. A woman can't expect everything.'*

Lou and TC finished off the dishes, then the ashtrays, as Carmel arranged crackers and cheese on a couple of plates. Sam came into the kitchen.

'More bottles there than hairs on a hound dog. Talk about boozers, no one could outdo this bloody mob.'

¶

Carmel and Lou were about to pick up the sink.

Sam said, 'Here, let me take that.' She took it by the handles and said, 'Where to?'

Carmel, Lou, and even TC were amazed at the ease with which Sam carried the tub outside and upturned it. Sam smiled at the three of them.

'There you go, TC. Everyone except you has always said I should have been a bloody man. Maybe they're right.' The four of them laughed as they entered the Shack.

Carmel was a very thin woman with beautiful, auburn hair. She wore a buttoned-up floral house frock with a belt. The dress looked as if it had seen better days, just as Carmel did. She wore no shoes, so Sam felt quite at home with her bare feet. Carmel would have been very pretty years ago. She was a friendly person who always made anyone and everyone feel welcome, no matter who they were or what colour. Who was she to be off-hand to anyone? She lived in a Shack after all. Better off than a lot of poor buggers who lived in tents or worse, still had nowhere to call home. She loved Jordan. Knew they'd never have much except each other. Their name was good, so they could always get tick from the grocer and the butcher, so there was always food on the table. Never fancy, but still food.

She made her way through the stirring bodies on the floor, then leaned over and extracted the beer bottle from the sleeping Jordan, then shook his shoulder. 'Wake up, Jordan. People will be coming soon. Want you to rouse up your mates so they don't get trodden on and killed in the stampede.'

Jordan opened his eyes, blinked a few times. 'What time is it, luv?'

'Almost seven.'

'Oh, shit, Carmel, why didn't you wake a man earlier? I was supposed to put some beer on ice.'

As he jumped up, he began rolling up the old mattress on which he'd been sleeping. After he'd thrown it in a corner, he clapped his hands loudly.

'All right, you drunken mob of bastards, on your feet. Work to do. Come on, hop to it.' Moans and groans emanated from the half dozen or so men, most of whom rose to their feet, appearing still to be asleep.

'No cold beer. The ice works is closed. Shit, we all get mad enough when the bloody stuff's cold. We'll be raving bloody lunatics if we drink it hot.'

Vance and Louise were cuddled up in the corner giggling as they observed the looks of disbelief on the faces of Jordan's suddenly wide-awake friends. They all wore expressions of terror as if doomsday had arrived and the Grim Reaper was taking them at last to where they always knew they'd go.

'Hope there's a cold beer in hell.'

'Because, shit, that's where I think I am.'

'My fucking head feels like it's gunna explode any second,' yelled Jordan. 'Why the fuck didn't you wake me, Carmel?'

Sam, TC, and Lou were standing at the back of the kitchen in silence. TC and Sam couldn't believe their eyes. Sam broke the silence and whispered, 'Feel like we're in a bloody movie. If a brawl breaks out, let's piss off quickly.' She edged TC towards the back door. Lou moved forwards towards her parents.

'Stop it, Dad. It's not Mum's fault. She's been working all day for three days while you sleep, and she can't sleep at night because of the noise and your Slim Dusty music records. Neither Mum nor I can stand to hear his voice any more for a damned long time. Poor neighbours must be going off their heads.'

'That's for bloody sure,' said a deep, loud voice from the back door of the Shack. 'Good on you, Lou. I've been stuffing cotton wool in my ears for a week. So have the rest of the family except poor mum. She took refuge with the nuns down at the convent four days ago. Threatened us all with a fate worse than death if we ever bring one of poor old Slim's records near the house. She reckons yours are close enough.'

Jake's family owned the ice works as well as the drapery store. They actually owned lots of things, milk depot, and a few houses. Jake's main interest was the drapery, though, because it generated the most money. One of his mates, Fred, ran the milk depot and ice works for Jake. Fred had phoned Jake an hour earlier.

'We've got an emergency, Jake. Old Jordan hasn't picked up any ice today. Don't like the thought of hot beer, mate.'

¶

'Well, throw ten or twelve blocks on the back of the ute. Don't forget to bring a couple of hammers so we can crack the bloody stuff.'

'What are all the sad faces for, boys? Start carrying those cartons out back to Fred. He's out there loading the tubs with ice.'

Sighs of relief from Jordan and his mates as they hurried towards the cartons stacked beside the front door. They all swore eternal devotion to Jake.

'Bloody great, young bloke you are, Jake,' said Jordan.

'Remind me to buy you a beer later, mate.'

'Yeah, Jordan, it'll be quite a while later, though, because a few of those cartons out there are already mine.'

'Know that, mate. Know that. I mean, after you've drunk your own.'

Jake turned his attention to TC, Sam, and Lou, who had returned to stand by the back door.

'Fred and I are going to my place to have a couple of coldies. We'll come back over here in an hour when the booze in the tubs has cooled down. Do you want to come across?'

'Get bloody real,' snapped Sam. Lou laughed.

Jake laughed, 'I didn't mean that. I live across the street. You can choose some better records, Lou.' Sam threw her arms around an astonished Jake.

'You're my kind of man. Got any Elvis, Little Richard, or Jerry Lee?'

'Don't know. Come on, let's go.' TC didn't move.

'I'll stay here with Carmel.' Jake looked at her with surprise.

'Why not?'

'Because I'd rather stay here with Lou's mother.'

Jake shrugged his shoulders as Sam and Lou preceded Fred and him through the door. TC had stayed behind with Carmel because she felt sorry for the woman who was staring into space as she leaned against the kitchen bench.

'Are you okay, Carmel?'

'Yes, TC, just tired, luv.'

'And sad, I can see it in your eyes.'

'Yes, luv, and sad … and embarrassed.'

'No need to be. You should be proud.'

'Why?'

'Because of your daughter and the way she handled things. Her father's still half drunk, I think.'

'TC, you don't even know him.'

'No, Carmel, I don't. My father used to carry on like that, but only when he was drunk. Sober he was a lovely, gentle, happy man. I've seen a lot worse than what happened tonight. Just like Lou, I'd have to step in. Takes a lot of courage, Carmel.'

'I think you and Lou will get along just fine, TC. Do you drink, TC?'

'My mother would kill me.'

'Good. Neither does Lou. Great. She needs a friend. Those snooty-nosed girls her age in Brolga reject her. The others are not her type ... too wild.'

⁋

A dozen or so people came to the front door at the same time. Mostly they were youngish, around thirty. All but two appeared to be married couples in ready-to-rage mode. Lots of laughing. The apparent couples were quite well dressed, while the odd-ones-out looked as if they'd been rolling around the sheep yards all day. Which is exactly where they had been.

One of the two men, who had a carton on his shoulder, enquired, 'Where's Jordan?'

'Out the back putting beer on ice, and if you've got coldies in that box, you'll be the most popular man at the party for an hour or so, even though you are covered in sheep shit,' Carmel replied. Vance and Louise laughed loudly at this comment. TC even suppressed a giggle.

In the next ten minutes, at least thirty new arrivals entered the front door. Most made their way through the crowded Shack and exited by the back door to where the grog was chilling in two old bathtubs. Jordan called them his open-air freezers.

'Easiest way to maintain a bar in the world,' he would skite.

'Bite the top off the bottle, fling the cap into the forty-four, drink the beer, then lay the bottle on its side on the stack. Anyone wants a bloody lunch, bring your own.'

⁋

As usual at Brolga parties, most of the females were segregated from the males. In this instance, the females remained inside the Shack and the men went directly to the open-air bar.

Jake, Fred, Lou, and Sam arrived back, all laughing. Sam and Lou were each carrying a foot-high pile of records. Jake and Fred were both swigging on beer bottles, obviously cold because condensation had formed on the outside.

'Time to party,' said a happy Sam. 'We lucked out with Jake's records, TC. Gunna show these local yokels what real music's all about, aren't we, Lou?'

'With a bit of luck, we might even convert dad from Slim,' replied Lou with a sigh.

'Pigs might fly, too,' added Carmel.

Jake spied Vance and Louise in the corner still cuddled up on the sofa.

'How are you, mate? Didn't see you when I was here before. You should have come over for a drink.'

'What? And lose the only fucking seat in the place?' laughed Louise. 'No bloody way. I'm too bloody frightened to go to the toilet in case one of these bastards claims it.'

'I'm drunk ... and happy,' replied Vance. 'I find Jordan's joint extremely amusing. Do us a favour, will you, Jake? Play musical chairs here with my girl while she goes for a pee.'

'Superlative idea, my dear. Oh, you are so clever, my sweet pea.' Louise jumped up and Jake sat down.

'Tell you what, Jake; if this party doesn't end soon, I'll be in heavy crap. Happy the cop is here most of the time. That way Delores can't find him, which means she can't find me. Figure I'm pretty safe for a few more days. I've got the car, so she can't piss off to Brisbane, thank God. Don't want to have to go get her again so soon.'

'She can take the train.'

'Shit. I never thought of that. Talking of trains, could you check at the railway station for me tomorrow? Probably a million bloody cartons of all sorts of things there for the shop. If I ever get to open it, that is.'

Louise came back.

'Your turn, lover.' She smiled adoringly at Vance. 'Why don't you ...' Vance didn't let her finish.

'Yes, I'll take a piss out by the car and bring in another bottle.'

'Exactly what I was about to suggest, you little mind reader.'

Jake slid into Vance's spot, and Louise resumed her position.

'Tell you what, Jake; I think I'm in love. He calls me his Roughly Rolled swag.'

Jake laughed. 'Why?'

'Because my surname is with another guy.' Louise paused as she lit a Craven A. After exhaling, she continued. 'All my lumps and bumps are in the wrong places, especially when I wear a belt with a dress. Appropriate, don't you think, Jake?'

Jake laughed. 'Very appropriate simile, Louise.'

Louise was short. She had long, black hair and incredibly beautiful eyes. A sense of humour and a quick wit to match anyone, man or woman. Not only Vance, but all the men she had ever known, were taken by it. She was not fat, chunky more like it. She did swear frequently; however, her diction was perfect, so she didn't sound rough like Sam. Vance returned with a new bottle of Bundy and a couple of bottles of Coke. Louise looked up at Vance.

'Now piss off, Jake, and let my Darling sit down.'

Jake stood up. 'I'll bring you some ice if you like.'

'Don't be bloody crazy. We don't want water polluting our drinks,' replied Louise. 'Now, go away, Jake, and leave us two lovers in peace.'

Jake found his way through the crowd, mostly women. He was looking for TC. She was standing with Lou and Sam by Jordan's old record player. Sam was obviously the unofficial DJ. She was rejecting record after record offered by TC and Lou.

'No, not that one. Got to start this joint reeling and rocking with something really special.'

As Jake walked slowly past TC, he paused, leant down over her shoulder, and said quietly, 'You're beautiful. I'm going to marry you.' TC spun around in shock. There was no one there. She looked the other way towards the back door. Jake Carmichael had his back to the door. He was talking to Fred and a couple of other men whose names she did not know.

TC looked at Lou, who said, 'I heard him, TC. He will, too. Jake gets everything he wants.'

'Well, he won't be getting me. Too damned sure of himself. Spoiled, rich brat.'

"Lordy, lordy, lordy, Miss Claudie. You sure look good to me." Elvis' voice came blasting from the kitchen on the highest volume Sam could manage. Apart from Elvis' voice, there was silence both inside and outside of the Shack. Everyone, apart from the three girls, Vance, Louise, Jake, and Fred were in shock.

One of the sheep-yard men yelled out, 'What's that bloody poofter music for? Where the hell is Slim?'

Carmel yelled back, 'He's taking a three-month holiday. So shut up and get drunk.' Eighty-five percent of the party-dwellers cheered. As they were so outnumbered, the other fifteen percent didn't matter. There were sixty-two people at the wake that night, not including Jordan, Carmel, and Lou. Rarely before had anyone other than Jordan and his closest cronies (the professional drunks of Brolga) stayed on to party all night. Most working people would usually leave around midnight. That night only seven people, including Vance and Louise, who went off somewhere for lovemaking, left before 6.30 am when Sam declared, 'That's enough. I'm buggered.'

Lou and TC had, hours before, taken refuge in Lou's tiny room. There was no point in trying to sleep from the noise of Sam's loud music and the laughter, yelling, and squealing of the party. They talked all night.

Sam came bursting from behind the curtain, which represented the door to Lou's room.

'I'll tell you what, girls, that chemist's a bloody fool for not having his shop open. Bet he could make a bloody fortune in pain potions today.'

The voice of one of the departing revellers yelled, 'Glad Slim's on holidays. Best party Brolga's ever seen. Thanks, Jordan. We'll spread the word, mate. See ya.'

'Let's clean the joint now,' suggested Sam. 'That way we won't have to pussyfoot around sleeping bodies later.'

'Better hurry. Dad and his lot usually crash around eight.'

Carmel had hit the gin that night and passed out, probably from exhaustion and the effects of gin, around midnight.

'Mum's a binge drinker,' declared Lou. 'Doesn't happen too often. This time I don't mind. She's had it. Four days, no sleep at all. Hardly any for a few days before that when Dad was making the coffins. Wish to hell I could get out of this God-forsaken town.'

'So do I,' sighed TC. 'Haven't been here a week yet. Feel as if I've been trapped here forever.'

'Shut up, TC. We are trapped here,' snapped Sam. 'Now, stop complaining. Let's clean up before we return to our, compliments of Romeos, luxurious apartment and most importantly some of Cheffy's breakfast.'

Jordan staggered through the back door just as the girls finished. 'Holy shit,' he said. 'The Shack looks like bloody Buckingham palace.'

Sam and TC returned to the hotel's staff quarters and showered under the foul-smelling bore water. Sam decided they should ask Old Cheffy if there was any chance of some food. Of course, there was, as Cheffy was, like every other non-wake attendee in Brolga, very interested to hear of the goings-on at the Shack. He started firing questions almost the same moment he placed their food on the staff dining table.

Sam avoided the issue. She began to ask Cheffy about himself. She saw no point in discussing the other people, especially when most of them were nameless to this point. TC sat silently as Cheffy told them his life story. Sam interjected periodically when she wanted him to embellish on some point which she found extremely interesting or intriguing.

Cheffy was a distant cousin of Bert and Jack Romeo. He had been a chef in Crete prior to the war. He had fled Crete for Australia with the help of his cousins in early 1943. He had worked as a chef for Great-Uncle Harry, who owned five of the seven hotels in Curloo, for six years prior to coming to Brolga some ten years earlier. Cheffy was a short, plump, kind man, always attired in immaculate white, starched trousers, shirt, and apron, along with a chef's hat that appeared two feet high. Due to the long hours he worked, he rarely left the confines of the hotel. His only living relatives were his Great Uncle and his two cousins. Consequently, Cheffy considered everyone who lived at the Empire Hotel as his family, and everything they did or said was his business.

Jack, Bert, Pia, Mara, and Jess always came to Cheffy for information and gossip regarding the dining room patrons, resident hotel guests, and particularly the staff. Cheffy liked most people, although he admitted only to himself that during his years in Australia, he had seriously contemplated purposely poisoning a hundred or so obnoxious persons he had unfortunately experienced knowing.

The two girls exited the kitchen via the back door as Jack and Bert entered through the door to the adjoining guest dining room.

'Doesn't that big one own footwear, Cheffy?'

'Don't know, boss,' as he looked towards Jack.

'Little one is always real neat. Very quiet, though.'

'Still waters run deep,' quipped Bert as he and his brother left the room.

¶

Peter, the hotel handyman, knocked on the girls' door a few hours later. Sam opened the door.

'Hell, if it isn't the hotel's slave. What brings you here to our exclusive abode?'

Peter smiled at the irony in her words. His expression became serious as he explained that Mrs Pia and Mrs Mara wished to see both girls in their office before dinner.

'What the hell do those old dragons want?' asked Sam. Pete shrugged and left.

¶

True to his word Jake had checked with the railway as to the whereabouts of Vance's pharmacy supplies. Two hundred and three cartons of various sizes had arrived on the Wednesday-night Flea. The station master explained to Jake that a half dozen or so had 'Keep refrigerated at all times' marked on the side, so he had asked the Greeks if he could store them in the cold room of the Railway Hotel, which was opposite the yet-to-be-established pharmacy. He also told Jake there were more cartons in Curloo as everything was unable to fit in the Flea's goods carriage. Whatever was still in Curloo would come when there was available space.

Jake went in search of Vance, whom he finally found down by the creek. Vance and Louise were asleep in her BMW. Jake thought to himself, *Thank God, they are parked under a tree. With all the grog in them, they would have dehydrated quickly in the heat of the full sun.* As Jake gingerly shook Vance awake, Louise stirred.

Both she and Vance yawned, stretched, and mumbled in unison, 'Where the hell are we?'

'Back to the real world, mate. A lot of your pharmacy gear's sitting on the platform at the station.' Jake also explained to Vance about the boxes in the cold room. Louise and Vance suddenly sat upright, both staring into space, each of them pondering on the reality of their individual situations. Jake sized up the scene.

'Okay, Vance. I'll see you later. If you need any help shifting things to your shop let me know.' Both Louise and Vance gave the back of Jake's car a wave as he drove off.

Louise realised that she had fallen in love with Vance. Sure, she'd known him less than a week; still, she knew she would love him for the rest of her life. The past days and nights spent with him were the best she had experienced in her thirty-three years of life. Vance was the most humorous, intelligent, uninhibited man she had ever met. Louise chose not to think about his wife, Delores, their children, or the fact that she had not yet seen the sober, serious side he usually displayed to the world.

Vance was thinking about Anna. He wondered where she was. He loved her so very much. He supposed he would have to call Delores soon. He imagined she'd been phoning the police at least a dozen times a day for news of him. He wasn't wrong. By now the police sergeant's wife and Delores were almost best friends. They had shared numerous discussions on the weaknesses of men, the evil of alcohol, and the responsibilities of raising children without the support of a normal husband. On one occasion the police sergeant's wife quipped, 'Buggered if I know what normal is anymore. Brolga does that to you.' Vance broke the silence.

'Well, Roughly Rolled Swagg, better take me back to the pub. I've got a lot to do.' Louise nodded her head.

'Anything you say, lover,' with an expression of false brightness on her face.

¶

Sam and TC entered the outer office of Pia and Mara Romeo's at exactly 5.30 pm. They noticed quite a few people entering opposite the bar.

'Well, girls, back to work tomorrow. Seems Old Jordan's wake is almost over. Our customers are coming back,' said Pia.

'TC, you will work with Jess. There's a shire council meeting in the morning; so, we will be busy come lunchtime.'

TC looked at Mara, 'What is a shire council meeting, Mrs Romeo?' Both women looked at TC as if she was an idiot.

'Well,' said Mara, 'It is a meeting of elected gentleman held once monthly at the Council Office to debate and decide the future of Brolga. The ultimate decision-making lies with the Shire Chairman, who is the equivalent of mayor in larger towns and cities.'

Sam mumbled, 'If they hit the bar at lunchtime, sounds more like an excuse for a piss-up and bull-shit session to me.' Pia Romeo glared at Sam.

'TC, you may go. Sam, we wish to speak to you in private. Please sit down.'

Sam sat down belligerently. 'What' she snapped. Both Mara and Pia wanted to fire Sam on the spot. They knew they could not. Their husbands always took care of such things. Apart from that, the girl owed them ten pounds for her train fare. Mara Romeo regained her composure.

'Sam, if you wish to remain employed by us, you really must do something about your overall appearance, particularly your hair. More importantly, we must insist that you wear some appropriate type of footwear. We can't have our staff going about their duties barefooted.

Not only is it bad for our image, it is also dangerous regarding your own well-being. The union will not tolerate this.'

Sam snapped, 'Okay. I'll tie my hair back.'

'You might consider brushing it first,' said Pia.

'Screw you. As for the appropriate type of footwear, I suppose you or the union will lend me the money to buy some.'

'Definitely not! You are the most obnoxious young woman it has ever been my misfortune to meet,' shouted Pia.

'Go see Jake Carmichael. He'll probably trust even the likes of you. The word is he gives anyone and everyone credit. In our opinion, he's a stupid, young man. Most of them won't repay him.'

'Bugger off, ladies. Thank you for your time' said Sam sarcastically, as she stood up and left the office.

¶

Sam found TC talking to Jordan's daughter, Lou, on the footpath at the front of the Empire.

'Are you all right?' enquired TC.

'All right as I can be after a session with those two old bitches. Hitler's sisters, if he had any, would have nothing on them. Looks like I'm about to give you a run for your money, TC. I have to brush my hair and tie it back. How boring! I also have to wear shoes—if I can talk Jake Carmichael into giving me a pair or two on credit.'

'He will,' nodded Lou. 'Half the people in town owe him money.'

At that moment, Jake pulled his Fairlane to a halt alongside the curb. He and Vance approached the three girls. Vance was wearing what would become known to Brolgaites as the pill-pusher's summer uniform, consisting of an R M Williams short-sleeved shirt with two breast pockets to accommodate his Craven As, long tropical shorts, beige leather belt, knee high socks, and beige, suede lace-up shoes. Obviously, he had located a can of hair spray, as every strand on his head was now perfectly in place.

Jake looked down at TC. 'Well, if it isn't my little bride-to-be.'

TC glared at him and walked away.

Jake laughed. 'What did I do to your little friend, Sam?'

'You bloody well scared her. Who'd want to end up with you? Anyway, Jake, I need a couple of pairs of leather thongs. Any chance of you trusting me for the money? I have none.'

'Sure,' replied Jake, 'as long as you promise to put a good word in for me with TC.' 'Consider it done. Can I get the thongs now?'

Vance muttered something about going to retrieve his car from the police station and phoning his wife. Jake and the two girls unloaded Vance's packages from Jake's car. They left them with Bert Romeo before walking to Jake's shop so Sam could make her purchase. Jake kept asking questions about TC. Sam was non-committal and Lou was bored as she knew nothing except that she hoped TC and herself would become friends.

¶

Vance knocked on the door of the police sergeant's residence, which was situated behind the railway station itself. Locals wondered why there was a police station at all as the only time it was open was when some big-wig police person of importance visited from the east. On the occasion there was a brawl in one of the Greeks pubs, the police sergeant would make a show of authority by arresting the perpetrators and throwing them into the one and only jail cell, which he didn't bother to lock. He knew, after sleeping off the booze, they would be the best of friends again in the morning. The sergeant's wife answered the door.

'My husband's asleep.' Vance knew for a fact that her husband was not asleep because he had seen the sergeant enter the Empire as he walked past.

'My name is Vance Callahan. I have come to collect my car.'

'I see. So, you're the drunken chemist. Heard a lot about you, especially from your wife. She wants you to call her. The keys are in the car; it's out back. Call your wife.' She slammed the door.

Vance located his car, which was covered in red dust due to the bulldust road between Curloo and Brolga. Inside the car was also a mess.

Disgraceful, he thought. His head was aching because of his need for a drink. His heart was aching because of Anna. The last thing he wanted to do was contact Delores. Vance parked his car in the back of the Empire, asked Pete to clean it when he could find the time, and slowly made his way to the phone box outside the Brolga Post Office.

Every call, be it local, or out of Brolga, was connected by a telephone operator. The three shift-working operators employed by the telephone exchange listened in to almost every call made into or out of Brolga. When bored, they would listen to local calls if only to give them something to gossip about, catch up on who was doing what, et cetera. Vance asked the operator for his number in Curloo. His hand was shaking. He wished he could escape to some far-flung place to live in seclusion for the rest of his life.

'Hello, he heard Delores say.

'Yes. It's me.'

'Where the hell have you been, Vance?'

'That's my business.'

'I've been frantic.'

'What about, Delores?'

'You, of course.'

'Don't waste your energy. I'm fine. Before you start, the answer is 'No' to every question you are about to ask me.'

'Vance, how the hell do you know what I was going to ask you?'

'Because I know you, Delores. No! The shop is not set up yet. No! I haven't found a house for us yet. No! I didn't forget to bring my clothes—I bought new ones. No! I don't miss you, and, No! I haven't been drinking. Say hello to the kids for me. Stop phoning the police sergeant's wife. I'll call you when I'm ready. In an emergency, phone the Empire Hotel.'

'How appropriate,' replied Delores.

'Delores, shut up.' He slammed the phone into its cradle.

The telephonist, who had naturally been listening in, thought, *Holy shit, there's a marriage made in heaven. Can't wait to tell my friends.*

¶

Jake and Louise were sitting at a table on the Empire's verandah when Vance returned. His face was like stone as he walked past them into the bar.

'What the hell is wrong with him?' asked Louise.

'Don't know. Don't want to know,' replied Jake.

After quickly downing two double rum-and-Cokes at the bar, Vance ordered a third with which he joined his new friends at the table. Vance scowled at both of them.

'If you two have an ounce of brain between you, don't ever get married. It sucks.'

Louise gently touched Vance's hand. 'Not even to you, my love? That is, if you weren't already married.' Vance shook his head and smiled.

'Especially not to me, Roughly Rolled Swagg. Let's go park at the creek.'

Jake sat deep in thought as they left. He knew he wasn't going to heed Vance's advice. He had every intention of marrying TC.

¶

Next morning the Empire was back in business-as-usual mode. Pia and Mara were appalled at Sam's choice of appropriate footwear.

'Leave the kid alone. Anything is better than nothing,' snapped Jack Romeo when the subject was brought to his attention.

Jake and Bert knew they would take a lot of money today. The three hotels would be busy. The council meeting was on, and Old Jordan would probably come by to pay for the wake grog. Over the years, Jack and Bert had manipulated a discriminatory, unspoken but usually strictly adhered to, ruling as to who could drink in each of their hotels. The Majestic, which was located on the far end of the block, was run down, and maintenance on the Majestic was limited to the exact amount required to render it appropriately passable when the liquor licence came up for renewal. The poor lost souls referred to it as the town drunks, and down-and-outers spent most of their waking hours (when they were in Brolga), between 10.00 am and 10.00 pm, at the Majestic, where there were frequent brawls, which usually broke out because someone would accuse their drinking mates of stealing their change off the bar when their back was turned.

In fact, these men were intelligent, honest, hard-working people. When they needed money, they would dry out and readily find work with a droving team, in the shearing sheds, navigating on the railway lines, or pushing a shovel for the shire council. Anything available would do. Without exception, they were, each and every one of them, doing their best to escape the reality of their struggles through life. While many were born and bred in Brolga or the surrounding district, others had come to the 'end of the line' in search of a new life to replace the heartache of what they had experienced in other towns or cities. Usually their pain was caused by unfaithful wives from whom they had walked. In many cases, there were children involved. Others did not want to accept that they had been betrayed by family or close friends, usually over money matters or jealously caused by same. A couple of others were rumoured to have run from the police in other states. In Brolga, nobody cared about such things. Most Brolga gossip was simply gossip. As the Seat-of-Knowledge gentry would say, 'Haven't done any harm to us. Leave the poor buggers alone.'

The Railway Hotel was known to Brolgaites as the Brick because it was the first-ever brick building to be erected in Brolga. One night very close to its completion, Jack Romeo remarked to the bar patrons of the Empire that the builders may be a brick or so short.

'I know how to fix that, Jack; you and Bert save your crap and make a couple. Will save you both money,' suggested a smart-mouthed son of one of Brolga's so-called elite families. After completion of the Railway Hotel, every time, for months that the young man and his friends cruised past the Brick, he would say, 'Looks like the Greeks took my advice. They shat a couple of bricks and finished the pub.' For years the most-used euphemism uttered by Brolgaites was 'Shit a brick and build a pub.' When Jack and Bert Romeo finally heard about it, they were both amused. Jack said, 'Cheeky bloody louts. Let them have their fun. Better not let on about the two extra pallets of bricks we have in the brewing room.'

In concurrence with Jack and Bert's unspoken rules, drinkers at the Brick usually consisted of Brolga's railway employees, including permanent fettlers, who were housed along with their families, if they had any, in railway-owned, shanty-type accommodations on the other side of the line, shearing shed cooks, and roustabouts when shearing was in season, oil exploration crews when they were on leave, and in-house guests. Only occasionally during summer when a small country-and-western band would come from Curloo to entertain in the beer garden of the Brick did the gentry of Brolga lower their standards, desert the Empire for the evening, let their hair down, and relax while listening to their favourite songs performed live. The group initially sounded mediocre. By the end of their performance some of the audience with more than a few too many beers under their belts would proclaim that Slim Dusty and Hank Williams should step aside. This group was better than both of them put together. Jack and Bert loved these now-and-then events. With the police sergeant's okay, they could keep serving at the Brick until the concert ended at midnight, while their 'reduced-to-skeleton' staff at the Majestic and Empire Hotels closed at exactly ten.

The Empire was old and stately, always immaculately maintained. There was a grandiose air about the winding staircase; huge, brightly-shined brass planters containing magnificent ferns, and highly polished floors. Off the bar area was a smoking room adjacent to a ladies' lounge with a discreet brass plaque proclaiming same above door. The formal dining room seated a hundred. Starched white, self-embroidered, linen tablecloths and finest Buckingham silver adorned every table. Almost everyone who entered the Empire for the first time felt a sensation of stepping back in time, perhaps to the turn of the century. In fact, in the front of the Empire alongside the footpath guttering was a relic from that era in the form of a hitching rail. Many years previously a council committee had decided to leave it there in memory of Brolga's old times.

The aristocracy of Brolga and surrounding districts had long ago deemed the Empire as the place to be seen in, meet up with old friends, and tell each other the most incredible, unbelievable lies. With every drink, the bullshit became more embellished until many of the storytellers began to believe them themselves.

Cattle-sale days and the annual horse-racing carnival would see Brolga and the Empire bursting at the seams as people came from far and near. Jack and Bert loved these times. They knew the three pubs would be very busy; and, when not yelling instructions at their staff, they almost visibly rubbed their hands together in anticipation of counting the day's takings.

Old Jess and TC began work in the bar early. Jess kept mumbling about how much she loathed council meeting days. Occasionally, she would stop, tell TC what to do, then wander back into mumbling mode. Jack threw the doors open as usual exactly at 10 am, briefly visited the bar, looked around, and nodded at Jess as he walked out.

'Big day today,' he said aloud to himself as he headed for the office. Vance, Jake, and the station master arrived a few minutes later. The three appeared hot and slightly dishevelled.

'Two beers and a double rum and Coke, please, Jess. Been shifting cartons to the pharmacy since six this morning. My helpers and I need a drink,' said Vance. Jess placed the two beers on the bar, then almost slammed the rum and Coke in front of Vance.

'An educated man like you should know better than to be hitting this hard stuff so bloody early,' snapped Jess, as she looked Vance directly in the eye.

'Thank you, Jess. You look really pretty today. Don't you agree, Jake?'

'Like a beauty queen,' replied Jake. The station master nodded his head. Jess threw her head in the air.

'Smart mongrels,' she said, as she took Vance's money and headed for the cash register. When she returned with the change, Vance added, 'Jess, keep them coming; we'll be here until the refrigeration in the pharmacy is cold enough to transfer the cartons from the Brick cold room.'

'Pity someone wouldn't throw you in the cold room,' Jess replied as she smiled sarcastically. TC had been observing while busying herself doing this and that to appear she was earning her wages. She had heard every word spoken, could not make much of the conversation, except it was obvious Jess didn't like Vance very much.

People began straggling in until the bar was almost full. TC was doing the best she could to follow Jess' shouted instructions.

Good heavens, thought TC, as she rushed about. *I hate this place.* She had deliberately been avoiding Vance and Jake. The station master had left to attend to his job. Jake got her attention with, 'Our glasses are empty; Jack and Bert won't like that.'

Vance said, 'Don't know what a kid like you is doing in a joint like this. Been watching you. Did you know that every time your breasts are hit, you run a greater risk of developing breast cancer? Been watching that cash register hitting you in the breasts every time you push the Total key.'

With that he placed a medical brochure on breast cancer on the bar. TC was embarrassed. Vance and Jake laughed uncontrollably. TC wanted desperately to disappear and hoped with all her heart that nobody else had heard as she took the brochure and crumpled it in her hand. Jess, with her ears like an elephant, had heard everything.

'Leave her alone, you idiots,' she hissed, as she briskly passed by.

⁋

By noon only Vance and Jack remained in the bar. A shearing contractor and a friend who had been drinking on the verandah moved into a far corner and had just settled themselves when the ten-strong committee of the Brolga Shire Council arrived. They were arguing amongst themselves regarding some matter brought up at the morning meeting. Jess, with TC's assistance, placed their drinks on the bar. Jess, as usual, pre-empted their order as they always drank the same, be it beer, spirits, or wine.

'Who's this lot?' enquired Vance of Jake.

'You see before you the decision-makers of Brolga's future. They meet once a month at the council office to consider any type of application that requires council approval. Load of bullshit, as far as I'm concerned. If the applicant is someone they like, immediate approval is given. On the other hand, if some non-descript Tom, Dick, or Harry submits the application, these arseholes hold it up as long as possible as a show of exerting their so-called power.'

By the time the councillors had finished their fourth round of drinks, they were extremely agitated and shouting at each other. Jack Romeo came in and asked them to 'keep it quiet, boys.' One man told him to fuck off and mind his own business. Mara Romeo came in a few minutes later and advised them that their lunch was ready and reminded them that the dining room closed at two. The same man said to her, 'You fuck off, as well. We'll be there when we are ready and not before. Jess, more drinks.'

'Like to throw their bloody drinks at them,' mumbled Jess to TC. 'Mongrels don't even know how to say "please".'

TC was on the verge of tears as she helped Jess serve them their next round. Most of them were swearing profusely. Two of them were pushing and shoving each other. Just as TC gingerly placed one of the beers on the bar, one of the pushing-and-shoving men threw his arms out and knocked it over. There was silence. The man glared at TC. 'Look what you've done, you stupid, fucking moron. Now clean it up.'

TC was crying uncontrollably. Without thinking, she threw the contents of a beer glass she still had in her hand directly into his face. Momentarily, she stood still in shock at what she had done, then ran sobbing into the adjoining smoking room.

The shearing contractor and his friend clapped loudly.

'Good on you, luv.'

Jess said, 'Serves you right, you mongrel. She's a good kid. If you spoke to me like that, you'd be wearing a keg of beer rather than a glass.'

The other Shire Council committee members stood silently with their mouths gaping as they observed their fellow committee member with his beer-soaked hair, face, shirt, and tie.

One of them finally said, 'Well, I guess it's time we had lunch,' as they filed out towards the dining room. The drenched man declared loudly and angrily that he would catch up with them after he'd reported to Jack and Bert what the fucking young moron had done.

Vance and Jake had seen and heard everything. Both had similar feelings about the incident but had said nothing. They were seated opposite the door to the smoking room where they could observe TC's shaking shoulders and back as she sat sobbing. Vance broke the silence.

'Poor little thing. I was wondering the other day what on earth an innocent kid like her is doing in this hell hole. Looks child-like with the ponytail and pink ribbons. Timid, shy, little girl, that's how I see her.' Jake smiled.

'Apparently not too timid or shy to throw a beer in the shire chairman's face. Lots of people in Brolga would like to have seen that one.'

'Oh! Shit!' exclaimed Vance in disbelief.

Jess had cleaned up the mess on the bar and was now attempting to console TC as she wiped TC's tears from her cheeks with a small, wet towel. TC's handkerchief was saturated. As she fumbled with it, she looked at Jess.

'Oh, Jess, what am I going to do? Now I won't have a job, and I owe the two Mr Romeos ten pounds for my fare. I'll have nowhere to live.' TC burst into tears again. Vance and Jake had been following the scenario in silence. Jake wanted to marry her there and then. In his eyes, she was the most beautiful girl he had ever seen. She had an air of innocence and propriety about her that he had never experienced before. Vance was thinking what a vulnerable little creature she was. He felt the need to somehow help her. He knew what it was like to be poor and broke. After all, his much-loved mother had grown and sold whatever her garden could produce to put him through pharmacy school.

Jess was still attempting to comfort TC when Vance got her attention.

'One for the road, Jess. Think that refrigeration unit will be cold enough by now.'

'Probably freezing,' snapped Jess. 'That girl out there crying is the best girl ever to grace this dump. I should know; I've been here for what seems a million years. She's too damned good to be sworn at and ogled by the mob of rats who frequent this place.'

'Thanks a lot, Jess,' said Jake smiling.

'If the cap fits, wear it,' replied Jess curtly.

With that Jack and Bert entered the smoking room.

'The troops have arrived for the slaughter,' whispered Jake.

Vance replied, 'Time for us to leave.' The shearing contractor and his friend who had quietly been discussing the event also left. TC took a deep breath and composed herself as best she could, then turned to face Jack Romeo when he addressed her.

'What happened, girl?'

TC didn't have a chance to reply. Jess glared at Jack with venom in her eyes and spat.

'The mongrel deserved it. Can't imagine he speaks to his wife or daughter the way he spoke to this kid.'

'That's not the point. He is the shire chairman,' replied Bert in a most oblique manner. Jess was desperately trying to control her anger as she almost screamed at Jack and Bert.

'Jack the bloody Ripper could be shire chairman of Brolga as long as he knew what arses to kiss to get the job. In fact, Jack the Ripper would, in my opinion, have more manners in his little finger than that mob of bastards put together.'

'Jess, calm down, girl. Someone might hear you,' said Jack with concern. With that, Jess went to attend to a couple of cattle station owners who walked in as Jack and Bert had TC follow them to the office.

¶

TC sat down as directed and looked straight ahead at the Romeo brothers, who had seated themselves opposite her. Jack Romeo spoke first.

'Well, girl, obviously, you'll have to go. Pity, with your youth and looks, you would have been a great draw-card to the bar.'

'Problem is,' added Bert, 'you owe us the ten pounds for your fare to

Brolga. You can work that off helping Cheffy in the kitchen. Or you can use the hotel phone to make a reverse-charge call to your family. We are sure they will send you money to get you back to the coast.'

TC felt as if she was seeing the Romeos for the first time. They were both short, round men, immaculately attired with highly polished shoes. Both had slightly greying, thick, black hair and bushy moustaches. Obviously, they cared more about money than other human beings. Even when those poor souls had died in that tragic accident the week before, they were more concerned about how much money they would make from the wake than they were for the grieving families. Now they assumed her mother had money to send to get her home. As for the reverse-charge phone call, her mother could barely afford food let alone a telephone. Why on earth did they think she had come to a place like Brolga if it wasn't to escape what was back there. TC nodded her head at the two brothers as she vowed to herself that, should she ever be in a position of money and power, she would always remember this day by treating people the way she would like to be treated herself. She would always project herself into the other person's situation, be understanding, and help them if she could.

After being excused by the Romeos, TC went looking for Sam, whom she found half asleep in their shared room at the staff quarters. Sam quickly became wide awake as TC calmly unfolded her story. When she came to the part about throwing the beer, Sam interjected in disbelief

'You what? And the shire chairman, no less! Never thought you had it in you, TC.'

'I couldn't stand it anymore, Sam. All that foul language, shouting, pushing, and shoving got to me. You alone in Brolga know how I grew up, Sam. Something snapped inside me today. I'm not cut out for a life where all I see and hear is drunken, brawling, foul-mouthed, arrogant, rude men.'

'Not all men are like that, TC,' said Sam.

'Perhaps not,' replied TC in a soft, feeble voice. Sam became frantic when TC told her about working the fare off and the remainder of the story.

'Fat, Greek pricks,' she proclaimed. 'I'm not staying here without you. How the hell are we going to get out of here?' Sarcastically, she added, 'Perhaps your wealthy mother can send enough money for both of us.'

'We'll see,' shrugged TC. 'Everything that happens is meant to happen. That's what my mother used to tell me.'

'Let's go park on the Seat of Knowledge. It should be vacant this time of day,' suggested Sam with a laugh of bravado.

¶

After the short walk to the median strip, they seated themselves and silently stared into space. Sam was thinking, *What the hell are we going to do?* TC was deep in thought wondering how long ago the seat was erected and how many people had sat on it since. She imagined hundreds, possibly thousands, over the years. Surely some of them must have been troubled and contemplating the worst with an uncertain future, just as she was now. She closed her eyes and could hear her mother saying, 'Keep your faith, and everything will be all right.'

They continued to sit there without uttering a word. The street was practically deserted apart from a couple of dogs wandering around and the occasional pulling-up to post or collect mail at the post office. There were a few parked cars along the block. They both heard a car door slam, but neither bothered to look around.

Suddenly a voice behind them said, 'What are two pretty girls like you doing here? Sunning yourselves? Better be careful. If the elders find out you've taken up squatters' rights on their sacred seat, there'll be trouble.' Sam looked over her shoulder.

'Sit down, Jake.' TC ignored him and continued to look straight ahead. As Jake seated himself next to Sam, Vance pulled his now-clean station wagon to a halt in front of them.

'See you soon, Jake. Have a nice afternoon, ladies. What's left of it, anyway,' and drove off. Jake explained that Vance was going to look at the house which he had bought a month ago. Vance hadn't seen it yet, but had surmised it would be okay. The house had been the bank manager's residence until recently when the bank had a new one built for the replacement manager, who had a larger family. Jake looked at Sam.

'How did your mate go with the Greeks?'

Sam told him every detail. TC wanted to throttle her friend when Sam told Jake how poverty-stricken her family was. Instead, she shrugged resignedly, thinking, *Oh, well, the truth is the truth, and there's no denying it.*

After a short pause Jake spoke to both of them while looking at Sam.

'Thought as much. I'm sure Jack and Bert love money more than they love their mothers. I won't mention their wives; everyone knows they don't love them. Vance and I were discussing the Greeks. He's new to Brolga, just as you two are. He's a clever man. Already has most of the population categorised. The ones he's met, that is.' With that he stood up. 'I have to go now. See how business is going. Been helping Vance all day. See you later, Sam. You, too, TC—I hope.' Sam nodded. TC nodded her head slightly.

Liar, she thought. *You and Vance were in the Empire bar drinking most of the morning.* Sam prodded TC's shoulder. 'He's crazy about you, TC.'

'Well, I'm not crazy about him,' replied TC belligerently. 'Let's go back to our 'sumptuous' room, as you call it. We'll probably be sleeping on the railway platform soon.' By the time they reached the quarters, TC was crying again. Sam never cried, but she sure felt like it.

¶

TC was woken by a knock on the door. She had no idea how long she had been asleep nor what time it was. She noticed Sam was not there.

'Open up, luv. It's Jess.'

TC opened the door. When Jess saw her swollen, red eyes, she touched TC's forehead gently.

'Poor little thing. I've just had strong words with Jack. Trust him to hide you in the kitchen until you've worked off their miserable ten quid, then get you out of town as fast as possible before word gets around as to the reason you threw the beer in that creature's face this morning.

Bert would have pushed him, of course. I know Jack backwards. We were lovers for years. Deep down, he has a kind heart. Bert, on the other hand, probably doesn't even have a heart at all, except when it comes to counting money. If you need any help, young lady, you let me know. I mean it.' With that Jess turned towards her room a couple of yards away, looked over her shoulder, and said, 'You're a good kid.' TC smiled.

'Thank you, Jess. You're a nice lady,' she replied.

¶

TC was sitting on her bed pondering Jess' words when Sam returned in a flurry. Old Jordan's daughter, Lou, was with her. Sam, as usual, was in a hurry. Without giving TC and Lou a chance to acknowledge each other, she began talking.

'Lou and I have been at the café next door. Greeks own that, too. Hope they're better than the Greeks that own the pub ...'

'They are,' interrupted Lou.

'Anyway,' continued Sam, 'we were on our way back here to check on you when Jake Carmichael came out of the pub. He wants to see you in half an hour. Said he'd meet you outside the café. Said he'd come meet you here except the Greeks have a rule that any males over the age of eight or under the age of eighty are not allowed in the vicinity of their illustrious quarters.'

'What does he want?' enquired TC.

'Think he wants to jump on your bones, TC,' quipped Sam.

'I'm sure he does,' added Lou. 'Lived across the road from him since we were kids. My Dad says he's a spoiled young arsehole who gets everything he wants. By the way, TC, Mum and Dad said you can stay with us if you want to. Everyone in Brolga knows what happened this morning.'

TC rolled her eyes and sighed. This was all getting to be too much.

'I'm not meeting Jake Carmichael. Not under any circumstances. Tell him to jump on someone else's bones.' Lou looked at TC.

'He won't have any trouble there. I assure you.'

'Are you certain, TC?' questioned Sam as she and Lou stood up to leave. 'Never mind. We'll meet Jake for you. He'll be disappointed. That's okay. Life's tough, then we go wherever!'

Sam and Lou returned ten minutes later. Sam handed TC an envelope addressed in the most beautiful handwriting she had ever seen. The letter was addressed "TC—Whatever your surname is".

TC opened the envelope. Inside were twenty-five pounds and a note hastily written, saying, 'Have paid the Greeks their ten quid. You're off the hook. My mother wants to meet you. Be a good girl.' said Jake. Sam and Lou were both flabbergasted.

TC thought for a while, before saying, 'Thank you, Lou. Please also thank your mother and father. I'll be happy to stay at your home, as long as I can pay my way.' TC then spoke to Sam who was obviously in shock.

'Well, Sam, looks like Jake Carmichael has just purchased me for the humungous amount of thirty-five pounds. The Greeks will be happy they've got their ten. God help me.'

Silence reigned.

¶

Early the next morning, TC thanked Jess for her kindness, said 'thank you' to the Romeo family, all of whom surmised TC must have seduced Jake at Jordan's wake, hugged Sam, both vowing they would be friends forever. TC with her meagre belongings walked towards Lou's parents' house wondering what the future held in store for her. Only the Lord knew.

Vance was busy talking to Delores on the telephone as TC passed the red phone box outside the Brolga post office. Louise was seated in Vance's adjacently parked station wagon, puffing furiously on a cigarette. TC waved to Louise, who did not respond. She just kept looking straight ahead as she inhaled deeply. Vance and Delores were yelling at each other. Lou was on duty at the telephone exchange listening to every word.

'How the hell will I get to Brolga, Vance? Don't want to go to the God-forsaken dump, anyway.'

'Delores, I'll come fetch you and the boys. The house is okay. Saw it yesterday. We'll put the furniture on a truck. The house is partly furnished, anyway.'

'Have you opened the shop yet?'

'No.'

'That would be right.'

'Delores, don't start. As usual, you'll never bloody well finish. See you in two days. Be ready.'

Vance hung up angrily. As usual, he wished he were a free man. He hated the responsibility of marriage. He lit a Craven A and faked a broad smile before he spoke to Louise.

'Creek?' he questioned.

'Wherever, lover,' responded Louise.

'Elmira Ferguson's grave?'

'No! Stop suggesting that, Vance, or, I swear, you'll be out at the cemetery with that poor woman.' Vance laughed loudly.

'We'll see, Roughly Rolled. We'll see.'

He drove off.

§

Late afternoon found Lou, her parents, and TC chatting at the Shack when Jake made his presence known at the front door. TC found it difficult to look at him. She was embarrassed by the fact that he had helped her. She thanked him, then went to Lou's room, which they would be sharing, and returned with fifteen pounds.

'Here's the ten you paid the Romeos plus five of the other twenty-five I owe you.'

Jake shook his head and said, 'No, I don't want it back.'

'I don't wish to owe anybody anything. If I find I have to go home, I'll send the money to you. Once again, thank you.'

'I, for one, hope you don't have to go home, wherever that is. Would you like to go out tonight?'

Lou and her parents looked at Jake enquiringly. Every Brolga resident knew the only entertainment available was the movies, pubs, or parking at the creek.'

Jordan liked this TC kid simply because his wife and daughter appeared to do so. Lou was a good girl. Usually a loner. Jordan was aware that most Brolga people laughed behind his back and that there was a certain stigma attached to 'being the daughter of the town undertaker-cum-handyman-cum-anything. After all, the Shack sign said it all. Jordan decided he would intervene on TC's behalf. Look out for her as if she was Lou's sister. Jordan was very much aware of Jordan's reputation. As long as Lou's new friend was under his roof, he would protect her with all his might.

'Just where do you intend taking her, Jake?'

Jake was surprisingly caught off guard and replied to Jordan's question with a quavering voice.

'Well, some of my friends are going to the creek for a party.'

'She's not going,' replied Jordan. 'I know what happens at those so-called parties. No!'

TC, who had been listening intently, was deeply touched by Lou's Dad's concern. She thought how lucky she was and realised they were obviously good, caring people.

'Well, Jake. Thank you for your invitation. No, I don't want to go to the creek. You did say in your note that your mother wants to meet me. When she's ready, I'd like to meet her, also.'

Jake was relieved, thinking, *She's no push-over, this girl. She really does want to meet my mother. Got the guts to do it, too. They'll love each other. They're both short.* Jake looked down at TC.

'Okay, I'll arrange it.' He turned and walked away towards his house across the street. He was deep in thought. *Oh, shit! What have I done? I'll have to get rid of all these other women. This one's special. Mum will love her.*

¶

Jake fell asleep that night feeling content that TC was safe across the road at Old Jordan's house. After talking for hours, TC and Lou fell asleep, each secure with the knowledge that they would be friends for as long as they breathed. Sam tossed and turned in her bed at the Empire's staff quarters. She realised that TC and she had reached a crossroad in their lives. She felt sad.

§

Vance and Louise were ensconced in each other's arms down by the creek after drinking too much rum and Coke and making love as if there were no tomorrow. Louise knew she was absolutely in love with Vance. As she drifted off into the land of nod, she could think of nothing apart from Delores' pending arrival in Brolga.

'What a mess. Will simply have to see how things turn out.'

Vance was contemplating and dreading his forthcoming trip to Curloo to collect Delores and the boys. He felt helpless and hopeless as he saw his future unfolding before him. Trapped in a marriage with a woman he respected but did not love. He loved Anna. He knew Anna loved him. He pulled the now-sleeping Louise closer to him and mentally resigned himself to the fact that he would drift from woman to woman for the rest of his life, while subconsciously knowing he would, as long as he lived, be searching for another Anna. He closed his eyes, thinking, *So be it.*

§

A small, unannounced cyclone struck Brolga in the early hours of the next morning. Brolga residents were unaware of the fact until they heard the ABC radio news much later. They had slept through the winds, lightning, thunder, and rain thinking Little Angela was simply a dust storm, to which they were accustomed. Sure, a few roofs had been damaged; but, as most locals thought, *We live here. Have to cope with whatever. Who cares? Dust storms—they come—they go. Part of the privilege of living here. Goes with the territory.*

The majority of the community were good people. Always there for

81

each other when hard times hit and the chips were down. Everybody helped each other. No one would ever go hungry in their little town.

It was the custom in Brolga that the small power house would sound a siren, five days a week at twelve noon, to alert the townsfolk that it was time for lunch, when every business apart from the hotels and cafes would close for one hour. The only other times the siren would sound was to alert the town that a dust storm was approaching.

The wall of red dust came from the west of Brolga carried by wild winds and sometimes followed by heavy rain. On the occasions the rain was involved, the locals would say, 'It rained mud.' This was true as the dust was extremely thick and would fix itself to the western side of the Brolga dwellings. When the heavy rain hit, the western side of the homes appeared to have had some crazed artist go berserk with a huge, mud-filled paint brush.

That night when the elders gathered on the Seat of Knowledge, their main topic of conversation was Little Angela.

'Thought it was just a bloody dust storm. Brolga will be famous for a while now. How stupid can a man be? Slept through a bloody cyclone! Upset those idiots at the power station, didn't sound the bloody siren.' said Jock.

One of his learned mates replied, 'Jock, the poor buggers have to sleep sometimes.'

'Yeah, I suppose so.'

'Yeah,' chorused the rest of the group.

Jock thought for a while, then spoke in his matter-of-fact voice.

'Pity those poor buggers who had their roofs damaged. They have to fix them. Prove their masculinity. When it's just a bloody dust storm, the women are the ones who have to race home and rip the washing off the line and later wash down the walls after re-dusting the bloody house. Anyway, let's just observe what's going on in downtown Brolga for a while, before we head home to our lovely, nagging wives.'

His friends all nodded in agreement.

Lou and TC had spent all day detailing the interior of the Shack. They didn't know about Little Angela until Jordan returned from the pub that evening.

⁋

Jake had been thinking about TC all day. He had made a dozen or so unnecessary visits home, hoping to catch a glimpse of her across the road at Jordan's Shack. His mother asked him repeatedly why he was home so often. Jake just shrugged his shoulders and left on every instance.

⁋

Vance and Louise knew nothing about Little Angela. They were oblivious. Vance dropped Louise off in front of the Empire at ten sharp after taking her to her friend's house to make herself presentable. Knowing TC was no longer employed there, Louise asked for an interview for the position of barmaid in the Romeo brothers' Empire Hotel. She got it. The Romeos liked her forthrightness. Louise was ecstatic; she knew Vance would be there every day from ten to ten (if he could be after Delores arrived).

⁋

Vance, stocked with his fully fuelled car, carton of cigarettes, and enough rum and Coke, headed towards Curloo, Delores, and his responsibilities. He felt as if he was going to the gallows. He'd felt like that frequently lately. Perhaps it was just guilt. Perhaps it was anything. He simply felt like shit. Anna kept popping into his mind.

⁋

Sam decided TC was history, and she would have to look for new friends. 'Don't know where I'll find them. Fancy leaving me for the undertaker's daughter.' Sam didn't realise that TC would always be her friend.

¶

Vance, Delores, and their two children, Jonathon and Andrew, returned to Brolga from Curloo a couple of days later. After dropping Delores and the children at the new house, Vance found Louise at the Empire.

'How is Delores?' asked Louise.

'Fine.'

'How are the children?'

'Fine.'

'How are you?'

'Take a wild guess,' replied Vance.

'Okay. I love you.'

'Give me a double rum and Coke. I need it after that trip. What time do you finish here?'

'Won't be soon enough. Ten. See you then.'

'I'll be around.'

Louise was not only in love with this man; she also felt sorry for him. She realised he really hated his life. Still, he was trying to do the right thing by Delores and the children.

Although Louise was an extremely intelligent, well-educated, young woman, she was so besotted by Vance that it did not enter her head that Vance was doing the wrong thing by Delores, just by being there waiting for her. Vance himself was appalled that any decent man could consciously dump his pregnant wife and two small children in a strange house, in a strange town, then less than an hour later be drinking like a man possessed while killing time until his latest girlfriend got off work so they could head for the creek for another night of sex and booze. Deep down, Vance knew it wasn't Delores from whom he was trying to escape; it was himself and the mess he'd made of his life so far. During his trip to Curloo and back, he had decided to get on with things, get his new pharmacy opened, and make the best of his lot in life with Delores and the boys. He hoped he could keep to his plan but knew he would not.

§

Early in the morning a few days later, Jake Carmichael knocked on the front door of the Shack. Jake had not glimpsed TC for what seemed to him an eternity. He explained to a disgruntled Jordan, who answered the door, that the last couple of nights he had been playing poker with Vance Callahan and the Greek owner of the café until the early hours of the morning. Money meant nothing to any of them. Easy come, easy go. There was an unspoken rule at these early times of camaraderie, two thousand—win, lose, or draw—was it. Then it was time to say goodnight—or good morning—shake hands, and go home.

Vance had half-heartedly opened the pharmacy. The local Brolga girl, whom he had engaged to be his assistant, sight unseen, simply was not suitable for the position.

'Wants to be a pretty show pony, not a worker,' Vance had told Jake.

'What about TC?' replied Jake.

'She's a barmaid,' said Vance. Jake looked at Vance.

'Yes, for four or five days. She's a good girl. I'm going to marry her if she'll have me.' Vance had appeared surprised when he realised Jake was serious.

'Hope that innocent little girl is astute enough not to marry a drinking, gambling, bullshit artist like you. She's hired, mate. Won't be easy getting her past Delores. Anyway, the kid's got the job.' It did not occur to Vance that he himself was a drinking, gambling, bullshit artist, the only difference being that he was older and more experienced in these areas.

Jake explained everything to Jordan, who, by now had elected himself as TC's unofficial guardian. Jordan agreed that this was a good opportunity for TC. This meant she could stay in Brolga and be a permanent friend for his daughter, Lou. Good heavens, in such a short time those girls had become like sisters. TC was in happy shock when

Jordan told her that she was going to be a pharmacy assistant.

Vance collected TC from the Shack that evening. He advised her that he was taking her to meet his wife.

'Don't worry,' he said. 'You've got the job, anyway. Just a stupid formality. I'll see you through it.'

Delores loathed TC on site. TC was taken aback because of the aura of elegance and authority that permeated from Mrs Callahan, who was beautifully attired and spoke with authority. Every word was enunciated perfectly. TC, at the same time, felt sadness and pity for Mrs Callahan, who was obviously unaware that Mr Callahan was involved with Louise.

Vance introduced TC to Delores.

'This is TC. She is coming to work in the pharmacy.'

'Oh,' replied Delores, as she scathingly looked TC over from toe to head and back again. 'Vance, I wish to speak to you in private.' Delores and Vance moved to another room.

A beautiful little boy appeared from nowhere.

'My name is Jonathon Callahan. What's yours?' he enquired cheekily. 'You're nice. Are you one of Daddy's girlfriends?'

'No,' replied TC. Jonathon looked angelically at TC.

'I know Daddy has girlfriends. Mummy and he yell at each other about it all the time.'

TC took the little boy's hand, looked into his eyes, and said, 'Well, Jonathon, I'm not one of them.' Neither toddler Jonathon nor TC realised the taking of his little hand in hers was the beginning of a lifelong bond of respect from Jonathon towards TC and motherly love towards Jonathon from TC.

In the adjoining room, Vance had informed Delores that he had employed TC. Delores was beside herself with anger.

'Where did you find her, Vance? I suppose it was in the pub? Is she a barmaid?'

Vance's voice was heated and raised as he replied, 'One might say so. She's just a girl.'

'Very pretty one, too, I may add,' screamed Delores.

'Delores, go screw yourself. I've given the girl the job. That's it.'

Vance emerged. 'Come on TC. You'll need some sleep. I'll take you to Jordan's and see you at the pharmacy at 8.30 sharp tomorrow morning.' Vance did not speak another word to TC as he furiously drove the short distance to the Shack and dropped her off before heading at breakneck speed towards the Empire and Louise.

As he drove, he was wondering how on earth 'born to shop' Delores, attired in the latest designer-labelled clothes, could possibly be so antagonistic towards this young, innocent girl, wearing a ribbon in her hair and shoes with bows on the front. What a bloody joke.

Vance met TC at the pharmacy at 8.30 am sharp. He spent one-and-a-half hours explaining to her that the numerous, so-far-not-emptied cartons, had to be arranged in alphabetical order from A to Z, both within the retail area as well as in the dispensary. He told her how to read a prescription with its roman numerals, et cetera, then painstakingly instructed TC as to how each and every brown-paper, string-tied package should be presented for mail truck haulage to customers who lived on outlying properties once the orders started coming in. At 10 am, Vance handed TC a set of keys to the pharmacy.

'If I'm not here, open and close. Good luck. If you need me, call the pub. If Delores calls, phone the pub and say it's an emergency. She's been told always to phone before she comes.' Vance left the pharmacy and headed across the street to the Empire.

TC was in shock. It seemed to her that there were a million cartons. She decided after a short period of meditation to sort out and place them in alphabetical order. She couldn't believe Mr Callahan's casual attitude. She was terrified at the thought of a prescription coming in. Especially the Latin part. She decided to worry about it when she was faced with it. In the meantime, there was obviously plenty to do.

TC worked at sorting things out until 2 am the next morning. She took no notice of the powerhouse siren for the obligatory lunch break, and locked the pharmacy doors at 4.30 pm. when Lou arrived to help her. TC was determined to have everything in order by the next morning when Mr Callahan arrived. With Lou's help she achieved her goal. Everything was alphabetically perfect in all areas.

When Lou and TC left the pharmacy, Jake Carmichael was parked outside waiting.

'Good morning, ladies,' he said as he debonairly opened the front passenger-side and rear passenger-side doors of his brand-new Falcon Futura. It was black with red stripes.

'New car, Jake?' enquired Lou while nodding her head. 'Guess I get in the back?'

'What do you think, TC?' asked Jake as he sought her praise and approval of his new pride and joy.

TC said nothing as she seated herself in the passenger seat. Truth was Jake had driven past the pharmacy after leaving Vance at the Empire around 8.00 pm, seen TC and Lou working, gone home, eaten dinner, talked about TC to his mother, Thel, called a nurse at the hospital, picked her up, drove her to the creek, shared wild, abandoned sex with the nurse for a few hours, drove her back to the hospital, then cruised around and around the streets of Brolga until he saw TC and Lou leave the pharmacy.

Jake drove to his mother's home in silence. He was upset that TC didn't appear to be impressed by his new car. He was even more upset when he pulled his car to a halt and TC, along with Lou, got out of his car, and thanked him in unison for the lift as they walked across the road to the Shack.

Little bitch didn't even give me the chance to open the car door for her, thought Jake. He made a mental note to get even with her sometime in the future.

¶

TC naively thought by the end of her first week at the pharmacy that Vance had a routine which consisted of arriving at 8.30 each morning, making a few telephone calls, spot-checking shelves for dust before leaving at 10.00 for the Empire. He gave her the same instructions each morning after she had collected any mail. Apart from that, he rarely spoke to her. In the early days of the Brolga pharmacy, there was no business, so TC kept herself busy by dusting. She was determined that Mr Callahan would not catch her out by finding one speck when he conducted his daily check. She was extremely grateful that he had employed her. Especially as she had overheard his conversation with his wife.

After a while, TC began to think the only reason for being there was to keep the premises clean and to allow Vance the freedom to spend his days at the Empire. She decided it was none of her business. She had employment. That was a God-send in itself. She often thought of Jake and how he had lent her the money after paying the Romeo brothers. She had a feeling he had asked Vance to employ her but she wasn't sure, as no one had mentioned it to her.

Jake had purposely been avoiding TC since the morning when she was so rude regarding his new car. He purposely drove up and down Brolga Street unnecessarily, knowing that she would have to notice him. He had been shocked one night when his mother handed him an envelope containing the residual of the money TC owed him along with a slip of paper with 'Thank you' written on it.

'That girl you are always talking about asked me to give this to you, Jake,' said Mrs Carmichael. Jake opened it and said nothing.

So, she's got principles as well as everything else, he thought. *I will marry her, no matter what.*

¶

The first prescriptions were presented at the Brolga pharmacy about six weeks after it opened. Previously, the hospital had dispensed all prescriptions issued by the flying doctor whenever he visited. Now, with a fully stocked pharmacy within the town, it was more convenient and less expensive to the government of the time to write the prescriptions at the hospital and have them filled at the pharmacy.

Somehow Vance had prior knowledge that the government was about to employ a permanent registered doctor for the Brolga hospital. This doctor could also operate as a general practitioner privately outside of hospital hours while being on call to the hospital in an emergency. This arrangement would take a load off the flying doctor, who had a lot of territory to cover.

TC was beside herself when the first person presented his prescription. She couldn't understand one word written on it except TDS, which meant three times daily. She did her best to retain her composure as she took the 6 x 4 pieces of paper from the man.

'Thank you. Please come back in ten minutes.'

'No. I'll wait,' he replied.

TC smiled, went to the telephone in the dispensary, and dialled the telephone exchange to be put through to the Empire. As she waited to be connected, four more people holding prescriptions in their hands entered the pharmacy. TC felt as if she was about to pass out as she observed through the one-way mirror from the dispensary two more people coming in, also bearers of prescriptions. There was no answer from the Empire. TC hoped everyone there had passed out, especially Mr Callahan. With as much composure as she could muster, she gently placed down the telephone and walked out into the dispensary, filled with what seemed to her a sea of faces.

'Oh. There's a slight problem,' she smiled. 'Please guard this place. I'll be back soon.' She was angrier than she had ever been in her young life. She strode determinedly across the road to the window of the Empire bar. There she saw Vance, laughing and carefree.

'Mr Callahan,' she yelled. 'Put that drink down, stop laughing, and get the hell back to your pharmacy now.'

Everyone in the bar began laughing.

'I mean now, Mr Callahan.'

Vance knew the kid meant it, so he nodded his head and moved quickly towards the door.

'Don't ever speak to me again like that, TC!'

'Don't ever leave me with all these prescriptions again, Mr Callahan. You told me if I needed you, I should call the Empire. Nobody answered.'

'Perhaps nobody heard the telephone.'

'Not my problem, Mr Callahan.'

Vance and TC entered the pharmacy, both smiling at the queue of anxious prescription-bearing Brolga residents as if everything on earth was wonderful. TC was thinking Mr Callahan would never grow up.

Vance was thinking, *Gee, she's a gutsy little thing.*

Mutual respect for each other was born that day. TC observed Vance professionally and quickly gathered and labelled prescribed medications and listened closely as he told her how to instruct each of the flying doctor's patients regarding dosage. None of these people had trust in or respect for Vance. That would come later. Everyone in Brolga knew that Vance was on with Louise and how he had literally dumped Delores and their children in the house before going off and marauding with Louise. Not only that, but he had hired a girl who had come to Brolga as a barmaid after declaring a local girl unsuitable.

§

'Going back to the pub, TC,' said Vance after the last prescription-bearing person had left.

'Don't think so, Mr Callahan,' replied TC. 'I need to speak to you about a few things.' Their conversation was brought to a halt when Jake and Louise entered via the back door.

Louise put her hands on Vance's shoulders as she said, 'So, you are a pharmacist after all, my love. Bet you impressed everyone, especially this kid,' as she gave TC a look that could be interpreted as admiration or hatred. 'I have the afternoon off. We can go anywhere you want, except visit Elmira Ferguson's tombstone.'

Jake very much wanted to speak to TC, but he was too well mannered to interrupt the conversation between Vance and Louise. He simply stood there observing the girl he had made up his mind to marry.

She's lovely, he thought. *Forget the nurses; forget everyone else; I want her.*

Vance and Louise left without a word to Jake and TC, both laughing loudly as they made their exit. Jake and TC looked at each other in silence. Jake spoke first.

'My aunt and uncle are going east to be close to their sons and need someone to caretake their home. They want to meet you.'

Jake's mother had listened to Jake speak about TC so frequently she wanted her to come to Sunday lunch, which was a family tradition. The family gathered for a weekly feast and all invited loved ones sat down together and enjoyed each other's company. TC could meet his aunt and uncle there.

'After all,' Jake said, 'you live across the street; I won't use any petrol collecting you. Anyway, things must be getting crowded at Jordan's Shack.'

'Not really. Lou and I will be friends for as long as we live. We have become very close. All I have to do is help Lou keep the shack clean and pay ten shillings a week for room and board. They are good people,' said TC as she extracted twenty pounds from her small, pink purse and placed it on the table.

'Thank you, Jake, for helping me. Thank you.' Jake was taken aback.

'She's not only the girl I'm going to marry. She's also honest. Bloody hell!' Tears glistened in his eyes. TC saw his reaction and reiterated her, 'Thank you.' Jake, who was rarely openly emotional, was eager to make a hasty retreat.

'See you Sunday?' he asked as he left.

'Thank your mother for the invitation. Yes. Lou's parents have been very kind to me, but I suppose I should move out if the opportunity is here.'

¶

Filled with trepidation TC was welcomed to the Carmichael home by an eager Jake, who had been sitting on the front verandah for what seemed an eternity to him. He so much wanted her to fit in with his family. He hoped with all his heart that his aunt and uncle would like her and approve of her as a suitable caretaker for their home. TC felt warm and contented when she entered Jake's mother's home. She could feel love. Thelma was in the kitchen retrieving a huge baking dish containing two roasted legs of lamb from the oven. Jake's little sister, three-year-old Carla, stood in a corner shyly sucking her thumb while silently scrutinizing TC before saying, 'Jake, you look very high next to her.'

Thel, Jake, and TC all laughed before Thel replied, 'Carla, this is Jake's friend, TC, and Jake is not high next to her. He's tall next to her. He's tall next to me, too. I think TC and I are about the same height.'

'Most men want to marry a girl like their mother,' said Jake.

TC was in shock. Thel obviously wasn't as she asked TC to place plates in the oven for warming. Carla was still in the corner. She was laughing uncontrollably, yet speaking at the same time.

'Jake wants to marry TC. Jake wants to marry TC,' she said repeatedly until Thel's sister and brother-in-law entered the kitchen, both questioning Carla in unison as to why she was laughing.

Thel said, 'Carla, stop being silly.' Then she introduced her sister, Flo, and brother-in-law, Doug, to TC. TC liked them immediately. Both of them obviously loved Thel, Jake, Carla, and Thel's other four children, who were away in boarding school. From conversation she realised that Jake was almost the same age as Flo and Doug's two sons and they were very close.

They ate lunch in what Thel referred to as the breakfast room. The breakfast room consisted of an extra-long, red-and-grey laminate table with stainless steel legs and twelve matching chairs. There were eight push-out windows and one door adjacent to which was a rainwater tank. TC wondered why the room was called the breakfast room and not the dining room, as obviously the breakfast room was the dining room. Everyone was talkative and happy. TC felt comfortable. She found herself wanting permanently to be part of this family as she offered to do the dishes while the family talked. Thel thanked TC profusely. TC gathered the plates and took them to the kitchen sink. There were no window screens in those days, and the left-over baked lamb, which Thel had left on the kitchen sink, was covered in flies. TC made a mental note never to eat sheep meat again. Not because she didn't like the taste, simply because obviously the flies loved it. She wasn't game to mention the flies to anyone. She made them fly away, found a tea towel to cover the meat, and prayed that nobody would eat it later.

After TC finished the washing up, she re-joined the happily chatting group in the breakfast room. After seating herself she looked enquiringly at Jake's aunt and uncle.

'I'm not certain what to call you as I don't know your surname. I won't feel comfortable referring to you as Doug and Flo; in my opinion that would be disrespectful given my age.'

'It's Delaney, girl,' replied Doug before directing his next words towards Jake, at whom he winked.

'Well, Jake, you've done it this time, young man. Not only is she good looking and can wash dishes; she also has principles and manners.'

'Why did you wink at Jake, Uncle Doug?' asked Carla. Everyone laughed. Carla's question was not answered.

'There it is, girl. You call us Uncle Doug and Auntie Flo. I have a feeling we'll be just that one day. You can move into our house tomorrow. It will give your Auntie Flo and me a few days to get to know you a little better before we go east. All you have to do is look after the place and pay for the telephone.'

A speechless TC, with tears glistening in her eyes, looked across the table at Doug and Flo Delaney and nodded her head in disbelief.

'No tears, girl' commanded Doug. 'I'm your uncle now, and in this instance what I say goes. Come around here and give your Auntie Flo and me a hug.'

TC's tears were out of control as she walked around the table to hug her new aunt and uncle, who both stood up and put their arms around her.

'Always wanted a daughter, didn't we, Flo?'

Flo nodded her head as she also burst into tears. A lifelong mutual bond of love and respect was born between the three of them during the brief moment they stood holding each other.

'Why are they crying, Jake?' asked Carla.

'Because they are happy,' replied an obviously touched Jake.

'Time for us to go home, Flo. Thanks for the meal, Thel. See you tomorrow, girl. Bye, Jake. Thanks for finding our caretaker for us. Bye, little Carla.'

As Jake's aunt and uncle left Jake's mind was racing.

Piece of cake, he thought. *Knew they would like her.* He had already conjured countless reasons to visit TC after Doug and Flo had gone east. He realised snaring TC was not going to be easy. She had hardly acknowledged him today.

I'll have to be patient. It will take a long time. Never mind. He decided he had plenty of time, and, after all, he was Jake Carmichael; he usually got everything he wanted. Why should TC be the exception?

Jake's mother showed TC to the bathroom so she could wash her face. As she looked in the mirror at her red, puffy eyes, she was thinking about how lucky she was to have met the Delaneys and what a kind and lovely couple they were. Perhaps, after all, coming to Brolga was part of her destiny. She had a nice job, liked her boss, Mr Callahan, even though she rarely saw him. Now she would have her own place to live where she could have her own bedroom and bathroom and no longer feel guilt over being a burden to Lou's family. Suddenly, she realised she owed everything to Jake Carmichael. Jake had paid the Romeos for her fare and lent her more money to see her through. Jake had got her the job at the pharmacy. Now Jake had found her a place to live. She shook her head in confusion as to why he kept helping her, and straightened her shoulders before joining Jake and his mother, who had been talking in the lounge room. It still didn't occur to her that Jake was purchasing her.

Their conversation stopped when TC entered the room. She felt uncomfortable, so decided she should leave in case they were discussing family or business matters.

'Thank you for lunch, Mrs Carmichael. Sorry about the tears. I didn't expect ...' Thel Carmichael interrupted before TC could finish.

'Don't worry about it, TC. You'll get used to us. Carla is having a nap and I'm about to join her. I'm sure Jake would like you to stay and keep him company for a while.'

TC felt trapped as she replied, 'Thank you, Mrs Carmichael.'

Jake was elated his mother had put TC on the spot for him without knowing what she had done.

'Don't play your music too loudly, Jake. I want to be able to sleep for a little while,' said Thel as she left for a while.

Jake didn't reply to his mother. He was too busy trying to come up with something to say to TC. TC seated herself in the chair furthest away from where Jake was sitting.

'I could move that chair out on to the verandah for you. Only problem would be we'd have to yell at each other and that would keep Mum awake,' said Jake sarcastically.

TC couldn't help laughing as she replied, 'Am I that obvious?'

'Not if I was stupid, blind, or both. I'm fortunate enough not to have those afflictions, TC; so, yes you are blatantly obvious.'

TC opened her mouth to speak.

'I'm not finished yet, TC,' Jake said seriously. 'Just what have I done to you that makes you dislike me so much? You didn't even like my new car,' as he stood up shaking his head and began pacing up and down the room.

How childish, thought TC. *Fancy bringing his car into it.* She was very much aware that Jake was in a foul mood. It was her first glimpse of what lay ahead in the future as she mustered up the courage to reply.

'Well, Jake, I do like you. How could I possibly not like you after all you've done to help me? As for your car, I like it as well. From what I hear from Lou, just about every eligible, pretty girl in Brolga likes you and your car. Even the nurses at the hospital like you and your car. Let's face it, Jake; you're the catch of the district. You can just about get any girl you want.'

Except you,' Jake snapped.

'And Lou,' added TC. Jake slumped into his chair opposite TC.

'I want you,' Jake said quietly as he looked TC directly in the eyes.

TC wanted to tell him that Lou had also told her that Jake Carmichael always got whatever and whomever he wanted and it was about time he missed out. Instead, she stood up to leave.

'Jake, I truly appreciate everything you've done for me. We can be friends. Apart from that, we hardly know each other and already your aunt and uncle have adopted me as their niece and are about to welcome me into their home and trust me to do the right thing by them. There's also the money you lent me, not to mention you asking Mr Callahan to give me work. You've changed my life with your kindness, and I shall always be extremely grateful for that. I have to go and tell Lou and her parents what I'm doing.' She hesitated. 'Jake, I didn't like to mention it to your mother, but when I went into the kitchen to do the dishes, the left-over lamb was encrusted with flies. Just thought I'd tell you.'

Jake watched her as she walked across to the Shack. He then went to the kitchen, wrapped the left-over lamb in newspaper, and threw it in the bin. He spoke softly to himself, 'Well, looks as if she's thoughtful as well as all the rest. I still intend to marry her, no matter what she says now.'

With that he picked up the telephone and asked the telephonist to put him through to the nurses' quarters. The telephonist on duty at the exchange just happened to be Lou, who thought TC would still be at the Carmichaels'. Lou automatically listened in as Jake made arrangements with an excited nurse to pick her up around eight. Of course, their destination was going to be down by the creek.

What an arsehole, thought Lou. *Probably been trying to con TC for hours. Now he's on the phone to one of the hospital harlots. Thank God, TC can see right through him. Hope she stays that way. Won't be easy with Jake.*

Lou in her innocence couldn't understand why Jake was hitting the creek bank that night when he was obviously besotted with TC. Lou actually liked Jake. They had grown up living across the road from each other. It never seemed to worry Jake, or any of the other Carmichaels, that her family lived in a thrown-together shanty called the Shack and, because they couldn't afford a telephone, and were using the Carmichaels' phone when one was needed. Lou simply didn't want her new, yet closest, friend to be charmed, then hurt by Jake.

A short time later, Lou who had literally run home from work, was surprised to find TC packing her few clothes into her tiny case. Lou, who had been desperate to find out how lunch at the Carmichaels' had gone and to report on Jake's phone call to the nurse, stood silently at the doorway to her bedroom. She was obviously disappointed and sad when she said, 'You're going to live at the Delaney's. I knew they would like you. I don't want you to go.'

'I know. I'll miss you, too, but I can't stay here forever. Your parents have been so kind to me, and you and I are like sisters. You guys don't have much of anything Lou, yet you welcomed me into your home without hesitation. Think of it this way, Lou; after tonight, you'll have your room back to yourself and I'll ask Mr and Mrs Delaney if you can come stay with me sometimes.'

'I hope they'll stay, "yes",' replied Lou softly.

TC looked down at her case filled with her worldly possessions.

'Know what, Lou? Don't know about you, but I always dreamed about growing up and having a wardrobe filled with beautiful clothes, multitudes of high-heeled shoes in every colour with matching handbags, of course, loads and loads of exquisite jewellery, a beautiful home and a big flash car.'

'No, TC. All I've ever dreamed about is getting out of Brolga. I know I'll do that one day. I also know you'll have all the things you dreamed of. I just know it.'

They hugged each other. Lou didn't bother to mention Jake and the nurse. She heard his car start up in front of his mother's place around a quarter-to-eight and thought to herself, *Hope your penis falls off, Jake.* She then continued talking to TC about movies and music.

¶

When TC told Vance Callahan the next morning about her arrangement with the Delaneys, he changed from his usual, 'I am the boss and you are the slave' attitude. He appeared very interested as he questioned her at length as to when the Delaneys were leaving, would she feel okay living by herself, and did she require an advance on her pay to buy anything she might need. He didn't bother with his 'checking for dust' routine that morning. He knew he didn't have to.

§

When TC returned from the post office with the mail, he said, 'TC, you're a hard worker and a quick learner. Despite what my wife says, I'm happy I employed you. You are a good girl; make sure you stay that way. You're young, extremely attractive, and you're smart. You can do anything you set your mind to. The world is your oyster, TC. I want you to do as I say. Never do what I do. Now that my lecture is over, I'm going.'

TC, while still digesting his words of praise and advice, asked, 'Mr Callahan, will you be at the Empire?'

'Not today,' he replied. 'Louise is off. We're going for a drive.'

'What if I get a prescription?'

'You'll work it out,' he replied as he walked out the back door.

TC was about to ask what she should do if Mrs Callahan called to say she was coming to the pharmacy, but he had gone. TC was happy that morning. She went about her work thinking how good Vance's words had made her feel. She decided to work extra hard to please him. To her surprise, a dozen or so orders were phoned in from outlying properties for next-day pick-up by the mail truck. Jake called her just as the one o'clock siren sounded.

'It's Jake, TC. How would you like me to drive you to the Shack to collect your gear?'

'No, thank you, Jake. I have it here. Brought it with me this morning.'

'What? All of it?'

'Yes.'

'Would you like me to pick you up after work and I'll take you to Doug and Flo's? Do you want to come home for lunch?'

'Yes, Jake, to the first question; no thank you to the second. I have things to do.'

TC put the phone down. Jake wondered what on earth she could have to do in Brolga during lunch shutdown except go to the café or one of the pubs. He knew she wouldn't be doing either.

¶

In fact TC was gathering the orders for the mail truck. She knew Mr Callahan liked everything to be packaged and labelled meticulously. With practice, she had mastered the boxing, brown paper wrapping and string-tying. The labels were a problem and took time—she had never needed to use a typewriter prior to coming to the pharmacy, so she decided to leave that until last. She would lightly pencil the name and address on the outside of the package, then place the label over it later. It was almost half-past-two when she realised she had not re-opened the pharmacy doors. She was entering details of the customers and purchases on the account card for the last of her orders and dreading the typing of the labels when the phone rang. Before answering the phone, she rushed to the door and opened in.

'Good afternoon. Brolga Pharmacy,' as she put the receiver to her ear.

'TC, its Delores Callahan. Is Vance there, please?'

'No, Mrs Callahan, he went somewhere.' TC was trembling.

'Where did he go?'

'He didn't say, Mrs Callahan,' replied TC.

'Good,' replied Delores. 'When he returns from somewhere, ask him to call me please.' Delores hung up.

The phone rang as two ladies who had prescriptions filled the week before came into the pharmacy. TC acknowledged them before answering the call. It was another order. She was about to serve the ladies when the phone rang again. Another order. Four more orders were called in while TC was attempting to serve the ladies. Both of them were very friendly and patient.

'Where's the chemist? You need some help,' said one of the ladies with a smile.

Her friend added, 'Well, I guess there's a method in his madness; he's thrown you in at the deep end. You'll learn quickly, kid.'

'I hope so,' replied TC. 'I'm sorry to keep you waiting. My name is TC, by the way.'

The women introduced themselves. TC didn't quite catch their names as she concentrated on ringing up their purchases on the cash register.

'What does 'TC' stand for?' enquired on of them.

TC looked up and smiled. 'I'd rather not say. Everyone calls me TC. Have done since I was born. Guess my mother made some mistake in interpretation of its meaning.'

'Oh,' replied the women in unison. Both were obviously suppressing their curiosity as they left.

The telephone rang. It was Delores Callahan again.

'Is he back yet, TC?'

'Sorry, Mrs Callahan. No, he's not.'

'Fine.' Delores hung up.

TC looked at the clock; it was four o'clock.

'Where on earth is Mr Callahan?' she wondered as she began gathering baby oil, shampoos, toothpaste, baby food, et cetera, for the first of her six remaining orders for the truck. TC worked as quickly as she could, keeping in mind everything had to be absolutely correct. Two more orders were called in just before five. TC muttered to herself that she would choke Mr Callahan on his return as she realised she now had five parcels left to put together as well as all that labelling. She locked the pharmacy door, before angrily gathering the items listed on the next order. Jake called.

'There's a commercial traveller from one of the companies we deal with in town. He's going for a few beers at the Empire, so I'll be a bit late.'

'Doesn't matter,' replied a relieved TC. 'I'll probably be here for hours. Can you please let your aunt and uncle know?'

'I already have. They understand. See you TC.'

It was eight-thirty when Louise and Vance came through the back door. They were both blind drunk and laughing loudly. TC was about to type the first of what seemed in her mind at the time a million labels.

She was tired and hungry and upset that she was late for the Delaneys.

'Any customers today, TC?' asked Vance.

'Two nice ladies came in,' replied TC without turning to look at her boss and Louise.

'Did they spend any money?'

'Almost twenty-five pounds.' TC was trying to concentrate on the typewriter. 'They bought cosmetics.'

'Good,' said Vance. He walked past her to the cash register and extracted twenty pounds. As he turned back to the dispensary, he was shocked to see the pile of neatly stacked boxes on the floor of the shop.

'Good heavens, TC. You have been busy,' said a surprised Vance.

'Yes, I have Mr Callahan. Mrs Callahan phoned twice. She wants you to call her.' Vance nodded his head before looking at a giggling Louise.

'Come on, Roughly Rolled, let's go to the Empire before it closes.'

Poor Mrs Callahan, thought TC, as she laboriously got on with the name and address labels.

§

TC was fixing the last label on the last box when she glanced across the road to see Bert Romeo close the door of the Brick hotel. She felt very tired as she sat down at the dispensary desk. She wondered what to do. Jake hadn't come back, and she had no idea where his aunt and uncle lived, and it was probably too late now to go to their place. She contemplated sleeping on the floor in the dispensary. She was startled when she heard banging on the front door. It was Jake. He was obviously inebriated. His head was slightly wobbling from side to side.

'Sorry, TC; I got tied up.' TC rolled her eyes.

'So I can see. Doesn't matter. I've just finished the mail.'

'You should ask your boss for overtime,' he slurred before continuing. 'Come on, let's get going; your new aunt and uncle are waiting for you.'

'It's too late,' TC said with defeat in her voice.

'No, it's not. Now come on.'

TC locked the back door, picked up her bag, turned out the lights, and locked the front door. Jake was already behind the wheel of his car. She opened the passenger-side door and sat down, holding her bag.

'Travelling light?' asked Jake.

'Got no choice at the moment,' replied TC.

With that, Jake slammed his foot on the accelerator. With breakneck speed, he drove to the end of the next block, did a screaming u-turn around the median strip, then almost instantly turned left into a long gravel driveway before screeching to a halt beside a house. Gravel flew everywhere, so TC wondered why he didn't worry about getting stone chips on his new car.

From the landing at the top of a short staircase at the rear of the house, Doug Delaney said, 'Jake, you're a wild, young bugger. Flo and I heard you from the moment you left up town. It's a bloody wonder you didn't kill yourself, not to mention this girl, when you came around the medium and belted up the driveway.'

Jake laughed. Doug directed his attention towards TC.

'Make sure this nephew of mine walks you home in the future. Come on in. Auntie Flo and I have been waiting for you. Your dinner's gone cold, but if you're hungry, you can have some toast and corned beef.'

TC declined; her hunger pains had long since disappeared.

'What about me, Uncle Doug?' asked Jake.

'You get your butt home to bed, Jake Carmichael, and don't bother driving like a lunatic.'

With that Jake saluted his uncle, jumped in his car, and carefully and slowly backed out of the driveway before taking off faster than a speeding bullet up Brolga Street. They could hear his car until he pulled up at his mother's house.

'One of these days that boy is going to get himself arrested,' his uncle said while shaking his head in concern.

Auntie Flo told TC she looked tired.

'Come on, luv, I'll show you your room and the bathroom. We'll talk tomorrow. When we leave, you can use our bedroom if you like. It's at the front of the house and much cooler.'

TC said 'Goodnight' to Doug and Flo, took a shower, climbed into bed, and was soon asleep.

The next morning Flo woke TC.

'Get ready for work, luv, then come have some breakfast.'

They chatted until TC left for work. TC still couldn't believe how lovely these people were to her. A few days ago, they didn't know she existed.

9

TC arrived at the pharmacy five minutes late. She didn't have a watch but the clock on the pharmacy dispensary wall said eight-thirty-five. The shop was already open. Vance was in the dispensary. He looked dreadful.

'You're late, TC. Make sure you're on time in the future,' he snapped at her.

'I'm sorry, Mr Callahan,' replied TC timidly. Vance glared at her.

'Move these bloody boxes to the front of the shop for pick up. You should have done that before you went home yesterday.'

TC was seething. She wanted to get the boxes and throw them at him, one by one. Instead, she did as instructed. She had not quite finished when Vance snapped at her from the dispensary door.

'Hurry up with that, then go get the mail.'

That was it for TC. She plonked the last box on the stack, then turned and strode quickly to the dispensary door. With hands on her hips, she burst out, 'Mr Callahan, I may be young and I'm certainly grateful to you for giving me a job; however, I am also human and I simply won't tolerate you speaking to me as if I'm a poor mongrel dog. Sure, I was five minutes late by the clock. Who's to say the clock isn't five minutes fast? I worked thirteen-and-a-half hours straight yesterday, while you were out doing God knows what with Louise. Mrs Callahan rang twice and was short with me. It's not my fault I don't know where you are. As a matter of fact, I prefer not to know where you are. Then I won't have to lie. You didn't even say "hello" to me when you came in last night at eight-thirty. Surely you could see I was struggling to type the labels, or perhaps you were too drunk to notice. Lastly, I would appreciate your making yourself available on future mail-order days and when the flying doctor is in town. I'm going to collect the mail now. If I still have a job when I get back, that's fine. If I don't, then that's fine, too.'

TC snatched the mailbox key off a hook on the wall and stormed out with her head held high. Vance, mouth open in shock, sat at his office desk. His mind was racing.

'Holy effing hell. Who would have thought she'd have it in her. What a little spitfire.' He began laughing as he extracted a Craven A from his cigarette packet. He was puffing on his cigarette when TC returned. She placed the mail on the desk, replaced the key on the hook, then looked Vance squarely in the eyes.

'What's your decision, Mr Callahan?'

Vance burst into laughter before saying, 'Perhaps the clock is five minutes fast. I'm sorry about the way I spoke to you. It's not your fault I've got a hangover from hell and had a row with Delores this morning. You're right about everything you said. Of course, you still have your job, and I promise I'll try to be more responsible where the shop is concerned.

TC nodded and replied 'Good.'

¶

Vance didn't go to the Empire that morning. Instead, he sat at his desk chain-smoking and deep in thought. He didn't speak at all until TC had finished stacking the shelves.

'TC,' he said, 'would you please make some coffee, then open and sort the mail. It's been piling up for weeks.' Vance signed countless cheques while TC was opening the mail. Neither of them spoke until the siren sounded; the phone had not rung all morning. They both stood up to leave for lunch.

Vance looked at TC. 'I meant what I said yesterday. You are a good girl and a gutsy one at that. When you finish sorting the mail, write the cheques for any accounts and get them ready to post tomorrow. Don't forget to fill in the cheque butts. I'll show you how and where to do the filing this afternoon.'

As they left the pharmacy, Jake with his mother and Auntie Flo pulled up on the other side of the street. Mrs Carmichael called out to TC.

'Come home and have some lunch with us, luv.'

Vance watched TC walk across and get in Jake's car before heading for the Empire. He didn't go back to the pharmacy that afternoon.

TC had never seen a cheque book before, so was filled with trepidation as she picked it up after sorting out the accounts. She was worried about the butt part Vance had mentioned. She figured it out very quickly and wrote until she ran out of signed cheques, then decided to fill in the few extra needed for Mr Callahan to sign. When she finished, she addressed the envelopes, stamped them, and placed them neatly on the desk. She wished Vance would come back so she could learn filing. Delores called at three-fifteen.

'Is he there?'

'No, I'm sorry, Mrs Callahan.'

End of conversation. Lou called at three-sixteen. She had heard the brief call.

'What did you do to Mrs Callahan, TC?'

'Nothing that I know of, Lou.'

They chatted for a while, then TC asked Lou if she knew anything about filing papers.

'Sure, TC. You put the paperwork in alphabetical order in the filing case next to the desk. It's that green metal cabinet with the pull-out drawers. I saw it when I was helping you unpack the boxes.'

'Piece of cake. Sometimes I'm such a dummy, Lou.'

'Don't think so. See you soon.' Lou was gone.

The filing was completed by five when TC closed up. TC was happy because she'd learned two things new to her that day—how to write a cheque and how to file papers.

§

Sam and Brad Lester passed by in his utility car as TC was walking down the block to the Delaney's house. TC waved but Sam averted her eyes, then looked straight ahead as they drove by. Sam had not been to see TC since she left the Empire. Sam knew TC would not go to see her at the hotel after what had happened. TC had seen Sam go into the café almost every afternoon. The café was next to the Brick Hotel, and through the wide frontage of the pharmacy there was a clear view of both buildings. TC was hurt that Sam had never walked across the street to say 'hello', but that was Sam. They had been friends since the first day they went to school. Sam would come looking for TC if something went wrong. She always had.

Truth was Sam was jealous of TC's new friendship with Lou; and, when TC started working at the pharmacy, Sam thought nothing would ever be the same between them. She was right. Things were never quite the same.

¶

Auntie Flo and Uncle Doug showed TC everything about their home that night. What could go wrong and what to do if it did. They were leaving the next morning. Uncle Doug told her the last thing before they all went to bed.

'Occasionally you might find a snake on the concrete path or in the bathroom. If the creek goes dry and it's really hot, they'll sometimes find their way up here and curl up under the house, where it's cooler during the day, and head for the bathroom at night. One day Flo found one in the laundry.'

TC went cold. She had just taken a shower in the bathroom, which was located next to the laundry opposite the back stairs. She had just walked across that path.

'Don't worry, girl,' added Doug. 'They usually slither away.'

TC was mortified and wondered what would happen if the snake or snakes didn't slither away or she accidentally stepped on one.

On seeing TC's reaction, Auntie Flo said, 'That's why the driveway is gravel, TC. Snakes don't like it. It's only now and then one will find its way across the front lawn. Now, go to bed. We'll call you in a couple of days.'

TC hugged them both.

'I'll be all right. I'll look after the house.'

That night TC couldn't get to sleep for hours. All she could think about was snakes, hundreds of them.

⁋

Auntie Flo had left an alarm clock for TC. When it woke her, she quickly got out of bed to say a final goodbye to Doug and Flo. They had already gone. TC felt alone for the first time in her life.

⁋

Vance was not at the pharmacy that morning. TC knew he had been there at some time because he had left a note, which read, 'Have signed the three cheques you needed. Fill them out and post. Will see you when I see you. Great job with the filing. Good girl.'

'Here we go again,' said TC to the walls. The phone rang a few minutes later. TC knew it was Delores before she picked it up.

'Have you seen Vance this morning, TC?'

'No, Mrs Callahan.'

'Well, when did you see him last?'

'Yesterday when the siren went for lunch,' replied TC.

'Tell him to call me when he arrives.'

⁋

Brolga pharmacy had a lot of customers that morning. They were mostly women, and all except two knew her name was TC. Obviously, word did spread fast in Brolga; half of them asked what TC stood for. She simply smiled at them and told them it was a secret between her mother and herself. Apart from the two who didn't know her name, everyone was friendly towards her. TC correctly assumed those two women were wives of property owners. She remembered with a smile what Jess had said at the Empire. By siren time, Delores had called four more times.

'Is he there yet?'

'No, sorry, Mrs Callahan.'

TC really wanted to go across the road to the café for a sandwich and a Coke, but couldn't afford to look at a Coke, let alone buy one. A sandwich to go with it, well, that was a dream. She walked the short block-and-a-half home and counted her blessings all the way. Flo and Doug had left their small freezer filled with meat and the refrigerator stocked with enough food to feed a family for a week. TC knew she couldn't eat it in a month. She opened the breadbox to find not only the bread but also an envelope with 'Girl' written on it. Inside was five pounds and a short message.

> "Don't be too frightened of the snakes. The poor buggers are just as frightened of us as we are of them. This few quid should help you along until payday. Uncle Doug. P.S. Don't tell Auntie Flo."

TC burst into tears. She read the note over and over again as she cried. She forgot about eating anything. She silently thanked God for directing her to Brolga and bringing so many kind people into her life. She had nothing to give them. They all knew it; yet, they kept on giving to her in so many ways. Incredible. She hoped she would one day be just like them.

⁋

The telephone was ringing as TC reopened the pharmacy door. It was Delores who sounded frantic.

'Is he there yet, TC?'

'Sorry, Mrs Callahan,' replied TC softly.

'Where on earth can he be?' said Delores as if she was speaking to herself before hanging up. This was the second day in a row TC felt sorry for Delores.

TC decided to fill in the three remaining cheques, then post them in case she became busy later. When she filled in the three cheques, she noticed that the next two cheques in the book were missing and the butts were blank. She decided Vance must have taken them for whatever reason. It was none of her business.

¶

When TC passed by the Empire after posting the mail, Jess was standing by the window. They exchanged 'hellos', and TC decided to ask Jess if she had seen Vance.

'He was here all afternoon yesterday. Left with Jake Carmichael around seven last night. Of course, he was drunk as usual. Some bloody chemist he is. Leaving a kid like you with all that responsibility. Your boss and Jake have been playing poker in the back of the café. The Greek who owns the place is also in the game. They've been at it all night. I could hear them carrying on through my bedroom window at the quarters. Silly mongrels are still there, as far as I know. All men are mongrels, TC.' A couple of men entered the bar through the rear door, and Jess went off to serve them.

¶

There were no customers that afternoon, so TC busied herself filling gaps created by the morning trade and answering countless calls from Delores, whom she could tell by the tone of her voice, was verging on hysteria. TC felt guilty that she knew where Vance was but could not tell Delores. She decided she had to do something about it if she could. At five she closed the pharmacy and determinedly strode across to the café.

'Is Mr Callahan here?' she politely asked the wife of the café owner.

'I'll see,' was the reply as the woman went through a door at the back of the café.

'Tell her I'm not here,' was Vance's reply when told TC had asked for him.

'Tell her I'm here for her anytime she wants me,' said Jake.

They all laughed. TC had heard everything. She was so angry she almost ran home where she immediately turned on the sprinkler hose to water the small lawn, then took a shower before the snakes came out, that is, if there were any. She was taking no chances. TC deliberated over phoning Delores to tell her Vance was at the café. She decided after much thought that her loyalty should be to Vance. How Vance and Delores conducted their marriage was none of her business.

Country music, courtesy of radio station 4CU Curloo, was playing as TC sat on the front top step, drying her hair and staring at the water spraying in a circle from the sprinkler. She missed the music she used to listen to before coming to Brolga. There was a radiogram in the house. Uncle Doug and Auntie Flo had told her she could use it any time. The records were mostly Frank Sinatra, Bing Crosby and Slim Dusty. TC wanted to hear Elvis, Little Richard and Jerry Lee Lewis–type rock and roll.

Never mind, thought TC. *Nobody gets everything.* She turned the sprinkler off before going indoors to put rollers in her hair. With her hair-rolling complete, TC made some toast on which she spread butter and vegemite, then filled a tall glass with ice and water. No way could she drink the bore water unless it was cold. Slim was singing on 4CU. TC took one of Auntie Flo's *Woman's Weekly* magazines from a shelf and sat down at the dining table. She had eaten her toast and vegemite and was reading an article on Elizabeth Taylor when she heard Jake's car scream down the street.

Probably going to the creek with some poor nurse, thought TC.

Seconds later she heard the gravel flying in the driveway and the screech of brakes at the bottom of the back stairs. Jake was out of his car, up the stairs, and in the room before she could get to the back door and close it. He looked terrible. Louise Swagg was with him.

'Love your hair, TC,' said a smiling Jake. TC rolled her eyes and glared at him.

'Thank you. What do you want?'

'Vance and I have been playing poker since last night. Between us, we just about cleaned out Con Kara, the Greek who owns the café.'

'I see,' said TC. 'I hope Mr Callahan has gone home.'

'No. As a matter of fact, he's here now.'

They all heard another car pull into the driveway behind Jake's. Within seconds, Vance and Louise were kissing and cuddling as if they hadn't seen each other for months.

'I've missed you, sweetie,' said Louise while looking adoringly into Vance's eyes.

He pulled away from Louise. 'Come on, Roughly Rolled, this is no way to set an example for the kid. Like your hair, TC.' TC said nothing. She was furious with her boss. He should have gone home to Delores. By now the poor woman must be beside herself. Both Jake and Vance recognised how angry TC was. Louise didn't notice; she was too busy clinging to Vance.

Jake spoke first.

'TC, I suggested Vance should meet Louise here. It's more discreet. This is a small town, and gossip travels like greased lightning. Vance does, after all, have a wife and children to consider.'

TC said nothing. She knew Jake was covering for Vance. Vance had made the suggestion, not Jake. Why on earth would Jake suddenly start worrying about town gossip? Vance and Louise left without a word. Jake and TC heard them laughing loudly as they got into the car. TC was disgusted.

'You go, too, Jake. If you've got any brains, which I doubt, you'll go home and get some sleep. You look like hell.'

'What if I don't want to go?' he asked seriously.

'Then I'll throw you down the damned stairs. Now go!'

Jake left. He purposely drove home slowly. TC shut and locked the back door. As she brushed her teeth at the kitchen sink, no way was she going down to the bathroom, there might be a snake there, her heart went out to poor Delores who was probably worried witless as she waited for Vance to come home. As TC set the alarm clock, then climbed into bed, Jess' comment that all men are mongrels ran through her mind.

In the morning, TC arrived at the pharmacy half an hour early. It was mail-order day, and she tidied before the phone started ringing. The flying doctor was also scheduled to be at the hospital. That meant prescriptions. As she unlocked the door, she was praying Vance would show up as he had promised. After switching on the shop lights, TC went to the dispensary. She was surprised to see Vance slumped over the desk. He had obviously been home because he wore fresh clothes. Still, he looked dreadful. He raised his head as he looked at her.

'Promised you I'd be here. Well, here I am. You hate me, don't you, TC?'

TC sighed before answering.

'No, Mr Callahan, I feel sorry for you. I also feel sorry for Mrs Callahan and your little boys.'

'Young TC, if only you knew what a troubled man I am.'

TC thought before replying.

'Mr Callahan, I may be young. I am not stupid. I believe you carry on the way you do because you are searching for escape from someone, something, or perhaps yourself. By the way, thank you for coming in today.'

TC took the post office keys from the hook.

'Going for the mail, Mr Callahan. I won't be long.'

As she left, Vance silently sought God's help to rescue him from the life he was leading. Show him a different path.

When TC returned from the mail, Vance said, 'TC, I think you must have lived a life or two before this one. You are a hundred or possibly two hundred-and-eighteen years old. You're far too wise to be just eighteen years of age. If I ever have a daughter, I hope she's exactly like you.'

The phone rang. It was the first mail order of the day. The orders kept coming in one after the other. At siren time, TC was worried Vance would go, then disappear for another day or so. Instead, he asked TC if she was going home.

She replied, 'No, too much to do. I'm fine.'

Vance was longing for and needing a rum and Coke, or two, or three, or ten.

'I really need a few drinks, TC. I'm going to the Empire. If I'm not back by ten-past-two, come and get me.'

TC nodded her head. 'Do you really want me to do that, Mr Callahan?'

'Yes, I do. Help me keep my promise to you, TC. Prescriptions will be coming in this afternoon as well as more mail orders.'

Delores called at ten-minutes-past-one.

'Where's Vance, TC? He said he'd be home for lunch.'

'He's gone, Mrs Callahan.'

'Thank you, TC.'

TC re-opened the pharmacy at exactly two. Prescription-bearing people invaded the pharmacy almost immediately. TC asked them to come back in twenty minutes. Some said they would wait. The phone kept ringing. She took it off the cradle. She still had half a dozen or so orders from the morning to collect and package. What a mess. Vance did not return by ten past two. TC politely and calmly asked the people waiting to guard the pharmacy for a few minutes. She had to go collect something urgently. They all smiled their okay. TC strode across to the Empire window. Vance was facing the window on the far side of the bar. She tried to catch his attention by just standing there but he was engrossed in deep conversation with Jake and another man. Jess saw TC and pointed at Vance. TC nodded her head. Jess told Vance that TC needed him. He laughed loudly.

'Tell her I'm not here,' then continued his conversation.

TC stamped her foot and literally screamed at him, 'Mr Callahan. You promised. I've got a pharmacy full of people with prescriptions, the phone won't stop ringing, and I still have orders from this morning to fill. Get the hell over there and help me now.'

TC wanted to kill him as she stormed back to the pharmacy. She forced a false smile as she entered and thanked everyone for minding things for her. Vance entered the dispensary via the back door only a few seconds later.

'You count the pills and get anything else together, TC. I'll do the labels and instruct the customers,' directed Vance.

They were still working furiously around an hour later when one of the post office employees came to enquire if there was something wrong with the telephone—no one could get through. The exchange had a dozen or so complaints. Neither Vance nor TC had noticed that the phone was still off the cradle. Vance righted the phone. It rang immediately.

'No, Delores,' he said. 'I'll call you later. I'm busy. I said I'll call you later.'

Orders kept coming one after another all afternoon. Vance was happy.

'The word is out, TC. You must have done a hell of a good job last mail day when I wasn't here.'

The last parcel was wrapped and stacked just on eight at night. Vance told TC to lock up before saying, 'You'll be happy, TC. I'm going home to my wife and boys.'

TC smiled, 'That's wonderful news. Mrs Callahan will be the happy one.'

Before leaving Vance said, 'Thank you for pulling me into line today, TC.'

There were more people around than usual. It was Friday night. The three hotels were full. Bert and Jack Romeo would be rubbing their hands together in anticipation of counting the day's takings. Lou and Jake walked across from the café when they saw TC close the pharmacy. TC was happy to see Lou, who had just finished her shift at the exchange.

'All right if we come to your place for a couple of hours, TC?' asked Lou. 'Jake has ordered hamburgers from the café. He's got some records in his car. He can have a few beers and we'll have a few Cokes. What do you think, TC?'

TC was certain Jake had put Lou up to this. Of course, he had. Why couldn't he talk for himself? She'd be happy to spend time with Lou and listen to some real music. If Jake was with them, so be it.

'Sure,' replied TC.

Jake who had not spoken a word, said 'Great! I'll pick up the burgers and some drinks.' With that he was off across the road to the pub and café.

'Sorry, TC. Jake can be pretty persuasive, especially when he wants something.'

'It's okay, Lou. I'm truly happy to see you; and, believe me, I sure am looking forward to listening to some music other than Slim and his mates.'

TC had been in the air-conditioned pharmacy. Now on the street, she felt as if she was in an oven. The heat coupled with the strong, dry wind from the west made it uncomfortable to stand there. TC undid the top two buttons of her blouse and rubbed her neck.

Suddenly there was yelling and foul language emanating from the Majestic Hotel. Almost immediately two men were brawling on the footpath. A third man joined then, then another. They were really into it. The Brick emptied quickly as patrons left their drinks and change on the bar to run down and see the action. Jack and Bert Romeo, closely followed by a few drinkers, raced towards the Majestic. TC had not experienced anything like this before.

'Lou, what if someone gets killed?'

'Don't worry, TC. Dad says drunks rarely get hurt too badly in a fight. Their bodies are too relaxed.'

TC flinched with the sound of every thud as someone hit the concrete footpath. Jake pulled up alongside the curb.

'Get in, ladies; let our party begin.'

The police car went flying by and came to a screeching halt opposite the Majestic. The police sergeant raced across to the fighting men.

Oh, shit, he thought. *One of me and four of them. The department must think I'm bloody Superman.*

As Jake and the girls drove past, they saw the sergeant himself knocked to the footpath. Jake laughed.

'Welcome to beautiful downtown Brolga, TC. It's Friday night, two shearing sheds cut out today, the fettlers are in town, there's a brawl outside the Majestic, the sergeant's been jobbed, and the mother of all dust storms is about to hit us.'

'She'll be a beauty, all right,' said Lou as Jake pulled into TC's driveway.

'How do you know a dust storm is coming?' enquired TC with great interest. Jake was up the stairs and on the landing before the girls were out of the car.

'Come on. Let's eat before Con's famous hamburgers go cold. He's probably laced them with rat poison because Vance and I won his money.' They all laughed. Jake was trying to open the door as he juggled the beer, Coke, and hamburgers. He put the drinks down and with his free hand tried again to open the door. No luck. He looked over his shoulder at TC and Lou.

'What the hell is wrong with the door?'

'It's locked,' replied TC as she produced the door key from her purse. Jake and Lou burst into laughter.

'What are you laughing at?' asked a confused TC as she unlocked the door.

Lou and Jake replied in unison, 'Nobody in Brolga locks their doors, TC.'

TC was amazed.

'Isn't anyone afraid of being robbed?'

'Nobody has to steal anything in Brolga,' replied Jake as he opened a beer. 'If anyone needs anything, they can borrow it. Mind you, sometimes they forget to give it back. If they need food, they can get it on tick. That's the way Brolga operates. Everyone helps everyone. It's good.'

That's unbelievable, thought TC, as she placed ice cubes in glasses for Lou and herself.

Lou got to choose the first record as she had hauled the pile of them from the car. They sat down to eat and talk with the radiogram in the next room blasting out Little Richard's, Good golly, Miss Molly.

'Don't care how much rat poison Con put on these hamburgers,' said Jake. 'Mine tastes pretty damned good. What about yours, ladies?' Both Lou and TC nodded their heads in agreement. They finished eating. Bobby Day was belting out, Rockin' Robin. Jake got up to get another beer and Cokes for Lou and TC.

'How do you know there's a dust storm coming?' asked TC again.

'Because we've lived here all our lives,' replied Lou.

'Lou's right,' said Jake, returning with their drinks. 'We just know.'

'But how?' questioned TC.

Jake scratched the back of his neck.

'TC, I'm not a meteorologist. All I know is what my dad told me when I was a little boy and experienced the first dust storm within my recollection.'

'What did your dad tell you?' asked Lou.

Even though Dion's, I'm a Wanderer was playing in the next room, TC and Lou were all ears for Jake's dad's explanation of dust storms in Brolga. Jake took a sip of beer and thought for a few seconds. He had to interpret what he was told as a small child into the vernacular of a grown man.

'My dad told me that the wild winds begin as a little willie wind in the red deserts of central Australia. They very occasionally go to the west, usually the east. We're in the middle of a drought right now, not much grass out there. As the wind heads east, it becomes stronger, crosses the barren land, picks up some dust, and there we go. Usually there's a spattering of rain before it really hits. Sometimes there's heavy rain immediately following the dust. Often there's no rain at all. That's about as much as I can remember,' said Jake. 'My dad may have been wrong. I doubt it.'

The three of them sat in silence as Del Shannon was singing, "Runaway".

❡

'Why do you think those men were fighting tonight?' questioned TC.

'One of them probably mistakenly or jokingly pocketed some change. Then mates stepped in to help. Happens all the time at the Majestic,' replied Jake.

'Thought you said nobody needed to steal in Brolga?' questioned TC.

'That's different,' replied Jake. 'Most of these poor buggers have been to hell and back for one reason or another. They are all mates. The booze has got to them.'

'Like Mr Callahan?' replied TC.

There was a loud banging sound as something smashed into the western side of a shed at the transport company across the road.

'It's here,' said Lou as she jumped up to close the back door. 'Close everything.' Between the three of them, they had every window and door within the house closed in less than a minute.

Smiley Lewis was singing, "I Hear You Knockin". It was bizarre.

Jake said jokingly, 'Get your gas masks, ladies. Anyone for a Coke?' He opened another beer.

The tin roof of the house was rattling, the louvered windows were shaking. The red dust began to secrete itself within the house. It found its way through every crevice, nail hole, gap in the walls, under, beside, and over the space between the doors and their frames. Everywhere. The dust viably floated around the room while the wind was howling outside. The wind passed, dust settled on everything, including their hands, arms, faces, and clothes. The furniture, floors, windows, even the wood stove were covered in red dust as thick as a fingernail. They all jumped up to open the windows and doors. Inside, the house was stifling. Elvis was singing, "Heartbreak Hotel".

'The King's not wrong there,' said TC. 'Know what I'll be doing on the weekend? Cleaning up.'

Lou felt lucky. Never much cleaning up to do at the Shack. The wind blew the dust through the open windows on the western side and out through the windows on the eastern side.

'Wonder how much dust the pharmacy copped, TC?'

'Yes, TC' said Jake with a smile on his face. 'Few thousand bottles and boxes to dust. Should keep you busy for a while.'

'Jake, don't be a rat!' said Lou.

TC sneezed, then again, then again.

'Let's sit on the front stairs while we have a drink. Looks like the dust has got to you, TC.'

'Then you'll have to go home, Jake. I have to go to work tomorrow,' said TC as she sneezed again.

TC turned the sprinkler hose on, hoping the water would take away the smell of dust. They sat on the front steps listening to the music on the radiogram. Johnny O'Keefe was singing, "Shout".

'Thank God for that,' said Jake. 'We have one Aussie rock star.'

'Don't you like Elvis?' asked TC.

'Not really,' replied Jake.

'Why?' asked Lou.

'He can get more women than I can,' replied Jake. Both girls laughed.

'That is ridiculous, Jake. Elvis is a rock star. He is in Memphis. You are in Brolga,' said TC.

Lou added, 'You should not complain, Jake. Elvis is the hottest guy in Memphis. You are the hottest guy in Brolga. I listen in to your conversations with half the young female population of Brolga. They all seem to love you, Jake.'

Jake stood up.

'I'm going home.'

He wanted to choke Lou for saying that in front of TC.

'I'm staying,' said Lou, 'if that's okay with TC.' TC nodded at Lou.

'Of course.' She looked at Jake and said 'Thank you for everything, Jake.'

'Yeah,' he replied.

Jake reversed out of the driveway like a maniac and drove at breakneck speed to his mother's house. Jake lay in his bed a little later after reporting to his mother that he was home.

Thel had made a rule. Her children, whilst they were living under her roof, had to tell her when they were going out and report in when they got home, no matter what time it was.

Jake couldn't sleep. He was thinking about TC.

'Did I say the right things? ... Lou should be reported for listening in to telephone conversations ... Fancy locking the doors! ... Poor little bugger has all that dusting to do ... God, I'm an arsehole.'

¶

Lou and TC sat on the stairs in silence until they heard Jake's car stop at his mother's house.

'He's a shit, TC,' said Lou.

TC thought for a moment. 'Yes, I know, Lou. He's been good to me.' TC sneezed again.

Jerry Lee Lewis was singing, "Honky Tonk Angel" as TC and Lou decided to go to bed. They both wanted to take a shower. It was so hot and they were both covered in red dust. TC kept sneezing. Between sneezes, she told Lou about the snakes. They both opted for a lick and a promise with the help of a towel plus water from the kitchen sink. TC brushed her teeth and made a mental note that she should always have a new spare toothbrush at hand for such occasions. Lou squeezed toothpaste onto her finger before rubbing it over her teeth with her fingers. She also made a note to always carry a toothbrush—just in case. Lou was allocated TC's bedroom. TC chose Auntie Flo and Uncle Doug's bed. Every window and door in the place was open. Even so, it was still hot. They would shower in the morning.

TC and Lou arrived at the pharmacy at eight the next morning. Dust was everywhere and on everything.

'Would you like me to help you clean up?' asked Lou.

'No,' came Vance's voice from the dispensary. 'She can do it by herself.' Lou left immediately.

'Good morning, Mr Callahan,' said TC.

Vance was sitting at the dispensary desk. As usual he looked dreadful.

'Did you enjoy yourself last night, TC?'

'Not really, Mr Callahan. I saw a fist-fight across the road, the police sergeant knocked down, and I managed to survive a dust storm.'

'Good for you. I had a terrible night myself.'

'What, from Delores and the kids?'

'I didn't want to be there. Too heavy, TC. I love the boys but I simply don't want to be there.'

'Mr Callahan, why did you marry Mrs Callahan? You both appear to be very unhappy.'

'Seemed like the right thing to do at the time,' replied Vance.

TC grabbed the broom, bucket, and mop. 'I'd best begin to clean up, Mr Callahan. There's dust everywhere. Not to mention the gaps on the shelves from yesterday's trading. What would you like me to do first?'

'I don't care,' replied Vance despondently.

Apart from helping the mail truck driver load the orders and serving a handful of customers who came to the pharmacy that morning, Vance sat at his desk and stared into space. By knock-off time at twelve, TC had from A to F, eight shelves deep, in immaculate presentation; G to Z had to wait until Monday. TC's wage was three pounds and ten shillings per week. Vance gave her this amount in a small envelope a few minutes before they left.

'See you Monday morning, TC. By the way, take this, buy yourself some different clothes. I'm getting tired of seeing you in almost the same outfit every day. You are a good girl. You are doing a good job.' He handed her a ten-pound note.

TC was speechless.

'Don't say anything,' said Vance. 'You earned it. Please lock up. I have to place a few bets.' Vance left the pharmacy and walked across the road to the Empire. TC went home to the dust-filled house. She finished cleaning right on seven as the train whistle sounded announcing the arrival of the Flea.

It was still hot. Snakes or no snakes, TC knew she had to bite the bullet. She went downstairs to take a shower. She needed to wash the dust off her body and out of her hair. After the shower, she gingerly opened the bathroom door, carefully scrutinising the path before running across it to the stairs. She tied her wet hair into a ponytail, then sat on the top stair, again watching the sprinkler whirling around. Jake's records were still there. She was listening to Buddy Holly singing, "That'll Be The Day". The telephone rang. It was Auntie Flo.

Is everything all right, TC?'

'Yes, Auntie Flo. There was a dust storm last night. I cleaned the house this afternoon.'

'Good girl,' said Auntie Flo. 'We only get half a dozen or so dust storms a year. They make a mess. Doug and I are in Brisbane. Call you soon. Take care of yourself. Take care of the house.'

TC sat herself back down on the step. She heard Jake's car scream down the block behind Brolga Street. She also heard it come to an abrupt stop, then start again.

Probably picking up one of the nurses, she thought.

TC was wrong. Jake's car came around the corner and pulled into the driveway. Louise was with him.

Not again, thought TC, as she heard them come up the back stairs. TC didn't turn around. She simply continued staring ahead. Louise had never acknowledged her, so she didn't see why she should acknowledge Louise.

'Quite the little housekeeper, aren't we?' said Jake from behind her. 'Move over so we can sit down with you.'

As TC moved across the stair, Vance drove around the corner and pulled into the driveway. Louise was through the house, down the back stairs, and in Vance's car within seconds. Jake sat down beside TC as Vance reversed out with Louise crouched down beside him.

'Is my boss drunk again?' asked TC.

'Pretty much so,' replied a surprisingly sober Jake. 'We were both lucky again today. Vance backed four winners and I backed three.'

'Looks like this is going to be the pick-up point for my boss and Louise,' remarked TC. 'I don't like the idea, but I'm hardly in a position to say or do anything about it.'

'I know,' replied Jake. 'I felt a bit the same way when I picked Louise up from around the corner.'

'I feel sorry for Mrs Callahan,' said TC.

'So do I, TC,' replied Jake. 'It's none of our business, so try not to dwell on it.'

They sat in silence for a while before Jake asked TC if she would like a Coke, as he needed a beer to cool off. TC got up to put another record on the radiogram while Jake got their drinks. They returned to the front step. The street was quiet apart from the occasional bang from the transport depot opposite. A couple of truck drivers were loading for their trip the next morning. There was very little traffic. A couple of cars had passed by in the direction of the creek earlier. Other than that, nothing.

'Some Saturday night,' said Jake.

'Did you meet the Flea?' enquired TC.

'No,' replied Jake. 'Won't be needing to meet it anymore.'

'Why?' asked TC. 'I've been under the impression that meeting the Flea twice a week is almost a must-do in Brolga.'

Jake looked at her seriously. 'The package I've been waiting for all these years arrived on the train with you.'

TC really wanted to ask him what was in the package. She didn't. Neither did she realise he was referring to her.

'Is Lou coming down tonight?' asked Jake.

'She's gone to the movies. She's coming down after they finish,' replied TC.

Good, thought Jake. *I've got her to myself for a few hours. That is, if she doesn't throw me out.*

'Is it okay if I keep you company until she arrives?' asked Jake.

'Sure, Jake. After all, they are your records I'm playing.'

'Good. I'll go up town and get you some more drinks. Would you like to come with me?'

TC declined. She didn't want to get known around town as one of Jake's conquests. The Seat of Knowledge elders would assume she was just that if they saw her with Jake. The news would spread through the town like wildfire. Neil Diamond was singing, "Song Sung Blue" when Jake returned half an hour later.

'So, you like Neil Diamond? I do, too,' said Jake as he sat down beside her and handed her a hamburger. 'Told Con his rat poison didn't kill us last night. He told me he added more tonight.' They both laughed.

'I should have been a professional gambler, TC,' said Jake between mouthfuls.

'Why is that?'

'Because I'm good at it and because I like it.'

'Aren't you afraid of losing your money?' asked TC.

'No. I actually get a buzz because of the risk. Apart from that, TC, I usually win. I love it.'

Jake went to the kitchen to get a beer. TC was looking at the sprinkler, wishing she could sit under it to cool off. Jake returned and sat down beside her.

'Auntie Flo's lawn must love you, TC. I think it's had more water in the few days you've been living here than it usually gets in a month.'

TC replied, 'I like looking at the water spinning around and spraying out in the perfect circle.'

Jake told TC about his family. How shocked and heartbroken they were when his father died prematurely. He worried about his mother, who still hadn't recovered from the shock. He talked for ages and by the time he finished she felt as if she knew them already. TC asked Jake if he had any favourites amongst his siblings.

'I suppose I love them all,' he replied. 'I don't get along too well with one of my brothers. If I had to choose a favourite, I suppose it would be Duke.'

'That's a strange name,' enquired TC.

'It's his nick name. Mind you, I call him Mike because his middle name is Michael.' Jake got up to get more drinks and change the record.

'What about your family, TC?' he asked when he returned.

'White and poor,' replied TC. She said no more.

A half dozen or so cars passed by.

'Lou will be here soon,' said Jake. 'Movies are over.'

Lou strolled up to the gate a few minutes later. She was carrying a small bag. It was a little after eleven o'clock.

'What's in the bag, Lou?' asked Jake.

'I robbed the bank, Jake, so it's filled with money,' replied Lou laughingly. 'It's my toothbrush and baby-doll pyjamas, if you must know Jake.'

'How about a fashion parade in your baby-dolls, Lou?' Jake suggested.

'Go to hell, Jake,' scoffed Lou as she joined Jake and TC on the stairs. Jake got up to fetch a Coke for Lou. Before doing so, he went downstairs and turned off the sprinklers.

'TC, if you let that thing run any longer, the town will be flooded out.'

'Yes,' added Lou. 'My shoes are wet from walking in the water. Not to worry, they'll dry out pretty fast in this heat.'

The path from the bottom of the steps to the front gate was covered in about three inches of water, which was draining across the footpath and running along the gutter for about thirty yards to the soakwell at the end of the street.

'Is it always this hot in Brolga?' asked TC.

'No! Winters are so cold the water freezes in the pipes sometimes,' replied Lou.

'Good heavens,' said TC, 'I don't even own a cardigan.'

'You'll have to cut a hole in a blanket and wear that, TC,' said Jake as he handed Lou an icy Coke.

TC didn't bother to speak. She simply looked at Jake and rolled her eyes.

What an idiot, she thought.

'So, what are you two young ladies doing tomorrow?' asked Jake.

'Sleeping in, I hope,' replied Lou.

'That is if it's not too hot, which it probably will be,' said TC. 'That sun blazes down on the tin roof from daybreak. Inside the house is like an oven by seven o'clock.'

'You'll get used to it, TC,' said Jake flippantly.

'All right for you, Jake. You've got air-conditioning,' said Lou.

'I'd settle for a cool breeze,' sighed TC.

Jake finished his beer then stood up. 'I'm going home, ladies; a man needs his beauty sleep.'

He gave TC's pony tail a slight tug, then patted Lou on the top of her head before leaving. Once more, he purposely pulled out of the driveway carefully and slowly before driving off at a snail's pace.

'Jake is besotted by you, TC,' stated Lou matter-of-factly. 'Never seen him like this over any other girl.'

'I don't think so,' replied TC. 'If he is, it certainly is not reciprocal. He's been extremely good to me, I appreciate it. End of story.'

They sat chatting about anything and everything for another hour, brushed their teeth at the kitchen sink, then went to bed. Jake couldn't get to sleep. His mind was too active. He was trying to come up with a feasible excuse to see TC the next day.

What the hell has happened to me? he thought. *I must be bloody crazy. Saturday night and I'm home in bed before midnight. Should have gone to the party at the nurse's quarters. I know I'm going to marry her. First, I have to get her to like me. Mum will be sleeping peacefully. She knows I'm safely home in bed. Somehow, I'll come up with something.* He continued to toss and turn until the early hours of the morning.

§

Lou was luxuriating in the double bed. Until the night before, she had never slept in one. 'I love it,' she said to herself before falling asleep almost instantly. TC thought about Delores and how sad she felt for her. Vance and Louise were asleep in each other's arms in his parked car down by the creek. Delores was in her bed. Her eyes were wide open as she worried about Vance and wondered where he was. Wherever he was, she hoped he was safe. Sam and Brad Lester were asleep on a mattress in the back of his ute, which was parked under the stars about five minutes out of town.

§

As predicted by TC, it was too hot to stay in bed the next morning. Lou appeared at TC's bedroom door around six-thirty.

'Come on, TC; time for breakfast. I've made some toast and boiled the jug.'

The toaster, jug, iron, and a small hotplate with a tiny oven underneath were the only electrical appliances in the house apart from the refrigerator and a small freezer. The hotplate was approximately eighteen inches long and twelve inches wide. Auntie Flo had always used the old, wood-burning stove to do her cooking. The girls sat down with their tea and toast.

'I can't believe that anyone could light that old stove day in and day out in this heat,' said TC.

'That's all most people in Brolga have to cook on,' replied Lou. 'As Jake said last night, you get used to it.'

TC had grown up with a wood stove which never seemed to burn out; she simply couldn't comprehend standing over one in Brolga's summer heat.

'Well,' said TC, 'I'd best do my laundry. If any snakes are downstairs, hopefully they are under the house sleeping.'

TC had washed her clothes in one of the three connected concrete wash tubs, rinsed them in the second tub, then put them through the hand wringer attached to the top of the third tub before hanging them on the clothes line to dry. In the laundry, there was also a wood-fired copper tub for boiling clean sheets, towels, and the like. Beside the copper, leaning against the laundry wall, was a four-foot long, well-used, round copper stick about two inches in diameter. TC looked at the copper.

'Think I'll leave the copper until next week,' she said.

'Good idea,' said Lou. 'If you've got plenty of sheets and towels, perhaps you can leave it until winter comes.'

TC smiled. 'Wish I could.'

'Let's go for a walk up into town while your washing dries,' suggested Lou.

¶

Half hour later found them in the Brolga newsagency flicking through fashion magazines. Although it traded as Brolga Newsagency, this establishment sold just about everything from newspapers to refrigerators. It had cigarettes, razor blades, hair products, perfumes, after-shave lotions, cosmetics, toothbrushes, toothpaste, records, radios, radiograms, washing machines, every electrical appliance available at the time, toys, books on just about any subject, sewing machines, et cetera.

'Talk about one-stop shopping,' remarked TC.

'I know,' said Lou. 'The owners are pretty upset about Vance opening the pharmacy next door, even though they own the building, and he's paying them rent. They think their sales in cosmetics will drop.'

'Probably will,' replied TC. 'Still, they've got a lot of other stuff to sell; doubt they'll go broke.'

Both girls saw Vance pull his car into the curb outside the pharmacy. They left the newsagency to speak to him.

'Hope you're not wasting your hard-earned money on magazines, TC,' said Vance. Lou answered him before TC could speak.

'No, she's not, Mr Callahan. Doesn't need to. My mum buys them, so TC and I can read them after Mum has finished with them.'

Vance nodded his head. 'Good thinking. Jake and I are going to play cards at the café. Con the Greek wants a chance to win his money back. Some bloke who works at the post office is playing as well. Should even up the odds.'

TC was alarmed.

'Mr Callahan, please remember tomorrow is an order day and you promised me you would be at work on order days.'

'I'll try, TC,' laughed Vance before he walked off to the café across the street.

The two girls headed towards TC's house. A few seconds later, Jake pulled up in front of the café. As he got out of the car, he waved to them and called out, 'Be good little girls today.'

'Not much chance of either of us being anything else,' said Lou. 'Let's get back to your place. We can play some of Jake's records while I watch you do your ironing.'

¶

Lou got only one weekend in four off with her job at the telephone exchange. Now that she had finally found a friend in TC, she hoped they would spend as much time together as their jobs would allow. Lou had been a loner since she had finished school. She had been lucky enough to get the job at the exchange shortly after. The shift work didn't allow her to participate in much of the limited social life available in Brolga. She was rarely invited to parties. The town snobs thought she was beneath them because her dad was the undertaker and whatever else he was. Others thought she was a prude because she didn't smoke, drink alcohol, use bad language, or allow herself to be mauled by any Brolga louts. As far as Lou was concerned, TC and she were so much alike that they could have been twins. Not in looks, of course, but in the way they thought and conducted themselves.

TC did her ironing on the louvred verandah on the eastern side of the house. The sun had moved to the western side, and the faintest breeze wafted through the louvred windows. Lou played Elvis records.

'Wouldn't it be great to be in Memphis?' said Lou. 'I'm sure if I lived in Memphis, I'd meet Elvis. He's so gorgeous.'

'You'd probably have to fight off a million or so other girls,' replied TC as she finished with the iron and placed a blouse on a coat hanger.

'Just the same, I might meet him,' sighed Lou.

Lou took a shower while TC made corned beef and pickle sandwiches. TC showered while Lou called Mrs Carmichael.

'Mrs Carmichael, it's Lou. I wonder if you could tell my mother that I am staying with TC again tonight. I have a late shift tomorrow, so I'll be home in the morning after TC starts work.'

'Of course, Lou' replied Thel Carmichael. 'Say "hello" to TC for me. She seems to be a nice girl, Lou, and I'm pretty sure Jake likes her. He told me he was with you two girls last night. I can't remember the last time he was home before midnight on a Saturday night.'

Perhaps my Jake is finally growing up, thought Thel Carmichael, as she put down the telephone.

Lou and TC sat on their favourite perch at the front of the house to eat their sandwiches. The easterly breeze coming off the creek became a little cooler as the sun went down in the west.

'This is great,' said Lou. 'Wish I lived at this end of town. Will still be as hot as Hades at the Shack. The sun will still be beaming down its heat waves. Sometimes, in the summer time, I think the Shack is the hottest house in town. I suppose that's understandable. After all, Dad built it out of scrap wood and tin. We don't even have a ceiling.' Lou paused before adding, 'TC, that's one of the reasons I think of you as a true friend. You didn't once comment on the Shack. You acted as if it's a normal house. Thank you, TC. Most other people I know think of the Shack and my parents as a joke. Consequently, that makes me a joke.'

TC shook her head before saying softly, 'Lou, please don't think that way. The Shack is a shack. Your mum and dad know that. Why else would your dad put that sign out the front of it? In my opinion, that is his way of saying to all and sundry, 'So, I live in a shack. So what?' You asked your parents to give me shelter when I needed it. They didn't hesitate to do so. Quite honestly, I'm so grateful to have had a place to stay that I didn't consciously notice the shack had no ceiling. Your parents are definitely not a joke to me, Lou. Neither are you. People who categorise you that way are probably self righteous and think only of themselves. I won't believe people should be judged by the type of house they live in, nor the amount of money they have to buy fancy trappings. Your parents and yourself are good people, Lou. Goodness comes from the heart. You are good, kind-hearted people. I am so proud to be your friend and honoured to know your parents.'

Tears were glistening in Lou's eyes.

'Thank you, TC. Guess I was feeling a bit sorry for myself.' TC ruffled the top of Lou's hair as she had seen Jake do.

'Happens to us all sometimes, Lou. I'm going to put another of Jake's records on the radiogram.' As TC stood up to do so the telephone rang.

'This is Jake, TC.'

'Yes, Jake. What do you want?'

'Don't ask me that. I might tell you,' replied Jake with a slurred voice.

'Bye, Jake' replied TC. TC returned to the stairs.

'It was Jake. I think he's blind drunk. I also think he's an idiot.'

'Most of the other girls in Brolga don't think so,' replied Lou.

'Good luck to them. They're welcome to him, as far as I'm concerned.'

Jake's car screamed around the corner from the back street and came to a screeching halt on Brolga Street, outside the front gate. Jake got out of the car, slammed the door, and was standing in the middle of the road, apparently oblivious to any traffic that may come by. He was unsteady on his feet, and his head appeared to be wobbling from side to side. He threw his arms out sideways.

'TC,' he yelled, 'I love you. I'm going to marry you.'

'Get off the road, Jake, before you get run over,' yelled Lou.

'Oh,' muttered Jake.

He staggered around the rear of his car, across the footpath, and fumbled while unlocking the gate before he made his way to the bottom of the stairs.

'Obviously, I've had a few,' he said with great concentration, focused on enunciating every word. 'I won two thousand quid this afternoon. Most of it from Vance. I'm drunk. I want to marry you, TC.'

'Are you crazy, Jake?' replied TC. 'We hardly know each other. You are extremely drunk. I don't care if you won two million pounds. You need a sleep.'

Ironically, Jerry Lee was belting out, Crazy Arms on the radiogram. Jake fell down, put his head between his upturned knees, and fell asleep. TC looked down at him from the top step.

'You know, Lou, Jake really is quite handsome. He always dresses immaculately. He's tall and slim, thick black hair and long sideburns. Charming. Has not said one word out of place to me, been very considerate, kind and generous; however, there's something about him I don't like.'

'He's also got a great car,' said Lou.

'Great car or not, Lou, I don't think he's capable of driving it anywhere at the moment.'

Lou and TC sat drinking Coke and listening to music until cars went past after the Saturday night movies were out. Jake was still sitting on the path. Now he was snoring.

Lou said, 'I'll put the sprinkler on, TC. That'll wake him up. Seen my dad do it many times when people have overstayed their welcome.'

'Seems cruel,' replied TC. 'I'll try some ice on his forehead first. Saw that in a movie once. Worked in the movie. Hopefully, it will work now.'

While TC was collecting ice from the freezer in the kitchen, Lou turned on the sprinkler. Jake awoke suddenly as the first drops of water touched the back of his shirt collar and ran onto his back and shoulders. He sat bolt upright.

'Bloody hell,' he said. 'A man is drowning.'

'A woman is, too' replied Lou, who was also dripping wet.

TC returned with ice cubes dripping in a tea towel.

'Give me those,' said Lou. 'I'll put a few down the front and back of his shirt. Seen my dad do that, too. Jake should be wide awake soon.' TC turned off the sprinkler before she got drenched herself. Jake looked up at Lou.

'You're a hard woman, Lou. I'm going to tell Mum not to let you use our phone anymore.'

'No, you won't, Jake. If you do, I'll have to tell your mum why you think I'm a hard woman.'

'That's blackmail, Lou.' Lou smiled and nodded her head in agreement. Jake stood up, pulled his shirt out of his trousers, and shook out the ice cubes before depositing himself on the stairs.

'I'll make you some black coffee, Jake,' offered TC.

'Thank you,' replied Jake 'Probably need a couple of gallons or so.'

Jake drank four cups of coffee while the three of them sat in silence. Without a word, he stood up, tucked in his by-now-dry shirt, and left. He drove away slowly in the direction of his mother's house.

'So, Jake wants to marry TC.' Lou threw her arms wide out imitating Jake. TC sighed.

'He does not, Lou. He was drunk.'

'You know what they say, TC. A drunken man speaks a sober man's mind.'

'I'm tired, Lou. Let's go to bed.'

As TC closed the front door, Vance and Louise drove past, returning from the creek.

Hope he's at work tomorrow, thought TC as she and Lou exchanged goodnights.

¶

Vance was in the dispensary when TC arrived at the pharmacy. He didn't reply when she greeted him; so, she took the mail key from the wall and went to collect the mail. TC was wondering what she could have done to upset her boss. She decided she'd done nothing. He would speak to her when he felt like it. TC returned with the mail, which she opened and placed in a neat pile on the desk in front of Vance before beginning to clean and dust shelves.

I loathe dusting, thought TC, as she sneezed uncontrollably. After about ten minutes of listening to TC sneeze, Vance came out of the dispensary and handed her two tablets and a glass of water.

'Take these; they should fix you.' He returned to the dispensary. Shortly afterwards, TC heard Vance talking very loudly. He was obviously extremely angry.

'I told you, Delores, I don't damned-well care.' He slammed down the phone.

TC was no longer sneezing, thanks to whatever pills the boss had given her. She would ask what they were when he was in a better mood. Only a handful of orders were called in. Vance was packing them immediately upon receiving them. TC was happy he was doing the orders.

'Great. Leaves me free to get through these shelves sooner.'

Vance walked past and around TC at least twenty times as he gathered bits and pieces for the orders. TC, while going back and forth through the dispensary to fetch buckets of clean water for washing the shelves, walked past Vance a dozen or more times. Still he did not speak to her. He was totally withdrawn and appeared to be trapped by whatever was on his mind. Suddenly she heard Louise's voice coming from the dispensary.

'Hello, lover. I've sneaked in the back way. I have to work tonight, so here I am.'

TC didn't hear Vance's reply. There was silence for a couple of minutes.

They're probably kissing and cuddling, thought TC. *Wish there was a radio in the place; then I wouldn't have to listen to every word spoken in the dispensary.*

Vance came into the shop. TC was on the small step-ladder cleaning one of the top shelves. Vance handed her a mail key.

'Go get the mail, TC.' TC looked down at him. She was confused.

'I know you've already collected it once. I want you to check it again. Don't come back until you see the front door open.' TC walked out in a quandary as to why. Vance closed and locked the front door of the pharmacy, returned to the dispensary, and placed the telephone receiver on the bench.

'Come here, Roughly Rolled,' he said to Louise.

TC checked the mailbox as instructed. Of course, there was nothing in it. She didn't know what to do until the door opened. The Empire wasn't open yet; so, she couldn't talk to Jess at the window. It was too hot to sit on the Seat of Knowledge. She walked into the small dress shop next to the bakery.

'Good morning, luv,' said an elderly lady sitting on a chair at the rear of the shop. 'You must be TC. I've been looking forward to meeting you.'

TC looked at her enquiringly.

'How do you know my name?'

'Everyone in Brolga knows your name, dear. You're the girl looking after the Delaney's house. Flo Delaney and Thel Carmichael are my nieces. Both Flo and Thel have told me you're a good, nice girl. My name is Carmel,' as she stretched her hand out to TC. 'Nice to meet you, TC,' as they shook hands.

'Nice to meet you too, Mrs ... Mrs?'

'Everyone calls me Carmel; why should you be different, dear? You call me Carmel. I'd like that.' Carmel invited TC to look at the racks of dresses, skirts, and blouses hanging on the racks.

'They are all lovely, Carmel. To be honest, I can't afford to buy ready-made clothes at the moment. I'm going to ask Auntie Flo if I can use her trundle sewing machine so I can make some clothes myself. I learned to sew at school. As long as I can buy some patterns in Brolga, I should be able to turn out whatever I need.'

'I'm certain Flo will allow you to use her machine, TC. When you need patterns, you come see me, I've got boxes of them.'

'Thank you, Carmel. I'll do that.'

'I look forward to seeing you again, TC.'

¶

TC walked to the median strip to look across to check if the pharmacy door was open yet. It was still closed. She needed to buy fresh bread. She started back across the road to the bakery, then realised she didn't have her purse, which was locked in the dispensary with her boss and Louise. TC resigned herself to the fact that she would have to wait on the Seat of Knowledge. She'd simply have to put up with the heat. A few minutes later, Jack Romeo threw open the doors of the Empire.

'What are you doing sitting there, girl?' he asked.

'Just waiting, Mr Romeo,' replied TC.

Jack Romeo shook his head as he walked inside the bar. TC looked repeatedly over her shoulder at the pharmacy door. 'Be patient,' she told herself. 'He can't keep it closed for too much longer.' TC saw Jess in the bar, so she walked to the window to say hello.

'I saw you sitting out there in the sun, TC. You'll get sunburned. Shouldn't you be at work?'

'I am at work, Jess. Mr Callahan is busy; so I have to wait for him to finish what he's doing before I can go back.'

'Huh!' Jess uttered in disgust. 'Not what he's doing, TC; you must mean who he's doing. You're such an innocent young thing, TC. I'll bet that Louise creature is over there with him.'

TC didn't reply.

'She doesn't start work until two today; so, of course she'll be over there. Your boss is a mongrel, TC. I feel sorry for his poor, pregnant wife and those two little boys.'

TC looked across the street as Vance opened the pharmacy door.

'I'd better go, Jess. I'll see you later.'

¶

Louise was gone when TC walked into the dispensary to put the mail key on its hook. She immediately saw the telephone on the bench, so placed it in its cradle. It rang immediately and did so every few minutes until siren time. Vance served the few walk-in customers and took most of the phone orders. TC packed, wrapped, tied, and invoiced the orders. She was way behind and hoped Vance would type the labels. Apart from telling her to take two pills, go to the post office, and wait until the door was open, he did not speak to TC all morning. He left and headed towards the Empire immediately when the siren sounded. TC decided to work through lunch hour. She wanted to get as many orders as possible together and packaged before the afternoon ones came in.

Don't like my chances of getting them all done in an hour, thought TC, as she picked up the pile of handwritten lists Vance had left on the bench. Once again, she wished they had a radio in the place. A radio would keep her company whenever she worked alone, which was most of the time. She wouldn't feel like a spy when Vance was talking on the phone, and it would break the silence when Vance wasn't in the mood to talk. At two o'clock, TC opened the door. She still had five packages to do from the morning orders. The telephone rang—another order. It was a re-occurrence of the morning. Every time TC began to gather stock for one order, another order would be phoned in. By three o'clock she had lost count of how many there were to contend with. It was obvious Vance wasn't coming back. She prayed there would be no walk-in customers. The phone continued to ring time after time after time. By four o'clock, TC was at the end of her tether. She picked up the telephone and took a deep breath before asking the exchange telephonist to please connect her to the Empire. One of the Romeo wives answered.

'Is Mr Callahan there, Mrs Romeo? It's TC speaking?'

'Yes,' came a softly spoken reply.

'May I speak with him, please, Mrs Romeo?' She heard whichever of the Romeo women it was tell Vance that he was wanted. She heard Vance reply 'Tell her I'm not here,' followed by lots of laughter. Mrs Romeo came back on the telephone.

'Did you hear that, TC?'

'Yes, I did Mrs Romeo. Thank you.'

'This is ridiculous,' she said to herself as she put down the phone.

TC was shaking with frustration and anger. Without hesitation, she stormed out of the pharmacy and across the road to the Empire window. Vance was sitting there in his usual spot. He was talking to Louise, who was behind the bar and laughing loudly. TC didn't wait for Vance to spot her waiting at the window. Instead, she literally yelled through the window.

'Mr Callahan, I suppose you think it's funny to say you're not here? Well, I don't. I haven't closed the pharmacy door. Quite frankly, it will serve you right if someone robs the place. You promised me you'd be there to help me on mail days. Instead, you're over here getting drunk again. I want you to come now. If you don't, I'll be closing at five sharp, and whatever I haven't got finished can stay unfinished.'

The half dozen or so other bar patrons were in shock. None of them dared speak. TC stood there tapping one foot, both hands on her hips. She glared at Vance.

'I'm waiting, Mr Callahan. Are you coming or not?'

Vance collected his change from the bar.

'I'll be right there, TC,' he said quietly.

TC nodded her head. 'Good.'

As she turned to go back to the pharmacy, she heard a male voice say, 'Holy shit, Vance, she's only a little thing but she sure packs a good punch.'

TC also heard Louise say, 'Fire the little bitch, Vance.'

She did not hear Vance reply. 'Mind your own business, Louise.'

¶

'I'm sorry, TC,' said Vance quietly as he walked quickly after TC into the pharmacy.

'So you should be, Mr Callahan,' replied TC in a calm tone of voice. 'I'm not a machine. You threw me in here and left me to sink or swim. Well, I'm swimming as fast as I can. I'm afraid I'll drown if you don't help me when necessary. There's lots of work to do, Mr Callahan. I'd be grateful if you would type the labels for the packages that are already done.'

Nothing more was said. A few more orders came in. When they were leaving Vance looked at TC.

'Thank you,' he said. He got in his car and drove towards his home and his family. TC said a silent prayer that he would stay at home with his wife and family.

He did.

¶

TC felt drained of energy as she slowly began the short walk home. Jake pulled alongside when she was about twenty yards from home.

'Want a lift?' he asked through the open windows of his car.

'I'm almost there, Jake.'

'What are you doing tonight, TC?'

'Going to bed after I take a shower. I feel tired.'

'Better be careful of snakes. Could be one curled up waiting for you in the bathroom,' he teased as his car moved along beside her. TC's skin crawled at the thought.

'See you, Jake,' as she opened the front gate. Jake stopped the car and jumped out.

'TC, I heard about you putting Vance on the mat today. Everyone in the Empire tonight was talking about it.'

'News travels quickly in this place, Jake,' she said as she unlocked the front door.

'Can I come in for a little while?' he asked.

'Jake, I told you I'm tired.'

'I can check downstairs for snakes.'

'Please stop mentioning snakes, Jake. Lord, you are persistent. Come in then, but you can't stay too long. I want to go to bed early tonight.'

'Can I come with you,' smiled Jake.

'Definitely not! Behave yourself, Jake, or leave now.'

'Do you wear baby-doll pyjamas, TC?'

'No.'

'Do you wear a short nightie?'

'No. Now stop it or leave.'

'Okay, TC, I promise I'll be good.'

TC went to the refrigerator, took out a beer, and handed it to him and then poured herself a Coke over ice before turning on the radio. She couldn't be bothered fiddling around with records tonight. They sat down at the dining room table. Jake produced a packet of Rothman's cigarettes and lit one. TC hadn't seen him smoke before, or perhaps she just hadn't noticed. She went to fetch an ashtray. There was a stack of them in the kitchen.

As she placed one on the table, Jake said, 'TC, I'm sorry about showing up here so drunk last night.' His tone of voice was serious, and the expression on his face told TC he was sincere.

'Did I say or do anything to upset you, TC? Truth is, I can't remember anything much except at some stage I was wringing wet and felt cold.'

TC laughed.

'No, Jake you didn't do or say anything to upset me. You were wet and cold because Lou turned the sprinkler on you and put ice cubes down the front and back of your shirt collar.'

'That's a relief,' Jake said softly.

TC finished her Coke.

'Jake, would you please go check for snakes. I need a shower.'

Jake was sitting with his beer on the back landing when TC was ready to shower.

'All checked; no snakes,' he said as she made her way past him and down the stairs.

'Thank you, Jake. I won't be long.'

Jake was still sitting on the landing when TC emerged from the bathroom. She had a white towel wrapped turban style around her head. She was wearing a yellow-and-white-spotted cotton knee-length dressing gown. Yellow jiffy slippers covered her feet with little white bows on the front.

Jake sighed, 'You look lovely, TC.' She was embarrassed because she knew by the way he said it he meant it.

'Perhaps in your eyes, Jake. Definitely not in mine.' TC would never forget Jake saying that to her, nor the way he said it.

'Jake, I really do need to get some sleep tonight.'

He stood up to go.

'I'll see you, TC. Sleep tight.'

She locked the front door behind him, checked the back door lock, ran her hairbrush through her wet hair, removed her dressing gown, turned off the lights, and fell into her bed, wearing a pair of bikini briefs and a singlet. The radio was playing softly in the next room. She was asleep within minutes.

¶

Vance beat TC to the pharmacy the next morning. He was sitting at his desk staring through the one-way mirror between the dispensary and the shop. He observed her unlock the door, pause to straighten a couple of packages stacked at the front of the shop, and look towards the shelves she had not yet cleaned.

TC said, 'Good morning, Mr Callahan.'

No response.

I hope it's not going to be another day like yesterday, thought TC, as she took the mail key from the wall and left. There were only a few envelopes in the mailbox. TC stopped at the bakery to purchase a loaf of bread. For some reason, looking at all the bread neatly packed on the racks made her feel nauseous. Vance was deep in thought at his office desk.

Good God, I'm a bastard of a man. I treat Delores like yesterday's garbage. I rarely see my two boys. I broke Anna's heart. That's why she left for God-only-knows where. Wish I could know where she went. All I'm good for is drinking, gambling, and screwing. Takes a fiery, straight-from-the-hip kid, whom I treat like a slave, to scream at me through the pub window to make me face what I have become. Please God, help me.

Vance heard TC returning. He snapped himself out of his soul-searching mode. TC put her purse and bread on a shelf before opening the mail, which contained cheques from account customers.

'They are fast payers. I haven't even sent them a bill yet,' said Vance. 'TC, make me some coffee, then sit down. I want to talk to you.'

'Are you firing me, Mr Callahan?'

'Just make the coffee and sit down.'

When TC was seated across the desk from him, Vance cleared his throat.

'You're too thin. How much weight have you lost since you started working here?' TC shrugged her shoulders.

'I don't know. I don't feel hungry very often because of the heat. When I do feel hungry, I'm too busy.'

'Lets' see what you weigh, TC. I want you to get on the scales.'

Vance stood beside TC as she stood on the shop scales.

'I thought so,' he said. Seven-and-a-half stone. Ninety-eight pounds. You should be at least seven pounds heavier. Your bones are protruding through your flesh, young lady. You're so thin, I think I'll name you Butterball.'

They both laughed.

'Come on, TC. I haven't finished yet.'

Vance put his hand on her shoulder and guided her back to the dispensary. Once seated, he looked across the table at her.

'Have you got any money?'

'Yes,' replied TC. 'I have eighteen pounds and nine shillings. Uncle Doug left five pounds for me, and I have my pay for last week and three pounds, ten shillings, plus the ten-pound bonus you gave me. I spent a shilling on the loaf of bread this morning.'

'What did you do with the other money you've earned? You never go anywhere, not even the movies. I haven't seen you in the café with the other young people around town, and you obviously don't blow your money on clothes.'

TC thought for a few moments, deciding what she should tell him.

'Mr Callahan, there's no explanation other than the truth. I don't go to the movies because not only have I been not able to afford it, but also I don't have nice clothes to wear. My wardrobe is extremely limited. I have noticed Brolga girls get really dressed up on movie nights. I haven't been to the café except once when I was looking for you, because I've been broke. Apart from that, I have nothing in common with any young people around town, with the exception of Lou and Sam. Jake helped me out with money; so, I saved every cent I possibly could, apart from board to Lou's parents and a few female essentials. I've repaid Jake. That makes me feel good. It was worth scrimping. Now I have eighteen pounds and nine shillings, and I do not intend to spend it flippantly. I know you told me to buy clothes with my bonus, Mr Callahan. Instead, if it's okay with you, I'd like to open a bank account with that ten pounds. I can sew quite well, so would prefer to make my own clothes. Until then, I'll make do with what I have.'

Vance was still, absorbing every word she had spoken. He handed TC the cheques from the table before smiling at her.

'Here, Butterball, go across the road and bank these. While you're there, open that bank account you want so much.'

'Thank you, Mr Callahan. Thank you. Thank you. Thank you.' TC was relieved and extremely happy as she made her way to the bank.

Bloody incredible, thought Vance. *I spend money like a drunken sailor. I'm not a sailor, but I sure am a drunk. Born-to-shop Delores would be hard pushed to thread a needle, let alone make a dress.*

TC came back from the bank waving her little grey-covered savings account deposit book. Vance noticed she was humming to herself as she collected water sponges and cloths for cleaning the shelves.

'I won't be long,' he said as walked out the back door.

'Mr Callahan, I don't care if you don't come back today. It's only mail days or if I don't know something. I really need you to come to the telephone when I call the hotel. Okay?'

'Okay,' he replied with a laugh.

Shortly later, TC was surprised to hear him call from dispensary.

'Come here, Butterball, I have something to show you.' TC was filled with curiosity as she stepped down from the ladder and dumped her cleaning cloths.

'What do you think?' he asked as he fiddled with the knobs of a new, latest-model radio positioned on top of the filing cabinet. 'Been meaning to get one for some time. I saw how much you love music at Jordan's wake.' TC was ecstatic.

'You are the best boss in the world, Mr Callahan. I have wished over and over for us to have a radio in the shop. I could hug you. I'm so happy.' Vance was laughing profusely.

'Don't get carried away, young lady. I'm probably the worst boss in the world. By the way, be careful who you hug.' Vance put his hand on TC's shoulder and said very seriously. 'I mean that, Butterball. Fatherly advice. Jake is my mate. Be careful; he's too much like me. On a lighter note, I'm off to the pub. My body is craving a few rums and Cokes.'

§

TC worked quickly and thoroughly. She loved having the radio in the background. She even heard a few country-and-western songs she considered catchy. The shelves all free of dust, TC decided she would re-stock them after lunch. She was crediting the cheques she had received that morning to the few accounts involved when Lou walked into the pharmacy.

'You've got a radio?' said Lou.

'Isn't it great? My boss got it this morning. Let's have lunch at the café,' suggested TC. 'My boss told me I'm too thin.'

'I agree with him on that one,' replied Lou, who was surprised that TC suggested having lunch at the café.

'I'm broke, TC. Dad borrowed my last few quid, and I don't get paid 'til Friday.'

'Don't worry, Lou, I'll pay today, you pay next time. Deal?'

'Deal,' replied Lou.

Shortly after siren time found them seated at a table in the café. The air- conditioning was cooler than that in the pharmacy.

'No wonder just about everyone flocks here in the summer time,' remarked TC. They both ordered a steak sandwich on toast and a chocolate thick-shake.

'When is Vance leaving?' asked Lou.

'Leaving for where?' enquired TC. 'He hasn't said anything about going away.'

'One of the other girls at work listened in to a call Delores made to her mother, who lives in Brisbane. Delores hates Brolga. It's too hot, there are no shops, Vance is never at home, and the little boys are sending her crazy. She's going to stay with her mother until their new baby is born. Then she's going to decide what to do. Vance is driving her to Curloo. She'll take the train from Curloo to Brisbane.' Their food arrived. Lou went to the counter to collect their thick-shakes. TC had never imagined a sandwich could be so large or so thick.

'Why didn't you warn me, Lou? I know my boss says I need to gain weight but I couldn't eat this in a week.'

'You're in the far south-west, TC. I didn't warn you because I've never ordered a steak sandwich on toast before. Don't think I ever will again.'

'No wonder it comes with a knife and fork,' said TC as she lifted the top eight-inch square piece of toast off her sandwich and placed it on the paper napkin beside her plate. She then eased the two fried eggs, beetroot, tomato, lettuce, cheese, and two pieces of steak off the bottom piece of toast and onto the plate. Lou followed TC's procedure.

'I'm not hungry any more,' said TC. 'I think the thick-shake will be enough for me,' as she picked it up and put the straw to her mouth.

'I feel the same. Dad says too much food on your plate can be a turn-off.'

'I agree with your father.'

The thick-shakes were magnificent. A meal in themselves. Both girls concluded they would definitely be back for thick-shakes. Next time, that's all they would order.

It was almost two. Time to return to work. TC paid for their lunch—five shillings and sixpence.

'Can't complain about value for money,' she said to Lou as they left the café.

The phone was ringing when TC entered the pharmacy.

'Where is he, TC?' demanded Delores.

'I'm not sure, Mrs Callahan.'

'Well, you'd better find him. When you do, tell him to come home and pick up the boys and me immediately.'

TC asked Lou to mind the shop, then ran across to the Empire window. Vance noticed her immediately when she beckoned him to come outside.

'What have I done now, Butterball?' he asked.

'Mrs Callahan is very angry, boss. She wants you to go home and pick up the boys and her. She wants you to do it now.'

'I'm taking Delores and the kids to Curloo. They are going to Brisbane for a while. I'll put them on the train in Curloo tomorrow night. I'll be back to help you with the mail on Friday.' TC nodded her head.

'Drive carefully, Mr Callahan. I'll see you Friday.'

¶

TC saw Vance's car head out of town about an hour later. Delores was driving.

The afternoon went quickly. Lou stayed until she had to leave for work at four o'clock. Lou helped TC fill the gaps on the shelves until she reluctantly left. Finished with gap-filling a while later, TC decided to sweep and wash the polished tile floor. With that done, she looked around the shop. She was satisfied. Everything was clean and perfectly in order. With brown paper-wrapped bread and purse in hand, she paused to look at the typewriter.

'Pretty soon I'll be belting out labels on you,' she said softly. She was startled when the telephone rang.

'Who on earth would call the pharmacy this time of night?' TC put the receiver to her ear. It was Vance.

'TC, what the hell are you still doing there? It's almost eight-thirty.'

'Still earning last week's bonus' replied TC.

'TC, I lost quite a lot of money playing poker with Jake the other night. I forgot to get more from the bank today. There are a couple of signed cheques under the cash register drawer. Fill one out for two thousand, cash it at the bank when it opens at ten, then go to the post office and wire the money to me at the Curloo post office. Call me at the Curloo Motel after you have sent it. It costs to wire money; so, take perhaps twenty extra from the till.'

'I understand. How did you know I'd be here, Mr Callahan?'

'Oh, for heaven's sake, Butterball, you're not exactly a social butterfly. I called the Delaney house; when you didn't answer, I knew you'd be at the shop. You be a good girl.'

As if I'd be anything else, she thought, as she turned off the radio and lights before leaving.

¶

TC was opening the front gate to her house when Jake's car turned towards the creek after it went around the corner from the back street. As his car passed under the corner street light only a hundred feet from where she stood, TC could see he had someone with him.

Oh, shit! She's seen me, Jake thought, as he automatically glanced in the direction of the front steps of her house and saw her at the gate. Well, that's put paid to the quick screw I had in mind for tonight.

A mile down the road, Jake turned to the nurse sitting beside him, saying 'Do you mind if I take a raincheck? I feel a dreadful headache coming on. Sorry, I just don't think I'd be any good to you the way my head feels.'

'Of course, I don't mind, Jake. You poor thing,' replied the nurse.

Jake was relieved, he knew he wouldn't be able to perform too well with the nurse when his mind was on TC. He turned his car back towards town, dropped the nurse off at the hospital, then drove up and down Brolga Street past TC's, hoping she'd be sitting on the steps watching the sprinkler. Jake gave up after half a dozen or so drive-bys. He decided to go home.

¶

Thel Carmichael was sitting in her lounge room reading when Jake Carmichael arrived home. She glanced at her watch when she heard his car pull onto the driveway. She looked up at her son as he came through the front door.

'What's gotten into you, Jake? It's not ten o'clock yet.'

'I know. Good night, Mum,' he said as he leaned down and kissed his mother on the cheek. She watched him disappear into his bedroom, shrugged, then resumed reading.

¶

The next morning at exactly nine o'clock by the pharmacy-wall clock, Jake walked into the pharmacy. TC was desperately trying to master the killer typewriter. Jake was standing at the dispensary door before she realised he had come in.

'Where did you go last night?' he asked.

'Not that it's any of your business, Jake, I went home, had a shower, and went to bed.'

'Would you like to go to the movies with me tonight? There's a Clint Eastwood movie on.'

'No, thank you, Jake,' as she continued to fiddle with the typewriter.

'Why not, TC?'

'Because I don't want to; also, because I want to learn how to use this typewriter before Friday in case my boss doesn't get back to help me with the mail. I have a feeling he won't.'

'Will take you ten years, not two days, if you keep going about it the way you are at the moment,' he laughed. 'Tell you what, TC. I'll pick you up after work and take you and the typewriter home to your place.

I'll teach you the fundamentals tonight; tomorrow night, too, if you like. You should be able to handle it with the use of three or four fingers after that.'

TC reluctantly agreed. She felt she had no choice.

'Okay, Jake, see you after work.' Jake turned to leave.

'You've got this place looking pristine, TC. Nice you've got a radio now.' Jake was excited as he left.

'How lucky can a man be?' he asked himself. 'Now I'll see her two nights in a row. Hopefully, I'll get the opportunity to accidentally touch her hands occasionally.'

The radio announced the usual, "It is now ten o'clock and the Commonwealth Bank is opened for business", as Jack and Bert Romeo threw open the hotel doors and TC crossed the road with the cheque.

'Mr Callahan told me to cash this,' she told the young bank teller as she passed the cheque across the counter to him. The teller looked at the cheque before taking it into a small office behind him. An older man returned to the counter with the cheque.

'I am the bank manager,' he announced in a very official voice. 'This is quite a large amount of money. Who filled in the amount?'

'I did. My boss told me to.'

'Why?'

'Because Mr Callahan is not here,' replied TC.

'Why does he need two thousand pounds if he's not here?'

'That's his business, sir.'

'Well, young lady, it's my business to be absolutely certain that Mr Callahan indeed did authorise you to write this cheque.'

'I write all the cheques to pay the accounts. Mr Callahan signs them. I fill in the amounts.'

'That's different, young lady.' TC realised with a shock that this stuffy, old bank manager must think she was robbing her boss. She was furious.

'Sir, Mr Callahan is waiting for a call from me as we speak. He is at the Curloo Motel in Curloo. I suggest you call him.'

The bank manager went to his office still holding the cheque. TC heard him ask the operator to connect him to the Curloo Motel.

'I believe you have a Mr Vance Callahan as a guest at your establishment?' Obviously he had been connected to Vance when she heard, 'Mr Callahan we have a young woman here with a cash cheque for two thousand pounds ... I see ... I see ... I'm so extremely sorry, Mr Callahan ... Of course, the bank values your business ... Of course, and your money as well ... There's no need to speak to me like that, Mr Callahan. On behalf of the bank, I am trying to take care of your best interests ... Yes, Mr Callahan, I am sure you are capable of taking care of your own best interests ... I'll do that, Mr Callahan ... Of course.'

Looks as if my boss has set him straight, thought TC, as the bank manager emerged smiling gushingly at her.

'How would you like the notes, Miss TC?'

'Hundreds will be fine, thank you, sir,' replied TC.

As the bank manager counted out the money and handed it across to TC, he said politely, 'I apologise for the confusion and delay, Miss TC.'

'Perhaps you should also apologise for assuming I'm a thief as well, sir.'

'I'm only doing my job,' he smiled.

'So am I,' replied TC with an exaggerated smile.

After TC had gone, the bank manager was openly furious as he yelled at his staff.

'Whenever that little jumped-up barmaid comes into this bank, give her whatever she wants. That drunken lunatic of a chemist had the audacity to tell me to pull my head out of my butt and mind my own effing business where his account is concerned. Even made me apologise to that girlfriend of his.'

'Excuse me, sir,' interrupted the more senior of the three bank tellers 'She's definitely not Mr Callahan's girlfriend. He races around with Louise from the Empire. TC only worked in the bar for a week or even less. She threw a beer in the Shire Chairman's face for using bad language. She seems like a very nice girl, keeps to herself.'

'So be it,' snapped the bank manager as he slammed shut his office door, slumped at his desk, and vowed to himself to get out of Brolga as soon as possible.

¶

Three middle-aged ladies were waiting outside the pharmacy when TC returned from the post office. She found it difficult to smile and appear happy but put on her best face when greeting them.

'We all want some cosmetics,' said one lady as she scrutinised TC, who wore only lipstick.

'You've come to the right place,' replied TC as she spread her hands and indicated the vast range of name-brand products.

'Please make use of the testers, ladies. I need to make a call to my boss. I'll be with you soon,' she smiled. As she was about to pick up the phone, it rang. She heard Vance's voice.

'So they gave you a hard time at the bank, Butterball?'

'Yes, the manager must think I'm a thief,' replied TC.

'Believe me, he doesn't anymore.'

'I wired the money, Mr Callahan, and I have some customers now.'

'Talk to you later, TC. Please try not to dwell on it.'

TC returned to the three ladies, who appeared to be having a great time as they tried this, then that. All three each purchased whatever they liked—cleanser, toner, moisturiser, eye cream, neck cream, foundation, loose face powder, compact powder, rouge, false eyelashes, mascara, eye shadow, lipstick, hand cream, body lotion, sun tan oil, everything.

TC thought to herself, These ladies must be extremely well off, as she totalled their individual purchases on the cash register. They must have read her mind.

'We won the Golden Casket Lottery, sweetie,' said the first lady.

'Been working together in a factory in Brisbane for twenty-five years. Never been able to afford all this stuff before,' said the second woman.

'Feel guilty buying it; still, it's only money.'

'What made you come to Brolga to buy it?' asked TC with a curious smile. The third woman explained.

'The three of us are devout John Wayne fans. If the end of the line is good enough for the Duke, it's good enough for us. Suppose you think we're crazy, sweetie? We've had a barrelful of fun getting here, even though the dirt road from Curloo to here is pretty rough. As a matter of fact, bloody rough.'

TC liked these ladies.

'That's almost the exact reason my friend and I came here,' she explained.

'How do you like living here, sweetie?' asked lady number two.

'It's quiet, most people are friendly, some have been extremely kind to me. I truly believe it was my fate to come to Brolga,' replied TC with a smile.

'Good luck to you, sweetie. We're staying at the Empire pub. Going back to titillate ourselves, have a few drinks this afternoon, then go to the movies to perv on Clint Eastwood tonight,' said lady number one.

'Not a touch on the Duke, chorused the other two, laughing.

What nice ladies, thought TC, after they had gone. She could hear them still laughing as they reached the Empire. I'm happy they won the casket. My boss will be happy, too. Between them they had spent a little over seven hundred pounds.

¶

The siren had long since gone by the time the ladies left; so, TC closed the door and sat down at Vance's desk to listen to the radio and meditate on anything and everything. Her mind was far away when she realised the phone was ringing. TC looked at the clock; it was ten-minutes-after-two. TC felt guilty as she picked up the telephone, realising she must have drifted off.

'May I speak to Vance, TC? It's Louise Swagg.'

'He's not here, Louise.'

'Where is he?'

'He has taken Mrs Callahan and the boys to Curloo.'

'He didn't tell me he was doing that. Tell the bastard I called,' she said angrily.

'I will, Louise.'

The afternoon was uneventful. A couple of walk-in customers. TC made a list of what was needed to be ordered from the drug houses in Brisbane.

§

Jake came back at closing time as agreed. He was happy and excited for some reason unknown to TC, who appeared miserable for some reason unknown to Jake. Once they arrived at TC's, Jake carried the typewriter from his car and positioned it on the dining room table. He then went to his car and fetched beer, Coke, and more LP records.

'Jake, the fridge is already almost full of beer and Coke you brought before.'

'Better throw out this food Auntie Flo left for you then,' after he opened the refrigerator to pack in the drinks.

'The corned beef is still okay. Rest of it has to go.' He began removing fruit and vegetables from the fridge and placing them on the floor beside him. 'Don't you eat anything, TC?'

'Too hot to eat, Jake.'

'No wonder you're getting so bloody thin,' replied Jake.

'Jake, I've already had that lecture from my boss. If I was overweight, you'd both be whinging about that. I'm taking a shower. If the snakes get me, it will be a blessing.'

Jake was trying to locate old newspaper in which to wrap the rejects from the fridge as TC rushed past the kitchen en route to the shower.

'Don't throw bread out, Jake.'

'Looks like you have yesterday's bread and corned beef if you want anything to eat tonight.'

'The newspaper is in the cupboard next to the fridge.'

Smart, thought Jake, as he searched for a couple of tomatoes worth rescuing before opening a beer.

TC emerged from the bathroom wearing her embroidered rock-n-roll shirt and a pair of pink pedal-pushers. Her wet hair was pulled back in a ponytail, as usual, and she was wearing her white jiffy slippers with the bows. She didn't think it appropriate to wear her dressing gown when taking typing lessons, especially from Jake. Jake was talking to Vance on the telephone.

'Here she is now, mate,' said Jake as TC ran up the stairs.

'What's Jake doing there?' asked Vance after TC had taken the receiver from Jake.

'Jake's going to teach me how to use the typewriter.'

'Make sure that's all he teaches you. Hope you remember what I told you.'

'Yes, I do, Mr Callahan. I remember everything.'

'I've just put Delores and the boys on the train. I have some business to do here in Curloo tomorrow. How did you go today?' TC told him about the three ladies.

'I mean how much money did we take today?'

'Eight hundred and fifty-two pounds and one shilling.'

'Excellent, Butterball. Make sure you eat. Talk to you tomorrow.'

TC realised she had forgotten to tell him Louise had called.

¶

Jake and TC sat once again on the front top step. He ate a corned beef and Holbrook sauce sandwich with a beer to wash it down. She ate a piece of toast with vegemite, with Coke to wash it down with. They sat in silence as they ate. No music in the background and no sprinkler.

When they finished eating Jake said, 'Come on, TC, let's get this typing lesson on the road.'

'Ready to rock and roll,' replied TC as she pointed to her blouse.

'Do you want to hear some music?' asked Jake.

'Sure. You choose, Jake.'

With Henry Mancini and his orchestra playing in the background, TC had her first typing lesson. Both Jake and TC realised after an hour that her fingers were absolutely uncoordinated. She had to resign herself to the fact that she would never excel as a secretary. TC really laughed for the first time that day as she put her elbows on the table and threw her hands out from the wrist.

'Guess I'll have to be great at something else, Jake. This is obviously not the avenue I should pursue.'

Jake laughed. 'I agree wholeheartedly. Let's go with the three-finger method.'

'Sounds good to me. It's so hot in here. Let's take a break so you can smoke a cigarette and I can enjoy my favourite pastime of watching the sprinkler whirl around.'

TC was on the front steps before Jake, who changed the record. Endeavouring to be a smart–aleck, he chose Slim Dusty.

That should get a rise out of her, he thought, as he went to join her. He pulled her ponytail as he sat down beside her. Silence. Not even a comment on poor old Slim's song. Jake was desperate for some sort of conversation.

'I see you like bows, TC,' he said as he glanced at the white bow holding her hair back and then at the slippers.

'Yes, I like pretty things. Suppose it's a throw-back to childhood.'

'What do you mean?' asked Jake.

'Doesn't matter.'

'It matters to me, TC. You have a captive audience of one.'

'You wouldn't understand, Jake.'

'Try me. Please.'

TC's mind raced back ten or twelve years as she considered whether or not to answer Jake's question.

'I'm waiting, TC,' said Jake, wearing the look of a curious schoolboy.

TC reasoned with herself. 'He's told me everything about his family and his life. I suppose I can tell him a tiny bit about mine.'

'My father was a gunny shearer in the central west. Off-season, he trained race horses for property owners. My mother was a spendthrift.'

'Your father trained race horses?' interrupted Jake.

'Yes. One horse he trained came from nowhere to be a runner-up in the Melbourne Cup.'

'What was its name?' asked Jake with great interest.

'I don't know. I was too young. All I know is what I recall my father said that it was a long shot, he backed it for a place, it ran second, he had put his shirt on it, and he won a lot of money.'

'Where's your dad now?'

'I don't know. Jake, you asked me why I liked pretty things.'

'Tell me now,' said Jake apologetically.

'Doesn't matter, Jake.'

TC changed the subject.

'The more I listen to Slim Dusty, the more I like him. A friend of mine told me years ago that the words in a song are more important than the beat. Slim sings some pretty good words.'

I'm a bloody idiot, thought Jake. She was just about to open up to me and I blew it.

'Jake, I think we should return to my three-finger typing lesson. It's my fingers that are the problem.'

Jake sat watching TC as she laboured with determination to beat the typewriter. He really wanted to pull her away from the damned thing, tell her it didn't matter that she couldn't type, wore bows in her hair and on her feet or that her rock-n-roll shirt was out of place in Brolga.

'What do you think, Jake?' asked TC on completing a pretend label. 'All I need now is speed,' she said excitedly as she turned towards him.

'I think you are beautiful. I want to make love with you. I've never met anyone else like you, TC. I believe I'm in love with you. I want to marry you.' TC could see Jake was serious and absolutely sincere as he looked at her adoringly. Her mind was racing.

'It's one thing to ask me in a drunken stupor, another thing to tell me like this. He's too much like my boss. Be careful of him. He's gone to private school, got money. We're both so young. He loaned me money and paid off the Greeks. He arranged for me to live in his aunt and uncle's house for free. His family have businesses. I have nothing. My family have nothing. He dresses like a prince. I dress like a peasant.' TC's list of comparisons was endless.

'Thank you, Jake. I'm extremely flattered. Jake, it's common knowledge around Brolga that you can get just about any girl you want.'

'Except you, TC. You're the only one I want.'

'That is, at the moment, Jake,' replied TC. 'We are both very young. In my opinion, too young to consider marriage. Also, Jake, I don't even know what "in love" feels like.'

Jake stood up, leaned down, took her face in his hands and kissed her on the forehead.

'I'm going home now, speed typist of the century. Pick you and your friend up in the morning,' he said as he looked towards the typewriter.

§

Vance phoned the pharmacy at precisely eight-thirty in the morning. Jake had just gone after depositing the typewriter on the dispensary shelf.

'How did your lesson go, Butterball?'

'Don't think I'll ever be a legal secretary.'

Vance laughed.

'What's on your agenda today?'

'I'm going to practice typing with three fingers.'

'Any calls?'

'I forgot to tell you last night, Louise phoned yesterday afternoon.'

'What did Louise have to say?'

'She seemed a bit upset you didn't tell her you were taking Mrs Callahan and the boys to Curloo.'

'All right, I'll see you tomorrow.'

§

Come siren time, TC felt confident that her three-finger method of typing would suffice. No longer would she be worried about mail days. If Vance wasn't there, she felt confident now that she could handle anything that came along except prescription day when the flying doctor was in town. From now on, she would concentrate on learning everything she could about reading and filling the prescriptions. In the afternoon, a few early mail orders phoned in, Louise called enquiring about Vance;

Auntie Flo called to see how things were going at the house. Auntie Flo told TC, of course she could use the sewing machine, and two jackaroos walked in to purchase hair oil. One of them returned to make three more purchases at three different times. On each occasion he appeared to linger longer than necessary and was hesitant about every word he spoke. Third transaction completed, there was an awkward few moments as TC waited for him to leave. The young man cleared his throat.

'Would you like to go out with me tonight?' he asked quietly. TC could see he was nervous as he waited for her reply.

'There's nowhere to go in Brolga tonight, apart from the hotel, that is' she smiled. 'I don't drink and I don't go into hotels. Thank you for your invitation, anyway.' The jackeroo was visibly disappointed.

'Perhaps next time?'

'We'll see,' replied TC with another smile.

What a nice young man he is, thought TC, as she watched him walk away. That was the first of countless such invitations TC would receive in the future from young men who worked on Brolga's surrounding cattle and sheep stations. She always declined, sometimes with difficulty since most of them were extremely well mannered and very handsome.

¶

Jake had not been able to take his mind off his conversation with TC the night before.

I'm a bloody idiot, he thought to himself. Laid my cards and my heart on the table to her. Should have kept my bloody mouth shut. What's a man supposed to do? Walk around with my dick in my hand until she decides we're old enough to get married? I'm not used to this kind of treatment from women. She doesn't know what "in love" feels like.' Well, I didn't bloody well know either until I clapped eyes on her. Bet she doesn't even realise how bloody adorable she looks in those bows and her stupid clothes. All I want to do is grab her and get it over with. I've had enough.

He picked up the telephone and recognised Lou's voice as she asked,

'What number, please?'

'Put me through to TC, Lou, and don't bother listening in.'

Jake's in a foul mood, thought Lou, as she connected him to the pharmacy. Of course, she was going to listen in, especially since Jake had told her not to.

'TC, it's Jake. Hope you've mastered that bloody typewriter because I don't want to have to sit in that house again tonight.'

TC was confused as she replied, 'You sound angry, Jake.'

'I am.'

'Have I done something to upset you?'

'You upset me every time I see you. That's the bloody point. You expect me to just sit, talk, and listen to Elvis when all I want to do is grab you and throw your cute arse on the bed.'

'I see. I'm okay typing the labels now. Thank you for helping me, Jake.'

She heard Jake slam down the telephone. TC sat down at Vance's desk as tears flooded her eyes. She wished Vance were there so she could ask him just how men thought.

After his outburst, Jake paced around his office for a short time before picking up the telephone again.

'You're some bit of business, Jake,' said Lou. 'Looks like you've finally met your match. Must be a blow to your good old male ego.'

'Shut up, Lou. Put me through to the nurse's quarters. Make sure you listen in this time, Lou. You can report it to your mate, TC.'

'It's Jake,' he said into the telephone.

'Oh, Jake, I've been waiting to hear from you,' replied a giggling voice.

'I'll take you up on that rain check tonight if you're available? I need to get laid.'

'I look forward to it, Jake,' she said still giggling.

'Pick you up at eight.'

Done, thought Jake, as he put the phone down. If I can't have what I want, I'll have to settle for what I can get. Better go to the pub and have a few beers so it will be easier to pretend I'm in a good mood tonight.

§

TC was closing the pharmacy as Jake pulled up outside the Empire. They ignored each other. TC felt lonely. She missed Lou's company and was happy Lou's week of four-to-midnight shifts finished the next night.

'Think I'll give the steps a miss tonight. Just take the routine shower and go to bed. Wish I had an air-conditioner. Never mind. Nobody gets everything.' TC suddenly realised she was talking to herself. She opened the front gate, ran up the stairs, went inside, and switched on the radio. Del Shannon was singing, "Runaway".

'Wish I could run away, too, Del,' she said aloud, shrugged her shoulders, then threw open the back door. The telephone rang.

'How are you, TC?' asked Lou.

'I'm all right, Lou. Looking forward to your shift change,' replied TC.

'Me, too. I heard what Jake said to you today, TC. Don't worry about him; he's a spoiled brat used to getting everything and every girl he wants.'

'He's been good to me, Lou,' replied TC.

'Sure he has, obviously with an ulterior motive in mind. He's a rat, TC. Please don't let your gratitude towards Jake drag you into his trap.'

'I don't want to talk about him, Lou.'

'Okay. I get paid in the morning. My spring for thick-shakes. Have to go. Lights are flashing all over the switchboard.'

TC was asleep several hours later when she heard the ringing of the phone. It woke her up. She looked at the clock through half-opened eyes. It was almost eleven o'clock.

'Who would call this late?' she asked herself as she dragged herself off the bed and staggered to the phone.

'Hello, Butterball,' said an obviously drunk Vance.

'What's wrong, Mr Callahan?' mumbled TC.

'Don't keep calling me Mr Callahan; it makes me feel old.'

'What should I call you, Mr Callahan?'

'Think of something, anything, except Mr Callahan.'

'I'll try to think of something tomorrow.'

'No, not tomorrow. Now!'

'You're drunk, Mr Callahan, and I'm half asleep.'

'There you go, Butterball. You called me that again.'

'Sorry, Boss,' said TC with as much sarcasm as she could muster under the circumstances.

'Good, that's good,' slurred Vance. 'From now on you call me boss.'

'Except when it's inappropriate,' replied TC, who was gradually waking up. 'What's wrong, Boss?'

'I'm drunk.'

'I know.'

'What are your favourite colours, Butterball?'

Why on earth does he want to know my favourite colours? thought TC, before replying, 'Can't understand why you need to know that at this time of the night, Boss. My favourite colours are yellow, pink, peach, and red. Now please tell me why you called?'

'Because I think I'm too drunk to drive to Brolga tonight.'

'Thank God for that, Boss.'

'Sorry, Butterball. Probably won't make it back in time to help you with the mail.'

'I half expected that, Boss. Please sober up before you drive.'

'You're a good girl, Butterball.'

'And you're a good man, Boss. Please try not to drink so much. Please drive carefully. Don't worry. Everything will be all right; so, don't worry.'

Silence, then TC heard him hang up. She couldn't get back to sleep, just lay in bed thinking about everything and everyone—her boss, Delores and the children, their baby on the way, Louise, the Romeos, Sam, Lou, Auntie Flo and Uncle Doug, Jake and how the boss and Lou had warned her about him. The sun rose at 5 am, TC got out of bed, took another shower, dressed for work, then sat on the back landing with a glass of iced water. TC's mind was blank. She simply sat staring into space for what seemed an eternity. She was startled back to reality when she heard a car door close and realised Jake was standing at the bottom of the stairs.

'I didn't hear you drive in, Jake,' said TC as she looked down at him. He looked terrible, had not shaved, and his eyes were bloodshot.

'Changed your posi?' asked Jake.

'No sun out here this time of day,' replied TC. 'What brings you here so early, Jake?'

'I couldn't sleep.'

'Join the club, Jake. You look as bad as I feel.'

'I got on the rum last night, TC.'

'I know. You smell like my boss.'

'TC, I'm sorry for what I said to you yesterday.'

'That's all right, Jake. You had to get it off your chest. I'm not your type, Jake.'

'Says you,' snapped Jake as he sat down on the second bottom stair. He sat with his back towards TC, put his elbows on his knees, and held his head in his hands.

'Good God, TC, it's hard to get through to you. You don't seem to hear anything I say to you.'

'I've heard everything you've said to me, Jake. You want everything and you want it yesterday. You move too fast for me. I'm flattered that you want to marry me. What girl wouldn't be? All I can offer you at the moment is my friendship, that is, if you want it. I suggest you go home and have a shave.'

Jake stood up, turned to look at her, shook his head, got into his car, and left.

¶

As TC had expected, mail-order day was chaotic. The phone rang incessantly all morning. At one stage, TC felt like smashing it to the floor. Lou came at siren time.

'Can't go, Lou. Too much to do.'

Lou walked across to the café and returned shortly after with chocolate thick-shakes.

'A deal is a deal,' said Lou. 'We'll drink as we work. I'll help you until I have to go to work.'

'I'll ask the boss to pay you some money.'

'Don't bother about money, TC. Ask him to give me some cosmetics.'

'Deal,' replied TC. They both laughed.

At two o'clock the phone started again. Lou answered the calls and took orders as TC concentrated on parcels. She closed up around ten.

Thank heavens for Lou, she thought, as she turned towards home. Without her help, I'd still be working at midnight. Hope the boss is all right. He didn't call today.

TC skipped the shower, cleaned her teeth, got into bed and fell asleep immediately.

¶

Jake was home in bed. He had not gone to work. He was hung over from the rum he'd consumed the night before and his head ached with a vengeance.

'I'll never drink rum again,' he declared to himself as he jumped up for the umpteenth time and ran to dry retch over the toilet.

¶

Vance was precariously driving towards Brolga about fifty miles from town. He was hot, covered in dust, and reeked of rum. Going back to Curloo brought back memories of Anna. After depositing Delores and the boys on the train, he had headed for the nearest hotel, where he drank doubles until closing time, then headed back to the motel with a bottle of rum and a couple of bottles of Coke. That was two nights ago. Apart from phoning TC a couple of times and going into a shop in Curloo, he could recall very little else. He told himself over and over again, 'Next time I go to Curloo, I'll buy fuel and keep on going.'

Vance didn't dwell too much on the fact that Delores had gone to her mother's with the kids. He knew she'd come back; she always did. He would go and fetch them after the baby was born. He felt sorry for Delores for the way he treated her.

'How can she possibly love a bastard like me? I treat her like crap.' He had asked himself just that at least a dozen times a day for years.

§

Delores was asleep in her mother's house in Brisbane. She had not heard from Vance since she had said goodbye to him at Curloo Railway Station. She had fallen asleep thinking about him and silently praying he was safe.

§

Sam and Brad Lester were having a vicious verbal fight down by the creek.

§

Vance was seated at his desk drinking coffee when TC arrived for work.

'Ah! Butterball, good to see you,' he smiled as if he meant it. 'See you were busy yesterday,' as he looked towards the mountain of packages near the front door.

'Good to see you, too, Boss,' replied TC. 'Yes, kept busy all day yesterday. Lou helped me until she had to leave for work. I told her I would ask you to give her some money. She said she would prefer some cosmetics. Boss, I hope you will give her something. This is the third time she has helped me.'

'What time did you close up?' he asked.

'Around ten. I'm so happy you are back. I'm going to fetch the mail.'

§

When TC had gone, Vance phoned Delores, who was happy and relieved to hear his voice. He then phoned through to the pharmaceutical companies in Brisbane and ordered the list of products TC had written for him.

This girl's a bloody one-man band, he thought. Better watch myself or I won't be needed around here much longer.

'No mail today,' reported TC on her return.

'This is for you, Butterball.' Vance pointed to a neatly wrapped brown-paper package on the desk.

'Don't know what this could be,' said TC in surprise.

'Open it and let's see,' said Vance as he handed her scissors to cut the string, which held the package together. 'Hurry up,' he urged.

TC began crying the moment she saw the contents.

On top were three paper dress patterns and beneath them three lengths of lovely material—one pink with white polka dots, one plain pale yellow with a white border of tiny flowers, and the third, a beautiful pale peach colour.

'That's this week's bonus, Butterball. Now stop crying. I described you to the woman in the shop; she chose the patterns and I chose the materials. Think I was more than a bit drunk at the time; so, I hope I chose right.'

'Everything is beautiful. You don't have to give me bonuses; I don't expect anything.'

'I know you don't. That's why I want to give you something now and then. Get these eyes dried out and go fill all those gaps in the shelves.'

TC looked at him with quivering lips.

'You are the best boss in the world.'

'And you are under an illusion, young lady.'

As TC went to the sink to wash her face, Vance added, 'Would have got you some red material as well but couldn't see a shade of red that would do your complexion justice.'

TC could feel tears welling again. She willed them back, dried her face, and began filling gaps.

¶

When the mail truck arrived, Vance helped the driver load the orders onto the truck. He then made a few phone calls. At ten o'clock he announced, 'I'm going to the Empire. When Lou comes in, give her whatever she wants. Within reason, that is.'

165

Jake and Lou arrived simultaneously just before siren time.

'Mum would like you to come home for lunch,' said Jake.

'Lou and I were planning on going to the café,' replied TC.

Jake looked at Lou. 'You come, too. Mum won't mind.'

'Sounds good to me,' replied Lou.

¶

As they ate lunch, Thel Carmichael asked TC if she had heard from Auntie Flo.

'Yes,' replied TC. 'She's called twice. She told me I could use her sewing machine; so, I'm going to make myself some new clothes. Heaven knows, I need them. Ready-mades are too expensive for me. I have plenty of spare time; so, I may as well make use of it.'

She sews as well, thought Jake.

'You'll need a lot of time, TC, if you plan to use Flo's old treadle,' said Thel. 'It will take you a thousand years. You had better borrow my electric sewing machine; I rarely use it.'

'I couldn't do that, Mrs Carmichael.'

'Of course, you can. I loathe sewing myself. You borrow my machine, and whenever I need anything mended, patched, or altered, you do it for me.'

TC smiled. 'Thank you, Mrs Carmichael.'

'Jake, take that machine when you go back to work. Put it on Flo's landing for TC.'

'Consider it done, Mum,' replied Jake.

Jake didn't have much to say during lunch. He sat quietly observing the interaction between TC and his mother. As far as he was concerned, Lou may as well not have been there.

Obviously his mother liked TC and TC appeared relaxed as they chatted about anything and everything.

'Time to go, ladies,' said Jake after collecting his mother's sewing machine and putting it in his car.

So that's what has brought about the change in Jake, thought Thel

Carmichael, as she washed the few lunch dishes. I'll bet it's TC. He hardly took his eyes off her through lunch.

¶

Lou chose one lipstick, an eyebrow pencil, and a tube of mascara as her remuneration for helping TC while Vance was away.

'Not enough, Lou' said TC. 'I'll tell the boss we still owe you.'

'Don't worry about it, TC. What I would like is for you to make me a couple of dresses after you've finished yours.'

'Deal,' replied TC happily.

'I'll buy some material before I go to work. Better get what I want before Dad puts the bite on me for more money.'

TC cut a tiny sample of material from each of her bonus lengths, checked the pattern for zipper lengths, then made a short list for Lou to take to Carmichael and Carmichael.

'Here's my list, Lou. I'll give you some money. Get matching cotton and zips for yourself after you choose your fabrics.'

'What about patterns?' asked Lou.

'Don't bother; we can make changes to these.'

Two snobby local girls who worked in the council office came in.

'We just want to look around, TC,' said one of them smugly.

'Yes, mostly at you, TC,' whispered the other one. They both giggled.

TC continued filling gaps. The two girls continued whispering and giggling. TC caught the words barmaid, shire chairman, Jake, Jordan's daughter, drunken chemist, same daggy clothes, and lots of laughter. They were fiddling with the lipstick testers. TC wanted to tell them to leave; instead, she walked past them to the dispensary and turned up the volume on the radio before returning to face them.

'There you go, ladies. Now you can converse with each other in a normal tone of voice,' she smiled. 'Are you interested in purchasing a lipstick?'

Both girls were visibly shocked. No smirks to be seen as they looked at TC with their mouths open.

'Not really. We already have plenty of lipsticks,' stammered one.

TC looked at the lipstick streaks on both girls' wrists.

'In that case, ladies, I suggest you leave the lipstick testers for the use of serious customers. Is there anything else I can help you with?' enquired TC with a smile.

They both shook their heads.

'In that case, ladies, I look forward to seeing you when you run out of lipsticks.'

They left in silence. TC turned the radio down as Lou returned. Lou ripped her parcel open.

'I've been talking to Jake. He told me he hopes we don't end up looking like the Bobbsy twins. He talked me into blue and emerald green. Here's your change. He didn't charge you for the dressmaking scissors. He said to be careful you don't stab yourself with them.'

TC was furious. 'How much were the scissors, Lou?'

'Five shillings.'

'Mind the shop for a few minutes, please, Lou.'

TC stormed down the street to Jake's shop. He was standing at one of the counters talking to two of his staff members. She had intended throwing the money at him, telling him to buy himself a pair of scissors, and stab himself with them. On seeing the other people with him, she smiled at Jake, who was obviously surprised to see her.

'There you are, Mr Carmichael,' she said as she handed him five shillings. 'You forgot to charge Lou for the scissors.'

Jake smiled at her.

'Thank you.' He took the money.

'Bad example for the staff,' she heard him say as she walked out. Jake and his staff laughed.

Vance was in the dispensary talking to Lou when TC got back to the shop. They both looked at TC curiously.

'What's wrong?' asked Vance.

'It doesn't matter, Boss,' replied TC softly as she shook her head from side to side.

'Of course, it damned-well matters. Now tell me what the problem is,' demanded Vance. TC told him about the two girls and Vance with the scissors.

'Perhaps I shouldn't have turned the radio up and been so rude to those girls. As for Jake, I don't want him to give me anything. He's already done too much for me.' Vance interrupted.

'TC, don't worry about those rude girls. They are obviously rude and probably jealous of you. TC, those two little tarts are lucky I wasn't here. I probably would have picked them up and thrown them through the door. As for Jake, he knows you have very little money; so, he was probably trying to be kind. After all, five bob is a lot to you.'

'Jake wants to marry TC,' said Lou. 'I heard him tell her. He was drunk when he told her. I told TC a drunken man speaks a sober man's mind. My dad told me that.'

TC could have choked her friend. Obviously, her dad hadn't told her about playing your cards close to your chest. Vance sat bolt upright when he heard Lou's announcement. His face appeared to have paled as he looked directly at TC.

'When did this happen?'

'About a week ago.'

'What did you say to him?'

'Nothing. He was so drunk he didn't remember.' TC decided she definitely wouldn't mention her conversation with Jake when he was sober. Vance glanced at the clock.

'Lou, you'd better be going if you start work at four.' Lou saw the time and flew off her chair.

'See you later,' as she rushed out.

Vance directed his attention towards TC. He was extremely serious as he spoke.

'Butterball, I told you to be careful of Jake. He's a man's man. I've told you before, you're a good girl. Not many like you around, especially in a place like Brolga. Jake and I are mates. We drink and gamble together. Jake's notorious around town as a ladies' man. Why on earth does he have to set his sights on you? You're far too good for him or any other mongrel around here. I told you before, you are special.' With that, Vance stood up.

'I'm going to see Jake now. Maybe he'll fancy a game of poker tonight.' He paused as he walked past TC.

'Be careful little Butterball.' TC nodded.

¶

Four shearers came in for toiletries. They were men perhaps in their late thirties, early forties. The four of them were immaculately turned-out for their weekend away from the shearing shed. TC had noticed most shearers, when not working, were almost always well turned-out. One of the four wore a punter's hat just like her father used to wear. They were all well spoken like her father, and so she was reminded of him.

'My father was a shearer,' said TC in conversation.

'Is that so?' said one man.

'What's his name?' asked another.

'He was known as Sykes within the shearing community' replied TC.

'Sykes?' they said in unison.

'Everyone knows Sykes, luv. Your dad's not just a shearer. The man's a legend.'

'Where's Sykes now?' enquired the man in the hat.

'Don't know,' replied TC wistfully.

'We'll keep our eyes and ears out for you, luv. By the way,' said the man in the hat as they were leaving, 'Sykes would be proud of you. He sure left his stamp on you; you look just like him.'

'Only you're a girl,' added one of the other men.

TC decided then and there she preferred to deal with men rather than women.

'I don't care if they are shearers, jackeroos, labourers, doctors, or lawyers,' she said to herself. 'Men don't daunt me. Most women don't like me.'

With that she closed the pharmacy and walked home with her precious package of fabrics, cotton, zips, and scissors under her arm.

On reaching home, TC automatically turned on the sprinkler and the radio and opened the back door. Thel Carmichael's sewing machine was not on the back landing as she expected. TC hoped no one had stolen it then thought Jake had probably forgotten to drop it off.

No sewing tonight, she thought, as she went downstairs to shower. She decided to trim her hair. It was getting too long on the top, front, and sides. It didn't matter how long it grew at the back. She ran back up the stairs to grab the scissors and was heading back to the shower when Jake pulled up beside the stairs. He burst into gales of laughter when he saw TC with the scissors in her hand.

'Been lying in wait for me, have you, Darling?'

'Don't call me 'Darling!" snapped TC.

'Come on, Darling, stab me in the chest,' as he put his hands behind his head in a surrendering motion.

'Jake, you are a drunken idiot.'

'Drunk I am; idiot I am not. Vance and I have been at the pub.'

'I can see that, Jake.'

'Vance is drunker than I am,' he mumbled.

'Is that so? Jake, why don't I make you some coffee?'

'No, no, no, no coffee. Vance is throwing a party at his place. His wife's away.'

'I know that, Jake.'

'Do you want to come?' as his head wobbled from side to side.

'Where to? The boss's party? Don't be ridiculous.'

'My mummy told me I have to leave this thing with you, Darling. I always do as my mummy tells me. Like hell, I do' he mumbled under his breath. Jake almost fell into the boot of his car as he reached down for the sewing machine.

'I'll get it, Jake,' said TC as she picked it up. Jake stood back and scratched his head.

'Darling, you're strong as well as everything else,' he garbled as he watched TC go up the stairs. Vance pulled into the driveway behind Jake. When TC saw her boss almost fall out of his car, she realised Jake was right. Vance was drunker than Jake.

'Butterball,' slurred Vance, 'come to chaperone you. Don't want this mongrel Jake alone with you.'

'You are both maniacs for driving around in your condition,' said TC as sternly as she could. 'If the police sergeant catches you, he'll put you in jail.'

'Not enough room in that little jail to fit in everyone who drives around drunk in Brolga,' murmured Jake with a ridiculous laugh.

'You're right on there, mate,' laughed Vance, who could barely retain his balance.

'I'll get you both some coffee.'

'No, no coffee; I told you that before,' from Jake.

'No coffee for me, either,' from Vance.

'All right, I'm going to take my shower and trim my hair. May God help both of you.'

When TC emerged from the bathroom half an hour later, both Vance and Jake were gone. Jake's driver's-side car door and boot were open. Vance's car door was also open. She closed their cars.

'Must have scared them off driving with my little lecture; so, they opted to stagger instead of drive.'

TC wound her hair in rollers. If her hair was curly, any gaps she'd made while trimming were camouflaged. She then went about trimming the paper dress patterns as she listened to the radio. It was 4CO's weekly non-stop rock-and-roll night. She got carried away with the cutting while enjoying listening to Fats, Jerry Lee, Little Richard, Buddy Holly, and, of course, Elvis. Once the cutting was completed, TC mixed and matched the patterns, deciding what sleeve or neckline or which style of bodice, et cetera.

The boss is right. I am a little bit thin, she thought, as she measured herself with the tape measure. Should get some food into the house. Probably just throw it out. I don't fancy eating alone.

TC suddenly remembered the sprinkler as the radio announced it was two in the morning. She quickly got up and went downstairs to turn off the tap. She thought she heard something as she came back into the house, stopped and listened, then heard it again.

TC turned on the verandah light. She was taken aback to see Vance asleep in the squatter's chair at the end of the front verandah and Jake asleep on the shearer's bunk behind him. Both of them were softly snoring. TC turned the light off, then on again. Neither of them roused. She tried speaking to them; they mumbled but didn't wake up. She thought of throwing some water on them but didn't dare. She thought it best just to leave them there. At least they were safe. She closed the back door, turned off the lights, and went to bed. She was awaken by a horn sounding, followed by doors slamming, just as the sun began to come up, went back to sleep, and woke up when the alarm went off at six thirty.

¶

As usual, when he was in town, Vance was at his desk when TC arrived.

'Make some coffee,' was his greeting.

She made him a cup of coffee and put it in front of him.

'Sit down. I want to talk to you,' he said.

'What have I done wrong?' asked TC.

'You have done nothing wrong. Jake and I are the ones who have done something wrong.'

'What did you and Jake do?'

'We've blown your reputation, TC. Brolga is a small town, and gossip is rife. The truck drivers from the transport depot across the road from your place pulled out on their mail run at four this morning. Without a doubt, they would have spotted our cars in your driveway. One of them sounded his horn as he drove past your house. That's what woke Jake and me. I'm sorry, Butterball. Know Jake will be, too, after he thinks about the repercussions on you.'

'I'm not quite sure what you mean, Boss. Do you mean people will think I was with you and Jake? 'I didn't know you and Jake were there until two in the morning. I tried to wake both of you but couldn't. I even thought of throwing a bucket of water over you.' TC sighed. 'Perhaps I should have.'

'Perhaps you should have,' agreed Vance.

A customer came into the pharmacy. Vance got up to serve her. TC drifted away into deep thought. She recalled hearing an elderly aunt a long time ago when she was a child.

'Gossip is cheap. If you do it, you wear it. If you don't do it, don't wear it under any circumstances.'

TC kept analysing those words over and over again. She felt a tap on her shoulder. It was Vance.

'Give me a hand, Butterball,' he said softly. 'The shop is full of customers.'

They were busy all morning; there was a Country Women's Association meeting in town that afternoon. Jake arrived via the back door as the last customer left. Vance closed the front door and gave TC her pay.

'Sorry about last night, TC,' said Jake. 'I have already told my mother what happened. Didn't want her to hear if from someone else and jump to conclusions about you. Mum told me it's my fault because I drink too much.' TC looked at Jake and then at Vance.

'You both drink too much. I'm going home.' She put her pay in her purse and walked out without saying goodbye.

'We are a ripe pair of bastards, Jake,' said Vance.

'I know. I should have taken that bloody machine and left it on the landing as I was supposed to. Suppose I thought it was a good excuse to see her.'

Vance started to say something, then changed his mind. Instead, he said, 'Let's go to the Empire, Jake. Think I'll have a few bets.'

'Sounds good. Meet you there. My car is out back; I've been to the railway station.'

❡

Lou was sitting on TC's front steps when TC got home.

'Thought I'd beat you here. Been to the grocery shop and bought some fruit, crackers, and cheese. That evens the score for the steak sandwiches.' TC gave her friend a half-hearted smile.

'Lou, you are exactly like me when it comes down to settling debts.'

'Could be worse, TC. We could be like those people who never settle. They cross to the other side of the street when they see the person who lent them the money coming towards them. Dad says if you owe someone money, be man enough to face them and tell them you can't repay them. Even if you pay them five bob a week, they'll respect you. That's what my dad says.'

'Your dad's right, Lou,' agreed TC. 'My sister, brothers, and I grew up taking notes to the butcher and grocer. More times than not, we were told, 'Tell you mother she can't get anything until she pays the bills.' Usually, an audience of other customers was present. My father religiously sent ten pounds a week. My mother blew it on rubbish, usually outings to the movies. The bank foreclosed on our house because my mother forgot to pay them one pound a month on the mortgage. We had no shoes, lice in our hair, and sure did see more dinner times then dinners. We were known around town as poor white trash. Jake asked me why I like bows and pretty shoes.'

'What did you tell him?' asked Lou with great interest.

'Nothing, really. I can tell you because you are interested. Once when I was around nine years old, I was invited to another girl's birthday party. I was very excited because it was the first one I had been invited to since I started school. I can remember pedalling my little bike like crazy to that girl's house. I jumped off my bike, threw it against the fence, and raced in. My hair was all over the place; I was barefoot, of course, and wearing a faded floral dress with half the hem falling down. All the other little girls wore frilly party dresses, pretty shoes and socks, and bows of ribbon in their hair. They looked at me as if I'd come from Mars before all of them except the party girl started laughing. 'Who asked you here?' 'Go home.' 'Haven't you got any shoes?' et cetera. I ran out of there, got on my old bike, and cried all the way home. From that day on, Lou, except for Sam, I was a loner at school. Sam was the party girl. We were inseparable until we came to Brolga.'

Lou was listening intently while TC was talking.

'Been the same for me here in Brolga, TC. Most Brolgaites look down on us. I still don't get invited anywhere, as I'm not good enough. I grew up in rags. I couldn't wait to start work so I could buy some decent clothes. Dad owes money all over the place, but he settles up when he can. I'm always broke before Friday pay day because my dad bites me for whatever I've got left on Wednesday.'

Silence for a few moments.

'Well, Lou, we should both put the past behind us. I know I intend to. Come on, I'll give you your first sewing lesson. We'll make one dress for you first, then one for me, one for you, and two for me.'

'I don't know about we, TC. I'm in a frantic frenzy if I have to put a hem up.'

'You'll learn,' laughed TC.

A few hours later, Lou was standing admiring herself in her new almost finished emerald green dress as TC pinned the hem.

'You look lovely, Lou. Jake sure did point you in the right direction with this colour; perfect with your auburn hair. The puffed sleeves, scooped neckline, and empire line look great. I suggest you put your hair up when you wear this one. You will look lovely.'

Lou was ecstatic.

'TC this dress has cost me less than five bob, including cotton and zipper. It's the best dress I've ever owned! It truly is, TC! Thank you,' as she gave TC a hug.

BY midnight they had a new dress each. TC had made up the pink with white polka dots material with a high curved neck at the front and a v at the back, straight-through tapered body, with short sleeves pleated highly on the shoulders.

'That's it for tonight, Lou' said TC. 'I'll teach you how to hem them properly tomorrow. You're doing well; you've mastered pinning the patterns to the fabric already.'

They sat on the front steps, each with an apple and a Coke. TC told Lou about Jake and Vance the night before, the truck drivers across the road, what the boss and Jake had told her would probably happen, and about Jake getting in first with his mother.

'Depends which truckies they are,' said Lou. 'Trouble is they all talk amongst themselves. Looks as if you'll be branded a scarlet woman, TC. Until something juicier happens, that is.'

Jerry Lee was singing, "Before you accuse, criticise and abuse, walk a mile in my shoes".

'How appropriate,' said Lou. 'Don't worry about what Brolgaites in general think about you. The few people who know you won't believe petty rumours.'

'Oh, well, Lou, if they do, they do. Jake, Vance, you, and I know differently.'

They brushed their teeth at the kitchen sink as had become their habit, then went to bed.

Come Sunday morning, Lou and TC were up early and back into sewing. By nine o'clock, Lou was slowly but meticulously sewing the hems and TC was sewing the blue dress for Lou.

'This electric machine is so quick, Lou,' remarked TC. 'Jake's mother is right. We'd still be only half-way finished with your green dress if I'd used Auntie Flo's treadle.'

'Little sewing circle ladies,' came Jake's voice from the back doorway.

'Didn't hear your car pull in, Jake' said Lou.

'I left it around the corner. Don't want to do Darling's reputation any more harm.' Both girls laughed at the way he accentuated darling's.

'I told you, Jake, don't call me 'darling.' Do you think parking your car around the corner is any less conspicuous than parking it in the driveway?'

'Not really, Darling. I parked it half-way between the nurses quarters and here, just to confuse people,' he replied. TC just looked at him and shook her head in disbelief.

'God, you're an arsehole, Jake,' said Lou with a smile.

'Yes, Lou, I know. But, you have to agree, I'm an irresistible one,' he laughed.

'Not to everyone, Jake' replied Lou.

'I'm aware of that, Lou,' he said seriously as he directed his gaze towards TC.

'What have you been up to, Jake?' enquired TC.

'Vance, Con, a guy who works for one of the oil companies, and I played poker until four this morning. Poor old Con lost again. So did the oil guy. Vance and I were lucky. We won a few quid each.'

'What do you want, Jake?' asked TC. 'We've got sewing to do.'

'Well, Darling, I could tell you what I want, but I'm afraid you'd throw me over the landing,' he said mischievously.

Lou and TC rolled their eyes and controlled their laughter. TC decided to ignore his darling. If she didn't bite, she hoped, he'd stop baiting her.

'Thought you might like to come to Mum's place for lunch.'

'Did your mother invite us?' asked TC.

'No, I'm inviting you. I'll tell Mum later.'

'In that case, no, thank you, Jake. I want to get this dress finished, do my washing, and make another dress before bedtime. Apart from that, Jake, I don't think it's fair to invite us before asking your mother, then telling her afterwards.'

'She always cooks plenty, TC,' replied Jake on the defensive. 'Think I'll settle in here for a little while, ladies. Interested in observing your sewing expertise.'

Both girls tried to keep a straight face but couldn't help laughing.

'You mongrel, Jake. You're only staying to annoy us,' said Lou.

'What makes you think that?' replied Jake, feigning innocence with a forlorn look on his face. 'Any beer left or have you two alkies cleaned it out?'

'Hardly,' replied both girls.

Jake extracted a beer from the fridge, collected an ashtray from the kitchen, and sat down at the table. He slowly and dramatically took his cigarette packet from his shirt pocket, lit a Rothmans, inhaled deeply, then exhaled the smoke. He held his head high and looked directly ahead as if the girls weren't there. Neither Lou nor TC could concentrate as Jake carried on with his theatrics. Both of them laughed uncontrollably.

'What are you laughing at?' asked Jake innocently while still staring straight ahead with his head held high.

'Jake, you look ridiculous,' said TC.

Still maintaining his pose and in a monotone voice, Jake said, 'I'm hurt, that's what I am. A man's been here less than half an hour; in that short time, I've been called a mongrel and an arsehole. Now I'm ridiculous. Suppose I'm a ridiculous, mongrel, arsehole. My mother will really appreciate that description of her first-born child.'

By now Lou and TC were in hysterics.

'You forgot drunken and gambling,' said Lou.

'I see, Lou. You are right, of course. That makes me a drunken, gambling, ridiculous, mongrel, arsehole. Good! Mum will like that even better,' as he shook his head in mock disapproval.

'Enough,' said TC attempting to be serious. 'Jake, please stop it. We do want to get on with this sewing.'

'All right, Darling, I'll go as soon as I've finished this beer.' Both girls sighed with relief. Jake finished his beer and got up to leave.

'Dread that long walk to my car. Must be at least a hundred yards.'

''Bye, Jake,' said the girls as he went down the back stairs.

'And good riddance,' said Lou.

'Agreed,' said TC. 'Although something tells me we haven't seen the last of him. At least he's not drunk today.'

'Just give him time,' said Lou. 'They don't drink much when they play poker. Booze dulls their concentration.'

With Lou's dress finished apart from the hem and TC's washing done, they decided on crackers and cheese for a mid-day snack.

'What do you really think of Jake, Lou?'

'He's never done anything wrong to me, TC. He's broken a few hearts around the town. Probably did when he was in Brisbane, as well. He's got a great sense of humour when he's in the mood. I have never heard anybody say they don't like him. Some of his mates might be jealous of him, the way he pulls in the women; think they all like him just the same. My dad says he's a nice bullshit artist. The rest is what you see. He gambles, drinks; he's tall, good looking, always has a flashy car and always extremely well dressed. Why did you ask TC?

'Just want to know.'

'Let's get back to our sewing.'

'I'm tired of sewing, Lou,' announced TC a couple of hours later. 'I have to do my ironing.'

'Yes and have our showers before dark,' said Lou, smiling.

'That's for sure. I try to forget there might be a snake waiting for me every time I use that bathroom. I try not to think about it, but I just can't.'

TC pressed the three new dresses and hooked the hangers over the top of the door then quickly got into her regular ironing, which was finished within less than an hour.

'Glad that's over. I hate ironing.'

'Those dresses are lovely, TC,' said Lou as she admired them hanging on the door. 'If all else fails, TC, you can always take up dress-making.'

'I hope not,' replied TC seriously.

'You take the first shower, TC. You look tired,' suggested Lou. 'Apart from that, I want to admire my new dress for a while.'

'You're not wrong there, Lou. I'm tired and hungry.'

'Me, too,' replied Lou.

When TC came up from her shower, she heard Lou talking on the phone.

'Tell your mother we love her for it, Jake. No, Jake, not you, your mother. See you then.'

'What did Jake want?' asked TC. 'I hope he's not coming here.'

'Sorry, TC, I told him he could. He told his mother that you are getting too thin; so, she's sending him down with some dinner for us.'

'In that case, he can come. Isn't that lovely of his mum to do that?'

'She's a nice lady, TC, and she sure must like you.'

'I like her, too' replied TC.

Jake wasted no time. He was there before Lou came back from the bathroom. He brought a large bowl of salad, a cold roasted chicken, a tub of ice cream, and a can of peaches.

'I decided to eat with you girls,' he said. 'Mum's into a good book, and Carla is asleep.' Jake put the food in the refrigerator and took out a beer.

'Want a Coke, Darling?'

'No, thank you, Jake. I'll have water with ice, and I'll get it. I'm trying to get used to the bore-water taste.'

'Never drink it myself,' as he took a sip of beer.

Lou appeared in her baby dolls. Jake whistled.

'Decided to give me a floor show, after all, did you, Lou?'

'Shut up, Jake. It's hot and you've seen a damned lot more than a girl's legs before.'

'Wish I could see TC's legs. What are your legs like, TC?'

'Short and thin, if you must know, Jake. Behave yourself or I will throw you over the balcony.'

'I think TC's serious, Lou. What do you think, Lou? Is Darling serious?'

'Let's sit out front for a while before we eat,' suggested TC.

'You brought your car tonight, I see,' said Lou jokingly.

'Nobody can see it around by the steps in the dark, and it's a black car, in case you ladies hadn't noticed,' replied a smiling Jake.

'Jake, I really don't care who sees what car here. The damage is done, and I don't care to be reminded of it,' said TC seriously.

'Isn't TC lovely when she's serious, Lou?' teased Jake.

'Your turn to change the record, Jake,' snapped TC.

'Better stop teasing her,' thought Jake, as he put on Elvis singing, "It's now or never". Then, 'Oh shit! She'll think I played this on purpose.'

'Smart,' said Lou when Jake returned to the front door.

'Let's eat Jake's mum's dinner,' said TC.

¶

They lingered over dinner for a couple of hours. Jake had the girls in fits of laughter as he told them stories about mischievous things he and his mates had got up to at boarding school, later at college, and hilarious experiences he had shared with his Uncle Doug's two sons teasing him when he was a little boy. TC decided Jake was quite nice and lots of fun when he wasn't drunk or taunting her. Lou understood why people liked Jake. Sure, there was probably a little bit of bullshit thrown in to embellish his stories, but they sure were funny. Jake made up his mind that TC was more relaxed when they weren't alone together. She had a great sense of humour and no way was he going to let her slip through his fingers.

'Don't like to break up the party, Jake, but we all have to work tomorrow,' said TC as she and Lou began clearing the table. 'I'll call your mum tomorrow and thank her.'

'She'll like that, TC.' He nodded towards the new dresses hanging on the door. 'Very nice.' He kissed both Lou and TC lightly on the cheek and left.

While driving home Jake made a mental note to make some sort of schedule whereas he could accommodate his needs. Surely he could come up with a plan where he could gamble and drink, fulfil his sexual needs, and court TC all at the same time.

Vance didn't show at the pharmacy until around ten. He looked tired and worried.

'What's the matter, Boss?' asked TC.

'Women,' he replied shortly. 'Make coffee, will you, please?' He phoned Delores. The conversation was brief. TC went about her normal routine of gap-filling while Vance drank his coffee and chain-smoked in the dispensary.

'I'm going to do the banking and collect the mail,' said TC, breaking the silence between them.

At the bank, TC handed over the shop's deposit book, then deposited five pounds in her savings account. The teller was over friendly, one might say even gushy. TC felt wealthy as she left the bank. On the way back from the post office, Carmel asked her how things were going. They chatted for a couple of minutes before Carmel said, 'TC, luv, Brolga is full of gossips. Don't let it get to you. If Flo and Thel like you, I like you.

'=Word must be on the street already, thought TC.

Vance was still drinking coffee and smoking when TC returned. TC began opening the mail.

'Leave that for a minute and listen to me,' Vance commanded. 'I want you to promise me you'll stay as you are, Butterball. I don't want you to become a demanding, greedy, or possessive woman. I don't want you to become a spendthrift, born-to-shop woman like Delores, and I certainly don't want you sitting around pubs, drinking and swearing like a man.'

'I don't know what you mean,' TC replied confused.

'I mean stay as you are!'

'I'll try, Boss.'

'Don't just try; do it! I'm going to the Empire.'

§

TC phoned Jake's mother to thank her for the meal. Thel told TC that Jake had explained everything and not to worry about gossip because it is cheap.

§

TC thought how great it would be if everyone phoned in their orders a day before mail day. Things would run a lot smoother on mail days, especially if the boss wasn't there. She decided to write a note requesting customers to phone in prior if possible. She would enclose the notes when the accounts went out. She got started on it immediately.

Lou and TC went to Con's café for a thick-shake at siren time. They were chatting when three young men came into the café. The men scrutinised the girls as they walked by to sit at a nearby table. Lou and TC could hear most of the conversation.

'No, not the redhead. It's the blond one.'

'You're kidding?'

'What? With the chemist?'

'Don't believe it.'

'Lucky bastard.'

'He's old enough to be her father.'

'Or close to it.'

'Let's go, TC,' said Lou.

'I think so,' replied TC, who wanted to throw her thick-shake over the foul-minded rats.

TC paid Con's wife, who smiled at her.

'Take the drinks with you, dear. Bring the containers back when the café is mongrel-free.' Both TC and Lou glared at the young men before leaving.

'Bloody mongrels,' said Lou.

TC was fighting to hold back her tears of rage and frustration.

'It's not fair, Lou. Why do people jump to conclusions?'

'They don't care, TC,' replied Lou compassionately. 'True or false, it makes for good conversation. It's the small-town syndrome. Don't let it get you down, TC. I'll stay with you until I have to go back on nightshift if you like.'

'That would be nice. Keep me from slipping into the realms of self-pity. Thank you, Lou,' replied TC softly.

'Apart from that, TC, you'll have a bona fide lady-in-waiting the next time Jake strikes,' laughed Lou as she left for work.

TC didn't feel like laughing. Poor Jake. Lou really stuck it to him every chance she got. TC continued on with her notes, her concentration broken now and then by a few early orders being phoned in. The notes and orders were done by closing time, when Vance stormed through the back door, closely followed by Louise. Louise was screaming at the boss, who was endeavouring to ignore her.

'You effing bastard, Callahan. Think you can drop me just like that? No effing way, my friend. Everyone knows Delores has left you. So what the fuck are you worried about? You knew it was my day off today, you mongrel bastard, you, you left me sitting on that fucking verandah, drinking by myself while you drank in the bar, chatting up that new piece of fluff barmaid.' Vance still said nothing. Louise turned her attention to TC, who felt as if she was bolted to the floor on which she stood.

'As for you, you little piece of shit, isn't Jake Carmichael man enough for you? You're the talk of the fucking town. Had to pull on your employer, as well, did you? You are nothing but a little slut. I'm going to smash your pretty fucking head in.'

Vance lost control completely as Louise lunged towards TC. He grabbed Louise by her left shoulder, pulled her right arm behind her back, and forcefully guided her through the back door.

'You are disgusting Louise. You are a disgrace to womanhood. Your mouth comes from the gutter. You are not fit to breathe the same air as that girl. Now get out of here and don't come back.' Vance slammed the back door. 'Don't worry about Louise, Butterball. She's upset with me, not you. She's also extremely drunk.'

The whole town could probably hear Louise bashing on the door and screaming.

'I know you spent the night with that little harlot. You fucking bastard. One of the fucking truckies told me. Suppose you will try to tell me you were discussing the fucking weather.'

Vance rushed to the door and threw it open.

'Get the hell out of here, Louise, or I'll call the sergeant.'

'That bastard doesn't scare me.'

'Is that so?' said the police sergeant, who had walked up behind her.

'What is this all about now? You're disturbing the peace, Louise. Now be quiet or I'll book you for disturbing the peace and drunk and disorderly conduct.'

'You can't do that,' snarled Louise.

'Watch me,' replied the sergeant.

Louise looked at Vance.

'You bastard. You reported.'

'No, he didn't Louise,' said the sergeant with authority. 'I had three separate complaints. The people living in Birdsville could probably hear you. Now I'm taking you back to the Empire. I want you to sleep it off.

If you don't want to do that, I'll have to put you in jail for the night.'

Louise began crying as the police sergeant walked her to the police car. She looked over her shoulder at Vance, who stood watching them get into the car. Louise called out to Vance.

'I'm sorry my love. I'm sorry. Please come to see me later. Please.'

'Not likely,' said Vance softly to himself.

TC looked at Vance when he came back inside. She now understood what he was trying to say that morning.

'I see what you mean by telling me to stay the way I am. Poor thing. Who would want to be like that.? I'm going home.'

Vance looked sad.

'I'm sorry about all of that Butterball.'

'I know.' TC collected her purse and walked out.

Once home, TC sat on the front steps to wait for Lou. Her mind was blank as she watched the water from the sprinkler catch the rays of the afternoon sun. Little green and orange spots seemed to appear, then fall onto the grass. Jake's car pulled up out in front of the house. Lou got out of the car, carrying a large, brown paper bag. Jake reached into the boot and picked up two more.

'One holds my clothes,' said Lou. 'I went to the grocer's after I finished at four. You owe me eight shillings and tuppence for your share. I conned Jake into picking me up from the grocer's and taking me home for my clothes.'

'What was the commotion at the pharmacy about?' asked Jake.

'Don't want to talk about it,' replied TC in a far-away voice.

'The sergeant was going to arrest Louise for drunkenness,' said Lou, who had heard about it at the grocery store.

'Doesn't make sense. Half the population of Brolga is drunk most of the time,' said Jake.

'My boss will tell you, Jake. If he wants to,' said TC.

Jake quickly went through to put the two bags of groceries in the kitchen. As he passed Lou and TC, he said excitedly, 'See you later, ladies I'm going to find Vance.'

Lou could tell TC didn't feel like talking.

'I'll put the food in the fridge and hang up my clothes, TC. Are we sewing tonight?'

'No. Maybe tomorrow night.'

Lou joined TC after putting one of Auntie Flo's Frank Sinatra records on the radiogram.

'Soothing songs. My mother loves these,' said TC reminiscently.

'Mine, too,' agreed Lou softly.

'Must have been a romantic era, Lou.' Silence. 'Tell you what, Lou. I'm very lucky Sam and I came to Brolga,' said TC.

'Are you crazy, TC? Why on earth do you think that? I can't wait to get out of this dump.'

'Because, Lou, I've learned more about the realities of life during my short time here than I did in my eighteen and a bit years I wasn't here.'

'What have you learned, TC? I'm listening. Please tell me.'

'There's a list; I have it in my head. Never expect friendship to last forever. People move on into different directions. Sam. Money doesn't buy happiness. Romeos. Marriage doesn't bring loyalty or happiness. My boss. We can love another person so much that we tolerate almost anything to keep them and financial security. Mrs Callahan. People who have the least usually give the most. Your parents. People in power are not necessarily well mannered and/or polite. They use their power to put down the underdog. Shire Chairman. Alcohol makes people feel happy up until a certain extent when sometimes it turns them into someone they are not when they are normal. Louise. Sometimes people will trust you on sight with their most precious possession. Auntie Flo and Uncle Doug. Not everyone judges us by the clothes we wear and where we work. Jake, my boss, Thel, Carmel. Sometimes a stranger will protect us for no reason obvious to us. Jess. Mates often fight for each other, whether right or wrong. Even knock down the police sergeant. Next day they are still mates. The people at the Majestic. Most, not all, people with title, property, or accolades feel superior to the normal working person. As Jess said, mostly inherited property and jumped-up governess wives. Some people judge us by what they hear, not by what they see. Fifty to sixty per cent of Brolga. My list will probably grow, Lou. Depends how long I stay in Brolga. The longer I stay, the more I shall learn.'

Silence.

'TC, this is all too much for me. Everything you said is right. I've never thought of most of those things before.'

'That's because you've been here all of your life, Lou. I'm the outsider looking in. Let's go get cleaned up, eat something, listen to music, and gossip,' TC said happily.

'About what?' asked Lou.

'I don't know. We'll make something up.'

⁋

Flying-doctor day and mail-order day. No Vance.

After yesterday, I'll probably commit suicide if he doesn't show, thought TC.

The telephone, once again, rang incessantly almost from the moment she arrived at work. TC was taking an order when she saw Bert Romeo open the doors of the Empire Hotel.

'Excuse me a moment, madam, I'll be right back.' She put down the telephone and raced across the road.

'Mr Romeo, should you see Mr Callahan, please tell him he's needed at the pharmacy. Mr Romeo,' she added, 'please tell him if he can't make it, I'll close the pharmacy and go home.'

'I'll keep an eye out for him,' said Bert Romeo with a smile.

TC ran back to the telephone, apologised for the interruption, and resumed taking the order.

Bert Romeo thought, Does that girl think I'm a mad man? Why would I tell that drunken chemist he's needed at his pharmacy while he's spending money in our pubs?

By midday there was still no Vance. Once more, she took the telephone off the cradle and stomped across to the Empire window.

'Mr Callahan, get the hell out of there,' she yelled. Vance ignored her as he cracked jokes with the woman behind the bar. Vance was blind drunk. Jess caught TC's eye and winked while nodding her head towards Vance. TC walked purposefully into the bar.

'Excuse me, Mr Callahan, here is the key to your pharmacy. I am convinced that, should I be stupid enough to continue working for you under the current circumstances, I shall be dead before I'm twenty. By the way, the door is not locked. I quit. I've had enough. Also the phone is off the hook.' TC went back to the pharmacy, grabbed her purse, and walked home.

I've got around twenty-five pounds, she thought. I simply can't put up with this rubbish anymore.

TC had not reached her front gate when Jake, with Vance in his car, pulled up alongside her.

'Go away, Mr Callahan. Go away, Jake. You're both the same.' Both men jumped out of the car.

Jake said, 'TC, if you leave the pharmacy, you'll have to leave Brolga. I don't want you to do that.'

Vance said, 'Butterball, I'm sorry. I'll be there to help you.'

'Were you in the Empire, too, Jake? You have a business to run. Are you as useless as Mr Callahan? Leave all the hard work to your underpaid staff?'

'No, TC. I wasn't at the Empire. Vance is my mate. He came to me to help him to get you to go back to work.'

'No! Not under present conditions. Seems to me if I didn't do everything, the pharmacy may as well not be there. It's prescription day this afternoon as well as every other damned thing that has to be done. I'm tired of that stinking phone ringing. I'm either being spoken to as a servant by Delores or down to by cockies' wives. Thanks to you and the boss, I have a reputation worse than some poor soul standing on a corner in Kings Cross. Why don't you help your mate, Jake?'

Silence.

'I need your help, Butterball. Need you to help me get these bloody mail orders ready for tomorrow morning. I'll be there for the prescriptions. I promise.'

'You've promised that before, Mr Callahan. I don't trust you anymore.'

'Jake, mate, will you be witness to my promise?' Vance fell to his knees and looked up at Jake.

'Of course,' replied Jake, looking down at Vance as if he was the Godfather of the world.

'This is ridiculous,' said TC. 'You really are lunatics. Okay, Mr Callahan, I'll do today. That's it. You are a married man with a pregnant wife and two little boys. All you do is get drunk, play poker, bet on race horses, and park by the creek with foul-mouthed women.'

'Think she's talking about you, mate,' Vance looked up at Jake.

'I don't think so, mate. I don't have a pregnant wife and two boys,' replied Jake seriously.

'Come on, mate. I'll take you home and you get your act together and we'll both give TC a hand this afternoon.'

Jake looked at TC. 'Okay?'

She nodded. 'Okay.'

Jake dropped TC off opposite the pharmacy, then took Vance home to freshen up. He may as well not have bothered. After Jake brought Vance back to the pharmacy via the back door, Vance immediately fell asleep in his office chair.

'I'll be okay, Jake. Somehow I'll handle whatever prescriptions come in. I may need help to get the mail orders together, that is, if I am able to answer the phone if it rings.'

TC called Lou at the exchange and asked her to tell anyone phoning the pharmacy with mail orders to please phone back just before five or leave a message with the exchange.

'I pray to our Lord I haven't made a mistake with these prescriptions,' said TC, as she looked up to the ceiling of the dispensary after the last prescription was filled. The telephone rang.

'I'm coming over now. Just about to knock off work. I have sixteen orders for you,' said Lou.

The telephone as usual kept ringing with orders until five.

They managed to finish by eleven. Vance was still asleep in the office chair.

'Poor bugger's a mess,' said Jake.

'He's a good man,' said Lou.

'We won't wake him,' said TC. 'He needs sleep.'

Jake went to his car and fetched a rug and covered Vance from the neck down. TC wrote a note stating, 'See you tomorrow.'

Jake dropped the girls home. They cleaned their teeth and went to bed. Jake drove up and around town to the nurses' quarters. He waited for a few minutes until a cutie-pie, strawberry blond appeared. She climbed excitedly into his car.

'Oh, Jakie, it's been a long time. I've been jealous. You've been taking my friends to the creek. Bitches. You are notorious around here, Jakie. Let's go, baby.'

Jake wanted to throw her out of the car. Let's face it, he thought, a screw is a screw. My mother would have a heart attack if I brought someone home who called me "Jakie". Can't possibly imagine TC and Lou referring to each other as bitches. Jake laughed.

'All right. Let's go to the creek. I promise I'll do my best to retain my reputation. We will go, I will come, then I'll bring you home.'

'Jakie, you do make me laugh.'

'Not as much as you make me laugh.'

❡

Vance looked the best he had for weeks.

'Marvellous what sleep can do,' remarked TC when she arrived at work.

'I'm sorry for everything, TC.'

'Mr Callahan, you are beginning to sound like a badly scratched record.'

'The booze has a hold on me.'

'Only you can fix that. Sooner or later, it will take its toll on you.'

'I want you to know I can't go on like this.'

191

'This place is a circus. I can't keep relying on Lou to help me. Last night, Jake helped as well. What if I make a mistake with someone's medication? You lecture me about what I should and shouldn't do. I think it's you who needs to be lectured. No wonder I've lost weight. Anyone would under the circumstances. Your life is a mess. I suppose what I'm saying is clean it up a bit or I can't stay. I'm going to the post office.'

Vance said nothing. He sat deep in thought until TC returned.

'You are right, Butterball. My life is a mess. I drink to escape the reality of that mess. When I've had enough to dull the pain of that reality, I have a change of personality. I do and say outrageous things I wouldn't dream of when sober. At the moment, because of something I'll probably tell you about one day, I desperately need that escape route. I don't want you to leave, Butterball. You are the one who keeps the business going. I know that. I'll try not to make any more promises that I probably can't keep.' He stood up.

'I'm going to the Empire and put an end to it with Louise. Last time I tried, we were both drunk and had an audience. This time, I'll try it while we are both sober and there are no other people around. See you later.'

'I hope so,' replied TC.

¶

The truck arrived to collect the mail. TC recognised the driver as one of the three young men who had been talking about her in the café. As she helped him with the load, he openly flirted with her and made several remarks with sexual connotations. TC completely ignored him as he waffled on. She wanted to throw the parcels at him rather than hand them to him.

As he was about to leave, he said, 'Looks like I'm not good enough for you to lower yourself to even speak to me. The drunken chemist has got more money than I can ever dream of having.'

'Go to hell,' snarled TC as she turned away from him.

Jake and Lou were waiting outside when TC closed at siren time.

They were both all smiles.

'Jake has invited himself to your place for lunch. His donation is a loaf of fresh bread,' said Lou. TC went back into the shop to fetch Jake's blanket. Jake smiled to himself.

'Missed that bloody thing last night. Had to throw my shirt out because of the bloody grass stain on it.'

Once TC was in the car Jake purposely hammered the car the short distance to the house.

'Jake, you are a mad man,' laughed Lou.

''Childish,' would be more appropriate,' said TC. 'I hope you're not in one of your moods, Jake. Had enough rubbish from a young man this morning to last me for a long time.'

'What do you mean?' asked Lou.

'Tell you over lunch,' replied TC.

Jake insisted on making sandwiches for the three of them. 'Camp pie and salad deluxe coming up. Nothing is too good for you two ladies.'

As soon as they sat at the table to eat, Lou asked TC again, 'What did you mean about a young man, TC?' TC relayed the story to them.

'Didn't he mention me?' asked Jake feigning disappointment.

'No, Jake, he didn't.'

'Jake, they probably didn't see your car,' said Lou.

'That would be right,' said Jake. 'Trust Vance to have all the fun. He's probably trying to steal my crown of notoriety,' laughed Jake.

'It's not funny, you rat,' said Lou. 'From my illicitly gained information, you haven't been mentioned, Jake. All the gossip is about Vance and TC.'

'You mean I confessed to my mother when I didn't have to?' said Jake, imitating a hurt child. Both girls laughed. 'Well, no point in crying over it; so, I might as well laugh.' Then Jake became serious. 'Anyone with half a brain would know it's ridiculous garbage.'

'The way the phones have been ringing, Jake, must be a lot of brainless people in and around town. One conversation I heard is that the two women agreed that TC is the reason Delores and the kids left Vance.'

'I've had enough. Let's change the subject,' said TC in disgust. 'Anyway, it's almost time to go back to work.'

¶

Back at the pharmacy, TC concentrated on getting the accounts ready to post. She couldn't fill all of the gaps until the new supplies arrived. TC had a few walk-in customers that afternoon. None of them were friendly to her. She pretended not to notice. 'Let them think whatever they want.' Lou came after she finished work and helped TC finish the accounts by putting them in the envelopes. At closing time, they walked across to post them. The Empire was full as they passed by. Of course, Vance was in the bar. TC and Lou heard a man say loudly, 'Hey, Pill-Pusher, there's your girlfriend.' They also heard Vance replying just as loudly, 'Wake up to yourself, you stupid bastard. She's just a kid and a damned good one at that.'

Neither Lou nor TC commented.

Once home, they went about the usual after-work routine. TC rolled her hair again while Lou foiled her fingernails.

'Think I'll finish that peach-coloured dress tonight, Lou. If I'm going to be scrutinised by everyone, I might as well be well dressed.'

'Thank the Lord for music,' said Lou as she changed the records. 'Without music, everyone in Brolga would be dead from boredom.'

'Don't know about everyone, Lou, but you and I most probably would be.'

TC finished sewing the dress; Lou pinned the hem.

'I'll sew the hem for you while you cut out the yellow one,' said Lou.

'Okay, then we'll call it a night.'

'It's too early for bed, TC; it's only half-past-eight.'

'I didn't mean go to bed, Lou. I meant for the sewing.'

'Front steps, here we come,' smiled Lou.

'I can hardly wait,' said TC with a smile and a shrug.

¶

Once seated on the steps, with the sprinkler running as usual, they sat in silence for a while, both staring into space and deep in thought.

'I can't wait to get out of Brolga,' said Lou wistfully.

'And leave all the excitement?' laughed TC. 'What will happen to me?' she said with a gesture of her hands.

'You could come with me,' replied Lou hopefully.

'The grass isn't always greener, Lou.'

'That means you won't come with me?' said Lou with disappointment in her voice.

'We'll see what unfolds.'

Jake's car belted around the corner and down the driveway. He was standing behind them in seconds.

'What a surprise to find you sitting on the stairs, ladies,' he said sarcastically.

'What a surprise to see you scream around the corner and into the driveway,' replied TC with equal sarcasm.

'Couldn't stay away from our illustrious beauty, could you, Jake?' said Lou.

'Something like that,' he replied. 'Like your hair-do, Darling.'

'I know. You've told me before.'

'Did the Empire run out of beer?' asked Lou with a laugh.

'Thanks for reminding me, Lou. Think I'll grab a beer from the fridge.'

Neither of the girls had turned to look at Jake as they had been bantering back and forth. Jake returned with his beer.

'Well, it's one thing to keep your backs to a man when he's talking to you; it's another when you don't move over and make room for a man to sit on the steps.'

Both girls sighed as they moved across the step.

'My mate, Vance, had some business to take care of; so, I thought I'd come and brighten up the night for you two delectable damsels.'

'Thoughtful of you, Jake. We're bored just about witless,' said Lou. 'I've been trying to talk TC into going away with me.'

'Is she going to?' asked Jake with alarm.

'I don't know, Jake. I hope so,' replied Lou.

TC cleared her throat. 'In case you two haven't noticed, I am sitting here with you.'

'You won't leave me, will you, Darling?' said Jake with a smile.

'I will if you don't stop calling me "darling",' said TC matter-of-factly.

Vance's car flew past, heading towards the creek just after ten o'clock.

'There goes Vance and Louise,' said Lou.

'Wrong there. It's not Louise.'

'Who is it?' asked Lou.

'Probably the new barmaid,' said TC.

'Remind me to never have a bet with you, Darling. I mean, TC. You picked it on the nose.'

'Wouldn't have to be Einstein to work it out,' said TC. 'Suppose that's the business the boss had to take care of.'

'What's her name?' asked Lou.

'Pauline,' replied Jake.

'You do realise we are gossiping,' said TC.

'What else is there to do?' asked Lou.

'I can think of a few things,' said Jake with mischief in his voice.

'Like what?' asked Lou.

'I can't tell you, Lou, because if I did, your adorable friend would push me down the stairs.'

'Keep it up, Jake, and I will push you down the stairs.'

Jake got up to fetch another beer, muttering, 'Keep it up, she says. It's up every time I look at her.'

When Jake came back, beer in hand, he said, 'Ladies, the record has ended. Think I'll put poor old Slim on.'

'No, you won't,' snapped Lou as she jumped up. 'One of the reasons I'm staying here is to escape Slim. As everyone in town knows, Dad plays nothing but poor old Slim.'

'Mum's grown to love Slim's songs. She listens to him all the time,' said Jake innocently.

'You're a mongrel, Jake,' said Lou. 'Dad plays him so damned loud; your poor mother is a captive audience. It's a wonder Slim hasn't driven her crazy.'

'You have to go home now, Jake,' said TC.

'Why, what have I done wrong?' asked Jake in his innocent, little-boy act.

'Nothing. It's midnight.'

'There you go, Lou. If your girlfriend isn't threatening to throw me over the balcony or push me down the stairs, she's telling me to rack off home. A man can't win.'

'You poor little thing, Jake,' said Lou with false sympathy.

Jake did his slow crawl backing out and down the street. He blew each of them a kiss as he passed.

'Jake's a madman,' said Lou.

'Yes, but he makes us laugh,' said TC. 'He's very entertaining at times.'

'That's what I mean,' agreed Lou.

'Let's get the teeth-brushing saga out of the way and go to bed,' said TC.

§

Vance and Jake were both sitting in the dispensary. TC could hear them laughing loudly when she came through the front door. They stopped laughing when she appeared at the dispensary door.

'Good morning, gentlemen. I hope I didn't interrupt anything.'

'As a matter of fact, you did, Butterball. Go check the mail before you do anything else, will you?'

'Sure. Sorry I interrupted you.' They started talking as soon as she went through the front door.

'Pretty wild, eh, Vance?' laughed Jake.

'You can say that again. Never had one like her before. I've got scratches all over my back. She's a wild cat. Incredible. She kept yelling, 'More, more, more. I was concentrating so hard I didn't have any more to give her.' They both laughed. Vance continued describing his sexual exploits of the night before. 'She's a beauty. That's for sure,' Vance was saying when he realised TC was back.

'TC, Jake and I have been discussing a race horse I'm thinking of buying.' TC took the broom to the front of the shop and began sweeping the floor.

'Do you think she heard much, Jake?'

'I hope not,' replied Jake as he stood up to leave. He paused as he went by TC.

'Think I like your hair today. Even better than last night's style.'

'Jake, go to work,' said a smiling TC. TC had indeed heard enough to know the boss wasn't talking about any race horse. As she swept the floor, she thought, I'm so happy I'm not that way inclined. I'd hate to have anyone talk about me like that. Am I crazy? The town's talking about me for something I didn't do.

The order from the drug houses arrived. To TC's surprise, the boss helped her unpack the dozen or so large cartons. Everything was unpacked by a little after twelve.

'Now you can fill the gaps, Butterball. I'm off to the Empire.' TC got started on gap-filling. She was on the ladder when she heard a female, attention-grabbing cough behind her.

'Are you TC?' asked the very attractive, tall, slim, brunette, at a guess around thirty years of age.

'Yes,' smiled TC. 'Can I help you?'

'Not really. My name is Pauline. I've heard all about you, TC. Thought I'd come in to check out the competition.'

'Don't believe everything you hear, Pauline,' said TC, seriously.

'I better not hear anything about you and Vance again. You got the message? For your sake, TC, I hope you have.' With that, Pauline walked out of the shop. TC was speechless.

This is ridiculous, she thought. That woman is working with Louise. Surely, she knows Louise has been the boss' girlfriend. Then it clicked. Louise must have told Pauline about the boss' car at her place all night.

Probably told Pauline I slept with him. I'm going to tell the boss about Pauline's visit. Some things are just too much. TC continued gap-filling until siren time. She was so angry about Pauline's visit she had almost finished. Jake and Lou were once again waiting for her.

'Let's finish off that loaf of bread,' said Jake. TC slumped in the back seat of Jake's car.

'What's the problem?' asked Lou.

'Repetition of yesterday, Lou. I'll tell you over lunch.'

'Don't tell us another young guy has hit on you, TC,' said Jake.

'No, I'll tell you over lunch.'

'There you go, ladies,' said Jake as he placed their sandwiches on the table. 'Now, TC, what's today's problem?' TC told them about Pauline's visit and what she had said.

'Stupid bloody woman's only been with Vance once to my knowledge,' said Jake.

'What does she plan on doing to you if she does hear anything?' asked Lou.

'I don't know,' replied TC.

'I'll put her straight, TC,' said Jake. 'Who the hell does she think she is? Daughter of a mafia boss?'

'Don't worry, Jake. I intend to mention it to the boss.'

'So you should, TC,' agreed Lou.

Jake was visibly extremely angry.

'I'm going to mention it to Vance, too, TC. Thanks to him and myself, you're putting up with enough crap at the moment. Vance told me about Louise abusing you. Yesterday you had that young truckie come onto you and now the Pauline thing. Enough is enough.'

'No need for you to be upset, Jake,' said TC. 'Thank you for caring. You too, Lou.'

¶

Jake dropped the girls off outside the café. Lou went to the post office. TC went across to the pharmacy. Jake went to the Empire to talk to Vance. As Jake expected, Vance was in the bar drinking doubles, as usual. Vance was talking to Pauline. They were both laughing.

I'd like to smack that smile of the bitch's face, thought Jake. Instead, he ordered a beer off her.

'How are you, Vance? Looks as if you're on the way again, mate.'

'Looks like it, Jake. Feels like it, too. What are you doing here this time of day?'

'I came to see you. I want to tell you something. Then I think I want to talk to Pauline.'

'You're not going to try to white-ant me, are you, Jake?'

'Not likely. Not my type. Apart from that, she's a bit long in the tooth for me.' Pauline put Jake's beer on the bar.

'Take it out of my money, then make yourself scarce,' said Vance. 'Jake and I want to have a talk.'

'Did you know she went to see TC this morning, Vance?'

'No. What for?'

'She told TC she wanted to check out her competition. Said she'd heard about you and TC and she'd better not hear anything again. Told TC it was for her own good and she hoped TC got the message.'

Jess, who was fiddling with glasses nearby, had heard every word. 'Bloody bitch,' she muttered under her breath. 'Every mongrel seems to be picking on the kid.'

'You have to be joking,' said Vance. 'How's TC?'

'How do you think she is, mate? Poor little bugger is copping it from all directions.'

'I know,' agreed Vance. 'Jess, tell Pauline to come here, will you, please?'

'Delighted to do so, Vance,' replied Jess. Pauline came up all smiles.

'You can wipe that smile off your face, Pauline,' said Vance. 'Did you go to my pharmacy this morning?'

'Yes, why?' replied Pauline.

'What did you buy?'

'Nothing.'

'Why did you go there?'

'I wanted to check out that little bitch who works for you.' Jake wanted to choke her; he was furious, and Vance could see it. Vance himself was ropeable.

'Let me handle it, Jake. I beg your pardon, Pauline. Did we just hear you refer to TC as a "bitch"?'

'Well, she is,' replied Pauline defensively.

'What the fuck makes you think that? You don't even know the girl.'

'Louise told me about you and TC. I wanted to warn her off.'

'What Louise told you is absolute bullshit.'

'I'll vouch for that,' said Jake seriously. He still wanted to choke her.

'So will I,' said Jess. 'There's a lot of bitches around here,' looking straight at Pauline. 'TC's not one of them.'

'Stay out of this, please, Jess,' snapped Vance. 'Pauline, how dare you go to my place of business and threaten TC. I've only fucked you once. Do you think you own me? Stay away from my shop. Stay away from TC, and stay away from me. Let's get the hell out of here, Jake.' Vance collected his money from the bar. Jake and he left the premises.

Jess went to the office and told Jack Romeo what had happened.

'Have to move that Pauline woman out of here,' said Jack. 'Can't afford to lose the chemist. He spends a fortune in this place.' Pauline was out of the Empire and working in the Majestic in less than an hour. Vance was feeling sober when he walked into the pharmacy.

'Know my body is plastered, but my mind is sober,' he said to himself. TC had finished the gaps and was sorting out hair dyes.

'Don't tell me you're even thinking of colouring your hair, TC? It's perfect the way it is.'

'No, I'm just tidying them up,' replied TC.

'Jake told me about that creature coming in here, Butterball. She won't be coming in anymore. That's one promise I know I can keep. You don't deserve what's being laid on you lately, kid. Once again, I'm sorry.'

'Mrs Callahan called a little while ago. She'd like you to call her back. Is it okay if I go to the bakers?'

'Off you go. I'll phone Delores.'

TC was talking to Carmel outside the bakery when Jess called out to her from the Empire window.

'Come say hello to me before you go back to work, TC.'

TC said goodbye to Carmel and walked across the road to Jess.

'Haven't seen you for a while, TC.'

'Been a bit hectic at work, Jess. I usually collect the mail before you are open.'

'I know, luv. I have something to tell you.' Jess told TC word for word what had happened in the bar.

'Anyway, Jack's moving her to the Majestic. Don't think she'll like it too much down there with all the hard-core drunks. Jack's got her in the office now, telling her she's out of here. That Vance is not as bad as I first thought he was, TC. Young Jake has also gained a few points with me lately. Goes to show, a woman can be wrong about people sometimes. Not often, just sometimes, TC.'

They both laughed. Pauline came into the bar as Jess and TC were saying goodbye. She glared at TC.

'You little bitch.'

'Call TC a bitch again and I'll have you fired instead of moved,' said Jess.

TC went back to the shop. Vance was talking to the sergeant about the trouble the sergeant had experienced recently in trying to control the drunks on Friday and Saturday nights.

'I've been asking the department for another man for months. They are finally sending me someone. Got a young constable just out of training arriving next week.'

'Where will he stay?' asked Vance.

'He'll stay at one of the pubs for a month or so. There's a pretty spacious storeroom out back of the jail. Nothing in the storeroom. It's supposed to be used to store files. Only a handful of files here. Hardly anyone ever gets arrested,' he laughed. 'Too much paperwork.' The sergeant was leaving as Louise came in.

'See you took my advice and slept it off, Louise. You look much better.'

'I feel much better,' replied Louise with a smile. 'All right if I talk to you, Vance?' asked Louise.

'Depends what you want to talk about, Louise.'

'I don't want to talk in front of TC. Can you send her out to the post office?'

'Not today, Louise. You didn't have any trouble screaming in front of TC the other day. You also screamed at her. If anything, you should apologise to TC and to me.'

'That's what I came for, to apologise to you. I'm not apologising to your staff.'

'Well, then, Louise. Please leave.' Louise began yelling. TC walked out of the shop and sat herself down on the Seat of Knowledge. She told herself, 'I've had enough abuse from Louise. No more.' TC sat there for what seemed an eternity. Lou came out of the post office and saw TC sitting on the seat.

'What's wrong?' asked Lou.

'Louise is in there yelling at the boss. Let's go home.'

'It's just four o'clock, TC.'

'I don't care. Let's go home.' Lou waited outside. TC walked into the dispensary, picked up her purse and the bread without saying a word. She doubted that either Vance or Louise realised she had come and gone. They were too deeply embroiled in their row. Jake was talking to a man out front of his shop. He pointed to his watch when he spotted the girls on the opposite side of the street.

'Finished early,' called Lou. Jake looked surprised as he nodded.

The girls didn't talk at all on the way home. Once there, TC suggested they do something different and sit on the front stairs with a cold Coke.

'Let's skip the beat-the-snakes routine for a little while, Lou. We have almost an extra hour up our sleeves. Why don't you put poor old Slim on while I put some ice in the glasses.' They both laughed. Lou selected Engelbert Humperdink.

'Have you quit your job, TC?'

'I'm not sure, Lou. Working in that pharmacy is like living in a horror movie. I'm still in my teens; yet, I feel like I'm an old woman. There's just one drama after another. I act as if I'm the boss' mother. He treats me as if I'm his daughter. On the other hand, he exposes me to the abuse of the people he associates with. I'm afraid he's going to drink himself to death. I know he's a good man. I respect him when he's sober and worry about him when he's blind drunk. I don't know how much more I can handle, Lou. If I didn't have you and Jake in my life, I'd be the loneliest person alive. When Jake's not stinking drunk, that is.'

'Are you falling for Jake, TC?'

'I don't think so.'

'I hope not.'

'He makes me laugh a lot. Haven't had much laughter in my life.'

'I know what you mean. I feel exactly the same way. Before I met you, I also felt I was the loneliest creature on earth.

¶

Jake rang just before five.

'Don't cook dinner. I'll get Con to make us some burgers. With rat-poison garnish, of course.'

'Jake, I have nothing to cook on or in except that tiny little hot plate and oven. I'm certainly not lighting that wood stove, even if I knew how. Lou and I would melt.'

'I forgot about that. Can I bring hamburgers? I enjoy taking a rise out of you and Lou.'

'All right, Jake. Thank you. We sometimes enjoy you taking a rise out of us. What time?'

'Seven-thirty.'

¶

Jake whirled into the driveway at exactly seven-thirty. Vance walked through the door behind him.

'Couldn't come without bringing my mate,' said Jake. 'I got the hamburgers. Vance got the Coke.'

'No rum,' said Vance with a smile.

'I'm impressed, Boss.'

'Me too,' said Lou.

'Want a beer, Vance?' asked Jake.

'No, I'll drink Coke with the girls.'

'Let's eat while they're still warm,' said Jake.

'Can't remember when I last ate,' said Vance. 'Guess the grog must give the body some sort of sustenance.' Vance and Jake did most of the talking. Hitting one-liners off each other, making the girls and themselves laugh.

Out of the blue in mid-conversation, Jake looked at Vance.

'Come on, mate. You'd better ask her. That's why you wanted to come, after all.' They were all silent looking at Vance and waiting for him to speak. Vance looked at TC, hesitated, then asked, 'Are you coming to work tomorrow, TC?'

'Why are you asking me this, boss?'

'I'm not sure if you signed yourself off this afternoon. Not too many secrets in this room. Honestly, I couldn't blame you if you run a million miles away. The joint's a bloody madhouse.' He looked so sad and vulnerable, TC felt sorry for him. Who could know how many and what demons he was fighting off within himself.

'Don't say anything else, Boss. It's mail day tomorrow. Of course, I'll be there. How could I possibly run away from the excitement of mail day at the Brolga Pharmacy?' Everyone, including Vance, laughed as a look of relief flooded his face.

'Don't tell me you think TC would pull a rat-deserting-a-sinking-ship deal, mate' asked Jake jokingly.

'Not for a moment did I think she was a rat,' replied Vance seriously. TC quickly stood up.

'Time for more music. Who do you like, Boss? Thanks to Jake, we have access to a wonderful collection.'

'Louis Armstrong if you have him.'

'Done,' smiled TC.

'I'll grab my rum out of your car now, Jake,' said Vance with a grin.

Just when I thought he was turning over a new leaf, thought TC, with a shrug and a sigh. Never mind. I'm sure he's trying.

The four of them sat on the front steps. It was a male-dominated discussion on everything from race horses to politics. Lou and TC listened intently, only speaking when spoken to or enquiring about record preferences. Time passed quickly; suddenly, Jake stood up and looked at his watch.

'Come on, Vance. We'd better go, mate. It's almost half-past-midnight. The ladies' curfew came and went a half-hour ago. That's right, isn't it, ladies?'

'Sure is,' replied Lou.

'That means the next time you darken our front door steps, Jake, you have to leave half an hour earlier,' said TC with a smile. Jake tugged at her ponytail.

'She doesn't mean that, does she, Lou?' said Jake, pretending disappointment.

'Get out of here, Jake. You, too, Boss.'

'Thanks for having me, girls,' said Vance. 'Very uncomplicated evening. See you tomorrow.'

¶

Once in Jake's car Vance said, 'Thought the kid had written me off, Jake.'

'I didn't. She's too loyal for that. Apart from that, she's grateful to you for giving her a job. She knows you copped a lot of flack when you hired her; so, I reckon she's prepared to cop some for you.'

'Much more than her share,' stated Vance.

'Vance has left his rum behind,' remarked Lou as they went to the kitchen to clean their teeth. TC glanced at the two-thirds-full bottle of rum on the dining room table.

'Good. That means he won't be drinking any more before morning.'

'He might have some at his house.'

'I doubt he keeps it at home, Lou. I'd like to pour it down the sink; instead, I'll put it away in the cupboard. Hopefully, it will be forgotten forever.'

¶

'Wonder what today will bring floating your way, TC,' said Lou as they were walking to work.

'Who knows, Lou? I'm filled with anticipation of the unknown.'

'See you at siren time,' said Lou as she went straight ahead to the post office and TC crossed the street to the pharmacy.

§

'Oh, you're here at last,' greeted Vance.

'I'm not late,' said TC as she glanced at the clock.

'I didn't mean you were late. I meant I'm happy to see you here,' replied Vance with a smile. The phone rang.

'Here we go. Mail-order day has begun,' said TC as she picked up the receiver. As usual the calls came in one after the other, after the other, after the other.

'It's a full-time job answering the phone,' said TC.

'Looks like it, Butterball,' replied Vance as he rushed around the shop collecting this, then that, to pack. Come siren time the backlog of call-in orders was a lot fewer than on past mail days.

'Thanks for staying and helping me, Boss,' said TC sincerely.

Surprisingly, Vance snapped at her. 'Got no bloody choice, have I?' TC was taken aback.

'What do you mean and why are you angry with me?'

'You don't want to know,' he replied offhandedly.

'You are wrong, Mr Callahan. I do want to know. Last night you were frightened I was leaving; today you're speaking to me as if I'm some poor, mangy dog. Keep this up and I'll leave right now.'

'If you must know, I haven't had a drink for thirteen-and-a-half hours,' he virtually snarled at her.

'So, go get one,' said TC angrily. 'Never stopped you before.'

'Do you think I'm crazy? I don't want to lay eyes on that Pauline ever again. Louise is a foul-mouthed lunatic when she's drunk and in one of her jealous rages, but she's certainly not as mad as that Pauline.'

'I see,' said TC with a controlled voice. 'You haven't been helping me because you think it's the right thing to do. You stayed here this morning because you don't want to face Pauline. For your information, Boss, she's not at the Empire anymore. Jack Romeo put her in the Majestic because he doesn't want to lose all the money you spend at the Empire.'

'How do you know?' he asked in a lower tone of voice.

'That's my business. Go and get drunk if you have to. I'd rather have you over there drinking yourself witless, than have you here snapping and snarling at me.'

'I'm sorry, Butterball.' Vance hit the release button on the cash register, extracted some money, and was gone.

'Where's Vance off to in such a hurry?' asked Lou as she came in carrying two thick-shakes.

'Take a wild guess!' replied TC in disgust. 'My turn to shout, Lou,' as she took the thick-shake money from her purse.

'Got much of a backlog with your orders?' asked Lou.

'Only about four or five. The boss helped me all morning. I don't expect to see him back this afternoon, though; so, looks like another late finish.'

'I'll help you, TC.'

'Thanks, Lou. Don't know how I'd cope without your help.'

'Got nothing else to do in beautiful downtown Brolga,' laughed Lou. They decided to buy material for more new dresses after TC's yellow one was finished.

'When are we going to wear them?' asked Lou.

'You can wear yours whenever you want to, Lou. I'm not wearing any of mine until I've got six. A different one for every working day. I also have to buy some shoes. I want high-heeled ones to match my dresses. Preferably pretty ones with bows, of course.'

'Of course,' agreed Lou.

❡

The few remaining mail orders were ready to go before Lou returned to work. The phone began ringing at exactly two o'clock.

No surprise, thought TC. I think people must sit by their telephone watching the clock to turn over the hour, then ring like people possessed.

Once again, there were half a dozen or so walk-ins. Today they all seemed to take a long time. Once again, TC took the phone off the hook. Once again, Lou took messages or asked people to call back later. Once again, Lou arrived a little after four. Once again, Lou took the calls. A man bearing a prescription in his hand knocked on the door only minutes after TC had closed it.

'Am I too late?' asked the man, who was covered in dust, windblown, and appeared to be extremely tired.

'Not at all,' replied TC with a smile. 'What can I do for you?'

'I have a prescription from a doctor in Brisbane. I got tied up with some friends in Brisbane, so didn't get to take care of it the way I should have.'

'Don't worry. Might take a little while.'

The man nodded his head. 'I'll go get a feed at the café.'

TC looked at the prescription. She could understand nothing except the man's name, the date the prescription was written, and that he should apply it twice daily.

Just what I need, she thought. She called the Empire and heard the boss say, 'Tell her I'm not here,' and once again she stormed across to the Empire window.

TC heard as she approached, 'You're in trouble again, Pill-Pusher. Here comes little Miss Dynamite.' The bar of the Empire was full as was to be expected on a Friday after five. TC asked a man leaning against the window frame to tell her boss she needed to talk to him.

'What about me, Darling. You can talk to me anytime.'

'Don't be ridiculous,' TC said venomously. 'Please clear my view. I know he's sitting opposite this damned window. This is important.'

'Poor little bugger,' she heard one man say.

'He's nothing but a lousy drunk,' she heard another.

'Let's clear the way so the kid can talk to the bugger,' said a third.

About a dozen drinkers moved aside. Vance was sitting, holding court with a group of men. One of them was Jake.

'Mr Callahan,' she shouted loudly. He didn't, or did not want to, hear her. Jess heard TC's voice; she also noticed that Vance and his group had ignored the kid completely.

'Shut up, everyone,' said Jess loudly and with authority. 'Mr Callahan, your slave needs your attention. She's at the window.' Vance looked towards the window and directly at TC, who was on the verge of tears.

'Mr Callahan, I have a prescription for ointment. I can't understand the writing. What do I do?' Vance looked back at TC with a stupid grin on his face.

'Well, Butterball, you take a wild guess and read the recipe book.' TC burst into tears of frustration, turned, and ran toward the pharmacy. Some people in the bar laughed; most didn't. Jess told Vance he was a hopeless mongrel and to go help TC since he was the chemist, after all.

'I agree with Jess,' said Jake, who walked out of the bar and followed TC.

'You better go, mate,' said a couple of men who had been drinking with Vance. The rest had moved away.

§

Vance staggered through the back door of the pharmacy and made his presence known by smashing an empty milk bottle in the sink.

'The drunken chemist has returned,' he said loudly. 'Does anyone care that I'm here?' He lay down on the floor and went to sleep in front of the sink. TC, Lou, and Jake heard the glass bottle breaking and Vance's voice.

'Keep getting those orders together, girls. I'll go take care of Vance.'

'Not this time, Jake,' said TC, who had stopped crying the moment she got back to the pharmacy and realised work had to be done. Both Jake and Lou followed TC as she went to the back of the dispensary, saw Vance on the floor, stepped over him, carefully took the smashed glass out of the sink, and threw it into one of the buckets she used for cleaning of the pharmacy. She picked up the other cleaning bucket, almost filled it with water, and without hesitation threw it over Vance. Lou and Jake jumped back as the water flooded over the floor. TC didn't give a tinker's that the only decent pair of shoes she owned were probably ruined. Vance stammered, threw his arms around, kicked his legs, cursed, and carried on.

'Get up, Boss,' said TC.

'Come on, mate' said Jake.

'Vance, come on,' said Lou. Vance sat up.

'Where the hell am I? Why am I so wet all over? What has happened?'

'TC threw a bucket of water over you,' said Lou.

'You deserved it, mate,' said Jake.

'Are you awake enough to put this ointment together?' asked TC.

'Where am I?' repeated Vance.

'Mr Callahan, you are sitting on the floor in front of the sink, behind the dispensary,' answered TC.

'I want to go back to sleep,' stammered Vance.

'You might drown in the water,' said Jake.

'I don't care,' mumbled Vance. 'Most of the time, wish I was dead, anyway.'

'Come on, mate' said Jake. 'I'll take you home and put you to bed. Try to stand up, mate; we have to get to my car.'

'You are not taking him out the front way; everyone will see him,' said TC vehemently.

'I'll get my car and bring it around the back,' replied Jake. 'Is that okay?'

'I'll get on with these stinking mail orders,' said Lou.

TC went to the café. The man for the prescription was just finishing his meal. He looked up as she approached him. TC smiled.

'Excuse me sir, are you by any chance staying in Brolga overnight?'

'Yes, I am,' he replied.

'Your ointment has to be mixed with several different medicinal ingredients. My boss is the pharmacist. He's not feeling well this evening. Is it okay with you to collect it around eight in the morning?'

'Been without it this long, luv; don't think another twelve or so hours will matter.'

'Thank you. See you around eight or so tomorrow,' smiled TC.

¶

Jake returned.

'Poor bugger's a mess, ladies. He's my mate. Don't know what to do for him.'

'Maybe we should tell Mrs Callahan,' suggested Lou.

'The poor woman is pregnant,' said Jake. 'Apart from that, she already has two little boys to look after. It would only worry her.'

'Let's get these orders done or they'll have no money to live on,' said TC.

§

They left the pharmacy just before closing time at the hotels.

'I'll take you ladies home,' said Jake. 'Take your showers. Beware of snakes. I expect toasted sandwiches in …' he checked his watch, 'exactly one hour and ten minutes.' Lou and TC each nodded their agreement. Jake drove up around and down the street to the nurse's quarters. Strawberry blond 'Jakie baby' was waiting for him. She climbed into his car and kissed him on the cheek; Jake drove to the creek, they had sex, strawberry blond told Jake she would love him forever, he drove her home, told her he'd give her a call soon. Jake presented himself at TC's back door within ten or so seconds of his predicted time.

'Where's my toasted sandwich?' demanded Jake as he checked his watch, then smiled.

'Rack off, Jake,' said Lou, who was in the middle of grating cheese.

'Where is Darling?' asked Jake.

'She's gone on a date with Clint Eastwood,' replied Lou.

'Oh, shit, Lou. I can't compete with Clint bloody Eastwood.'

'I know; so does TC. That's why she's gone with Clint.'

'I need a beer,' said Jake as he opened the fridge.

'You need more than a beer, Jake. You need to grow up.'

'You're back, Jake?' said TC from the verandah doorway.

'Darling, I just asked Lou where you were.'

'Jake, please stop calling me "darling".'

'All right, Darling. I'll try,' he said sincerely. 'Difficult not to call you "darling" when I'm head over bloody heels in love with you.'

'You've seen too many movies, Jake,' smiled TC.

'Food's ready,' called Lou from the kitchen.

'Great,' said Jake. 'I'm hungry.'

Before eviction-of-Jake time, it was agreed that Jake would check on Vance on his way home and make certain Vance was at the pharmacy by seven the next morning.

'I promise you, TC, my mate will be there. Even if I have to carry him.'

❡

Jake kept his promise. He and Vance were in the dispensary drinking coffee and chatting when the girls got to the pharmacy. TC looked at Jake.

'Did you have to carry my boss?'

'No, Butterball, Jake didn't have to carry me,' said Vance sheepishly without looking at TC. He kept his eyes directed at the desk. His voice was soft. 'Thank you for douching me, TC. Think I've needed someone to throw a bucket of water over me for a while now. Hopefully, I have come to my senses.'

'I hope so, too, Boss,' replied TC with head raised and affirmatively. 'Now, would you please look at this?' She threw the prescriptions at Vance.

'Thank you, TC. I'll take care of it immediately,' he said as he picked it up from where it had landed beside his chair. Jake and Lou were speechless as if in shock.

'Think I'd better go, mate,' said Jake looking at Vance.

'I'm going, too,' said Lou.

'That goes for me as well,' said TC as she placed her shop keys on the dispensary desk. Vance stood silently holding the ointment prescription in his hand. He directed his gaze towards TC.

'You've had enough, Butterball?' TC nodded.

'Time to grow up, Mr Callahan. I can't keep rushing across to the Empire window yelling at you and being ridiculed any longer.'

'See you later, mate,' said Jake.

'See you later,' from Lou.

'Time to grow up, Boss,' sighed TC, shaking her head. Vance felt abandoned as he watched Jake, Lou, and TC leave.

A man has to grow up. The kid is right, thought Vance. My life is a bloody mess. Anyway, I've known that for a long time. He shrugged in resignation as he went about collecting the ingredients for the ointment, which would prove to be the beginning of a remarkable turning point in his life.

§

Jake went off to Carmichael and Carmichael, thinking about his mate, Vance. 'Wish I could think of a way to help him get back on track.'

TC cried silent tears as she and Lou walked towards home.

He is the best boss in the world! What on earth am I going to do? I hope he does sort things out. I'm worried about him.

Lou was thinking, Good. TC might leave Brolga now. We can go to Brisbane or Sydney or anywhere we damned-well want to go.

§

'Think I'll light up that old copper, Lou. Perhaps I can work off some of my frustrations with everything while I stir the sheets and towels around in the boiling water.'

'You are so fired up, TC, you'll probably break the stirring pole,' replied Lou.

'The way I feel about things at the moment, I'd like to break it on a few backsides of human rats in this town. I'm not talking about my boss, Lou. I'm meaning the so-called saints who ridicule him.'

Lou answered the ringing telephone.

'What are you ladies up to?' asked Jake.

'TC is about to murder the sheets and towels in the copper,' replied Lou. 'Think she is wishing she could throw a couple of barmaids and hypocrites in, instead.'

'In this heat, Lou? Has she gone bloody crazy?'

'Nothing of the headstrong little bugger now.'

'She'll melt, standing over that bloody copper. I'll call Mum and tell her TC needs to use the washing machine. Tell TC to bundle up the stuff; I'll be there to collect you in a few minutes.'

'What if your mother says "No", Jake?'

'Don't be ridiculous, Lou. See you shortly.'

'Jake will be here in a few minutes, TC,' said Lou as she raced down the stairs to the laundry where TC was about to fill the copper with water from a short hose attached to one of the laundry taps.

'I'm not going, Lou,' replied TC sharply. 'I have done little apart from accepting charity since I arrived in Brolga.'

'It's not charity,' replied Lou just as sharply. 'Brolgaites are mostly like that, TC. After a while, we begin to ignore the rest. Stay here long enough, TC, and you'll understand,' added Lou in a softer voice.

Jake's car hurtled in. He jumped out, looked at the heap on the laundry floor and then at TC.

'You've gone bloody mad, woman!' as he opened the boot of his car and began hauling the laundry in. 'I thought you had at least part of a bloody brain.'

'Well, Jake, your aunt is much older than I am; if she can handle the copper, so can I.'

'This bloody thing hasn't been used in years! She's had a washing machine since they came into fashion. My Auntie traded it in for a new one recently. Of course, they took it with them. 'Why wouldn't they? Now get in the bloody car, ladies, or I'll throw you in,' he laughed. TC grabbed a packet of detergent from the laundry bench; Lou rushed to close the front and back doors of the house; then Jake drove them faster than they could believe to his mother's home, where he unceremoniously opened the boot before plonking the laundry on the front path.

'Mum's gone to a meeting. Make yourselves at home, ladies. Just wash! Don't hang anything on the clothes line. I'll collect you in three hours,' as he looked at his watch. 'Take care, Darling,' he smiled at TC. 'You, too, Lou,' as he closed his car door and sped off.

Lou and TC carried the washing around the house to the outdoor laundry enclosure. They sat on the perimeter of the laundry concrete floor in silence as one load after another finished its cycle. Occasionally, each of them walked to the rainwater tank adjacent to the laundry to cup their hands under the tap to gulp some water. As each load finished, they straightened it out, partly folded it, and placed in the Carmichael's wash tubs.

Jake, bearing a cane laundry basket, presented himself.

'Ready to go, ladies?' he looked at TC. 'Once more, I think you are definitely a mad woman, Darling. Let's get this basket and you ladies back to Auntie's house. I'm going to meet Vance at the Empire. We'll have a few bets and a few beers. By the way, TC, Vance asked me to give you these.' Jake handed over keys to the pharmacy enclosed in an envelope with TC's pay and another envelope containing a note which read, 'Know I keep repeating myself but here goes. I'm sorry, TC. Not only to you, but also to my wife and sons. Have another child coming. You are a good girl. Please come to work on Monday? Had a very long conversation with the man for the ointment. Will tell you later. Thank you for being you. Thank you for believing in me.'

What can I do? thought TC. Jake reached into his pocket and fetched out a five-pound note.

'Vance gave me this to give to you; said it should cover for throwing the water over him.' Jake, TC, and Lou all laughed.

'Think you do have the best boss in the world,' said Lou.

Jake shook his head. 'My mate's a smart bugger, all right, and conned me into being his messenger. Come on, ladies. Let's go. Gotta meet my mate, drink some liquor, and place some bets. Drop you off and see you later.'

§

Jake and Vance came to the house around seven in the evening. They were both happy after drinking at the Empire all afternoon. They had both once again won a heap of money on the race horses they had backed. Jake carried beer and Coke, Vance a bottle of Bundaberg and hamburgers from Con's Café. TC was standing in the dining room in her almost-completed yellow dress; Lou was pinning the hem.

'You look lovely, Darling,' said Jake.

'You are drunk,' replied TC matter-of-factly.

'Louise is coming later. Hope that's okay,' said Vance.

'After what she said to me?' questioned TC, rolling her eyes. 'There is a limit to what your bonuses buy.' Then to herself, 'What's the point?' She sighed.

'Let's put on poor old Slim,' said Jake as he looked at Lou and winked.

'Go to buggery, Jake,' replied Lou.

'Let's eat,' said Vance as he plonked the burgers on the table. 'Where's a glass, TC?'

'I'll get you one,' said Lou.

TC went to her bedroom to change. 'What on earth does the Boss want to tell me about the ointment man?'

❡

A short time later, when they were all seated on the front steps with the sprinklers running, she asked, 'What are you going to tell me about that man for the ointment, Boss?'

'He's a very interesting man,' replied Vance. 'I didn't know before, but some people used to mine opals around here. He's on a sentimental journey. Relatives of his had an opal mine not too far from Brolga. They did pretty well out of it. He told me Chinese immigrants had a go at opal mining in the area a long time ago, also.'

'What's opal?' asked Lou.

'Some sort of gemstone,' said Jake.

'Never heard of it,' said TC.

'Heard of it, but don't recall seeing it,' said Vance. 'Guess I'll have to do some investigating.'

'Good. Might keep you out of the Empire,' from TC.

'Not much chance of that,' laughed Vance. 'My mate, Jake, might miss my company.'

'Not to mention barmaids,' quipped Lou.

'What a coincidence. Here comes one now,' laughed Jake. Louise was approaching the front gate as they looked towards the footpath.

'Fancy seeing you here, Roughly Rolled,' said Vance after inhaling deeply on his Craven A and deliberately blowing the smoke in Louise's direction. Louise smiled at Vance.

'May I come in, lover?'

'Not until you do something I asked you to; you know the rules,' replied Vance. Jake, Lou, and TC silently looked at Louise curiously.

'I don't want to do it in front of Jake and Lou.'

'Well, turn around and take yourself back to the pub, then.' Vance laughed before purposely turning his attention to Jake and the girls, all of whom, including TC, felt more than a little sorry for Louise as she continued standing outside the gate gazing at Vance.

'You really are a prick, Vance Callahan,' snarled Louise.

'I'm very well aware of what I am, Louise. No foul language in this area, please. Don't want Lou and TC to end up with a vocabulary like yours.' Vance blew more smoke towards Louise.

Louise snapped, 'Okay, you win, Vance,' before very loudly continuing in a monotone. 'TC, I'm sorry for saying the things I said to you the other day. Jess has put me straight on the way you are. So have Vance and Jake. A regular little Miss Lilly Milk White, that's you,' with sarcasm. 'Almost feel sorry for you.'

Jake stood up angrily.

'TC doesn't need pity from you or anyone like you, Louise.'

'More TCs in this hell hole, it would be a much better place,' said Lou who was also angry.

'Couldn't help yourself, Louise?' from a seething Vance. 'For your information, I've lectured TC on never becoming what you and your kind are.'

Somehow seeing Louise standing at the gate reminded TC of herself at that little girl's birthday party years ago and how Sam had become her friend.

'Everyone, it's all right. Come in, Louise. I've been the odd one out for most of my life. It's not a good feeling. Time for a Louis Armstrong record,' as she stood and went inside.

'Want a drink, Louise?' asked Jake as he picked up Vance's almost-empty glass. Louise nodded her head.

'I'll help you, Jake,' said Lou.

Jake took drinks to Vance and Louise, who were arguing on the steps.

'You seem to have sobered up, Jake,' remarked Lou when Jake returned inside.

'My mate has, too,' replied Jake. 'Never seen such a reversal of 'Do unto others' as TC. I'm a staunch Catholic, but buggered if I could have done that.'

'Yes, Jake, the Great Book also says, 'Turn the other cheek," added Lou.

'Yes, and who was it that said, 'There but for the grace of God go I'?'

'Let's leave it alone,' said TC, as if deep in thought. 'All I can say in this. 'Louise is in love with the boss. Poor Boss doesn't seem to know what he's doing most of the time. I don't think he loves anyone because he doesn't love himself. I wish Mrs Callahan would come back soon. At least he has great respect for her as his wife and mother of his children. That's it. I'm saying no more.' Silence except for the raised voices of Louise and Vance emanating from the steps.

'By the way, ladies, heard Pauline is taking off on the Flea tomorrow,' said Jake. 'Jack Romeo sacked her for hitting some poor old bugger over the head with a King Brown Beer Bottle. He's in hospital. Seems she didn't enjoy working at the Majestic. Too many down-and-outers.'

'I'm turning on the radio,' said Lou.

'I agree,' said Jake. 'Turn it up loud. Hopefully, it will drown the noise from the row out front.' As Lou stood up, they heard another, much louder male voice. It was a trucker from the transport company across the street.

'Keep it down, will both of you! My mate and I are trying to load up for tomorrow's trip. Can't concentrate on our job. Can't even hear 2 bloody-well UE on our radio. Can only get that station late at night.'

'Sorry, mate,' said Vance.

'And Louise here,' said Louise as she got up and walked towards the trucker.

'So, it's you the pill-pusher is on with, Louise? Interesting. We all thought it was the kid.'

'You thought wrong,' said Louise with a smile. 'Now be a good boy and go back to your truck. We'll keep it down, won't we, lover,' as she glanced across her shoulder towards Vance.

Vance nodded. 'Sorry, mate. Wait here, Louise,' as he stood up, lit a Craven A, and walked inside. 'Jake, will you drive me home after dropping Louise off at her quarters?'

'Where's your car, Vance?' asked Lou.

'Like me, Lou, it's broken down. Thank you, TC. You're a good girl, too, Lou.'

'See you later, ladies,' said Jake as he and Vance walked towards the front door. They heard Jake's car leave within seconds.

'Well, TC, I didn't think of you as a wimp,' said Lou aggressively. 'You have the courage to race to the pub window and tell Vance Callahan to haul his butt out of the place. You obviously do not have the courage to stand up for yourself to the likes of Louise.'

'I'm no wimp, Lou,' replied TC just as aggressively. 'I get the boss away from the pub only when I have to. If I don't, his livelihood is on the line. So is mine! Not to mention his responsibilities to his family.'

'He's got plenty of money, TC,' argued Lou. 'He plays poker, bets on race horses, and drinks like a man possessed.'

'That's his business, Lou! Let's drop this subject. Now!'

'Think I'll turn off the radio and put poor old Slim on,' laughed Lou.

'Whatever you want to do,' replied TC.

¶

Time passed as time does. Some days the hours seemed to go so slowly; sometimes extremely fast, on mail days in particular. Never seemed to be enough hours in the day.

Delores phoned frequently. The baby was due soon. Vance appeared more anxious after every call. Lou became almost a full-time resident at Auntie Flo and Uncle Doug's house with TC. She returned to the Shack for a few days occasionally whenever she felt she had to just to check that her parents were okay.

TC managed to run the pharmacy with only an occasional storming of the Empire window. Jake continued to visit Lou and TC after playing poker, betting on race horses, and satisfying his male needs with the nurses from the hospital. Vance drank more and more. He was at the pharmacy only on mail days for as little time as possible. He and Louise became closer. Their relationship was the main point of gossip for the majority of Brolgaites.

One morning Vance was sitting in the dispensary, signing blank cheques for TC to fill out and dispatch to various creditors.

'TC, what on earth am I going to do? Delores is about to give birth, I hardly know the two boys, and I'm drunk most of the time. It's my escape route from reality. I hate this fatherhood role. I was never cut out for it. I'm a lonely man even though my façade says differently. I married Delores for all the wrong reasons. She's tolerated my gambling and drunkenness and turns a blind eye to my indiscretions with other women. Delores is either the smartest or most stupid woman on earth. What on earth am I going to do, Butterball?' asked Vance tears glistening in his eyes.

TC felt extremely sad to see Vance so sincerely distressed.

'I don't know, Boss,' replied TC softly. 'Why did you marry Mrs Callahan?'

Vance stared at the ceiling for a few seconds before looking TC directly in her eyes and replied.

'Seemed like the right thing to do at the time. I'm sure I have told you that before. Make sure you never make the same mistake.'

'I'll try not to, Boss,' replied TC. 'I feel so sad for you, Mrs Callahan, the boys, and your new, about-to-be-born baby.' TC was fighting back tears. Vance changed the subject.

'Like your dress, TC. Is that one of the pieces of material I got for you in Curloo? Hope you have been saving your money.'

'Yes, Boss, I have a different dress for every day now. And I have one hundred and twelve pounds in the bank. Lou wants me to go to Sydney with her.' Vance's eyes opened wide in alarm.

'What? You are not going!' TC was surprised by his reaction. She had no intention of going to Sydney or anywhere else. She wouldn't dream of deserting her boss, especially the way he was at the moment.

'I'm not going anywhere, Boss. Someone has to take care of things.'

'Good girl,' replied an obviously relieved Vance as he stood up after closing the chequebook. 'I'm off to the Empire.'

¶

Vance started throwing impromptu parties at his house. He and Louise delighted in spiking the drinks of party attendees with pure alcohol, which was tasteless and odourless. On occasions, it had disastrous effects on the unsuspecting consumers. At one party, Vance and Louise accidentally double-spiked the drinks of a young truck driver, who literally passed out while standing on his feet. He fell to the floor, face down. The impact when he hit the floor caused a huge gash in his forehead. Vance thought the young man had suffered a heart attack; he panicked; so did Louise. He phoned Jake to help him get the passed-out truckie to hospital. After twelve stitches to his head and a diagnosed concussion as a result of his fall after his intake of an unknown quantity of pure alcohol, the young man was hospitalised for two weeks. After release from hospital, he made a point of seeking out Vance at the Empire.

'You did me a favour, mate,' he said as he reached out his hand to Vance.

'Why do you think so, mate?' replied Vance as he shook the truck driver's hand.

'Get real, Pill-Pusher! I'll never leave my drink unattended again. I will be like a bloody eagle hawk whenever I'm drinking around you.'

'Buy you a beer?' asked Vance with a mischievous grin on his face.

'Sure,' replied the truckie, 'as long as you show your money on the bar before putting your hands in your pocket; Jess serves the beer, not Louise; and I sit on the pub verandah under a bright light to drink it.' Everyone laughed.

Next day Vance told TC never to charge the young truckie for anything whatsoever that he purchased from the pharmacy.

¶

Delores did not call in the morning, as was her usual routine. She called late in the afternoon. Vance was at the Empire, and TC took the call.

'TC, tell Vance the baby is coming. Tell him to get to Brisbane NOW!' TC raced to the Empire window.

'Mr Callahan, Mrs Callahan called. The baby is coming. You have to go to Brisbane NOW!' Vance went into panic mode; TC could tell by the look on his face as he put down his drink on the bar and took a deep breath.

'Reality time has struck,' he said as he looked around at his drinking mates. 'I'm about to be a father again.' Jess looked Vance in the eye.

'Sure hope you can find more time to spend with the coming new little one than you spent with your other little boys.'

'Mind your own business,' snapped Louise as she followed Vance out of the Empire bar. 'So, Delores snaps her fingers and off you race to her side,' snarled Louise. Vance was on the median strip, briskly walking towards the pharmacy, Louise only a couple of feet behind him. Vance came to an immediate halt, turned, and looked at Louise with absolute disgust.

'Louise, you really are a piece of work. At times like these I am disgusted with myself for having anything whatsoever to do with a creature like you.'

'Suppose you would prefer someone like Little Miss Milk White?'

'Don't be ridiculous, Louise. Why do you always bring TC into everything? This has nothing to do with her. Delores is my wife. She is about to give birth to my child. What sort of a bastard would I be if I didn't go?'

'The bastard that you always are,' screamed Louise. If Vance had ever wanted to hit anyone, it was now. He grabbed Louise by her shoulders and shook her.

'Wake up to yourself, Louise.' He shook his head and walked away.

By now the entire complement of drinkers at the Empire Bar were on the footpath. Jess was leaning on the window. Everyone was on the street, including the baker and his mother. Con and Lisa Kara were outside the café observing. Even the bank manager and his staff were in front of the bank as audience.

'Screw you, Vance!' screamed Louise.

'Know you already have,' came a voice from one of the onlookers. Vance paused at the door to the pharmacy. He turned towards Louise.

'Don't know what came over me. Must have been desperate.' Everyone clapped.

'Good on you, Pill-Pusher,' yelled one man.

'Go to your wife. It's about time,' from another.

'Drive carefully and God bless you,' muttered Jess softly.

Louise screamed, 'Bastard' before running off to the quarters.

'Takes one to know one!' called a voice from the crowd.

The crowd dispersed back to wherever they had emerged from. Jack and Bert Romeo had missed the entire scenario. They had been counting money in their counting room. Both of them were always alert, even when counting their money, as to the sound of the cash register clanging in the bar. Jack and Bert emerged from the very private office when they realised the sound had resumed.

'Were we quiet for a while?' asked Jack.

'Didn't hear anything being rung up for around ten minutes,' added Bert.

'Just missed a great show,' replied Jess, rolling her eyes.

'Where's that Louise girl?' asked Jack.

'She's not feeling too well, Jack. I told her to go take a rest. I can handle this dump and this lot of mongrels with my eyes closed.'

'Okay, girl,' said Jack Romeo as he and Bert headed back to their money room.

¶

Jake Carmichael knew nothing about the event until Con Kara telephoned him.

'Mate, you missed a great show with our mate, Vance, and that Louise person.'

'I've been busy with a travelling salesman,' replied Jake.

'That's what you get for being located at the other end of the block, my friend. Better go see our mate soon. His wife is about to give birth; so, he's off to Brisbane. Fill you in later, mate.'

Jake told the travelling salesman he had to leave and would meet him at the Empire in half an hour. He walked briskly across the street and down the block to the pharmacy where he found Vance and TC in the dispensary.

'What happened, mate? Con called me; told me there has been some drama with Louise.'

'Don't want to discuss it now, mate. The bank manager and his mob saw the show. Just called the bank about cashing a cheque to go to Brisbane. No answer. I know they are there. That manager is a rat!'

'How much do you need, mate?' asked Jake.

'Couple of thousand quid,' replied Vance.

'No problem, mate. I'll go get it now.' Vance filled out a cash cheque for two thousand pounds.

'TC, cash this tomorrow and give the money to Jake.'

'Get on your way, mate, and greet your new baby.' Vance shook Jake's hand and gave TC a kiss on the cheek.

'Here I go, about to be a father again. I'll call you, Butterball; let you know what happens.'

'Go, Boss, go. Everything will be fine here. Drive carefully, and call me when the baby comes. Good luck, Boss,' from TC.

'Good luck, mate,' from Jake.

'Looking at you two, I already have good luck,' replied Vance as he left via the back door of the pharmacy to fuel his car and head off on the long drive to Brisbane, where Delores, his boys, and possibly a new baby by the time he got there, would be waiting.

¶

Twenty minutes later, Vance was driving at break-neck speed across the narrow bridge that spanned the creek. Cannot believe Louise and her attitude, he thought to himself. His mind was racing all over the place. Jake is a real mate; came up with three thousand quid without blinking an eyelid. Lou will help TC with the pharmacy. Wonder if Delores will have another boy or a baby girl. The boys must have grown a lot now. Hope they recognise me. I'm not much of a father. Have to try harder. Have to quit the booze and be a good husband and father. Wonder where Anna is? A man is an asshole. That is what I am! His mind kept racing on and on as he sped his car recklessly over the red dust road into Curloo.

¶

Vance pulled up at the service station.

'What time is it, mate?' he asked the same young man who had attended him on his initial trip to Brolga. 'The pubs are not closed yet, Callahan.'

'Who asked about the pubs?' smiled Vance.

'Nobody,' replied the young man. 'Simply meant it's not quite ten yet.'

Vance looked at the young man and smiled. 'Check the tyres, fill the car with petrol, and please clean the windshield, check the water and the radiator. I'll be back soon. Have to go to Brisbane in a hurry. By the way, I hate Curloo.'

Some things never change, thought the young garage attendant, as he watched Vance walk briskly towards the Curloo Hotel. Poor Mr Callahan, I think he's still in love with Anna. Must hurt him when he comes to Curloo. Suppose he's always reminded of her.

¶

Vance silently told himself, I won't buy any rum, only Coke. When he reached the drive-through window, 'Bottle of Bundy, mate.'

'Coke as well, Mr Callahan?'

'What do you think?' replied Vance. 'Got an opener for the Coke?'

'Anything for you, Mr Callahan,' replied the drive-through attendant as he placed a bottle of Bundaberg rum, a four-pack of Coke, and a bottle opener on the small counter.

'Mate, take this,' said Vance as he put a twenty-pound note on the counter. The attendant was in shock when Vance said, 'Keep the change, mate. Does the kid at the service station drink booze?'

'Beer,' replied the attendant.

'Take him a carton of whatever he drinks when you close up.' Vance handed over another twenty-pound note. 'Give him the change,' added Vance. 'Tell him not to end up like me.'

'I'd be proud to end up like you, Mr Callahan,' was the reply.

'That's what you think now. Talk to me in twenty years.' Vance headed towards the petrol station.

'Need to use your telephone,' he said to the young service station attendant, who had quickly washed Vance' car as well as fulfilling Vance's other requests.

'As long as you make it reverse charges, Mr Callahan. The boss will think I'm phoning my girlfriend, and I'll be in trouble when the phone bill comes.'

'Wouldn't want that,' smiled Vance as he picked up the phone. 'Reverse charges call to Brolga 118,' said Vance to the Curloo telephone exchange operator. Vance heard Lou's voice answer when the Curloo operator contacted Brolga exchange.

'The pharmacy has closed; I'll put you through to the manager's house.' Vance cracked up laughing. Good on you, Lou, he thought. Play it to the hilt.

'I have a reverse charge call from Mr Callahan in Curloo. Will you accept the call and pay the charges?' TC answered her telephone and smiled with relief when she heard Lou's question regarding taking the reverse charge call from Vance. Vance had obviously reached Curloo safely.

'Of course, Lou. Please put my boss through.'

'TC, I want you to do something for me,' said Vance.

'Thank you for being safe,' replied TC.

'Butterball, the house is a mess from my party-throwing saga. Please clean it up before I bring Delores and the kids home.'

'Sure, Boss,' replied TC. 'I hope you are not drinking rum and Coke on your way from Curloo to Brisbane?'

'Just bought some, Butterball,' admitted Vance.

'Throw it away, Boss,' commanded TC. 'You have a new baby coming, new start. Call me when you get to Brisbane.'

'I love you, Butterball. You're a good kid.' Vance hung up the phone and walked to the bin outside the service station, looked at the service station kid. 'Pity you only drink beer, mate,' as he was about to place the bottle of Bundy in the bin.

'Please don't, Mr Callahan. Some of my mates like Bundy and Coke.'

'Good on you, mate' replied Vance.

'They'll have to buy their own Coke; I'm taking mine with me,' as he handed the bottle of Bundaberg to the young man. 'How much do I owe you?' Vance counted out the exact amount of money. 'Your tip will be delivered. Thanks for washing the car,' he said as he drove off towards Brisbane. The young service station attendant watched Vance drive off at break-neck speed and thought, Good on you, Mr Callahan. You are a bloody good bloke. Good luck and please drive carefully.

¶

As Vance drove off at breakneck speed towards Delores, his boys, and the birth of his new child, his mind was racing.

'Another child. I really am a rat. Hardly see the two I already have, poor little buggers. Poor Delores. What a fool she is for loving me. She spends money faster than I can make it, but, so what! She loves me. At least, I'm pretty sure she does. Why the hell would she put up with the crap I lay on her? Don't know how on earth I'll get to Brisbane without a drink. Wish I hadn't given that kid the bottle of Bundy. Starting to shake already. Withdrawal symptoms are setting in. I feel guilty. I still love Anna. I use TC as my touchstone. Poor little bugger covers for me all the time. Louise, well, Louise is Louise. Need to say goodbye to

Louise soon. Need to turn over a new leaf. That's what a man has to do.' He pulled his car to an abrupt halt, jumped out, and took a leak alongside.

¶

Meanwhile, Delores was in labour in a Brisbane Hospital. Jake, Lou, and TC were sitting on the front steps of Uncle Doug and Auntie Flo's house, listening to poor old Slim on record. Louise, in the company of a shearer from Tasmania, was sitting in her car down by the creek.

'Louise, I think I'm in love with you,' said the young shearer as he put his arm around her shoulders.

'Don't get carried away. Let's have another drink, darls,' replied Louise. As the shearer handed the drink to Louise, radio station 4CH blasted out some song about, when a man loves a woman. 'What about when a woman loves a man?' demanded Louise as she slammed her left hand down on the dashboard, threw the drink the shearer had given her out through the car window, and said, 'Come here, lover.'

'Are you sure, Louise?' asked the shearer in a soft voice.'

'Certain! The pill-pusher can go to hell as far as I'm concerned. Let's make love.'

They did. They married three weeks later in Curloo. They had a private ceremony with two of the young shearer's mates as witnesses. As the Anglican minister was reading the marriage rights, Louise was thinking, This guy's a good, simple man. Too bloody honest! My heart will always be with Vance.

Louise's about-to-be husband was thinking, Hope to God I'm doing the right thing. I know her reputation. Still, she sure is hot in the cot. Time will tell; always does.

Marriage vows complete, Louise, her husband, and the two witnesses moved off to the Curloo Hotel, where they proceeded to get plastered beyond belief. When the hotel closed, they moved upstairs onto the hotel verandah, where they were eventually joined by the half dozen or so houseguests who could not sleep because of the noise caused by the wedding party. Of course, Louise was the star of the party. Her sharp sense of humour and wittiness became more and more amusing as the early hours wore on.

The hotel manager joined them around 3 am.

'A man can't sleep with all this bloody noise. Thought I may as well join your mob of bloody drunks.' He handed Louise a bottle of Bundy and plonked a carton of cold beer and some Coke on the verandah table. 'Here's to a happy future for the newlyweds,' he said before biting the bottle top off a beer and taking a swig.

The party ended when all the grog was gone around six-thirty in the morning.

'Great wedding night,' slurred Louise as she and her groom staggered giggling towards their room.

'Bonza,' laughed one houseguest as he fell onto his bed.

'Bloody bonza, all right,' replied another as he urinated through the hotel verandah railings.

'Hope there're no poor buggers on the street copping your piss,' said the hotel manager. 'Think I'll join your mate. A lot of bastards in Curloo need pissing on,' as he opened his fly and followed suit.

'Not what I expected on our wedding night,' sighed the young shearer as he lay down on the bed beside Louise, who was already asleep. He also was asleep in seconds. And so their life together as man and wife began.

❡

Louise had told no one in Brolga that she was getting married. She had simply requested a week off from Bert and Jack Romeo. Said she wanted to go to Brisbane for shopping. She believed, mistakenly, that Vance would be shocked and heartbroken when he returned to Brolga to find her married.

Truth was, Vance had not given Louise a second thought since shortly after driving away from the Curloo service station. His body was fighting off the demons of alcoholism. En route from Curloo to Brisbane, he pulled over several times to throw up, then dry-retch when there was nothing left in his stomach to bring up. He sat for two hours with his head cupped in his hands against the steering wheel.

This is it, he told himself. His body was shaking so much by the time he reached Brisbane that he had difficulty holding the steering wheel of his car as he pulled into the motel car park. He was perspiring profusely as he reached for his bag, then walked to the motel reception office.

'Are you okay, sir?' enquired the receptionist.

'Not really,' replied a ghostly white, shaking, and perspiring Vance. 'My wife has probably just given birth to our new baby. Suppose it's news I need to lay down for a little while.' The receptionist quickly took down Vance's particulars and directed him to a room.

Poor man, she thought, as she watched him walk towards it. Heard about new fathers reacting like this but never seen it in anyone.

¶

'Bloody hell' murmured Vance. 'Just made it.' As his blood pressure dropped, he fell onto the bed. He attempted to reach for the telephone as he passed out.

The hotel owner knocking on the door, 'Are you all right, Mr Callahan?' awakened Vance fifteen hours later. Vance was disorientated, didn't have a clue where he was. The door opened.

'Sorry to bother you, Mr Callahan. The office girl told me you didn't look too good when you checked in. Thought I'd look in on you, make sure you're okay.'

'Thanks, mate,' said Vance groggily. 'Had a long trip; just tired, I guess.'

'Would you like some breakfast?' enquired the man. Just the thought of food made Vance want to dry-retch.

'No, thank you, mate. I'll get up for a shower soon. Thank you for your concern.'

'No problem,' replied the man with a smile as he closed the door and walked away, thinking, Poor bugger looks like he's been to hell and back. Glad my old woman and I couldn't have kids if that's the way it can do a man in.

Vance quickly drank three glasses of water, turned on the cold water tap in the shower, undressed, then slumped on the shower's tiled floor as the cold water played over his body.

This is enough, he thought. Going to join the AA joint. If ever a man needed saving, it has to be me. In my opinion, I'm a pretty good candidate. He opened his eyes, looked at the water spurting directly into them. Oh, dear Lord, please help me, please. Vance sat there for what seemed to him like an eternity. He was meditating deeply. Have to pull myself together, have to present myself to Delores and my children as a passable husband and father. Have to phone TC and tell the kid I'm still alive. Hope the business is okay. Make the call to the AA mob. Hope they can, in some manner, shape, or form, help a bastard like myself. Vance abruptly stood up, stepped from the shower cubicle, grabbed a towel, dried himself off, clothed himself, reached for the telephone directory, found the number for Alcoholics Anonymous, and dialled it. 'My name is Vance. I need help.' Vance was on his way to a new life.

§

Arrangements were made for him to attend a meeting for people in similar circumstances as himself. He telephoned the hospital. Delores had given birth to a baby girl. 'Cute,' he was told by the nursing sister he spoke to.

'Please tell my wife I'll be there soon. Please also tell her "thank you" for loving me.'

Vance then phoned TC. 'How are things?'

'Great, Boss. I'm so happy to hear from you. How is Mrs Callahan? Any baby yet?'

'Proud father of a baby girl, TC. Haven't seen her yet. Going there to the hospital soon.'

'Don't worry about anything,' replied TC. 'Lou and Jake will help me. Say hello to Mrs Callahan. Congratulations.' Vance hesitated before saying, 'Delores hates you, TC. Don't know why!'

'Neither do I, Boss,' said TC, shaking her head. 'Go see your new baby girl, and please, please, please remember to be loving towards Jonathan and Andrew. Poor little darlings don't see much of you. They will feel left out if you pay too much attention to the baby girl.'

'Thanks, Butterball. As usual, you are right.'

Vance paid for his motel room in advance for a few more days. He cabbed it to the hospital, hugged Delores, held the baby, and waited until Delores' mother arrived with Jonathan and Andrew, hugged them, had a family photograph taken, needed a drink, excused himself, and almost ran to the front of the hospital, where there was a queue of waiting taxi cabs.

He jumped into one. 'Take me to this address,' the cab driver was told as Vance handed over a slip of paper. The cab driver looked over his shoulder at Vance.

'You an alcoholic, mate? Been there myself. Good on you! People like us need all the help we can get.' The cab driver dropped Vance off at the designated address, which was a well-known Charity Meeting Place Hall.

Great' thought Vance, as he paid the cabbie. not too far from wherever I need to be.

⁋

A man really is a bastard, he thought to himself, as he stood in front of fifty or so people in the hall and said, as instructed by the person who had greeted him, 'My name is Vance. I'm an alcoholic. I have not had a drink for I can't remember how may days. The way my body feels, seems like a thousand. In reality, more like three or four. I've been a pathetic gambler, womaniser, and drunk. With the help of God, whom I have neglected for too long, I now hope to become a better person. I feel I have reached rock bottom. I sincerely want to be a better person, better husband to my wife, and better—or at least passable—father to my children. Been to hell and back. Think everyone in this hall has done the same. Thank you for listening.'

'You'll make it, mate,' chorused a dozen or so as everyone clapped and wished him luck in one manner or form.

Vance walked out of the hall feeling like a new person. He held pamphlets with contact help-line numbers in his left hand, reached into his pocket for his pack of Craven A with his right hand, flipped open the top of the cigarette box, grasped a cigarette between his teeth, deposited the small box back into his pocket, sat down on someone's concrete fence wall, and deposited the paperwork on the footpath under his right foot so it would not fly away on the breeze. He reached for his box of matches, struck one alight, lit his cigarette, inhaled deeply, sat in silence meditating on the 'Prayer of Serenity' until his cigarette was just a butt filter, picked up the pamphlets from beneath his foot and set out on his walk to the motel, which was only a mile or so away.

'Know I can be a better man. Poor bloody Delores. Poor bloody kids. Poor, poor Anna. This is the turning point! Has to be.' As Vance walked towards the motel and his car, his mind wandered to the story the ointment man in Brolga had told him about opals. 'Sounds good to me. Let's see what a man can do. Who knows? I sure as bloody well don't!' Once back at the motel, Vance researched via telephone everything he could think of regarding opals.

'Dear, sweet Jesus, please help me. Don't care about the money, dear Lord, only about doing the bloody right thing for a change. Anyway, I'm a gambler. Perhaps it's time to gamble on something tangible that I can hold in my hands rather than a couple of poor, bloody race horses fighting their way under the jockey's whip to the finishing post; poor, beautiful creatures are more often than not pulled by the jockeys being paid well to lose the race. Some poor horses never reach their full potential because of human corruption. Dear Lord, please grant me the wherewithal to reach full potential, within my capability, that is.'

A million thoughts raced through Vance's mind. Louise, Anna, Delores, the boys, the baby. All guilty thoughts of everything he could remember doing wrong. Hurting people! Didn't think of how he had hurt himself or of the kindness he had shown to countless people who had come to him with hard luck stories. Unbeknown to Vance at that stage, subconsciously he felt guilty about his success. His father had been an alcoholic who had died prematurely. His poor bloody mother had grown and sold some sort of bloody fruit or vegetable to educate him.

At least I owe it to my poor, darling Mother, whom I have ignored for years, to make something of myself. She made all those sacrifices for me. Made me wear a long-sleeved shirt and a hat whenever we went near a beach and the sun; I must have looked like a real wimp. My mother and my sister had me wrapped in kid gloves as if I were something special. Like the Christmas gift of the bloody century! Some prize I am for all their bloody trouble. Rarely think of them. Too damned busy being a drunk, womaniser, and lousy father and husband. Holy suffering hell! I really am a mongrel! Like to get in that stinking car and drive off the side of the Story Bridge. I really and truly don't want to be here any damned more.

As Vance walked past a hotel bottle shop, he thought of his escape route—rum and Coke. He entered the premises, purchased two bottles of Bundaberg, half a dozen bottles of Coke, and a bag of ice. After paying and giving a tip, he then asked the bottle shop attendant to call a cab. Once back in his motel room, he decided to call TC. It was mail-order day. When Vance got through to the Brolga exchange, Lou was working.

'Hello, Lou. It's Vance Callahan. Please put me through to TC.'

'It's mail-order day, also cattle-sale day and flying-doctor day. I was helping her during my break and before work. She's flat-out like a lizard drinking. I'll help her after I finish working, as well.'

'Please put me through, Lou.'

'Sure, Mr Callahan. See you soon.'

TC was racing around the pharmacy like a chook with its head cut off while the telephone kept ringing, ringing, ringing.

'Hello, Brolga Pharmacy.'

'TC, it's me. I'm about to get drunk.'

'What's new, Boss? Stop feeling sorry for yourself.'

'I just need a drink, TC. Butterball, please understand,' he sounded desperate.

'Okay, Boss, have as many drinks as you need. Please don't leave the motel room. Please get some food in! I shall call you when everything is done here. Please promise me you won't drive your car.' Silence. 'Promise, Boss!'

'Okay, Butterball, I won't leave the place; I'll get some food in. I won't drive the car.'

TC asked everyone in the pharmacy to please wait while she dialled the exchange.

'Lou, please charge this call to my home number. Phone the motel where the Boss is staying in Brisbane. Please ask them to look after him. Poor Boss doesn't know what he's doing right now, Lou.'

'At his age?' Lou replied.

'Must go, Lou. Thank you. Talk to you later.' TC went off to attend to the prescriptions, mail orders, account-paying, cattle- and sheep-station owners, who were mostly nice, and their uppity wives purchasing cosmetics as if they were high society or royalty. Old Jess' words rang in TC's ears.

'Nothing but a mob of jumped-up housemaids and governesses, come to the west to nab a cow cockie's son for themselves.'

So, what! thought TC, as she tried to keep everyone happy, counting prescription pills and typing labels at a furious pace. Wonder I don't kill some poor soul. Should I ever make a mistake with these things, may God forgive me!

¶

That night after the Romeo Brothers shook the police sergeant's hand out front of the Empire Hotel, the occupants of the Seat of Knowledge applauded.

'Silly pair of bastards you are,' called Old Jock. 'You let that TC kid go. There she is, over there at the pill-pushing joint, still working like a dog; even your bloody pub's closed.'

'My kid's helping her,' came a voice from across the street as Lou's dad, Old Jordan, came around the corner, carrying a carton on his shoulder.

'Yes,' said Jock. 'So is that smart-aleck rat, John Carmichael, born a conman, smart, young prick.'

'Hope that young TC is smart enough not to get mixed up with that sweet-talking, good-looking young bastard,' added one of Jock's mates as they left the Seat of Knowledge to return to their homes where their loved ones were sleeping and/or simply waiting for their husbands and fathers to return from their night of observations and gossip. Almost always when the Seat of Knowledge gentry folk returned home, their families would breathe a sigh of relief and immediately go to sleep. Their wives knew they would get all the gossip the next day. The children didn't really care as long as they could go to slumberland with the knowledge that Dad was home and Mum would be happy.

¶

That night around midnight, Jake, Lou, and TC left the pharmacy. Jake drove the girls home and said, 'I'll see you tomorrow,' as he blasted off at break-neck speed as usual towards the nurses' quarters.

'Jake surely is a mongrel,' said Lou.

'Why is that, Lou?' asked TC.

'Everyone knows he's crazy about you. Everyone also knows he's an alcoholic. Think even the poor, much-used nurses know that about Jake.'

'Who cares, Lou,' replied TC. 'Jake is okay. He's a show pony. One day he'll get his come-uppance.'

'I hope so, TC,' replied Lou sincerely.

'At the moment, Lou, my friend, let's listen to that rock-and-roll station in Sydney, if you can organise it on the radio.

'Sounds good to me, TC. Poor Old Slim is becoming a little stale. By the way, Lou, I heard from one of my aunts that Slim's wife is my cousin.'

'You have to be joking, TC'.

'No, I'm not!'

As TC and Lou tuned into radio station 2UE, listened to rock music, showered, toasted bread, and piled the toast with tomato, canned beetroot, and stale lettuce, Vance was already drinking himself witless in a motel in Brisbane and Jake was making out with one of Brolga's nursing sisters down by the creek.

Vance was thinking, Please, God, help me!

Jake was thinking, Wish I could get this over with; really want to be sitting on those bloody steps with TC and Lou.

After their toast was ready, TC and Lou sat on the front stairs of Auntie Flo and Uncle Doug's house, watching the truck drivers across the road getting the trucks loaded to go in the morning.

'Poor buggers,' said Lou. 'Look at them. Looks like they are getting ready to go to hell and back.'

'Lou, they keep looking over here. Looks like they want to come over and watch the sprinkler go, listen to 2UE, and eat some toast.'

'You truly are naïve, TC. I'll call Dad and ask him about these guys. If Dad says their okay, then they're okay.' Lou phoned Thel, who, as usual, was up waiting for Jake to come home.

'Sorry, Mrs Carmichael. Know it's late. Could you please ask my dad if the truckies working across from Uncle Doug and Auntie Flo's house are okay?'

'Known those boys since they were born, Lou. They're fine. Good kids! Say hello to TC for me. Hope Jake is there with you.'

'Thank you, Mrs Carmichael', replied Lou.

Lou and TC walked across the road

'You look bored,' said Lou.

'Waiting to go pick up a late load for the mail,' the two young men replied in unison.

'Would you like to come to Uncle Doug and Auntie Flo's house, sit on the steps, watch the sprinkler go round, listen to rock-and-roll music from radio station 2UE, and eat some toast with whatever on it?' asked Lou.

'Sounds good,' said the young, blond, mail-truck driver with a smile that would melt a thousand hearts.

'Your wife, Corinne, wouldn't think so,' said his six-foot-two, bulkily built friend.

'Corinne will understand. These are good girls.'

'Everyone in Brolga knows that, mate,' replied his friend.

Lou went off to make sangas. Over her shoulder, she said, 'Jake has left some beers here. Would you like one?'

'No,' was the reply. 'Have to drive a long way tomorrow.'

'Like the music' said the blond truck driver as Lou returned to the steps with the food. TC turned off the sprinkler.

'What is a truck driver mailman's life like?' she asked. The two young men looked at each other and began to recite together something they had heard from a veteran truckie mailman for the stations somewhere, sometime. They couldn't remember when, where, or by whom. They relayed the story in unison as if they were school children reciting a poem—

The mailman's lot is not the life that it's made out to be.
For ten long years I ran a mail, a life of misery.

You never get a Sunday off like others in the town,
For that's the day you run the mail across the red-hot downs.

Each station has two bosses, the cocky and his wife,
And from either one the mailman is never out of strife.

The butter is all melted and the bread has gone all stale.
It couldn't happen anywhere, only on the mail.

His truck is overloaded and just as he pulls out,
The postman rushes to his side and lets out a mighty shout.

"Mrs Mitchell-Grass is on the phone; she needs spuds and margarine,
A couple of drums of petrol and one of kerosene."

And then when you arrive there, she will meet you at the gate
And say, "Why is it, mailman, that you're always running late?"

I one time had a parcel that looked so neat and square
With written in big letters "BOOTS: Handle them with care."

Next day I was returning and heard along the track,
"The bloke you brought the parcel for is drunk and got the sack."

I proceeded then with caution; for I knew what had been done:
The parcel marked as "BOOTS" was a bottle of O.P. rum.

You may strike a lot of trouble when the roly-polies roll
And then choke up the bore-drain and the water overflows.

Then you dig away for hours; for your trucks bogged near the drain,
While the women sit and grizzle, "That mailman's late again!"

Now you can help your mailman to keep from running late:
Write your mail the night before and hang your bag upon the gate.

And always ring in early for your spuds and margarine,
Your petrol and your stubbies and home-lighting kerosene.

'Sounds like some famous author wrote that,' said Lou.

'Just a truck-driving mailman out of Brolga,' replied the blond Frank Michaels. His friend shrugged and agreed. TC didn't know then that Frank Michaels and his wife would become lifelong friends. They all heard Jake's car go around the corner from the creek to the nurses' quarters.

'Think we had best go. Sounds as if Jake will be here soon.'

'Can't compete with him,' said the larger, bulky man.

'Who would want to?' said Frank Michaels before adding, 'Jake's a bullshit artist. Has been since he was born. Known him forever; he's a rat.'

'I agree,' said Lou.

TC didn't comment on Jake.

'Love the unknown truck-driving mailman's story. Will remember it for all my life. Please drive safely,' she said as the two young men walked across Brolga Street to finish loading their trucks.

Lou and TC closed the front door as Jake pulled into the side driveway of the house.

'Tell him to go away, please, Lou,' said TC. 'Tell him we are tired.'

'Jake, please go away. We're tired,' yelled Lou through the louvred windows. Jake didn't bother to reply.

Stupid bloody women, he thought to himself, as he reversed like a lunatic out of the driveway.

'What a rat,' remarked Lou as she and TC walked into the kitchen to brush their teeth.

'What else is news, Lou?'

'I'm buggered,' replied Lou.

'Me, too, Lou.'

'Seems to me the world is full of bullshit artists, TC.'

'You are probably right, Lou. In the meantime, thank you for being my friend.'

PART II

MINING

Time passes quickly in Brolga as time passes quickly everywhere. One night, Lou and TC were sitting on the stairs.

'Know what, Lou, my friend?' said TC. 'Ten years is only five hundred and twenty weeks.'

'What about leap years?' asked Lou. TC stood up and rolled her eyes, strode to the radiogram, and placed Slim's record in the player after turning off 2UE.

'Well, it's a lonesome way,' sang Slim.

'You can say that again,' yelled Lou as she jumped up, slammed the front door, and joined TC, who was cleaning her teeth at the kitchen sink.

⁋

Jake. of course, helped TC and Lou during busy times at the Pill-Pusher's Joint, as the locals now referred to the pharmacy. Vance was being totally indoctrinated at AA in Brisbane. Delores had gone home from hospital to her mother's house. One day, Vance called TC.

'Coming home! Is the house clean?'

'Sure is, Boss,' replied TC. 'Looking forward to seeing you.

⁋

Louise and her husband had returned to Brolga. Louise resumed work with the Romeo Brothers. Her shearer husband took a job with a contractor in New South Wales. Vance and Delores returned to Brolga in the early hours of one morning.

§

'Vance, did you tell TC to fill the refrigerator?'

'No, sorry, Delores.'

'Look, Vance. Everything is here.'

'Bloody hell,' said Vance. 'Kid thinks of everything!'

In fact, it was not TC who had thought of everything. It was Lou's dad, Old Jordan. When Lou had told her parents she was helping TC clean the Callahan house, Jordan said, 'Better make sure the refrigerator is filled. Also better have a bottle of Bundy there for the pill-pusher in case the poor bugger is thirsty.'

'No, Dad. He's off it. TC told me he's joined some alcoholics group. Mr Callahan has quit the booze, Dad.' Jordan looked at Lou in shock.

'As much chance of that, my dear daughter, as there is of some poor bastard walking on the moon.'

'We'll see, Dad.'

'We'll bloody well see, all right,' laughed Jordan. 'All right. Tell TC to take some of that powdered milk in tins to the pill-pusher's house. Sure the baby hasn't given up milk yet.' He laughed loudly as he walked out of the Shack and headed towards the pub.

§

Although Vance thanked TC and Lou profusely for cleaning the house, he even thanked Old Jordan for his thoughtfulness in the suggestion to the girls to buy him a couple of cartons; Delores didn't say a word.

TC heard from pharmacy customers who had seen the baby that she was a beautiful little girl but did not see the child until she was three months plus. Occasionally, Delores would come to the pharmacy, after being pre-announced with the obligatory phone call of her arrival, rush in like a cyclone with Jonathan and Andrew, grab things on her list from the shelves, nod at TC, then scurry out to the station wagon, where the baby was ensconced in a bassinet. TC could never understand why the boss' wife didn't like her.

One night sitting on the stairs with Lou, she asked, 'Lou, why do you think Mrs Callahan doesn't like me?' Lou thought about it for a few seconds, smiled, and looked at TC directly in her eyes.

'Because, TC, you are too damned pretty! Not only that, TC; you are nobody's fool. Work your bloody heart out, as my dad says. Everyone in town respects you except Vance's wife and his golf-playing cronies. That's because you worked for the Romeos. Mob of bloody s-holes is Dad's opinion. My dad says, 'Evil thinkers, evil doers.' The way I have been treated in Brolga because my Mum and Dad drink and he is, apart from many other things, the local undertaker, makes me realise my Dad is correct. Let's make a pact, TC,' suggested Lou.

'What sort of pact?' enquired TC with great interest before adding, 'By the way, Lou, I believe everyone in town, should they ever have the courage to take a good look at themselves, would respect you, as well; you have never done anything wrong to anyone except live to be the undertaker's daughter. What's the proposed pact, Lou?'

'Let's get out of this dump, TC. Please!'

Silence. TC thought for a few minutes.

'We'll see, Lou. Promise you, if I leave Brolga with a friend, it will be with you.'

❡

Vance was "a man on a mission", so to say. He was not drinking, always at the pharmacy, and there all day at crucial times. Louise called a lot; TC knew her boss was still meeting for 'creek outings' because they met in TC's driveway. Lou once said, 'No wonder the whole town thinks you are on with your boss, TC.'

'No wonder Delores hates you,' added Jake.

'Don't care,' replied TC firmly. 'The boss and I know the truth.'

'So does bloody Louise!' snapped Jake as he left the stairs and briskly walked down the passage towards his beers, grabbed one, then stormed back onto the top step, where he plonked himself down in obvious frustration.

'What makes you better than Louise, Jake?' asked Lou seriously.

'She's married to one of my bloody mates, Lou. Poor bastard is away working.'

'Excuse me. Don't think you should talk too much about the boss and Louise, Jake. At least they obviously have deep feelings for one another while all you do is go race off to the hospital and literally use the female staff bodies for your own satisfaction. You then race in your fast, fancy car back here to sweet-talk TC and me. Pretend to the world and yourself that you are perfect. Have to be a lot of stupid people in Brolga, let alone the world,' said Lou seriously with a great deal of sarcasm in her voice as she glared at Jake. Jake stood up as if he were a child in a tantrum, threw his beer onto the grass.

'Screw both of you,' he said as he tried to restrain his anger at having heard the truth about himself.

'Pretty sure you won't, Jake,' said Lou. TC looked at her in disgust.

'Leave, Jake. You are supposed to be a good Catholic man. Don't you recall, "Do unto others …"?' Jake looked at Lou and TC with a look of frustration and resignation in his facial expression.

'A man can't win with you two!'

Jake carefully and slowly reversed his car out of the driveway and drove slowly home to his still-awake-and-waiting mother's home.

'That you, Jake?'

'Yes, Mum.'

'What time is it, Jake?'

'After twelve, Mum,' his usual stock answer.

'See you tomorrow, Love.'

'Okay, Mum.'

Jake lay in his bed, trying to sleep. Couldn't. Mind kept racing. 'Those two little bitches are right. I am a bloody hypocrite. Somehow I'm going to get that bloody TC.' A silent voice in his head told him, 'Will have to be pretty illustrious somehow. I'll work something out,' he told himself. 'Shit, I'm Jake Carmichael. I can manipulate just about any bloody thing. Have managed to so far, anyway.' Jake decided he'd work something out, closed his eyes, and slept like the egotistical, 'I can do anything,' spoiled young man he was.

¶

'Get the hell out of here, Jack and Bert!'

'I will speak to you later.'

'Once again! Everyone except Sam, Lou, and TC, piss off now!'

The hordes left, some mumbling, some laughing, some silently wondering what on earth had occurred to drive a young man, born and bred in Brolga, to point a .303 rifle at his head and pull the trigger.

'Get a mop and bucket, Lou. Clean the bloody floor!'

'What on earth possessed you to throw Con's shakes onto the floor?' demanded the sergeant.

'I was upset!'

'Because Sam was pushing my friend around,' replied Lou as she filled the bucket with water at the dispensary sink. TC was racing around, endeavouring to restate the cosmetic stand to its former illustrious, grandiose appearance. Lou had removed the telephone from the cradle ages ago.

'Where the bloody hell is Vance?' asked the sergeant with authority.

'I don't know,' replied TC.

'Why the hell did you come here, Sam? Why didn't you call me?' yelled the sergeant with great antagonism towards Sam. 'I am supposed to be the law in this crappy, shithouse town! Whenever anything dramatic occurs, it comes to my mind that I am usually the last bastard to be notified.'

Sam sat on the floor next to the filing cabinet. She was picking at Brad's blood spots, which adorned her clothes. Sam was crying, coughing, and convulsing. TC picked up the telephone and placed it in the cradle. It rang immediately.

'TC, this is Delores. Where is Vance? I've been trying to call the shop for ages.'

'Mrs Callahan, I do not have a clue where the boss is. Suppose it's a matter of bad timing, Mrs Callahan. The moment I see the boss, I promise I shall tell him you called.'

'Thank you, TC,' was the response as Delores slammed down her end of the telephone. Lou finished cleaning the floor.

'Last time I'm buying Con's stinking thick-shakes,' she said as she emptied the contents of the bucket down the sink before rinsing it and hurling the bucket and mop out back of the dispensary.

'I'm out of this dump! See you later, TC. Good luck, Sam.'

'What about me?' asked the police sergeant. Lou looked him directly in the eyes.

'Why don't you ask my dad about that, Sergeant?' smiled Lou. The police sergeant cracked up.

'You have spirit, girl! If I hang around Brolga long enough, I suppose your old man will be responsible for my burial. Think I had best, for my own future good, be nice to you.'

The telephone rang. Lou picked up the telephone.

'Brolga Pharmacy. Due to unforeseen circumstances, I shall call you back to take your order in around five minutes.' Lou put the phone down. 'I'm out of here, TC.'

'Looks as if I'll be taking orders for this joint again all afternoon!'

'I'll see you after I finish at the telephone exchange.'

'Thank you, Lou,' said a smiling, grateful TC.

'Fuck off,' snarled Sam.

'Tell your dad I think you are a great kid!' laughed the police sergeant. 'Hope he believes me!'

'For your sake, I hope he does, also,' replied Lou as she left.

As Lou exited via the front door, Vance, Neil, and his brothers, along with Faith and Little Joe, entered via the back door. Sam scrammed from her space on the floor near the filing case.

'What the fucking hell is going on here? People coming and going!! What about poor, bloody Brad?'

'Calm down, Sam,' said the police sergeant. 'Mr Callahan is the pharmacist; far as I know, he is the boss here.'

'He might be the fucking boss,' replied Sam loudly and sarcastically.

'Far as I know, my friend, TC, runs the fucking place.' Vance looked around before eyeballing TC.

'Came to collect some money, TC. Think my friends and I should do just that.'

'Great idea, Boss,' agreed TC as she pushed the open button on the cash register, extracted notes, and thrust them at Vance. 'Mrs Callahan called.'

'Okay. If she calls again, tell her I'll see her later.'

'We're going to be opal mining, Little Flower,' said Faith as Vance led the group out the back door.

'Why are you calling the kid "Little Flower"?' asked Neil.

'Because that's what she bloody well looks like,' slurred Faith. They all laughed, including Vance.

'Come on,' as he led them back towards the Majestic.

'Some great business man the pill-pusher is,' said the police sergeant. TC glared at him. How dare he put her boss down! 'Please lock the front door of this joint, TC. Then we'll get to the bottom of this Brad Lester deal with your friend here.' TC went to close the door as instructed. Sam began yelling.

'Don't bring her into it! She's been my friend forever!'

'What happened, Sam?'

'Hell, nothing really,' replied Sam. 'He's been asking me to marry him for months now. Don't think I'm ready for that sort of crap yet. He's threatened to bump himself off a couple of times before. Now the stupid bastard has done it.' Sam was hysterical. Had been for what seemed an eternity to TC.

'No, Sam, he has not killed himself. The bullet just grazed his head.'

'I threw the fucking ring at him,' replied Sam in a quiet, resigned voice. 'Blood went everywhere when he pulled the trigger.'

'He must be a clever shooter,' replied the sergeant. 'He grazed the side of his head, blew off one ear. That's where the blood came from.'

'That means the bastard is going to be okay?' The sergeant nodded.

'He will need reconstruction of his ear; other than that, Brad will be just fine.'

TC leaned down towards Sam, who was crying, either in relief or disappointment—who could tell with Sam?

'Come on, Sam, you are still my friend. We have known each other forever.'

'Sure, that's why I came running to you when all this crap happened.'

'Well, I'm here with you and the sergeant, Sam.' Sam looked up at the sergeant, who was sitting in Vance's chair, wearing an expression of 'Let's get this bloody drama over and done with.'

'I want to see Brad,' said Sam quietly.

'We can organise that. First, we had best go to the police station and get your statement on paper.'

'Fuck you,' snapped Sam. 'I've already told you what happened. What? Are you fucking deaf or something?'

'Please calm down, Sam,' suggested TC.

'Fuck off, TC. You're such a bloody limp-wrist.'

The police sergeant stood up.

'That is definitely enough, Sam. Come on. We're going to the cop-shop, as I believe people like you call it.'

'What's up your butt?' yelled Sam as she looked up at the seething face of the sergeant.

'I'm disgusted with you, Sam! That's what's up my butt! Your boyfriend shoots off his ear, you run over here to your old friend, cause a drama in this God-forsaken town, so much so that the entire joint closed down while all and sundry of who's who in Brolga watched your act unfold. The only person who has stuck by you is your own self-professed best friend of forever, and you have just called her a limp-wrist. Now, come on. We're going to the police station. After I have taken your statement and you have read and signed it, I shall take you to the hospital to see Brad. In my opinion, off the record, of course, the man should run like the wind away from you.'

Sam stood up, wiped each of her cheeks quickly, and looked at TC.

'Sorry, kid. I'd best go with this prick, sign the bloody statement, then go see Brad in the bloody hospital.' TC nodded her head.

'I'm always here for you, Sam.' Sam hugged TC.

'If you had any bloody brains, you would take this asshole cop's advice and also run like the wind from me.'

'Never do that, Sam,' said TC as she squeezed Sam's hand. Sam looked at the sergeant.

'Let's get the fuck out of here, mate.'

'I'm not your mate!' said the sergeant as he marched Sam through the back door of the dispensary. TC felt helpless, knew she couldn't help Sam or Brad, placed the telephone in its cradle, and raced to open the front door as the phone rang.

'Oh, good heavens, it's mail day! Forgot! Where's the boss?' she asked herself as she picked up the phone.

'TC, its Delores. Is Vance there?'

'No, Mrs Callahan, I'm sorry.'

'Where on earth is he?'

'I don't know, Mrs Callahan.'

'Tell him to call me when he comes in, please, TC.'

'Yes, Mrs Callahan, I shall tell him you called and would like him to call you.'

The phone rang once again.

'TC, it's Lou. I have fourteen orders for you.

'Uh, oh, here comes another one. Looks like we'll have a late night. Tell Vance I don't need any more cosmetics. We'll have to come to some other arrangement,' laughed Lou.

'If I ever see the boss, I'll tell him.'

'Putting your call through, TC.'

Poor Sam, poor Brad, TC was thinking, as she automatically spoke into the telephone.

'Good afternoon, Brolga Pharmacy, TC speaking.'

'TC, it's Jake. I'm in Curloo. What the hell has happened there?'

'Jake, how do you know anything happened if you're in Curloo?'

'Bad news travels fast in the bush, TC. I grew up in Mum's house, almost opposite to Brad Lester's parents' place.'

'I'm feeling pretty drained, Jake! Sam threw away a ring Brad had bought for her when he proposed. From what I gather, Brad attempted to shoot himself with his .303 rifle. He shot off his ear and is in hospital. Sam is at the police station, making a statement to the sergeant, who will take her to the hospital to see Brad after she has signed the statement. I have to go now, Jake. The Boss is on the booze again, it's mail day, and I've just about had enough.' TC put down the telephone, which immediately rang again. TC took the order from the cattle-station owner's wife, then phoned Lou at the exchange.

'I'm going to find the boss, Lou. Please do me another favour and take any orders that come in.'

'No problem, TC. Let's get out of this dump soon.'

'Thinking about it, Lou. At the moment I have to go find the boss.'

TC walked furiously across to the direction of Vance's favourite drinking spot.

'Not here, luv,' said Old Jess. 'Haven't seen him all day.'

'He's drinking with the down-and-outers out back of the Majestic,' came Jack Romeo's voice from the smoking room in the Empire.

'Thank you, Mr Romeo,' TC replied through the wooden wall. TC ran down Brolga Street to the Majestic Hotel, through the bar, and into the backyard.

With hands on her hips and emotionally on the verge of tears, she called out, 'Mr Callahan, get back to the shop now! You're a liar, Mr Callahan! You told me you wouldn't drink again. You need to grow up, Mr Callahan. Lou is right, I have to get out of Brolga.'

'Don't be like that, Little Flower,' chorused Faith and Neil. All of them, including Vance, were laughing. TC stamped her foot on the concrete path.

'Mrs Callahan wants you to call her. Mr Callahan. You appear to have forgotten it is mail-order day. Lou has fourteen orders last time I spoke to her. I have taken more than a few. Lou is probably taking more as we speak. Brad Lester shot off his ear. The sergeant has taken Sam to the police station. You are drunk. Mrs Callahan speaks to me as if I am garbage. I expect to see you back at the shop as soon as possible. I need help with the orders!' TC burst into tears, turned, and stormed off via the bar and ran across the street to the pharmacy.

'Little Flower has burst her banks,' said Faith.

'Poor little bugger is beside herself,' added Neil. Neil's brothers and little Joe nodded their heads in agreement. Vance put down his drink and stood in a swaying fashion.

'Better go help her.'

'She's a good kid.'

'Sounds as if she's been to hell and back today while I've been drinking with you poor bastards.'

'If what you have told us is true, Pill-Pusher, you won't be too bloody poor for long,' said one of Neil's brothers.

'We'll see,' said Vance as he staggered away. 'Whatever happens, I'm telling you men, if I make it big, you will all be looked after.'

'We'll see,' said Faith.

'Promises, promises,' said Neil. Little Joe said nothing, just nodded his head. Neil's brothers were out of it. Too far gone to be bothered to respond.

§

TC was crying while collecting goods to pack for a customer when Vance arrived at the pharmacy.

'Please don't speak to me, Boss. Straighten yourself out and call Mrs Callahan, please.' Vance washed his face over the dispensary sink, shook his head, then picked up the telephone.

'Where the hell have you been, Mr Callahan?' demanded Lou.

'Mind your own business, please, Lou. Put me through to Delores.'

'Connecting you now,' replied Lou.

'Vance, where on earth have you been? One of my friends from the Brolga Ladies Golf Club called me and told me just about everyone who is anyone was in the pharmacy today.'

'So?' questioned Vance.

'So, what happened, Vance?'

'Delores, how the hell would I know? I was not here.'

'Where were you, Vance?'

'Delores, I was not here. I'm hanging up now. It's mail day!' Vance picked up the telephone again. 'Lou, keep taking the orders, will you, please?'

'Sure, Mr Callahan,' replied Lou. 'Already told TC I don't need any more make-up.'

'All right, Lou. I'll pay you in cash instead of in cosmetics.'

'See you soon, Mr Callahan. Have mail orders coming out of my ears.'

'Thank you, Lou.'

'Don't thank me, Mr Callahan. Thank TC; she's my friend, not you. See you soon, Mr Callahan. Knock off here in exactly twenty minutes.'

'Thank you, Lou' said Vance.

'Pleasure,' replied Lou sarcastically.

Louise walked in via the back door.

'Hello, lover,' she said to Vance, who was about to speak to TC. TC was furiously putting together a mail order. She was also crying quietly. A customer walked in the front door.

'What's wrong, TC?'

'Perhaps a little dust from one of the shelves got in my eyes.'

'Sure, luv,' said the wife of Old Jock from the Seat of Knowledge. 'What's the problem, luv?'

'Everything,' replied TC quietly as she attempted to compose herself by wiping the tears from her cheeks.

'Do you want to talk about it, luv?'

'No, no, thank you.'

'Usually, things sort out one way or another. I'll come back tomorrow, Luv. You look after yourself,' said Jock's wife.

'Thank you,' replied TC as she felt more tears welling and her voice shaking.

'Take care of yourself, luv,' said Jock's wife as she left. Seconds later, TC heard Louise yelling in the dispensary.

'You rotten bastard, Vance!'

'Louise, you are a married woman.'

'You're a bloody married man. That never stopped you before.'

'Louise, TC is in the shop. She can hear everything we are saying.'

'So, tell the little bitch to piss off to the post office.'

'Louise, it is mail day!'

'So?' screamed Louise.

TC placed the order items she had been gathering on the floor and walked out via the front door, which she closed firmly behind her. She was crying as she talked to herself.

'I'll sit on the Seat of Knowledge while I wait for Lou to finish work and bring the orders.'

As always, Jess was in the bar of the Empire awaiting with concealed loathing the 'afternoon rush of assholes,' as she privately referred to the so-called hierarchy of Brolga as they gathered five days a week after finishing their so-called work for the day. Jess spotted TC crying as she sat down on the Seat of Knowledge.

'You okay, sweetie?' she called from the pub window. 'What a stupid, damned question; of course, you're not okay. You are crying, you poor little bugger. Any mongrel in this hell-hole of a town hurts you, I promise I will take great pleasure in adding rat poison to their drinks.'

TC smiled, once again wiped her cheeks, stood up, and walked over to the Empire window and Jess.

'Come here, young lady,' said Jess as she threw out her arms towards TC, whom she hugged.

'Jess, you'd get into a lot of trouble with the police sergeant if you poisoned anyone.'

'TC, I'm too smart for that,' laughed Jess. 'I'd poison a hundred or so and the police sergeant is so hopeless, he'd think the plague had struck Brolga.'

'I love you, Jess,' said TC as Lou approached them.

'I love you, too, kid,' replied Jess. 'I suggest you get out of this dump while you are still young. Don't want to see you end up like me.'

'I couldn't agree more,' said Lou as she joined them, holding a bundle of notebook pages in her hand.

'Bye, bye, girls,' said Jess. Both TC and Lou smiled at Jess before walking across the road to the pharmacy.

'Best knock loudly before we go in, Lou,' suggested TC.

'Why? TC, these are all the bloody orders to be put together,' replied a tired Lou.

'Louise is in the back with the boss.'

'Screw her,' snarled Lou as she threw open the door. TC collected the items she had previously placed on the floor as Lou loudly announced their presence. 'Mr Callahan, TC, and I are here. I have a handful of phoned-in orders. Will probably take us until midnight at least to get them organised. If you are still there, Louise, I suggest you leave now!' said Lou loudly. 'Unless, of course, you want to stay here half the damned night to help us.' TC and Lou entered the dispensary as Louise made a hasty exit via the back door and Vance adjusted his clothing.

'Okay, girls, let's get to work,' smiled an obviously guilty Vance. Lou slammed the pile of orders on the desk.

'Bloody good idea, Vance. Remember, I'm on cash now!'

'How could I forget?' laughed Vance.

The three of them worked until just after two in the morning. Delores phoned five times before Vance left the telephone off the cradle.

'Never get married!' he said to TC and Lou. Both girls nodded in agreement.

¶

'Here you are, Lou,' Vance said when they had finally finished with the last package stacked by the front door. Vance handed Lou a ten-pound note.

'Ten quid?' said Lou in shock. 'What about TC?'

'She'll get hers later, Lou.'

'Sure, Mr Callahan. You treat her like a mongrel dog.'

'Got to be tough to be kind, Lou. In the meantime, I have to get home to Delores and the kids before she takes off on another bloody spending spree!' Vance brushed his teeth at the dispensary sink and smiled at the girls before leaving via the back door. 'See you girls tomorrow.'

TC pushed the button on the back of the door lock as Lou sat down in Vance's chair, picked a pencil and a blank piece of paper, and began sketching.

'Want a laugh, TC?'

''Anything to make me happy, Lou,' smiled TC. Lou quickly sketched her impression of Vance and Louise having illicit sex on and over Vance's desk. Lou collected the piece of paper and showed TC.

'What do you reckon?' asked Lou.

TC laughed before saying, 'You should leave that on the desk for the boss to see. Let's go home. Been one hell of a day! Sam's boyfriend shot his ear off. Blah, blah, blah, blah!' Lou smiled.

'Yes, let's go home.'

As they left the pharmacy, both girls realised it was cold. Wind from the west was blowing furiously.

'Winter is here,' said Lou as she clutched her hands shoulder to shoulder. 'Think we should run, TC.'

'I think so, too,' agreed TC, also clutching her hands shoulder to shoulder while straightening her back. They ran to the house.

TC sat on the back landing with a blanket around her while Lou took a shower under the hot water. Lou sat on the landing with two blankets wrapped around her while TC took a shower. When TC emerged from the downstairs bathroom, she said, 'Hope it's too cold for the snakes, Lou,' as she raced up the stairs.

'I think it probably is," replied Lou.

A car came screeching to a halt out front of the house, reversed and screeched into the driveway.

'It's Jake,' said Lou.

'So?' replied TC. 'I'm cold and I'm going to bed.'

Jake flung open his car door, raced up the back stairs, and knocked furiously on the door.

'Come in,' said Lou.

TC said, 'Jake, it's late; we are cold. Please go home. It's four in the morning.' Jake entered the room.

'I know it's cold. I've just come from Curloo. I have brought you this coat, TC. I want you to wear it to the movies when I take you on

Saturday night. Want you to be warm.'

'I don't go to movies, Jake.'

'I know,' replied Jake. 'I believe there's a first time for everything.'

Lou laughed.

'Jake, rack off. You must know you are talking to a brick wall when TC is concerned.'

'I'll leave the coat, anyway, TC,' said Jake, as he left by the back door. 'Please lock it,' he yelled.

'Done,' said Lou.

'Let's get some blankets for our beds,' said TC as she went to a closet and saw Auntie Flo's blankets neatly stacked.

'I hate Brolga, Lou. One minute we are hot, then we have a storm that rains dust and mud; now we are all cold.'

'I hate Brolga more than you do,' replied Lou.

'Let's grab these blankets for our beds; I'll see you in the morning.'

¶

Doing the right thing, even though he continued to meet Louise for creek outings, obsessed Vance. One morning TC arrived at the pharmacy to find Vance sitting at his desk.

'Want you to read this, cover to cover and back again,' he said as he pushed a maroon-covered, large Bible-sized book towards her. 'Also want you to be a good girl. Don't want you to be run-of-the-mill. Want you to be perfect!'

'What have I done?' replied a shocked TC.

'Nothing! That's the point. Want you to be a good girl.'

'I am, Boss.'

'Do as I say!' as he threw the Bible-like book across the dispensary towards her. 'By the way, the word for today is perfect. No dictionaries allowed. Give me your translation before the lunch-time whistle sounds.'

TC was crying as she collected the maroon-covered book from the floor.

'Perfect means without imperfections, faultless, always does the right thing, et cetera. Anyway, I've had enough, Mr Callahan.' TC threw the shop keys at Vance. 'Mr Callahan, I liked you much better when you were drinking rum and Coke over at the Empire!' Vance looked at TC with sadness in his eyes.

'Take the AA Bible. I'll have Delores bring the keys to you in the morning. The word for tomorrow is misery.'

TC collected her purse, the AA Bible as instructed, and left the pharmacy. She looked over her shoulder and replied, 'Misery means sad and hopeless. That's what I feel for you, Mr Callahan.'

Vance watched TC walk out the door. 'Poor little bugger, I'm so bloody tough on her.' He collected his thoughts. Won't be business today. Think I'll go to the Majestic, talk those drunks into working for me when I go mining for opal. Don't know how I'll afford a tractor, bulldozer, whatever the hell I'll need. Anyway, one way or the other, I'll do it. I'll do it!

§

The Romeo brothers' pubs had just opened as the announcement came on over the radio station 4CL, "It is 10 am and the Commonwealth Bank is open for business".

Vance closed the front door of the pharmacy, didn't bother to lock it. Who the hell in Brolga would pull a heist on a house, pub, or anything else, let alone a pharmacy.

Bert Romeo had just opened the doors of the Majestic. What the hell is the bloody pill-pusher doing here? he thought. Bastard should be at the Empire.

Five men who looked like they'd been to hell and back straggled through the rear door of the Majestic Bar as Vance entered via the front door. Three of them were brothers grown up in Brolga. Their father had been an alcoholic, long since passed away. He had been a good man. The Seat of Knowledge folk always agreed to that. 'He was a nice, poor bugger. The grog just got to him. After he passed away, his wife had tried her best to keep her family together. The three sons are down the tube. Poor bastards.' The fourth man was a repat from Yugoslavia. Nobody knew very much about him. He was a strong, wiry-looking person. Looked as if he could and would take on the world. He was known by Brolgaites as 'Little Joe,' a name that grew out of Brolgaites sense of humour. The fifth man was the grandson of a pioneer Brolgaite who had come to the area in the early days. His name was Faith. Named by his parents because of his grandparents' hope for success on the land. They had, indeed, been successful; Faith had married a governess who came to work on their property. She broke his heart when one night he returned home early from a muster to find her in a bed with a jackeroo who worked on the station. Faith left almost immediately and decided to end his life by drinking himself to death. Faith was best mates with the oldest of the brothers, whose name was Neil. Neil, like Faith, had been wronged by a woman. Often, they would talk about how the wrong woman could break their bloody hearts and turn a man to drink.

The five men looked pretty seedy to Vance as he approached them. They all slumped over the bar as they waited in anticipation of the beers they were about to have placed on the bar in front of them by the bored barmaid. Just another day selling grog to losers, thought the barmaid, as she looked at their tired, dry faces.

'I'm Vance Callahan,' he announced. 'Seen you about. Been researching opal in the area. Need some good, hard-working men. We all have something in common.'

'What's that?' asked Neil.

'We are all bloody drunks,' replied Vance. Everybody laughed, including the barmaid. 'Don't know how I'll get the equipment. Don't know how I'll . . .'

'We'll do anything.'

'Just need to shake your hands; then I know we have a deal'.

'You have a deal, Pill-Pusher,' said Neil as he stepped forward to shake Vance's hand.

'Me, too,' added Faith.

'All we do around here is drink grog, work on the railway or for the council—when there's work, that is! Fight or bullshit each other the rest of the time.'

'You are late,' snapped Vance when TC arrived ten minutes past starting time.

'I worked late, Mr Callahan. Don't you remember?'

'Don't talk smart to me, TC. Go check the mail. I have to make some phone calls.'

'Here are your keys, Mr Callahan. I quit! And please don't send Mrs Callahan to fetch them to me. I quit! You want the mail? Go get it yourself. By the way, the word for today is rodent. That's what you are!'

'You're joking, TC?' said a shocked Vance.

'No, I'm not, Mr Callahan! You treat me like a mongrel dog. Mrs Callahan loathes me! You and Louise commit adultery every time you are together. That, of course, is none of my business. The bit that upsets me is the fact that she scarcely acknowledges me; when she does, it is to abuse me. Not only that; you meet her at my house so just about the whole town gossips that I am your girlfriend, not Louise. What about her poor husband? What about Mrs Callahan and your children? What about you giving up drinking to go opal mining? What about everything? 'You are forever telling me to be a good girl. Don't do this, don't do that. All I do is come to work. What about you, Mr Callahan?'

Vance's mind was racing. 'She really means it this time! How on earth am I going to handle this bloody joint without her?'

'TC, I was upset when I found this on my desk.' He held up Lou's sketch.

'So, Lou and I thought it was funny. Lord knows, there is rarely anything to laugh about in this God-forsaken place.'

'TC, it is not nice to laugh at other people expense,' replied Vance angrily.

'What do you think the people at the Empire and the shops opposite are doing when they observe me sitting on the Seat of Knowledge for an hour or so two or three times a week? Everyone except Jess laughs at my expense every time I have screamed at you through the Empire window. You laughed along with them. It was always extremely embarrassing, especially when I didn't know what a wench was. The whole town still laughs about that occasionally. Lou hears every phone call when she's on duty; remember? I could go on and on. Sorry, perhaps you'll grow up if you don't have me here to cover for you all the time. You are the best and worst boss in the world.'

Vance was speechless. Everything TC said was true. He was grateful she had not mentioned Anna.

'Please stay, TC,' asked Vance quietly. 'I promise things will get better.' TC stood up.

'I have to go now. Don't know when or where I'll go for now, but I'm going home to finish reading your book. I shall return it when I finish it. I have read it before, only then it was called the Holy Bible.' Vance watched TC's back as she walked away.

What a bloody bastard I am, he thought. A man's a real shit-head. Poor little bugger. First Anna left Curloo because she could no longer work with me. Now TC is leaving Brolga because all and sundry, including myself, treat her as a joke or a dog's body. I was in love with Anna; still am. I also love TC but in a different way. She's like a daughter to me. Suppose that's why I'm always harping at her. If my little girl grows up to be half as fine a person as TC, I'll be a happy man. Vance sat in silence for a few minutes before abruptly standing up to make a phone call.

'Do you want to buy the pharmacy?' he asked his manager in Curloo.

'Yes, Mr Callahan. I sure would like to. Haven't had the courage to ask you if you would like to sell. It's a great business.'

'I know,' replied Vance. 'I want to do other things. Come up with a hundred thousand and it's yours. It's a great business and, if you don't have the money, I'll put in a good word to my old drinking mate who manages the bank in Curloo.'

'Fine,' replied the astonished pharmacist. 'Thank you, Mr Callahan.' Vance picked up the telephone again.

'Suppose you heard that, Lou?'

'Sure did. Which number do you want now?'

'Before you get me any number, Lou, I must say I appreciate your artistic talents.' Vance then asked for the number of a huge second-hand earth-moving-machinery company in Brisbane, had a conversation on what was available and prices, agreed to travel to Brisbane in a couple of weeks' time, put down the phone, picked it up again, asked Lou to take messages, closed the pharmacy doors, and walked across the street to the Empire.

'Are you slumming it?' asked Jess sarcastically when he ordered a double rum and coke.

'No, Jess. I missed your pretty face,' replied Vance with a smile.

'Smart bugger,' said Jess as she all but slammed his drink on the bar in front of him before taking his money. Vance looked around; the bar was empty apart from Jess and himself.

'Where is everyone?' he asked when Jess returned to place down his change.

'You are early; only just opened the doors,' replied Jess.

'You are friends with TC, aren't you, Jess?'

'She's a bloody good kid. That's why I told you to give her a job.'

'She's leaving, Jess.'

'When and why?' snapped Jess.

'She walked out of the pharmacy this morning. I don't know when she's leaving Brolga. Why, well, I suppose for a lot of reasons.'

'I'll bloody well tell you why, you stupid mongrel. She spends too much bloody time on the sacred seat while you entertain your trollops behind the locked doors of your place of business. You've turned her into your slave. She works till all hours of the night on mail and flying-doctor days. She's ridiculed by all the drunken mongrels in this joint whenever she comes looking for you to help her. The poor little bugger has not killed some poor bastard with the wrong medication; just as well she's as smart as she is or she could have.'

'I know, Jess. Give me another drink, please. Has TC been complaining to you, Jess?' asked Vance when Jess returned with his drink.

'I talk to her a lot, Vance, but never once has she uttered one derogatory word about you or anyone else. I think that kid would stick up for you through thick and thin,' added Jess. Vance nodded his head, gulped down his drink, and put his glass on the bar.

'Keep them coming, Jess. Going to be one of those days.'

'Good! I'll warn Jack and Bert,' snapped Jess.

Other drinkers staggered into the bar. Vance ignored them. He sat on the bar stool silently in deep thought and consumed drink after drink. After a couple of hours, Jess became concerned, so went to call Jake Carmichael.

'Tell him to get up here as soon as he can because I'm worried about his mate, the pill-pusher.' Jake was there in a few minutes. Jess caught him at the door of the smoking room.

'What's wrong with Vance, Jess?' asked a concerned Jake.

'He's been sitting there silently for a couple of hours. Just staring into space and drinking like a man possessed. He's not showing any signs of being drunk but he's drinking doubles and he's already gone through a bottle and a half of Bundaberg.'

'Okay, Jess. Thank you. I'll see what I can do.' Jake looked down at Jess as if he were seeing her for the first time. He suddenly realised there was a soft, gentle, caring heart beneath the tough, blunt façade Jess usually portrayed.

'What's the problem, mate?' asked Jake as he seated himself beside Vance. Vance nodded but did not reply.

'Going to buy me a beer, mate?' asked Jake. Vance nodded again. Jake was alarmed.

'On second thought, don't need a beer. I'd best get you out of here, mate. I'll get a bottle of rum and some Coke, and we'll go somewhere to drink it and have a yarn. That okay with you?' Vance nodded his head before saying softly, 'Get two bottles and double the Coke.'

'Okay, let's go,' said Jake when he returned from Jack's bottle room with the booze.

'We'll go to the shop. There no one there,' muttered Vance.

'Where is TC?' questioned a surprised Jake.

'She's reading the Bible,' replied Vance. Jake was confused but said nothing. Vance gave Jake the key to open the door to the pharmacy. Jake opened the door, and Vance walked through to the dispensary, where he turned off the shop lights except for one small light in the dispensary.

Con Kara saw Jake and Vance; so, he quickly crossed the street and spoke to Jake, who was about to lock the door.

'People been coming and going all morning, asking why the joint is closed,' said Con in his heavy Greek accent.

'Do us a favour, Con. Tell them the truth, and tell them you don't know.'

'Smart bastard, aren't you,' laughed Con.

'Con, you can do us another favour,' said Jake.

'Anything, mate,' replied Con.

'I think we'll run out of ice before the grog is finished. Also would you knock us up a couple of your world-famous steak burgers? Give me a call when ready and I'll open the door for you. I'm warning you, though; you can't come in.'

Con nodded. 'You got it, my friend.'

§

Vance sat silently at his desk as Jake poured drinks before turning on the radio and sitting down opposite.

'What's the problem, mate?' asked Jake. 'Not like you to be quiet. Usually, a man can't get a word in after you've had a few.'

'That's me,' replied Vance. 'Always the bloody life of the party. Not today, Jake. Been doing more than a little soul-searching. I'm a low bastard, that's who and what I am.'

'What on earth has brought this on, mate?' enquired Jake with concern.

'Everything, Jake. Just everything. I'll tell you about Vance Callahan, Jake. I'm always the life of the party, but only when I'm drunk. Which, of course, is most of the time. I have a complete personality change with the booze, which I use as an escape route from reality. I do this because the reality of my life is too bloody painful for my own self-tolerance. I have managed to make one hell of a mess of myself. I have bulldozed my route through life, never caring about myself, let alone anyone else. I drink like a maniac, gamble like a man possessed. I'm a womaniser. I've lost count of the women I've had. Ninety-nine percent of the women I've had are faceless. Not ever a memory, Jake. Isn't that bloody terrible?'

'Wish I couldn't remember some I've had, mate,' laughed Jake.

The telephone rang.

'Get that, will you, Jake. I told Lou to take messages.'

'What are you doing answering the phone?' asked Lou.

'That's my business, Lou,' replied Jake.

'Con is coming across. He said to let you know. Mrs Callahan has called five times; she's frantic. Can't blame her. She wants to know why TC isn't answering the phone and if Vance is there. I want to know, too.'

'Okay, Lou. Have to go. Talk to you later.' Con was at the door; Jake took the food and thanked him. 'Con, remember, mate; no one here.'

'Got it,' nodded Con as he walked away towards his café.

'Delores is frantic, mate. Perhaps you should call her.'

'Later!' said Vance, who was facing Jake but looking past him. 'I need another drink. This time, don't be a Scrooge.' Jake laughed.

'Didn't think you'd notice.'

'Two things you can't fool me on, Jake. One is grog, and the other is women. You know, Jake, the reason those women are faceless is because for some reason they get switched on by my drunken, outrageously promiscuous behaviour. Poor sorry souls must be bloody desperate. I have zero respect for them because they possess none for themselves. It's tragic.'

Jake offered Vance a burger.

'Here, mate, you should eat. Con will be upset if he find out you didn't eat it.'

'Screw Con, Jake. I'm trying to have a heart-to-heart with you.' Jake nodded.

'I understand, Vance. I don't feel hungry, either.'

'Look, a poor, bloody Delores stuck at home with the kids whom I rarely see and hardly know. Poor bugger takes off when things get too damned tough for her to tolerate. I know she loves me. I'm just not capable of returning to hear what she gives to me. That's probably why I put up with her spending sprees. I suppose subconsciously I'm trying to make up for the pain I cause her by not giving myself to her. Why would any sane man prefer to spend time with someone like Louise rather than be at home with his wife and kids?'

'Buggered if I know,' replied Jake. The sirens sounded. Almost immediately, they heard someone knocking on the door. Jake looked through the dispensary's one-way glass.

'It's Lou,' he said to Vance.

'Take the messages and get rid of her,' replied Vance in alarm. Jake picked up the packet containing Con's burgers and walked quickly to the door.

'Can' talk Lou. We are having a meeting.'

'Here are the messages. Where on earth is TC?'

'Here, lunch for you and TC. She's at home reading the Bible. Now off you go, Lou. Tell TC I'll come see her tonight.'

'What about me, Jake Carmichael?' asked Lou with feigned disappointment in her voice. Jake laughed as he firmly closed and locked the door.

'Before you sit down, Jake, how about a refill?' requested Vance.

'Gee, mate, perhaps you should slow down.'

'No! I intended to drink until I pass out.'

'Why would you want to do that?' asked Jake.

'Because if I don't, I may be tempted to head for the creek with Louise when she gets off work. She is one bad habit I have to give up. I feel sorry for that poor bloody shearer she married.'

'So do I,' agreed Jake. 'Rumour has it she married him to get even with you.'

'Yes, to make me jealous. Stupid, damned woman. Got some rough mouth on her. Perhaps that is what amuses me. You ever been in love, Jake?'

'Not sure what 'in love' is supposed to feel like. Do know I have never felt for anyone the way I feel about TC.' Vance at last looked Jake directly in the face.

'Leave her alone, Jake. She's too good for you. You are too much like me. That is the reason we get along so well. We are both drunken, womanising, gambling, bullshit artists!'

'Hang on there, mate. I don't drink as much as you do,' replied Jake defensively.

'Not yet! That's because you are a lot younger than I am. Mark my words, Jake; when you are my age, you'll be at the pub drinking, gambling, bullshitting to the barmaids while the poor, unfortunate woman who has been unfortunate enough to marry you will be at home alone wondering where and with whom you are. Leave TC alone, Jake. You can have any Brolga girl you want.'

'No, I can't Vance. I can't get TC, no matter how hard I try,' replied Jake seriously.

'That's because she's not a Brolga girl, and she's far smarter than you are,' smiled Vance. 'And I hope she stays that way, my friend. You know, Jake, I have been in love; still am.'

Jake looked at Vance in surprise, ears alert, waiting anxiously for Vance's next words. Vance told Jake about Anna and how she went away. How she was the reason he came to Brolga. Jake couldn't help but feel sorry for Vance as he told his story with such obvious heartache in his voice. Vance finished his story by saying, 'The only other person I have talked about Anna to is TC.'

'I wonder if you will ever see Anna again, mate,' questioned Jake.

'I don't know. Isn't it ironic. I love and respect only three living females. Delores, who puts up with all the crap I lay on her and is the mother of my children. She leaves me repeatedly. My darling Anna, the love of my life, left me. Just went away. Now dear little TC, whom I love as a daughter, is going away, leaving.'

'Where? When?' asked Jake in shocked alarm.

'Don't know, Jake. Don't think the kid knows herself. Anyway, I'm going opal mining. Perhaps I'll fall in love with Opal,' laughed Vance. 'Give me another drink.'

'Think you should look at these messages, mate,' suggested Jake as he handed the pieces of paper to Vance. Vance flicked through them.

'Delores, Delores, Delores, Delores, Delores, two orders, pharmacy manager in Curloo, Delores,' mumbled Vance.

'Vance, mate, don't mean to tell you how to run your life, but perhaps you should call Delores. Poor woman is obviously worried witless about you. Personally, I don't blame her.'

'Suppose you're right, Jake,' replied Vance as he stood up and approached the telephone in a staggering fashion. As he was about to pick up the telephone, it rang.

'It's Lou. I'm back. Do you want me to keep taking messages?'

'Thank you, Lou. Before you go, put me through to my house, please.'

'About time you called Mrs Callahan,' replied Lou.

'Just do it, Lou, that's the girl.'

'It's me, Delores,' said Vance hesitantly into the receiver.

'About time. I've been out of my mind with worry. Where have you been?'

'Here,' replied Vance innocently.

'Don't lie, Vance. I have been calling all day,' snapped Delores.

'I told the telephonist to take messages because I have been in an important meeting.'

'What meeting and why couldn't TC answer the phone?'

'An important meeting, and TC is busy taking care of a project I gave her. What do you want, Delores?'

'I just wanted to know you are all right.'

'Delores, I assure you that should anything occur rendering me not all right, you would know in a heartbeat. Bye, now.' Vance put down the phone and staggered back to his desk.

'Think I'll make you some coffee, mate,' suggested Jake. 'How about we drink a couple or three cups, then I'll drive you home. Delores loves you; she's worried about you. She'll feel better if she knows you are safely at home when you go to sleep.'

'Coffee won't put me to sleep, Jake. It will wake me up.'

'Okay, then, how about you drink some iced water, brush your teeth, and wash your face with iced water; then I'll drive you home.'

'She'll be in a terrible, bloody mood, Jake.'

'No, she won't. She'll be relieved to see you. Come on, mate, clean your teeth, get rid of your Bundy breath. I'll bring some ice.'

'You are a great friend, Jake,' said Vance.

'So are you, Vance,' replied Jake.

¶

Jake pulled his car to a halt in front of Vance's house.

'Thanks. I'm going to have a sleep,' said Vance as he got out of the car, straightened his shoulders, and walked up the stairs.

Incredible, thought Jake, he's walking as straight as a sober judge.

Vance did not announce his arrival. He laid down immediately on the bed on the front verandah and immediately fell asleep. Delores was unaware that Vance was home until she went to close the front door quite a while later. She felt surprise, love, and relief simultaneously. Jake drove to the Empire after leaving Vance. He wanted to talk to Jess.

'Thank you, Jess. My mate is in a pretty bad way. Today, Jess, I have learned a very important lesson from you and Vance. We should never judge a book by its cover. My mother has been telling me that since I was about ten years of age. Today I realised she is absolutely correct. TC is leaving Brolga, Jess.'

'I know, Jake,' replied Jess with a sad smile.

'Anyway, I'd best get back to work, Jess. Thank you once again.'

Jess watched through the Empire window as Jake got into his car and drove off. She said silently to herself, 'The arrogant young play boy does possess a few fine qualities, after all.' Before shrugging her shoulders and donning her tough persona, 'Still a mongrel,' she muttered to herself. 'They all are.'

Once in his shop, Jake phoned Lou.

'Hi, Jake. I'm just about to finish for the day. I have more messages for Vance. I'll put them under the door on my way home.'

'I'll pick you up, Lou.'

'Sure, Jake. I have to buy some groceries; so, if you drive me, we'll save wear and tear on my shoes. Like that Elvis guy with his blue suedes, Jake. I love my shoes.'

Jake collected Lou, drove her to the grocery shop, waited while she shopped, pulled by the pharmacy so Lou could slide the messages under the door, then drove her home. Lou got out of the car, collected her purchases, closed the car door, and smiled at Jake, who was also out of the car.

'Thank you, Mr Carmichael; I shall recommend you to all of my friends as a superb car service. I'm sorry I can't invite you in; Miss TC is not receiving guests today. See you later, Jake.' Lou laughed as she walked away. She would remember that look of shock and dismay on Jake's face forever. Serves him right, she thought, as she heard the gravel fly and Jake's car torpedo up Brolga Street.

The police sergeant was talking to Jack and Bert Romeo out in front of the Majestic when Jake's car flew past at break-neck speed.

'I'll catch that smart young bastard one day,' said the sergeant, shaking his head from side to side.

'You'll have to be pretty quick, my friend,' said Jack Romeo. They all laughed, then went their separate ways.

Jake was furious. He drove to the end of the bitumen road about five miles west of Brolga, parked under an old gum tree, and embarked on a silent journey of soul-searching. Jake snapped out of his thoughts when he realised it was dark and he was feeling cold. He turned the ignition key, turned his car around, and drove slowly to his mother's house. Thel Carmichael was surprised to see Jake home so early.

'You are early, Jake. It's just past seven-thirty.'

'Got a headache, Mum,' replied Jake after kissing Thel on the cheek. 'I'm going to bed, Mum.'

Thel Carmichael was relieved. She thought, I'll have a night off from worrying when I hear his car pull into the driveway. Raising her head to the ceiling, 'Thank you, dear Lord,' she said quietly.

¶

Lou and TC were huddled up in chairs, each wrapped in a blanket. They had managed to master the art of lighting Auntie Flo and Uncle Doug's kerosene heater, which was gradually heating the small lounge room. 'Where the Boys Are' was playing on the stereo.

'They sure are not here,' quipped Lou. TC shrugged.

'Who needs them, Lou?'

'Obviously, you and I don't,' replied Lou. 'Have you finished Vance's book?'

'I'll finish it tomorrow.'

The record was finished. They could hear the glass louvres on the western side and the front of the verandah rattling.

'Dad was right, as usual,' remarked Lou. 'He said we'd get a dust storm this week.'

'Oh, no!' from both of them as they stood up. TC raced downstairs to retrieve a few items of clothing from the clothes line and firmly shut the laundry and bathroom doors while Lou bundled up the pillows and covers from the verandah bunks, fetched them inside, and closed all the inner doors under which they jammed old towels as a feeble attempt to keep out the dust.

TC had not yet mentioned to Lou that she had quit her job. Lou assumed Vance, in one of his idiosyncratic moods, had ordered TC to go home and not to come back until she had finished reading his revered book.

As they settled themselves back in front of the heater, 'Lou, how come it gets so cold here so quickly?'

'Never bothered to ask, TC. Have you tried on the coat Jake brought you yet?'

'No!'

'TC, it's beautiful. Have you even had a good look at it?'

'No!'

'Why?' asked Lou as she stood up.

'Think I'll turn on 4CL. Perhaps we'll hear Old Slim if we are lucky.'

The telephone rang alongside where TC was sitting.

'TC, it's Jake.'

'Yes, Jake.'

'I want to come see you.'

'Jake, Lou and I are busy. Apart from that, the wind is howling.'

'I know, TC. There's a dust storm coming.'

'I'm not afraid of some wind and dust.'

'I want to come see you.' TC sighed.

'Look, Jake, the fact of the matter is that my boyfriend from Memphis arrived in Brolga this afternoon. He's come a long, long way to see me; so, the least I can do is give him my total attention.'

'What's his name?' asked Jake seriously.

'You wouldn't know him, Jake.'

'Try me.'

'Well, if you must know, his name is Elvis Presley.'

Bitch, thought Jake, as TC hung up her end.

The wind grew stronger. Slim was belting out, When the Rain Tumbles Down, on 4CL.

'What about the dust blowing in, Slim?' asked Lou, staring at the radio. 'TC, I really do loath living in Brolga. It must be the worst town in the world.'

TC shook her head.

'Doubt that, Lou. I always thought my home town was the worst place on earth. Now I know it's not. Besides, there are some nice people here.'

'Name me a dozen,' demanded Lou. TC nodded her head and thought for a few seconds.

'Your parents. You. Thel Carmichael. Con Kara. Jess. Carmel from the little dress shop. My boss. Jock's wife. The two truckies across the road. Auntie Flo and Uncle Doug. There you go, Lou; that's thirteen.'

'You can't count Uncle Doug and Auntie Flo because they are not here,' argued Lou.

'Fair enough, Lou. I'll take them away and reluctantly add Jake; that's twelve.' Lou gave one of her 'I surrender' shrugs.

'Okay, TC, you win.'

The wind blew furiously. The dust came and enveloped the town. It permeated every nook and cranny. Even though the girls had buffered the bottom of the inner doors, the dust still managed to cloud the lounge room where they sat.

'Think of all those white shelves, bottles, boxes, packets, and everything else you'll have to clean, TC.'

Poor Boss, thought TC.

'You are probably a little bit right, Lou. This is probably one of many potential "worst towns" in this part of the world.'

'Let's get out of here, TC,' Lou all but begged.

'Probably, Lou,' replied TC quietly. Lou couldn't hide her excitement. 'We could go anywhere—Brisbane, Sydney, Melbourne. Anywhere.'

'Not quite, Lou,' from a very serious TC. 'We don't have very much money, and we are both leaving great jobs behind.' Lou interrupted.

'TC, admittedly I have a great job. Yours is a different story. If it weren't for Jake and me helping out, you would be dead by now. No wonder you're so thin.'

'Well, Lou, the boss helped me when he gave me the job. He's been good to me. I have learned a lot from him. He's a good boss, Lou; he's just a bit troubled.'

'A bit!' exclaimed Lou.

'Lou, let's leave this conversation alone.' Lou nodded her head in agreement. TC stood up, stretched, and said, 'Let's go to bed, Lou. You have a day off tomorrow; suggest we get up early and get rid of the dust.'

'Sounds good,' from Lou as she turned off the radio and the lights. 'See you in the morning.'

§

The girls were sweeping and hosing the wooden verandah when Vance arrived. TC saw him first.

'Oh, no, Boss, please don't ask me,' she said. Vance smiled when he reached the top step.

'Doing a good job there, ladies. I've got a pharmacy up the street that needs a good clean-up. Are you interested after you're finished here? Got flying-doctor and mail day tomorrow.'

'How much are you paying, Vance?' asked Lou with great interest. 'I need all the money I can get at the moment.' Vance laughed.

'I'll pay you two quid an hour, Lou.' He looked directly at TC, who had been ignoring him. 'What about you, TC? Will you help me out?'

'I told you I didn't want the keys.' Vance nodded.

'That is not quite correct. You told me not to send Delores with the keys. I didn't; I brought them myself. Please, TC,' he said with a desperate expression on his face.

TC shrugged and sighed.

'I'll think about it. Don't leave the keys. That means you'll have to be at the pharmacy and not in the hotel when and if we come.'

Vance smiled. 'You're a tough girl, TC.'

'I had a good teacher in you. Perhaps we'll see you later.'

Vance was gone.

'Come on,' said Lou. 'Let's get cleaned up here so we can go help Vance. Two quid an hour, TC. I can't turn my back on that. How many hours do you think it will take to do the job?'

'Usually takes me three days with interruptions if I start early, skip lunch break, and work late. You already know that, Lou. Anyway, I haven't decided to do it yet. After all, I did quit yesterday. If I do it, I shall do it only because I feel sorry for the boss. Lou, I really, sincerely hope he goes opal mining. At least it will get him out of this hopeless place where getting drunk at the Romeos' hotels is the only outlet he has.' TC finished closing the louvres. 'I'm going downstairs to hose down the outside now.'

'Okay, I'll start inside,' said Lou.

¶

By 10 am, when the hotels and banks were opening, the house was as dust-free as it would or could ever be. Everything was clean.

'Come on, Lou, let's go clean up the pill-pusher's shop. Better take our bucket and duster; there's only one of each up there.'

Jake was on the footpath in front of Carmichael and Carmichael, chatting to a couple of nurses, who were laughing loudly when TC and Lou passed by on the opposite side of the street.

'Good morning, ladies,' yelled Jake from across the road. Lou waved and TC nodded.

'They must be a couple of Jake's harlots,' said Lou.

'Who cares,' TC replied.

'What a nightmare,' grimaced Lou when they entered the pharmacy.

'Tell me about it, Lou. I figure out it's faster and easier to start at the front and work towards the back. Looks like there's been a delivery,' said TC as she spotted twenty or so large cartons lying willy-nilly all over the floor. Vance was on the telephone in what was obviously a serious conversation.

'Okay, Lou, let's stack these cartons in the middle of the floor; that way we can work around them.' They stacked the cartons neatly.

'You can take one side of the shop and I'll do the other. I'm going next door to borrow a ladder while you fill the buckets with hot water and suds.' TC returned a few minutes later.

'Let's get started, Lou. if we're lucky, we'll be finished by midnight.'

Vance eventually got off the telephone. TC didn't give him a chance to speak.

'Mr Callahan, please don't go to the hotels today because when customers come in or the phone rings, I'll have to get down and let the cleaning wait.'

'Fair enough, TC. I've just sold the Curloo shop. That means I'm definitely going mining.'

'That's wonderful,' smiled TC.

'Sure is,' chirped Lou. 'Perhaps you'll put this dump on the map.'

'I hope so. I know it won't be easy. I know virtually nothing about it apart from what I have read. Anyway, we'll give it a go.'

Vance was at the counter when Jake's voice came from the doorway.

'See you've got your char ladies on the job, mate.'

'Rack off, Jake. Some of us have to work for our money instead of standing around on footpaths flirting,' snapped Lou without turning her head to look at him.

'What, Lou, don't tell me you are jealous?' asked Jake sarcastically. Lou ignored him. 'How's TC?' asked Jake. 'Suppose your boyfriend has gone back to Memphis? Got scared by the dust storm?' TC also ignored him. Vance rolled his eyes.

'Come in, mate. I have been advised that I am not allowed to leave the premises. Thank God, we have some leftovers from yesterday. You have no idea how I'm hanging out for a "hair of the dog".' Jake laughed.

'Can't say I blame you, mate. It was a bloody big dog. You knocked off a bottle and a half at the Empire and two-thirds of a bottle here.'

'No wonder a man is crook,' laughed Vance as he retrieved ice and Coke from the refrigerator.

'Do you remember what you told me?' enquired Jake quietly.

'I don't know. I do recall we were here for quite a while, and I remember waking up on the verandah bed at home in the middle of the dust storm.'

'Some storm, wasn't it, mate?' said Jake as he lit a Rothman cigarette and Vance a Craven A. Jake didn't bother to tell Vance he'd had a terrible night. Not only because of the storm, but mostly because of his talk with Vance. They picked up their glasses, wished each other good luck as they clicked and put their first drink of the day to their lips. That first drink was followed by many more. They sat there talking mostly about Vance's forthcoming venture into opal mining until siren time.

'TC, is it all right if we go to the Empire now?' asked Vance.

'Not up to me,' replied TC.

Once the two men were outside with the door closed behind them, Jake said, 'Vance, mate, we don't want a repetition of yesterday. How about coming home to Mum's for lunch? There's always plenty of tucker at Mum's house. Besides that, she'd enjoy talking to you.'

'All right; sounds good, Jake.'

The girls kept working. They were a third of the way down the main shop when Vance and Jake returned from lunch. Each of them was carrying a plate with corned beef and salad and a slice of buttered fresh bread.

'Jake's mother sent this for you workers,' said Vance, who also produced a tea towel containing two knives and forks.

'How lovely of her,' said TC.

'I agree,' added Lou.

'I told Mum I am taking both of you to the movies on Saturday night. She has invited you both for a meal before we go. Mum said she will go with us if that would make you feel more comfortable, TC.'

You are a manipulating rat, Jake, thought TC. I already told him I won't go; so, he invites Lou and has his mother inviting us to dinner. No choice now; Mrs Callahan is a really nice lady. Lou could see TC was seething.

'You always get your own way eventually, don't you, Jake?'

'Usually, Lou,' Jake smiled and nodded his head.

'Spoiled rat, that's what you are, Jake Carmichael,' spat Lou.

'I'll call your mother and thank her, Jake,' from a resigned-to-the-situation TC.

The girls quickly ate their food and resumed work. Vance and Jake resumed drinking until closing time, when they left.

The girls finished cleaning the shelves in the main shop around ten, then began to unpack the new stock and transfer it to the now-clean shelves. When done, they flattened the large cartons and put them out at the back of the shop.

'You sweep the floor, Lou; I'll follow you with the mop,' suggested TC.

It was three in the morning when everything, including the dispensary, was finished. They were both beat.

'I'm buggered,' mumbled Lou as she yawned.

'That make two of us,' agreed TC.

'TC, let's skip our showers and just have a lick and a promise before we go to bed.'

'Suits me, Lou. Let's go,' answered TC as she collected the door keys Vance had left in a convenient, not-to-go-unseen location in the centre of his desk. Lou picked up the bucket and duster and wet cleaning cloths as they left. Naturally, the street was deserted at that time of the morning. There was a slight cold wind blowing.

'We'd better run again, Lou; don't know about you, but I feel as if I'm freezing.'

'Let's run.' They did so, as fast as they could both bolding the handle of the bucket between them.

Brushed teeth and licked and promised, they were in their beds and asleep in twenty minutes. Both girls' last thought before they feel asleep was, 'Hope we get out of Brolga soon.'

§

A little before 8 am TC was woken by Lou pushing her on the shoulder.

'What's the matter, Lou?'

'Perhaps I'm sleep-walking. You are wanted on the telephone.'

'If I have to get out of bed, I will be sleep-walking as well. Who is it?'

'I don't know. I'm going back to bed. Do me a favour. Leave the phone off the hook. I want to get some more sleep. I'm working four to midnight today.'

TC stumbled to the telephone.

'Hello, whoever it is; I'm still asleep.'

'TC, it's Vance. I'm calling from Curloo. I had to come here to sign some papers for the pharmacy.'

'So? Why couldn't it wait until tomorrow? It's doctor day; also mail day.'

'I know. That's why I'm calling you. Will you handle the place for me today? Couldn't wait till tomorrow; it's Saturday. The bank and lawyers are closed.'

'I told you I quit three days ago. What on earth are you going to do when I'm not here to call?'

'I don't know, TC. I'm worried witless about that. Please do it for me, TC! Please!' TC knew she had no choice.

'All right', she replied, shaking her head in disbelief.

'Thanks, kid. See you when I see you.' Vance was gone.

'Who was that?' asked Lou from her bed as TC passed by on the way to the shower.

'The boss. He's in Curloo. I'm going to work.'

'I didn't recognise his voice. I must be tired,' replied Lou softly before turning her back to her bedroom door and hugging her pillow. 'I'm going back to sleep; don't have to start till four.'

When TC emerged from the bathroom Lou was sitting on the top back step clutching a towel.

'Thought you were going back to sleep, Lou,' came from a surprised TC.

'Don't be crazy, TC. From nine to four is seven hours. That means I will earn fourteen quid. Wild horses couldn't keep me away.'

'Thank you, Lou. We had best hurry. The phone orders will begin to come in at exactly nine.'

¶

As predicted, the telephone was ringing when they walked into the pharmacy at exactly nine. It kept ringing until siren time when the station people assumed the place would be closed for an hour. There were at least twice the number of orders as usual because the weather had suddenly turned so cold that people were stocking up on provisions of cold and flu potions. Coupled with that, the prescription-bearing doctor's patients began arriving around eleven. There were also many more of them than usual as a result of the dramatic change in the weather.

When TC closed the doors at siren time, Lou said, 'Good heavens, TC, Vance sure knows when to desert a sinking ship! This place is bloody bedlam.'

'I know, Lou. I'm so grateful you are here to answer that damned phone. I have to get moving on filling these prescriptions. I have around a dozen people coming back after two. I'll gather the medication and you type the labels, okay?' Lou nodded her head as TC started counting pills.

'Delores has called for Vance four times,' came from Lou. 'She obviously doesn't know he's in Curloo.'

'Some things never change, Lou.'

¶

They finished with the prescriptions a little before two.

'Wish I had you here all the time, Lou.'

'Perhaps we can sublet the joint from Vance,' quipped Lou.

'Sure, Lou,' laughed TC. 'I only qualify as a practical pharmacist. There is also an essential successful course in theory required before I could acquire the necessary piece of paper to make me legal.'

The telephone rang. It was Delores.

'TC, where is Vance and why is Lou there answering the telephone?'

'He's not here, Mrs Callahan, and Lou is here helping me because she doesn't start work at the exchange until four today.'

'Does Vance know she's there?'

'Yes, Mrs Callahan. It's very busy—it's doctor day and mail-order day.'

'Tell him to call me when he comes in.' Delores was gone.

TC put down the telephone and went to open the door to receive the people wanting their prescriptions. The next hour passed quickly with TC explaining their medications as they signed their prescriptions, paid, and one by one left.

TC had long ago noticed the patience displayed by the majority of these bush town inhabitants when it came to waiting their turn. She apologised for the seemingly slow, long drawn-out procedure as she hurried as best she could. Not one of them seemed to mind at all. If anything, they appeared grateful. TC mentioned this to Lou when the last script recipient had gone.

'That's because they have never had a pharmacy here before Vance opened up. They are grateful for the convenience of just popping in here immediately after they have seen the doctor. Before Vance, often they would have to wait a week or more if the hospital didn't have the medication the doctor prescribed.'

'I see. Didn't think of it that way. Lou, will you keep answering the phone while I start collecting these orders? How many are there, Lou?'

'Lost count,' replied Lou as the phone rang. Lou kept taking phone orders, and TC got on with collecting, charging, packing, wrapping, and labelling orders until a quarter to four, when Lou broke their verbal silence to say, 'I'm off now, TC. Feel like a rat leaving you with all this.' Lou handed TC another fistful of orders. 'I'm going to Con's to get a thick-shake, then straight to work. I'll take the afternoon orders if you would like. Call me after closing time and I'll give them to you.'

'Thank you, Lou. As your dad would say, your blood's worth bottling.' Lou laughed as she walked out the door. TC kept at it. She was on a mission. A few more prescriptions were brought in. She filled them calmly and methodically.

'No point in stressing out,' she told herself. She had already resigned herself to the fact that it would be another all-night deal. 'I should bring my bed here,' she said to herself. She closed the doors at five-thirty before calling Lou.

'How are you progressing?' asked Lou.

'Looks like I'll be here 'til three again, if not later.'

'You'll be old before you're of age, TC.'

'I'm old already, my friend,' sighed TC.

Lou thought for a few seconds before replying, 'Yes, I suppose you are ... I've nine more orders. I'll bring them after I finish at midnight. And Vance called. He said to tell you he's going to Brisbane to buy a bulldozer or tractor or something like that. He said to tell you he's going to ask you to look after the place until he gets back. He seemed relieved that he got me instead of you. I told him he should call Delores. Poor woman has called twice more since I came to work at four. He said he would call her later.'

'I can't believe this, Lou. Think I'll throw some pipe cleaner down my throat. I'd slit my wrists except I can't stand the sight of blood after seeing Sam the other day.' Lou ignored TC's threat of suicide.

'Vance said I should help you whenever you need me. At his expense of two an hour, of course. See you when I finish work, TC.' Lou hung up from TC, then called Carmichael and Carmichael, hoping she would catch Jake before he headed for the Empire. She was in luck; Jake answered the phone.

'Jake, I'm sorry I have to decline your kind invitation to accompany you and TC to the movies tomorrow night. That means I also miss out on one of your Mum's great meals. Suggest you tee it up with your Mum to make it next week because I know TC won't go unless I do. TC is flat out, pushing sand uphill at your mate's pharmacy. She's got orders to the ceiling. I think it would be a grand and endearing gesture on your part if you happened to drop by and offer your assistance. I'll see you both around midnight. Don't let me down, Jake. See you.' Lou hung up, smiling to herself. 'That will fix Jake and his 'I get everything I want' attitude.'

Jake stood holding the telephone in his hand. Women! he thought. A man couldn't get a bloody word in. He called his mother, told her to put the roast on hold until next week, and not to stay awake worrying about him because he would be helping TC at the pharmacy until late. Thel Carmichael was happy her son was going to help TC; that way she didn't have to worry about him getting drunk at the Empire, then driving at break-neck speed to the hospital, then to the creek with one of those tarty nurses in tow. Thel never mentioned to Jake that she was aware of his wild ways. She gleaned her information from her Auntie Carmel, who knew everything about everybody. After all, it was Carmel who had first old her what a nice lass TC was.

¶

Jake pulled alongside the kerb in front of Brolga Pharmacy, walked across to Con's Café, and ordered a couple of burgers for around seven. 'Please deliver, will you, mate?'

'Sure, mate,' Con answered, with his usual smile. 'By the way, mate, when are we having a game of cards?

'Soon, mate, soon,' from Jake as he headed for the Empire to buy some beer and Rothmans. A few minutes later, Jake walked through the rear door of the pharmacy, opened a beer, sat at Vance's desk, and lit a Rothmans.

TC was unaware of his presence. She was busy and had turned up the radio after she locked the front door; so, she did not hear him come through the back.

Jake sat sipping his beer and enjoying his cigarette as he silently observed TC through the dispensary's one-way mirror.

'Bloody hell, she's lovely. Not only that, she's smart as well as being fiery and a bloody hard worker. Why the hell can't I get her to like me? She always heads me off at the pass. She must have ridden with John Wayne in a former life, I reckon. Little bitch.' With that Jake realised his other beers were not in the fridge. He stood up and purposely coughed loudly as he opened refrigerator door.

TC heard his cough and turned in surprise.

'What are you doing here, Jake?'

'You should remember to lock the back door. Jack the Bloody Ripper could creep up behind you'.

'In Brolga? I doubt it, Jake. I must, however, remember to lock it to keep the likes of you out.'

'Don't be like that, little TC. I have been summoned by Miss Lou to help you with your burden.'

'Thank you, Jake. I appreciate it. You can pack, wrap, tie, and label; I shall collect and charge.'

'You're on, Boss,' smiled Jake sarcastically.

They worked without speaking until Con knocked on the front door. Jake went to open it.

'Put them on plates for you, mate. Also brought a shake for the little one. Poor kid has been here all day without anything. Where the hell is pill-pusher?'

'I don't know, replied Jake. 'You know Vance, mate; he could be anywhere. Where is Vance?' enquired Jake, as he turned to look at TC. TC rolled her eyes.

'He told Lou to tell me he's gone to Brisbane to buy a bulldozer or tractor. I might run over him with whatever he buys when he gets back.' Con smiled at TC.

'I detect a little bit of anger in those words, young lady. I better go; the wife will be after me with a meat cleaver if I'm away too long. She keeps a pretty close eye on me.'

¶

'Let's eat, TC; you must be starving.' TC went to the sink to wash her hands. She's clean, too, thought Jake, as he followed suit.

'I think I need to sit down for a few minutes more than I need food, Jake. I'm more than a little tired.'

They ate while listening to the radio station 4CL. Both of them burst into laughter when Slim came on.

'Poor Old Slim follows us wherever we go, doesn't he, TC?' TC nodded her head, laughing.

'You can say that again. Sure, Lou and I know his entire repertoire word for word.'

'He's a nice bloke. He's done a few concerts here. The town hall was packed out each time,' said Jake seriously.' TC couldn't stop laughing.

'Poor Slim must have been pretty desperate for a dollar to come to Brolga, Jake.'

'Not at all. He likes coming here, and the people here like him,' stated Jake defensively.

'I'm sorry, Jake. I mean no offence to either Mr Slim or the people of Brolga. It is simply that his songs are played on the radio at least a million times a day,' replied TC seriously.

'Well, Slim is a bushman, you know. I imagine people in Memphis get tired of hearing your boyfriend, Elvis, all the time, as well. What's the difference?'

TC stood up.

'Time to get back to work. Thank you for the food, Jake. By the way, are you jealous of Elvis, Jake?' Jake scowled.

'Of course, I'm bloody well jealous of the mongrel. He can probably get any woman in the world if he takes a fancy to them.'

'Well, Jake, I suggest you learn how to sing and play a guitar.'

'I heard he can't play the guitar; he just pretends.'

'That's okay, Jake; he can still pull in the women. We don't care if he can play the guitar or not.' Jake smiled once more with sarcasm.

'Well, he's in Memphis. I am here.' TC ignored him.

They worked methodically. Jake attempted to make jokes for a while. TC ignored him; so, Jake decided he drink his beer and ignore her as well. The telephone rang a little before midnight. Jake was close; so, he answered it.

'Yes, Lou.'

'It's not Lou. It's Vance. What are you doing there, Jake?'

'I'm helping TC. Been a bummer day here, mate. Lou's coming soon with more orders to fill. You'll have to put me on the pay roll,' laughed

Jake. Vance laughed on the other end of the phone.

'Sure, mate. I'll pay you the same as I pay Lou—two quid an hour. Get TC, will you, Jake?'

'I'd like to,' replied Jake.

'I told you, Jake; she's too bloody good for you. Leave her alone.'

'Don't think I've got much choice, mate. TC, your boss wants to talk to you.'

'Yes,' said TC into the telephone. 'Where are you?'

'Some petrol stop in the middle of nowhere. Had to wake some poor bugger out of his bed to sell me fuel.'

'I'm not happy, Mr Callahan. You tricked me. You do recall I quit, do you not?'

'You didn't mean that, TC,' he laughed.

'Yes, I did mean it and, by the way, you are drunk. Drive carefully; pull up when you are tired.' TC hung up.

¶

Lou arrived and changed the radio station to 2UE. Jake became inebriated as he drank beer after beer. It was almost four in the morning when the last package was placed on the huge, neatly stacked pile at the front of the shop.

'I'm buggered,' said Jake as TC turned off the lights and locked the doors. Both girls nodded their heads in agreement.

'It's freezing,' complained Lou as they stepped into the cold westerly wind.

'Freeze the do-das off a brass monkey,' added Jake. 'Jump in. I'll get you home.'

Frank Michaels and his mate were at the trucking yard as Jake drove by. Jake sounded his air horn and they waved.

'Those poor buggers must be cold,' said Jake. The girls jumped out of the car and bolted towards the top of the stairs and the front door.

'I'm not even brushing my teeth; I'm going straight to bed.'

'That'll do me, too, Lou. Doubt our teeth will decay beyond

redemption in just a few hours. Wish tomorrow was Sunday so I could sleep in.'

'Well, I sure am sleeping in, TC. Good night. I'm taking the phone off the hook so it can't wake me.' Both girls were asleep the moment their heads hit the pillows.

¶

TC groggily reached for her alarm clock the moment it sounded at 8 am.

Hope it didn't wake Lou, she thought. She was showered, dressed, and at the shop at eight forty-five to meet the truckies who would collect the parcels.

'No wonder you were working so late. Must be half the bloody chemist shop in these.'

'Not quite,' said TC as she carted the orders to the truck.

'How do you know I worked late?'

'My mates told me when I got to work this morning. Where's your boss?' enquired the young man.

'He's in Brisbane. He's working on going opal mining and he's gone to buy some sort of earth-moving machine.'

'So, it's true, eh? Heard the mad, drunken prick was talking about having a go at that.'

TC sighed, threw the packages she was carrying onto the back of his truck, saying, 'Just who do you think you are? Don't criticise my boss! Carry the rest yourself!' she called out as she stormed inside.

'I should learn to keep my bloody mouth shut around her. This is the second time we've had a run-in. Little bitch is Little Miss Bloody Dynamite, all right.'

¶

The morning went quickly. There were quite a few customers, mostly for cough and cold medicines. Two of Jake's nurse friends came in for lipsticks.

'Do you know Jake Carmichael?' asked one of them.

'He's my boss' best friend,' replied TC politely as she imagined Jake's mouth plastered with these lipsticks at some time in the near future.

'Is he your friend, as well?' asked the second nurse.

'Not really. I tolerate him. Will that be all, ladies?' They left and TC heard them giggling loudly once they were outside the shop.

Come closing time TC was surprised when she realised the telephone had not rung all morning.

'Thought the boss would have called. Hope he's all right.' Surprisingly, not even Mrs Callahan had called.

Con waved to her as she closed the shop. She remembered his plates and milkshake container, so she went back inside and collected them. She was feeling foolish crossing the street with Con's plates and container in one hand and a loaf of bread in the other when Jake parked his car almost in front of Con's and stepped out with the two lipstick-buying nurses.

'Hello, TC. Care to join us for a few drinks?' invited Jake. TC rolled her eyes.

'Jake Carmichael, wake up to yourself.' Jake and the nurses all laughed and walked off towards the Empire.

'Don't worry, TC.' smiled Con. 'Jake is just trying to show off in front of those tarts.'

'I'm not worried, Con. Thank you for these,' she said as she handed him his things.

TC went home and directly to bed. She didn't hear Lou leave for work. She was awakened by a loud knocking on the front door. It was dark. She stumbled out of bed and switched on her bedroom light before making her way to the door.

'Who is it?' she asked through the door.

'It's Jake the Bloody Ripper again.' She heard Jake's voice and opened the door. 'What's wrong?'

'You're wrong, that's what is wrong.'

'Why?'

'Vance has been trying to contact you all afternoon, not to mention my mother trying to reach you for me, for that matter. Vance just phoned

Mum in panic mode, so Mum called me at the Empire, and here I am. Who are you, TC? Rip Van Bloody Winkle? It's almost nine o'clock. Vance is going to call you at nine.'

'Jake, I remember Lou took the telephone off the hook because it's so close to her bedroom it wakes her up.' Jake charged through to the lounge room, switching on lights as he went, then slammed the phone into its cradle. 'I'm supposed to be happy. I won two thousand quid today. Instead, I'm here babysitting you,' he said angrily.

'Please leave, Jake. I don't need you to babysit me. As for the boss, if I want to sleep on my time, I can. I did quit, remember?! He went away without having the courtesy to tell me, let alone any other damned thing. I'm sorry if my having a sleep and not remembering the telephone was disengaged has inconvenienced your mother. As for you and the boss, I really don't give a tinker's. Just go! Please leave me alone!'

'TC, we were worried about you,' replied Jake in a calmer tone of voice. The telephone rang.

Vance's voice, 'TC, I've been worried about you. I couldn't get through to you. Are you all right?'

'Yes, Mr Callahan, I'm okay. Your shop is okay. When are you coming back? I have plans to make.'

'TC, don't start on that again. I will be going on Monday to look at machinery. Might take a day, might take a week to find the right piece of equipment. To be quite honest, I'm not even certain what I'm looking for.' TC heard Louise's voice.

'Tell her she's an employee; you'll be back when you are good and ready.'

'Mr Callahan, you really are a piece of work.' TC hung up as Vance began to say something. Jake was sitting, drinking a beer he had taken from the fridge. 'Jake, I'm going back to bed. Drink your beer and close up when you leave, please.'

'I have to get out of this God-forsaken place,' TC told herself as she climbed back into bed.

¶

Lou came home just after midnight, passed TC's room, and saw her sleeping. She was surprised to find Jake asleep in front of the heater in the lounge room. She shook Jake awake. Jake woke up with a start, mumbling between yawns and shaking his head.

'Make me a cup of coffee, will you, Lou? Probably had more beer than I should have today. Feeling a bit seedy.'

'What else is news, Jake? I'll make you a coffee; then you have to leave.'

'That's all I ever hear in this place. 'Jake, leave.' 'Jake, go home.' Why doesn't she like me, Lou?' Lou ignored him as she put his black coffee in front of him. Jake drank his coffee and smoked a Rothman before standing to leave.

'Suppose a man will have to throw the towel in where TC is concerned.'

'Looks like it, Jake,' agreed Lou as she followed him to the door. TC woke when she heard the door close.

"Hi, TC. Bye, TC. I'm off to bed,' from Lou. TC was wide awake.

'No way can I go back to sleep. Think I'll try to finish the boss' book. Hope one day he gets around to reading it himself.' She was still reading when Lou got out of bed around nine next morning. Lou came to TC's door.

'Oh, no, TC, you are still reading that book?'

'No,' replied TC. 'I just finished,' she replied as she closed the back cover, placed the book on the small table beside her bed, jumped out of bed, and stood to attention. Still in their pyjamas, they ate breakfast, sitting in the sun at the top of their favourite front stairs.

¶

Vance and Louise were in the midst of a drunken row somewhere in a Brisbane motel room.

Delores was at home with three children worrying about Vance.

Jake was back in bed after attending the obligatory early morning Sunday Mass with his mother and little sister. I hate bloody Sundays, he was thinking.

The soon-to-be-sober future opal miners, Faith, Neil, and Little Joe, were asleep on the floor in a room behind the Majestic. All of them were reeking of booze and oblivious to anything and everything.

§

'I've told you before, TC, do as I say, not do as I do! I'll call you soon.' Vance hung up.

Tired of Scrabble because TC had won three games in a row, the girls moved to the little lounge room. Lou was going about sketching.

'TC with rollers in her hair,' is the caption for this one,' said Lou. 'Think I'll ask Vance if we can hang it in the dispensary. Perhaps we can hang it next to the one I did of him and Louise "at it" over his desk.' They both laughed. The heater was on, and Jerry Lee was singing, "You shake my nerves and you rattle my brains".

'You can say that again, Jerry, my friend,' said Jake from the doorway. 'I see you are both sporting my favourite hair-do, ladies.'

'Rack off, Jake,' scowled Lou as she continued sketching. TC didn't bother to acknowledge him. Jake went to the fridge for a beer before making himself comfortable in a lounge chair next to TC.

The young aristocracy of Brolga were sleeping off the theatrics of the night before. Only the newsagency and Con's Café were open. Apart from a couple of wandering dogs and an occasional car pulling up at the newsagency, Brolga Street was deserted.

'All go, go, go here,' said Lou. 'Could fire a cannon up the main drag without any worry of injuring a soul.'

'Sure is exciting. I agree with you there, Lou.'

'Better get our washing done.'

'Now that is definitely an exciting idea,' laughed Lou as they left the steps and closed the door. With records blasting from the radiogram, they went about their business. A couple of hours later, they were in the dining room playing Scrabble when the phone rang.

'TC, it's Vance. I have been trying to get through to you for ages. What have you been doing?' TC rolled her eyes; seemed to be a regular occurrence lately.

'If you must know, we had records playing loudly while we did our washing, showered, washed our hair, and put each other's hair in rollers. We probably didn't hear the telephone because of the loud music and the fact that we were mostly downstairs. Apart from that, it does happen to be my day off from the job that I quit almost a week ago. Between you and Jake, you are like what I imagine the manner in which the C.I.A. operates.'

'Okay, okay, okay,' laughed Vance. 'Louise and I had a fight. I'm finished with her for good this time.'

'About time. It's a pity you ever got started with her.'

'She'll be back in Brolga on the Wednesday night Flea.'

'What about you, Mr Callahan?'

'I'm not sure. I told you that.'

'Have you called Mrs Callahan?'

'That's my business,' snapped Vance.

'Fine! Then what I do is my business!'

'When's my mate coming back? Con wants a game of cards. So do I. I'm getting bored.'

'Join the club,' quipped Lou.

'Let's go to the movies tonight,' suggested Jake.

'No! Take one of your nurse friends to the movies, Jake,' said TC. Jake was indignant.

'Don't be ridiculous, ladies. I'm not going to be seen at the movies with a nurse.'

'Hypocrite, that's what you are, Jake,' stated TC seriously.

'Me a hypocrite? That's it! A man has to go,' he said, as he stood up and placed his now-empty beer bottle on the table. Lou finished the sketch and handed it to TC.

'The rollers look good, Lou, every little detail.'

'What about you?' asked Lou in a concerned tone.

'I think your pencil has been over-kind to me.' Lou was obviously hurt.

'Go look in the mirror and hold it next to you.'

'Honestly, Lou, it's lovely. Perhaps too lovely—that's what I meant.'

'Well, I don't think so, TC,' said Lou quietly as she took the sketch from TC and briefly looked at it before placing it on the table, then got out of her chair to change the record from Jerry Lee to Elvis.

Twenty minutes later Lou and TC were sporting blue-coloured facial masks and painting their manicured nails with baby pink-coloured polish when Jake once again appeared at the lounge room door. Jake took one look at the girls with their rolled-up hair, blue faces, and carefully applied nail polish.

'God strike me pink; I've seen it all now! Glad you said "No" to the movies. Perhaps taking one of the nurses would be less embarrassing. Hear you're listening to that mongrel from Memphis again. Don't think he'd find either of you two appealing in your present condition.'

'Jam it up your jumper, Jake,' snarled Lou.

'Jake, didn't they teach you at that fancy college you attended that good manners require you to knock before entering?' asked TC in an indifferent tone of voice.

'Yes, especially when it's someone else's house,' added Lou.

'Well!' said Jake as he turned to deposit his armful of beer and Cokes in the refrigerator. He returned with a beer and cigarette and sat down. 'Well, as I was about to say, this is my aunt and uncle's home. I made it possible for you to live here rent-free and, if you ladies are too stupid not to lock the door, what do you expect?'

Both girls ignored him as they waited for their nails to dry before going downstairs to remove their blue beauty masks. When they came back upstairs, Jake was holding Lou's sketch in his hand, studying it.

'This is incredible, Lou. I didn't know you were this talented. Incredible! Can I have it?'

'No!'

'Why not?'

'Because I want TC to have it as a memory.'

'Fair enough, Lou. Then, do you ladies want a Coke? I noticed you had none.'

When Lou emerged, her beautiful, long, thick, auburn hair looked lovely curled around her face and shoulders. Jake stood with his car keys in hand.

'Lou, you look gorgeous! If you hadn't grown up opposite me, I'd take a run at you.' Lou laughed.

'Would have to be a damned fast run, Jake. Let's go or I'll be late for the gossip pit.'

TC removed her hair rollers which were beginning to hurt her scalp. Her hair bushed out. She remembered to lock the back door before beginning her ironing, which she was just finishing when she heard Jake's car pull up alongside the back steps.

Oh, no, Jake's back, she thought, while once more rolling her eyes. She opened the door to find Jake nursing a pile of records on one arm; on his other side, he was holding his little sister's hand.

'Hello, TC,' said Carla. 'I wanted to come with Jake to see you.' The little cutie was moving her head from side to side coyly and kept lifting her right foot onto her toes.

'Come in, sweetie. It's cold out there.'

'Thank you, Darling. Don't mind if I do,' smiled Jake. TC said nothing to Jake. Instead, she concentrated on chatting to his little sister. Carla strolled around the house, touching this and that before grasping Jake by the arm.

'Jake, I want my ice cream with chocolate flavouring now.'

'Okay, we'll go to Con's now,' replied Jake as he sat Carla on his knees.

'I want TC to come with us, Jake. Will you come with us, TC?' TC felt trapped. She didn't want to be seen with Jake at Con's any more than Jake wanted to be seen at the movies with a nurse.

'I don't think I can, Carla. I have to put my ironing away.' Carla put her head on Jake's shoulder and started to cry.

'I want you to come to Con's, TC.'

'All right, Carla, don't cry. I'll come with you.'

§

Con could not conceal his surprise when Jake, TC, and little Carla entered his Café. He stretched out his arms in a welcoming gesture.

'Come in. Come in, my friends.' Jake seated Carla and TC at a table on the aisle half-way down the length of the café before going to place the order with Con.

No wonder Jake high-tailed it out of here, thought TC, as she returned her attention to Carla, who had surprisingly by now finished her ice cream. TC once again wiped Carla's face.

'Is your tummy full, Carla?'

'Yes, TC. My tummy is cold, too.' TC took the coffee cups and ice cream dish to the counter. Con's wife handed her a note from Jake.

'Sorry, TC, a man is a mongrel. Meet you and Carla in the car.' Jake was sitting in his car when they reached it. TC helped Carla into the front seat next to Jake, then climbed into the back seat herself.

'I've got a cold tummy, Jake; I want to go home to Mummy.'

'Yes, Jake, and I would like to go home to my place. Is it okay with you, Carla, if Jake takes me to my place first, Sweetie?'

'That's okay' smiled the little girl.

Once at her house, TC got out of the car.

'Bye, bye, Carla. Say "Hello" to Mummy for me, will you?'

'Okay, TC.' Jake sped away. Ten minutes later the phone rang.

'Sorry, TC,' said Jake. 'I saw them walk in and felt as if I was about to fall off a cliff. I want to come back to your place so I can pick up Lou when she finishes work.'

'No! Lou will be all right. She'll run. That's what we usually do.' TC hung up, lit the kerosene heater, and put a Ray Charles record on the stereo before putting her ironed clothes away.

'The boss loves to listen to Ray Charles,' she murmured to herself. 'Wonder what the boss is up to? Hope he's okay.' TC sat down, listening to the words of the songs. Beautiful, she thought. Like life—some happy, some sad.

Jake called again.

'TC, I'm sorry our first date turned out the way it did.'

'Stop right there, Jake. That was not a date. I went only because your little sister asked me to. The way you bolted when those nurses came in was disgusting. In my opinion, Jake, they are not very nice people, and, quite honestly, I don't think you are a very nice person.'

'I'm sorry, TC. I got a fright. I didn't know what they might say to me in front of you and Carla.'

'Who cares, Jake? Please do not call me again tonight.' TC hung up. Her mind was racing. 'I have to get away from here. Wish Lou didn't have to work tonight. Wish Auntie Flo would call so I can tell her I plan to go away. Hope the boss comes back before mail day.' The Louis Armstrong record finished playing; TC turned off the heater, brushed her teeth, then went to bed.

¶

Louise was on the train when it arrived on Wednesday night. Her husband was at the railway station to meet her. As far as he was concerned, Louise had gone to Brisbane to visit her family and do some shopping.

Two mail days, one doctor and mail day, then another two mail days passed. Lou was happy. Her two pounds an hour were mounting up, and she was rubbing her hands together in anticipation of Vance's return and being paid. The weather became colder, Jake kept nagging TC to go to the movies with him, but she continued to decline. Auntie Flo rang. TC told her emotionally that she planned to go away. Auntie Flo said, 'Never mind, luv, you'll be back. We will ask Jake to keep an eye on the place while you are away.'

'I don't believe I'll come back to Brolga, Auntie Flo. I am feeling a little afraid because I'm not even sure of where Lou and I will go.'

'That's normal, luv,' replied Auntie Flo. 'That is just the fear of the unknown versus the familiarity and security of the known. I'll call you every week until you have something definite, TC. Talk to you next week, luv.'

Without prior notice, Vance was sitting at his desk in the dispensary on a Monday morning when TC arrived at the pharmacy. Vance smiled broadly at TC when she entered.

'Hello, TC. I bought a loader.'

'Hello, Boss. Obviously, you had to go to America to find it.'

'Don't be like that, TC. I have been busy. My life has changed. Did you finish my book?'

'Well, Boss, I have been busy, too. I have had to withdraw money from my savings to live on.'

'TC, you could have taken your wages from the till,' interrupted Vance.

'I could have, Mr Callahan, but you didn't tell me to and I certainly was not going to ask. As for your book, I have read it cover to cover, then gone back through it, bracketing passages that may be of interest to you. I would like to finish up next Saturday. Lou and I are leaving on the Flea on Sunday morning.'

Vance sat in silent shock for what seemed an eternity.

'TC, I can't believe you are serious about this. You have everything here. You have a house to live in free of charge, a good job where you virtually please yourself as long as you get the job done, which you do. You have a real friend in Lou, Jake is crazy about you, and, quite frankly, I don't think I can function without having you to look after this damned place.'

'That's exactly it. I'm still a teenager; yet, I live the life of a middle-aged, married woman. I'm married to my job. All I do is come to work, go home, sew, clean, wash, and iron. Lou is the same. The greatest excitement in our lives is listening to records on the stereogram and Slim Dusty on 4CH. As for Jake, I think he's an insincere poser. I admit he visits us a lot and is kind-hearted, but I'm sure he has some ulterior motive. Quite frankly, I think he's had just about every girl in town except Lou and myself. Too bad for Jake. Lou and I are outcasts here. Lou, because her father is the undertaker-cum-Jack-of-all-trades, and me because you rescued me from the Empire. You'll just have to learn to manage without me, Mr Callahan. You can teach someone else.'

Vance realised TC was serious.

'Not like you, I can't,' he said as he stood up, then walked out. TC swept and mopped the floor, then closed the door and went to fetch the mail. As she passed the Empire window, she heard Vance and Jake laughing.

So much for the boss' life changing, thought TC. She purposely walked back to the shop via the other side of the street.

'Lovely day for sitting on the Seat of Knowledge, luv,' said Carmel as TC passed by the bakery and Carmel's shop. 'Don't suppose you'll get the chance to soak up the sun, though, luv. Saw Vance and Jake go into the pub when it opened.' TC nodded as she walked by.

'Some things never change, Carmel.'

'You can say that again, luv. Still, where there's life, there's hope,' added Carmel.

¶

TC was filling out cheques when Lou came in after she had finished work.

'Write one for me, TC,' she laughed.

'Not a problem, Lou. I can write you a cheque; however, you'll have to ask the boss to sign it.'

'Did you tell him we were leaving next Sunday?'

'Yes, I did.'

'How did he take it?'

'He's in the Empire with Jake.'

'No, he's not; he's in the Majestic. I saw him walk in there as I was coming here, and Jake's car is outside Carmichael's shop.'

¶

'I won't be long, Lou; only a half dozen or so to go!' The telephone rang for the first time all day. Lou answered it. Delores was on the other end.

'Why are you answering the phone again, Lou? Where is TC? Can't she even answer the telephone? Lord only knows what goes on in that shop!' Lou saw red and experienced great difficulty in controlling her tone of voice.

'Work is what goes on here, Mrs Callahan.' TC took the telephone from Lou.

'Sorry, Mrs Callahan, I was doing paperwork.'

'Where is Vance?' demanded Delores.

'Sorry, he's not here.'

'Is he at the Empire, TC?'

'I don't think so, Mrs Callahan.'

'Tell him to call me immediately when you see him, TC.'

⁋

Delores was furious after she hung up and began talking to herself.

'Who the hell does TC think she's fooling? I know she knows exactly where Vance is all of the time. Little Miss Goody-Two-Shoes thinks she owns the damned place. She's nothing but a jumped-up barmaid. Trust Vance to hire a barmaid.' The baby began crying, so she stopped talking to herself and went to take care of her.

⁋

TC had stormed across the road to the Majestic. Sure enough, she found Vance out the back leaning against a wall, drinking with the would-be opal miners. She heard Vance speaking as she stood unnoticed.

'Now you have a week to wean yourself off the booze.'

'What about you, Pill-Pusher?' enquired Little Joe.

'I'll be all right, mate,' replied Vance with a laugh. 'It's not me I'm worried about; it's you lot of no-hopers.' They all laughed. They sat bolt upright when they finally noticed TC.

'How long you been there, Little Flower?' asked Faith.

'Long enough, Faith. Long enough to know you are all drunk.'

'You look angry, Little Flower,' came from Neil.

'Nothin' to be angry about, luv,' came from Little Joe.

'Yeah, be happy like us,' added Faith.

'You are all drunk,' snapped TC again. 'Mr Callahan, you wife wants you to contact her. I suggest the sooner, the better.' She turned and left them sitting there. Jake called out to her as she left the Majestic. She waited as he walked towards her.

'So, you really are going, TC? You sure know how to break a man's heart.'

'Sure, Jake. What?'

'Mum heard from Auntie Flo that you are going away for a while; so, she told me to invite you and Lou for a meal tonight.'

'That would be nice, Jake. Like to say goodbye to your mother and little Carla.' As she walked away, he was silently hoping his mother could talk them out of leaving.

¶

Although Jake and his mother came up with countless reasons why the girls shouldn't go, neither girl changed her mind.

'Make sure you remember me,' came Carla's little voice as she held her mother's hand.

'Put the kettle on, ladies. I'll be back for a cup of coffee and to tuck you in bed in about one hour from now.' He drove off. Lou and TC both pretended not to hear his car pull up at the hospital before heading off for the creek.

TC and Lou sat in the lounge with the heater and music both turned up high and made individual notes on where they should go and what they would like to do. Both of them realised that everything depended on money and that they wouldn't have nearly enough to do much before they found work. Still, they had agreed that it didn't hurt to dream.

¶

Jake returned as predicted. Lou put the kettle on as they heard his car pull into the driveway. The telephone rang as they sat down to drink their coffees. Lou answered.

'Is Jake there?' asked Vance in a somewhat frantic voice. She knew he was calling from the phone box outside the post office.

'Jake, it's for you.' Lou handed the telephone to Jake.

'You are where, mate? Bloody hell, mate, what are you doing there? Okay, mate, we'll be there faster than a speeding bullet.' Vance didn't get the chance to say "don't bring the girls" before Jake hung up. Jake pulled up adjacent to the tiny, red telephone booth outside the post office. Vance got into the car next to Jake.

'Sorry, girls. You can't come. Jake, drop the girls back home, will you, mate? They don't need to come with us.' Jake drove the curious girls to the house.

'I'll see you later, ladies,' said Jake. Once they were out of his car, Jake drove at break-neck speed along Brolga Street heading west.

'What the bloody hell were you doing at the cemetery in the middle of the night, mate?' asked Jake. 'You can't be that bloody drunk.'

'I've been trying to talk Louise into doing something she fends off for a long time now. As I have to get sober and stay sober pretty soon, I thought I'd give it one more try. She wouldn't come to the party with my plan. When I gave up trying to convince her, I turned the key in the ignition and the bloody car wouldn't start. I walked to the post office and called you. I've got grass and crap all over me because every time a car came along the road, I dived into the bushes so no one would see me and gossip all over town. Thank God, there were only a few cars.'

Jake began laughing uncontrollably as he imagined his friend running for cover every time he saw headlights coming in his direction or heard a car coming up behind him.

'Where's Louise, mate? Did she walk home?'

'No, Jake, she's locked in my car at the cemetery. Poor thing must be scared witless.'

Jake couldn't believe his ears and almost went into convulsions with more laughter. When his laughter finally subsided, 'You really are an asshole, Vance. Fancy leaving a poor bloody woman out there in the dark with all those poor dead bastards.' Jake turned off the bitumen road onto the dirt track to the Brolga Cemetery. 'You'll have to wash my car tomorrow, Vance,' he said as the dust swirled everywhere. When

Jake pulled his car to a halt next to Vance's, Louise, white faced, furious, and freezing cold, jumped out of Vance's car and clambered into Jake's.

'You fucking bastard, Vance. What took you so bloody long? Feel as if I've been here for a thousand fucking years. Not only that; it's fucking freezing.' Jake handed Louise a blanket from the back seat of his car.

'Come on, Vance, let's get the jumper leads hooked up, mate. I want to get away from here pronto.'

'You are not the only one,' snarled Louise.

Vance's car engine turned over in less than a minute.

'I'm staying in Jake's car,' stated Louise. 'I've had enough of that fucking contraption of yours to last me three lifetimes.'

'You are the one who insisted I leave the lights on,' replied Vance. 'That's why the damned battery went flat.'

'Okay, children, I've had enough of this place. I'm out of here like a rat up a rope. Wait for you at the bitumen, Vance.' Jake drove furiously along the winding dirt track.

'Slow down, Jake, or we'll be spending eternity with those poor bastards back there.' Jake pulled off to the side of the bitumen around a hundred yards from the cemetery turn-off. Seemed like forever till Vance's car finally emerged from the track. He pulled over behind Jake's car.

'You blinded me with your tail dust, Jake. Thought I'd choke on it. Come on, Louise, I'll take you home.'

'I want Jake to drive me. I told you, I've had enough of your bloody car.'

'Up yours, Louise,' said Jake seriously. 'I don't want your poor bloody husband after me. I've done my bit by rescuing you.'

'Weak, gutless bastard you are, Jake Callahan,' she spat as she reluctantly got out of his car.

'Thank you, Louise. Next time you are stranded at the cemetery in the middle of the night, don't expect me to rescue you,' replied Jake seriously before he drove off.

Jake went straight home. He knew Lou and TC would be all questions. He also knew they would be waiting for him; so, when he got to his mother's house, he immediately called them

'Where did you go, Jake?' asked Lou. 'What was wrong with Vance?'

'Nothing much, Lou. His car broke down near the cemetery turn-off.'

'Is that all? Why didn't he want us to come?'

'Because it's so cold, Lou. Say goodnight to TC. See you tomorrow.'

§

TC was addressing envelopes for the cheques when Vance arrived at the shop the next morning. TC looked up at him.

'You look dreadful, Boss.'

'I feel it, too, TC. I won't be here long. I see you've written the cheques. I'll sign them while you go and get the mail. Then I'm out of here.'

'Not to the hotels again, I hope,' said TC as she took the post office box key from its hook.

'Don't start, TC. Delores is right. Sometimes you overstep the mark,' he snapped.

'Well, neither you nor Mrs Callahan will have to tolerate me much longer.'

'God, I'm a bastard. No need to take everything out on the kid every time I have a blue with Delores.'

TC returned with the mail.

'Mr Callahan, is it okay if I go have a look at suitcases before you leave?'

'No! You're on my time. Do your shopping on your own time. Clean the shop. When you've finished that, get these cheques in the mail. Don't think you can sit around here all day and do nothing.' TC was stunned. This was not her boss speaking; this was Mrs Callahan.

'Mr Callahan, the shop is spotless, the shelves are full, the filing is done, and the cheques are written. I cleaned everything yesterday.'

Vance had just signed the last cheque. He stood, pushed his chair away, threw his pen on the desk, and almost shouted.

'Well, clean it again. Are you deaf, stupid, or both?' TC looked at him in disbelief.

'Why are you doing this? I don't understand. I think I'd best go now. Don't forget, it's mail day tomorrow,' she reminded as she collected her purse and jacket before walking out.

Vance slumped back down in his chair. He felt desolate.

'You've "really" done it now, you stupid, rotten bastard,' he told himself.

¶

TC walked home slowly, deep in thought and totally confused. The moment she was inside the house, she burst into tears before throwing herself on her bed. She cried until no more tears would fall, then got up and washed her face. The telephone rang. It was Vance. She hung up. A few minutes later, it rang again. It was Lou.

'TC, Vance asked me ...'

'Forget it, Lou!' TC hung up again. Ten minutes or so later, the ringing sounded again. It was Jake.

'TC, Vance asked me to say ...'

'I'm taking the phone off the cradle.' She did so, placed the Ray Charles record on the stereo, then went to bed. Lou found her asleep when she came home just after four. She gently shook TC on the shoulder until she woke. Lou saw her friend's puffy, red eyes.

'What happened, TC?' she asked softly with concern.

'It doesn't matter, Lou. Perhaps we will talk about it some other time. I just want to stay in bed for now.' Lou nodded her head, patted her friend on the head, and left the room as she heard TC say, 'Sometimes our best just isn't good enough, Lou.' TC woke up a few hours later when Lou and Jake came into her room and sat down on the side of her bed.

'Come on, girl, get your cute butt out of this bed before I drag you out,' commanded Jake. 'You look bloody terrible. Do believe I prefer the blue-face-and-roller look.'

'Go away, Jake. I'll be there in a minute,' murmured TC.

'Good. I'll make some tea and toast,' said Lou.

TC slowly got out of bed, put on her dressing gown before brushing her hair, then joined Jake and Lou in the lounge room.

'What's this sleeping-all-day business?' said Jake before lighting a cigarette, deeply inhaling, then filling the tiny room with exhaled smoke. TC yawned before replying.

'Well, Jake, probably because I'm lazy. The boss thinks I am, as well as being deaf, stupid, or both.' Jake stood up, puffing furiously.

'Bullshit, TC! He does not think that!'

'Yes, he does, Jake. He told me,' replied TC, softly and matter-of-factly. Lou interrupted.

'Jake, Delores Callahan implied that TC is lazy to me on the phone yesterday. I became angry. Everybody knows TC works like a drover's dog. Vance is paying me per hour almost as much as TC gets per week except when he feels guilty and flings her a bonus.'

'Lou, that's enough. Leave it alone,' interrupted TC. 'He's worried about having to give up the drink, going opal mining, who will look after the pharmacy, and probably a million other things.'

'That's not your fault, TC. We all know you wouldn't have agreed to go away with me if you weren't taken for granted by just about all and sundry who come and go in that place. Sorry, TC. That includes your revered ex-boss. You haven't been paid for God-knows how long. Vance forgets such incidentals; he's too damned busy disappearing, boozing, and running around with Louise.'

'Lou, I said leave it,' commanded TC. 'That's none of your business.'

Jake had been walking in and out of the tiny lounge room, all the time puffing furiously on cigarettes one after the other.

'Screw it! I'm going to find Vance.' With that he was out the back door and into his car.

'Lou, you should not have said anything about my pay. How did you know, anyway?'

'A teller at the bank told his mate on the phone that Miss Scrooge from the pharmacy was actually withdrawing one pound a week from her precious savings.' TC was somewhat taken aback.

'I can't believe this place, Lou. People will gossip about anything. I can't wait for Sunday to come.' They heard Jake's car arrive. He was in the lounge room in seconds.

'Vance said to tell you he's sorry, TC, he'll see you tomorrow, and to remind you it's mail day.'

'Not this time, Jake,' replied TC firmly. 'What use would a lazy, deaf, stupid creature like me be to him?'

'TC, he said he wasn't angry towards you. He was and is angry with other people, not you. Mostly himself, he said.'

'Come on, Jake,' snapped Lou. 'Why not take his anger out on the people he's pissed off with? All TC did was go to work and get abused.'

'Stop it, both of you.' TC had enough. 'I'm not going into the pharmacy tomorrow and I don't care if it's mail day. Let the people the boss is angry with help him or let him do it himself. After all, it is his business. I'm going back to bed,' she declared as she stood up and left the room.

'Buggered if I know what the bloody hell to do, Lou,' said Jake as he opened a beer and poured Lou a Coke.

§

'Do nothing, Jake. It's not your problem.' Jake drank his beer, smoked a cigarette, then left to go home.

Next day was Lou's last at her exchange job. When she was leaving for work, she told TC she was going by the pharmacy after finishing.

'Going to pick up my pay, TC. Want me to get yours?'

'No, Lou. I'll see him tomorrow when we go to buy our Flea tickets and a suitcase.'

§

Sam phoned TC early in the afternoon.

'Got a news flash that you are getting out of this dump, kid!' said Sam in her usual flippant manner. 'I must be the last bloody person to know. Do you plan on coming back, TC? Where are you going, Sam? Well, Brad has asked me to marry him again. Don't know what I'll bloody well do. After all, the poor bastard did try to do away with himself for me. I'll probably marry him. Who knows? Anyway, I have to go. Take care of yourself, kid.'

TC smiled to herself.

'That's Sam. Never draws breath. Suppose I'll write her a letter to answer her questions when Lou and I get where we are going.'

¶

When Lou went to collect her money from Vance, he was busy in the shop, so she went through to the dispensary. Louise was sitting at Vance's desk.

'What are you doing here, Lou?'

'I could ask you the same,' replied Lou icily.

'Hear that you and that little bitch, TC, are quitting this place.'

'I know who the bitch is, Louise, and it is certainly not TC. I'm out of here, Vance. I suggest you disinfect the place after you get rid of that garbage piled up on your chair.'

The telephone rang. As Vance went to answer it, he asked Louise, 'What was the problem with Lou?'

'I don't know,' replied Louise, shrugging her shoulders.

After several constructive calls, Vance told Louise she should leave because he'd be tied up for a long while.

'Missing your little slave, are you, lover?' asked Louise sarcastically.

'Yes, Louise, as a matter of fact, I am. I took the poor little bugger for granted.'

'Little bitches like her are a dime a dozen, Vance.'

'No, Louise, you are wrong there. Women like you are a dime a dozen. Now, please get the hell out of here so I can get some work done!'

Louise paused at the back door, yelled, 'Screw you!' and took off.

You already have, Louise—me and God only knows how many countless others, thought Vance, as he locked the back door behind her.

¶

That morning Vance had received confirmation of successful

applications for mining leases on two of the three sites for which he had applied.

'Don't know how I'll handle this bloody place once I go mining. Have to open mail days only until TC comes back.' There was no doubt in his mind that she would be coming back. On the spur of the moment, he called her.

'TC, it's me.'

'Yes?'

'Did you miss me?'

'What's the problem, Mr Callahan?'

'I miss you being here.'

'You'll get used to it. I'll come to collect my pay tomorrow if that's okay with you.'

'Are you certain you want to go, TC?'

'I think so. I'll see you tomorrow.' She hung up.

Vance then phoned Jake.

'Come to the pharmacy after you close up, Jake, that is, if you don't have other plans. Bring something to drink. Looks as if I'll be here half the bloody night.'

'Sure,' laughed Jake. 'I can pack, wrap, tie, and label for you.'

¶

Con wandered over around midnight. Both Vance and Jake were half-plastered.

'How much longer will you be?' asked Con.

'A while yet, mate', replied Vance.

'I thought we might play a game or two. I think you boys are frightened I'll win all your money', laughed Con. Both Vance and Jake nodded.

'You're on, mate. See you soon.'

'Let's go now', suggested Vance.

'Still a lot to do here, mate', replied Jake.

'I'll get that done early in the morning.'

'You're the boss. Let's grab the grog and go.'

❡

They played poker until nine in the morning. Vance completely forgot about the orders he hadn't finished and the truckie coming to collect them.

Jake looked at his watch when Con's wife told them for the last time to break it up.

'Vance, mate, it is bloody nine o'clock. What about your mail orders? The truckie will have been trying to collect them hours ago.'

'Oh, no!' Vance jumped up and virtually ran out of the café and across the street to his shop. Jake was hot on his heels.

'I told Con we'll sort out the money later. I'll throw the finished ones into your station wagon, mate, while you get started on the others.'

They worked furiously. Vance didn't bother to ring up and enclose dockets. He could do that later. Just after ten the last lot was thrown into his wagon. Vance jumped in the driver's seat, and Jake wished him luck.

'That mail truck's long gone, mate', laughed the young mechanic at the truck depot. 'If you drive fast, you might catch him at the second station on the route.'

'Oh,' muttered Vance. 'What a bloody mess,' as he hustled in reverse onto Brolga Street, negotiated the U-turn at the median strip, and drove like thunder in pursuit of the mail truck.

'This is lunacy. I can't believe it.' He glanced at the fuel gauge with a sigh of relief. He had three-quarters of a tank.

❡

As predicted by the mechanic, Vance caught up with the mail truck as it was leaving the second station. The truck driver laughed.

'I thought of throwing a crowbar throw your shop window, mate. I could see all the mail stacked up, but couldn't get to it.'

'My fault, mate. I overslept,' smiled Vance as he threw one after another package to the truckie. Just glad I caught up with you here instead of two more stations along.'

When he finished loading the truck, the driver told Vance he would drop off whatever there was for the first two stations when he came back through to collect their outgoing mail. Vance drove back into town to his house, ignored countless questions from Delores, showered, dressed and went into the pharmacy. Jake walked in as Vance sat down to smoke a cigar.

'Poor old Con lost again, mate,' said Jake. 'You won twelve hundred, and I won eleven-fifty.' We started with five hundred each,' he reminded as he counted out one thousand and seven hundred pounds to Vance, then sixteen hundred and fifty to himself.

'Con's old woman said if Con doesn't have a win soon, we'll have to draw our winnings in food.'

'Poor bloody Lisa,' laughed Vance.

'Poor bloody Con, that's what I reckon,' laughed Jake in return. 'Fancy being stuck with your wife twenty-four hours a day?'

'I don't ever want to think about it,' replied Vance seriously. 'I rarely see poor bloody Delores, and sometimes that's still too much.' Vance kept looking at his watch. 'Wish bloody siren time would come. I need a drink.'

'Yes, I'm feeling a bit seedy myself, replied Jake. 'I could go and get something, but I really don't think it's a good idea to be drinking on the job. Think it's a habit I can do without.' Vance nodded his head.

'You are right, mate. I wish TC were here. Then we could go and drink in the Empire.'

'Strange, isn't it, mate, we all tend to take people and things for granted until we haven't got them anymore,' Jake said seriously.

'You are not wrong there, Jake,' agreed Vance.

'Which reminds me,' Jake said, 'Lou told me they were going to buy a suitcase each this afternoon. I want to beat them to the punch. I'm giving them each one as a going-away present. See you at siren time, mate.'

⁋

When the girls returned home after visiting Lou's parents, they were surprised to find Jake's gifts on the back landing with a note—'The maroon one is for Lou. Will match her hair. The other one is for TC. It will match her overcoat, which, to date, I have not seen on her. These are a bribe, not a gift. You are leaving Sunday morning, and I expect to be seen at the movies on Saturday night with both of you (safety in numbers, TC).' They both laughed.

'He never gives up, does he, Lou?'

'Not our Jake,' replied Lou. 'Have to give him full marks for tenacity.'

¶

A little after siren time Vance and Jake were standing at the bar in the Empire.

'The usual, Jess,' requested Vance.

'One double Bundy and Coke and one beer coming up. When's the little one going?'

'Sunday,' replied Vance and Jake as if one. Jess returned with their drinks, took their money, and returned with the change.

'Poor pair of losing mongrels, you two are.' They both looked at Jess in anticipation of her next words. 'Well, Pill-Pusher, pharmacist, chemist, or whatever you call yourself, you threw that kid in at the deep end. Everyone in town knows she's been running the joint since day one while you have been drinking yourself witless and cavorting about the town with that Louise creature. First mail day after TC quit, you played poker all night, then had to chase the mail truck. Picked you as a mad mongrel the first time I saw you. I have not changed my mind.'

'Suppose I'll have to do something to change your image of me, Jess. Fill us up again, will you?' smiled Vance.

When Jess returned, 'As for you, Jake Carmichael, you were born with a silver spoon in your mouth. You have never wanted for anything. Everything you have ever wanted, you got, until TC came along, that is. Everyone knows you are crazy about her. Could that possibly be because she is too smart to get mixed up with the likes of you? Thank God for that! All you do is drink, gamble and litter the creek several times a week with the trash from the hospital. When ball time comes around, you find yourself one of Brolga's little up-themselves tarts to hang on your arm. I'm glad TC is leaving this God-forsaken town. Will teach you two a bloody lesson.'

'Thank you, Jess,' said Jake. 'Get us another drink, please.'

'Actually, no,' said Vance. 'Get another two, Jess, and could they come without the dressing down on the side?'

Jess smiled, 'Mad mongrels,' and went off, head held high, to fetch their drinks.

They took their drinks and change to go sit in the ladies' lounge.

'Old Jess is spot on, Jake,' remarked Vance as he stared into space over Jake's head. 'Young TC is the hardest-working, most loyal person I have ever met, and between us we have made her want to go away.'

'You sure are right there,' agreed Jake. 'She's also smart, clean, fiery, and can sew. Don't know if she's much of a good cook!' he laughed. 'Then, again, she's got nothing to cook on except Auntie Flo's old wood stove.' They sat in the ladies' lounge mostly in silence except when one or the other went to buy more drinks until Jess interrupted them.

'Excuse me gentlemen, there are two young ladies at the pub window looking for you, Mr Callahan.'

'What about me, Jess?' asked Jake.

'It is three in the afternoon, Jake. I suggest you get back to work.' Both men looked at their watches in shock. Jake went quickly to his car. Vance left the hotel and looked to the left to see TC and Lou talking to Jess.

'Probably won't see you again, young TC. No doubt I will see you again, Lou; your parents live here.' Jess walked through the main door to the bar and into the footpath.

'Come here, sweetie,' she gushed as she put her arms around TC and hugged her before kissing her profusely on the cheeks. 'You are a good girl. Stay that way, won't you, luv? Always remember, you are special. You are a good girl, too, Lou. Against all odds, you have turned out damned great.'

'What's this?' asked Vance. 'Must be tear-drop city because the three of you are weepy-eyed'. Old Jess pulled away from the girls and wiped the tears from her cheeks as she glared at Vance.

'I've already told you once or twice today, you are a mongrel. Now I'm telling you again.' She quickly escaped back inside to the bar.

'I'd like to collect my pay, please, Vance,' smiled Lou.

'Sure, Lou.' Vance pulled a wad of notes out of his pocket.

'Not here. People will think I'm putting the blight on you. I did the work in the pharmacy, so I think I should be paid in the pharmacy.'

'Fair enough, Lou. Let's go.' Vance laughed as they turned to walk across the street. 'Have you bought your train tickets yet?'

'No, we'll buy them later.'

'Hope the Flea is not as bad as I remember it,' said TC.

Once in the dispensary, Vance asked Lou how much he owed her. Lou, in a very business-like manner, handed him a page from a small notepad on which she had written dates and times. Vance looked at it.

'You are a wealthy woman, Lou. Fifty-three hours at two quid an hour,' he exclaimed as he handed her a hundred and ten pounds. 'There's an extra couple of quid there for wear and tear.' He smiled.

'Now you, young lady.' He smiled at TC. 'What do I owe you?'

'I don't know. You paid me the Saturday before you went to Brisbane.'

'I also owe you your holiday pay, TC.'

'Whatever,' shrugged TC. Vance turned his back on the girls.

'Go across to Con's and buy me a Coke, will you, girls?'

When they returned, he handed TC an envelope.

'I think this should cover things, TC. Should either of you run short while you are away, call me.'

'Thank you. I don't think so, Boss. Have to learn to stand on my own two feet.' TC. Smiled.

'Me, too', added Lou.

'I think you both already are. I'll see you Sunday,' said Vance, and they were gone.

Vance called Jake.

'Are you busy, Jake?'

'Not really mate.'

'Good. Meet you back at the pub in five minutes.'

'You can count on that. See you then.'

§

They stayed at the Empire until Jack and Bert Romeo threw everyone except the police sergeant out at ten o'clock.

'Go home, boys. Too bloody cold to be drinking all night,' said Jack Romeo.

'Bet you wish we could, Jack, cold weather or not,' yelled one man who could hardly stand up.

'You are not wrong there, my friend,' replied Bert Romeo, while making a gesture of rubbing his palms together. 'Blame the cop here; it's him who makes us close at ten.'

A few stock and station agents looked at the Sergeant, who smiled and outstretched his arms insomuch as saying, 'That is the law; what can I do about it?'

Vance and Jake made their way to Con's Café.

'Come to let me win my money back?' asked Con, hopefully.

'No, mate, we came for a feed,' replied Vance.

'We haven't had any sleep since the night before last,' added Jake, who had a wobbly head caused by too much booze in conjunction with lack of sleep.

Con cooked steak and eggs for the two hungry men, who ate as if they hadn't seen a meal in weeks. Two cups of coffee and they were on their way home to bed.

Mum will be happy, thought Jake. It's not even midnight. Vance hoped Delores would be asleep. He was not in the mood for questions. Once they were safely home, and in their beds, it could actually be said that Brolga was asleep apart from the late-shift workers at the small power house, telephone exchange, and hospital.

§

Vance was up early the next morning. He went to find and check up on the condition of his opal-mining crew. He was correct in assuming they would be huddled up on the floor in the room behind the Majestic with only the few old blankets to keep them warm.

What a motley-looking mob they are, he thought, as he opened the door and observed them. Poor bastards, bet there was a woman somewhere in the past of all these poor buggers. Like me, the pain was/is so unbearable they sought/seek escape and refuge in the booze. Drink enough for long enough, there's no pain at all. Just a numbness. Trouble is the pain comes back once sober; so, we seek the escape route again and again.

'Come on, you lot,' said Vance, loudly. 'Come on, time to get cleaned up. This joint smells like an outhouse.'

'We do, too,' mumbled Neil as they all began to stir.

'You're not wrong, mate!' laughed Vance. 'Do you mob of no-hopers have any clothes other than what you've been wearing for the last week or more?'

'Somewhere,' replied Neil as he slowly rubbed his forehead between yawns.

'All right, wake yourselves up while I go find some soap and towels.' Vance went to the pharmacy and phoned Jake.

'I know it's early, mate. I've just woken up my crew. They are in a mess in more ways than one. I want to get them fitted out. How about I meet you at your shop in ten minutes?'

'Sure,' replied a still half-asleep Jake.

Vance gathered soap, toothpaste, toothbrushes, shampoo, razors, blades, and shaving cream from the shelves. As he was leaving, Jake drove by and pulled up in front of Carmichael and Carmichael. Vance quickly joined him.

'Jake, to begin with, I need a half dozen towels all different colours and your help in getting these poor bastards cleaned up. Then we'll come back here and get them fitted out with whatever they need.'

¶

'Now, men,' said Vance, 'before I get carried away spending my money, do any of you want to pull out?'

Neil's two brothers both nodded their heads.

'No, mate. I speak for both of us. We are happy getting work when it comes up; at least when we get a break, we can enjoy ourselves.'

'Yeah, 'til the money runs out,' said Neil.

'Okay, you two are out,' said Vance. 'I do need at least four men. Do you know anyone else, Neil?'

'Me,' came a voice from a head that surprisingly emerged from under a blanket.

'Who are you?' asked Vance.

'My bloody name is Yappy. They call me Yappy because of my squeaky voice and because I talk a lot'.

'All right, Yappy, you are hired.'

Yappy threw off the blanket and stood up. Neither Vance nor Jake could believe their eyes.

Neil, Faith, and Little Joe were incapable of shaving themselves; their hands were too shaky as Vance and Jake took on the task. When they were shaved, showered, and shampooed, they went off to Jake's store.

'Come on, men. We'll get you some work clothes and boots; don't forget socks and underpants; three sets of everything except boots. Better throw in a windcheater, each a different colour.'

'I'm going to find Yappy,' said Vance as he walked out.

Vance went to the shower room behind the Majestic to collect the towels and toiletries. There he found Yappy, whom he hardly recognised as the bedraggled little creature he had previously hired this morning.

'Where the bloody hell have you been? Leave a man stranded like a shag on a bloody rock!' asked Yappy, one hand on his hip and his other hand in the pocket of his beautifully pressed, dark-grey trousers, complemented by grey leather, highly polished shoes, pale grey shirt, and navy sports coat. On his head he wore a dark grey punter's hat.

'What? Are you going to the races, Yappy?' laughed Vance.

'Don't be a smart bastard, Callahan. People judge a man by the clothes he wears.'

'Not everyone does, Yappy' replied Vance. 'Come on, let's find the other men, then go to Con's for some breakfast.'

¶

When they reached Jake's shop, Neil, Faith, and Little Joe were dressed in their new work outfits and sporting brightly coloured windcheaters. They looked like different men and obviously felt like different men.

'The men decided on one pair of long khakis and two pairs of shorts,' said Jake, 'khaki shirts and they chose their own socks and underpants.'

'Fine,' replied Vance. 'Everyone happy?'

'I'm not happy,' interrupted Yappy. 'I didn't know they were going to get one of those jackets. I think I need one of those.' Vance looked at Jake and smiled.

'Jake, find a girl's size windcheater for Yappy, will you? Preferably in pink.'

Yappy stood no more than five-foot-two and weighed no more than a hundred and fifteen pounds, if that.

'What are you bloody-well lookin' at?' asked Yappy indignantly. 'Haven't you ever seen a once-famous jockey before?'

'I think we had best make you the cook and general hand, Yappy,' smiled Vance.

'I can work as hard as any bastard,' replied Yappy.

'I'm sure you can, Yappy. I'd still like you to be the cook.'

'All right, all right, all right! You are the bloody boss. No need to buy me any gear; I've got plenty. Even got a proper room in this pub somewhere. I think I'd better go find it before the bastard runs away.' Jake and Vance laughed as Yappy wandered off in search of his room.

'I like him,' said Jake.

'I like the little prick, too,' smiled Vance. Everyone laughed except Yappy.

'Smart bastard! A man wouldn't be seen bloody dead in pink. Give me any other colour.'

'How about navy blue, Yappy?' asked Jake.

'That's more like it, mate. A man wants to look like a man.'

'Even if he is a small man,' stated Vance.

'Exactly,' agreed Yappy.

'That's it,' said Jake as he handed Vance a docket and a pillowcase containing the towels and toiletries. 'I'm going home to get ready for work,' said Jake. 'See you later, Vance.'

'Come on, men,' said Vance. 'Let's go eat.'

Neil, Faith, and Little Joe each held two large, brown-paper bags, one containing their new work gear and the other their soiled clothes with their initials printed on the outside.

'You men go inside and order. I'll put these in the pharmacy,' Vance said as he took the bags from them.

'What about this?' said Yappy as he pointed out the little navy windcheater he had folded over his arm.

'Give it here, Yappy,' smiled Vance.

§

Over breakfast, Vance told the men he had a loader on the tracks arriving any day. While in Brisbane he had also purchased everything he could think of to set up a camp.

'The guy at Army Disposals was very helpful. If there's anything lacking, all I have to do is call him and he'll have it on the next train for us. I want you men to sober up over the next few weeks. Yappy, I'm going to put you in charge of the weaning after I get rooms at the Majestic organised for Faith, Neil, and Little Joe.'

'Why am I in charge?' asked Yappy. 'They might beat the crap out of me if they go into the horrors.'

'Because you don't have to be weaned off the booze, Yappy. It is obvious to me by your presentation that you only hit the grog occasionally instead of all day, every day. They won't beat the crap out of you, Yappy, because you will give them a drink when they really need it. Other times, you make sure they drink lots of water and eat something at least once a day. Okay, men?'

'Won't be easy.' Said Neil seriously.

'That's for sure,' added Faith

'You can say that again,' answered Little Joe.

'I'll be back soon,' said Vance. 'Don't go anywhere.' Vance found Jack and Bert Romeo in the office of the Empire.

'I want to rent rooms at the Majestic for Neil, Faith, and Little Joe. It ain't to dry them out the way you men did for me.'

'Didn't last long,' laughed Jack.

'That's all about to change,' smiled Vance.

'We'll see,' nodded Bert.

Vance explained about Yappy being caretaker. After a short time, it was agreed that they would open the door between two connecting rooms. There were to be two beds in each room, one for Yappy and one for each of the other men.

'Yappy needs to be in the same room as the others so he can keep a close eye on them,' said Jack Romeo.

'Yes,' added Bert. 'He also better go to the crapper with them and keep the doors locked whenever he goes out for food or booze.'

¶

Vance and Bert collected the men from Con's Café and went off to the Majestic to organise the accommodations and get the men locked in before the pubs opened.

'Yappy, go to Jake's and get warm pyjamas for them; otherwise, the poor buggers will freeze.'

'Right on, Boss, you think of everything.'

'Want a pink pair for yourself, Yappy?' asked Jake as he selected three pairs of pyjamas from a wall cupboard.

'Don't be so bloody smart, you young pup. Keep it up and I'll deck you.'

'Sure, Yappy, I'm terrified,' laughed Jake as he looked down at Yappy.

'I'll go buy a radio so you can listen to the races while you babysit, Yappy,' said Vance. 'You get your charges settled in first.'

¶

Vance returned sometime later with a radio, a box of forty-eight chocolate bars, and a half dozen or so books.

'I have to go now, Yappy. I'll check on you after siren time. You're all on the payroll as of now, Yappy.'

It didn't dawn on Vance until he was seated in the dispensary that not one of the men had asked what pay they would receive.

Bloody hell, he thought to himself, the poor buggers are so eager to be rescued they don't care about money.

¶

Jake phoned TC around midday.

'Did my bribes work?'

'They are lovely, Jake. Thank you from both of us. Yes, we will be delighted to go to the movies with you on Saturday night.' Jake couldn't believe his ears.

'Should have bought you a couple of suitcases earlier,' he laughed.

'I'll even wear the overcoat. Lou is wondering when she will get one.'

'Well, she won't be getting one from me because I don't plan on marrying Lou; I plan on marrying you.'

'Don't be ridiculous, Jake. How is the boss?'

'He had a tough day and night yesterday. He's okay today.'

'Is it okay if I come and waste time with you ladies tonight? I'll bring food for dinner.'

'See you then, Jake,' replied TC.

¶

Lou and TC had been sorting out their clothes when Jake phoned; so, as TC returned to Lou, she told her friend that he was bringing some food for dinner and to make certain they remembered to return his records.

'I'll miss some of them,' said Lou. TC laughed.

'Me, too, especially poor Old Slim. Wonder if I should take these, Lou?' as she held up her pink embroidered Elvis, Jerry Lee, Rock 'n' Roll shirt and pedal-pushers. Lou laughed.

'Why not? They'll be more appropriate anywhere we go than they are here.'

'We sure have done a lot of sewing,' remarked Lou. 'I have nineteen dresses, all home-made.'

'I have about the same,' replied TC. 'I am going to buy some shoes and matching handbags when we get to the city, that is, after we find somewhere to live and a job.'

'How much money have you got, TC?' enquired Lou.

'I'm not sure. I have around two hundred in my savings and whatever my pay was, which will be around six weeks, including holiday pay.'

'Haven't you counted it yet, TC?' asked a somewhat shocked Lou.

'No, didn't think about it 'til now. Suppose my mind has been on other things.'

'Thanks to Vance and his hundred-and-ten quid, I've got two-hundred-and-seventy. Do you think that will be enough?'

TC shook her head. 'I don't know. Suppose we will find out soon enough. It's mail day tomorrow, Lou. I'm going to help the boss.'

'When did he ask you?'

'He didn't. I just simply decided that I am helping him.

❡

At siren time, Vance went directly to the Majestic to check on his men. He took with him a pack of cards.

'How are they, Yappy?' he asked when his knock on the door was answered.

'We are all bloody bored,' said Neil loudly.

'They are a bit cranky,' replied Yappy, rolling his eyes and smiling.

'I can tell,' whispered Vance.

Once inside the room, Vance asked the men if they were hungry.

'No. We want a drink,' replied the three in unison.

'Plenty of water there,' replied Vance as he indicated two large jugs of water on a small corner table.

323

'We don't want effing water! We want an effing real drink!' from Neil.

'You can have one later. Yappy will get you all a drink later, won't you, Yappy.'

'I sure will,' replied Yappy.

'All right, I will see you men later,' said Vance. 'Yappy, come outside for a minute, will you, mate? Give them one drink each in a couple of hours, Yappy. Sooner if they get stroppy. See if you can encourage them to eat those chocolate bars. Their bodies will be craving sugar pretty soon. Do you want something to eat, Yappy?'

Yappy shook his head. 'No, had a big breakfast.'

Vance left. 'See you all later, Yappy.'

'Can't blame the poor buggers for needing a drink, I need one myself,' as he headed to the Empire.

¶

'How are they doing?' asked Jake, when Vance joined him at the bar.

'As you'd expect. I feel like a hypocrite, Jake. I've got those poor bastards locked up, and here I am in the pub about to knock off a rum and Coke, or two, or three, or more.'

Jake said nothing, deciding to change the subject.

'I'm going to see the girls tonight, and I am taking them to the movies on Saturday night,' Jake laughed. 'I still can't believe it.'

'In that case, thank God TC is going away, Jake. I told you before, Jake, you are not right for her.'

'Thought you wanted her to stay?' replied Jake.

'With all my heart but not if she looks like ending up with you. I'm going.' Vance picked up his change and walked out. Five minutes later, he was chatting with Lou and TC in their dining room.

'Jake told me he's taking you to the movies.' Both TC and Lou nodded.

'He gave us a suitcase each as a bribe,' said Lou.

'I see.' Vance looked at TC.

'Be careful of Jake, TC.'

'Boss, I'm going away on Sunday. Apart from that, he knows that I'm not his type.'

'That is exactly what I'm afraid of, young lady,' he said, as he stood up and left via the back door.

¶

Jake was sitting in his car in front of the pharmacy when Vance re-opened after lunch break. Jake got out of his car.

'What's the problem, Vance?'

'Every damned thing, Jake. Just everything.'

'Well, can I help you, mate?'

'Nobody can help me, Jake. I've committed myself to this opal mining project. This joint will be closed more often that it's open. Delores is fed up again. Says she's going. I've got three full-blown alcoholics locked up in a room in the Majestic with a poor bloody binge drinker playing nurse to them. TC has quit her job with me and is going away because I took her for granted and allowed all and sundry to treat her like crap. Louise is being the bitch that she is. Latest is she has threatened to tell her poor bloody husband and Delores what has been going on. As if they don't already know. I have reached the stage where I would like nothing more than to walk away from this whole bloody mess, find Anna, and disappear into thin air.'

'Sounds like chronic depression to me, mate. I'm no doctor, but seems to me you have had a gutful of everything.'

'You have hit the nail on the head, Jake,' agreed Vance. 'I feel locked in like a caged animal, no escape route, unless I can find the key. Problem is, where do I start searching for the bastard?'

Jake shook his head slowly with an extremely serious expression on his face.

'Don't think you have much choice other than to carry on, mate. You have a wife and kids, this business, your mining gear, plus you have now adopted and taken under your wing four poor buggers for whom you will be their salvation. Everything will turn out in the end. People will become accustomed to erratic hours in this place. Delores will go away;

then again she will come back; she always does. The men will dry out and probably prove to be the hardest-working poor buggers on earth. Louise will eventually fade into oblivion. TC will eventually return to Brolga because Lou will; at least, we both hope she will, for our own individual reasons. As for Anna, I think you should try to forget her, mate. She's long gone. Get out there, find the opal and become a bloody legend.'

They both laughed, then chatted for a while until the phone rang and Jake said 'See you later.'

⁋

The rest of the afternoon passed quickly, except, that is, for the confined locked up at the Majestic.

Yappy had given them one drink each as instructed. Bloody strong ones too, he had thought as he poured them. They all wanted more. When Yappy refused and offered them water and chocolates, Neil threw a jugful of water all over Yappy's immaculate clothes, and Little Joe upturned the carton of chocolate bars.

'This cold-turkey crap is bullshit,' snarled Faith. 'I'll kill that bloody pill-pushing bastard when he shows up.' Yappy kept looking at the locked door, praying Vance would show up soon.

⁋

At closing time Vance took the men's bags full of soiled clothes to Neil's mother, who took in washing and ironing to make a few bob here and there. Vance told her about Neil, Faith, and Little Joe.

She was happy and thanked Vance profusely. He collected a large tray of pre-ordered sandwiches, a large aluminium pot of fresh hot, black coffee and a cylinder of plastic cups from Con's Café. He grabbed a handful of sugar cubes from a bowl on the counter and made his way to his crew.

⁋

Jake went directly home from work. Thel Carmichael was openly in shock.

'You are early, Jake,' she said as he kissed her on the cheek.

'Yes, I want to get cleaned up, and then I'm going out for dinner.'

Thel knew better than to ask where and with whom. She smiled at Jake.

'That's nice, Jake.'

'Yes, I'm going to TC and Lou's place,' replied Jake as he walked towards the bathroom.

Thel sat in silence, wondering how on earth the girls were going to cook dinner on the tiny little hot plate-cum-oven that was bought on the spur of the moment a few years ago. She could still hear Flo saying repeatedly, 'The damned thing is useless.'

When Jake emerged quite a while later, Thel could not help but comment on how handsome her son looked in his obviously new, white, polo-necked sweater and matching cardigan contrasted against his black hair, blue eyes, and black trousers, belt, and shoes.

'You look very handsome, Jake. Wish your father could be here to see you.'

'I wish he could be here, too, Mum,' replied Jake softly. 'See you later,' after he kissed her cheek.

Ethel sat silently remembering her late husband and the happy years they had shared until Carla came rushing in from her toy room crying because the head had broken off one of the many dolls.

Anyone would think a man has never been to Flo's house before, thought Jake as he pulled his car out of his mother's driveway. Jake made a quick stop at Con's to discuss details of the special dinner Lisa was preparing for the girls.

'Where are you going, young Jake?' asked Con.

'You know where I'm going, Con,' replied Jake with a smile. 'Obviously, after last week, I can't bring her here anymore. I could kill those bloody nurses for coming in when they did.' Con laughed loudly.

'Mate, you had better think twice before you kill the nurses. You would be killing your sex supply.' Jake joined Con in laughter. 'Smart, bloody Greek, see you at seven-thirty sharp.'

¶

TC and Lou, both dressed in cute, flat shoes, jeans, and sweaters with bow-tied ponytails, heard Jake's car pull to a stop. Next thing, he was opening the back door and inside.

'Jake, you look great,' said Lou. 'I mean it, Jake; you look really handsome.'

'Mum thought so, too,' smiled Jake, who was looking at TC.

'I thought we were going to the movies Saturday night,' said TC with a smile. TC then gave him a nod of approval. Yes, Jake, you look pretty good.'

'You smell good, as well' added Lou.

'This is the third last night I'll have for a while to impress TC,' he smiled. 'Isn't that so, my darling, sweetheart girl?' as he looked directly into TC s eyes. TC looked away and shook her head.

'Jake, stop being ridiculous or you will have to leave now.'

'Okay, princess, I promise to be good. Put on some music, Lou. I'll get us some Cokes and a beer. And you, TC, darling, should set a table for three.' TC glared at him.

'Jake!'

'Okay! Okay! Okay! No more darlings, sweeties, or princesses.' Jake went off to fetch drinks.

¶

Jake and Lou sat in the lounge happily chatting while TC set the table.

'Jake, how much money do you think TC and I will need?'

'Don't know, Lou. I strongly suggest you both have a good time, spend every cent you have, then come back. Treat it as a holiday.'

'That's what you would do, Jake. You are not TC and I.'

'Of course, that is what I would do because it's the smart way to go.

How much money have you got, anyway?' continued Jake.

'I have a bit less than three hundred. TC is not quite sure how much she has.'

'About time she found out,' said Jake as he puffed on a cigarette.

'I'm about to find out,' said TC, who appeared at the lounge room door holding the envelope Vance had given her. 'It's none of your business whether or not I have enough money, Jake Carmichael.' Lou jumped up.

'Give me the envelope, TC. I'll open it. If it was me, I would have opened it ten seconds after Vance handed it to me.' Lou ripped open the envelope and stared open-mouthed at the contents.

'It's twenty-pound notes, TC. A lot of them!'

'Show me,' said TC as she reached for the envelope before extracting the money and a note from Vance. The quickly written note said, "TC, you have earned every penny of this and deserve much more. Please stay the way you are—a good girl. Boss." Tears filled TC's eyes. She placed the money back in the envelope and put it on the small telephone table before going in search of tissues. Lou picked up the envelope, read the note, and counted the money.

'No wonder she's crying. There's five hundred quid here.'

'Lou,' said Jake. 'It's not the money that made her cry; she didn't count it. It's the note that has caused TC to cry. Incredible. She comes across like strength unlimited; yet, a simple note from Vance brings out the soft side. After all the crap she has had to tolerate, it's unbelievable she's feeling guilty because she's leaving. I have to go talk to her, Lou. You get you and me another drink.'

§

Jake found TC sitting on the edge of her bed crying softly.

'Come on, TC, I have ordered a great dinner for the three of us. Lisa Kasa has probably been busy all afternoon preparing it.'

'I feel as if I'm deserting the boss, Jake.'

'No, you are not. You'll see. He will appreciate you more when you come back.'

'I'm not coming back, Jake.'

'Yes, you will. Vance and I both believe that; otherwise, we wouldn't let you go. Now, come on, go wash your sad face and replace it with a happy one.'

'Thank you, Jake. I'll be fine. Go put Louis Armstrong on the stereo, and I'll be there in a minute or two.'

¶

As promised, TC joined Jake and Lou shortly after.

'Lou, I am definitely going to help the boss with the mail tomorrow.'

'I'll come, too,' agreed Lou. 'Free of charge this time.'

'Good. That's settled,' sighed Jake, looking at his watch. 'I am going to collect our dinner. Lou, how about coming with me to lend a hand? TC, you stay here and mind the house.'

Last thing I bloody need with TC the way she is tonight is to run into those bitchy nurses again, thought Jake, as he and Lou ran down the stairs.

¶

TC shifted the heater into the dining room, then closed the lounge room door to keep the warm air in. Jake and Lou arrived back with two trays, one huge and one medium, both laden with food covered by thick white towels.

With great fanfare, Jake removed the cover of the larger tray to explore a beautifully presented assortment of food, including a gleaming baking dish filled with what looked like lasagne but didn't smell like lasagne, a Greek salad plus a garden salad, an assortment of freshly home-baked small, warm bread rolls along with a small bowl containing butter cubes topped off with sprigs of fresh parsley. On the side of the tray was a card which read, "Please enjoy—Con and Lisa Kasa."

'We'll enjoy, all right,' said Lou.

'Looks delicious,' agreed TC.

'Don't know what this is called but Lisa served it up one night when we did one of our many daylight-'til-dawn poker games,' explained Jake. 'Let's eat, ladies. Give me your plates and I shall serve the mystery dish. Better ask Lisa for the recipe after we get married, TC.'

'Wake up to yourself. Jake,' said Lou as she handed a salad bowl complete with a beautiful set of Lisa's silver salad servers to TC.

'Pretty good tucker, isn't it, ladies?' asked Jake as they ate. Both girls agreed immediately. Lou smiled.

'I imagine this is just like eating in a restaurant.'

Jake took a sip of his rum and Coke. 'Just about, Lou. Pity you ladies don't drink; red wine would go well with this meal.' Lou looked at Jake in confusion.

'If red wine goes well with the meal, how come you are drinking rum and Coke, Jake?'

'Simple, Lou. I don't like red wine.' They all laughed. Lou stood up.

'I think I'll play a Dean Martin record; he is always drinking red wine—I read so in a magazine.' Jake shrugged.

'Well, Lou, if you read it in a magazine, it must be true.'

¶

When they finished eating, Jake suggested they return to the lounge room for coffee. The girls cleared the table and rinsed the plates and cutlery while the kettle boiled. Jake covered the left-over food before taking the smaller tray into the lounge and removing the cover. When Lou and TC took in the coffee, Jake was sitting back smoking as he looked at the ceiling. He was waiting for the girls' reaction to his surprise.

Both girls spotted the cake at the same time. It was a double-decker sponge with cream and shaved nuts on the ends and sides, while on the top there was cream with piped-chocolate icing reading; 'Be good girls' and a piped-chocolate 'Come back soon' and a heart on opposite ends. Alongside the cake was a crystal bowl full of chocolates, three cake plates, a cake knife, and three dessert forks individually wrapped in white linen napkins.

Lou and TC were speechless. TC broke the silence.

'Can't think of anything to say, Jake, except thank you.' Lou smiled.

'Me, too, Jake. Thank you.'

'My pleasure,' replied Jake with a smile. 'I think I'll have another Scotch and Coke while you ladies drink your coffees.'

In the meantime, Vance was holed up in the room at the Majestic with Neil, Faith, and Little Joe. He had sent Yappy to his room to get some sleep.

The three men were restless and cranky. They all complained of being hot one minute, then shivering cold the next.

Poor bastards, thought Vance. Wish there was an easy way to do this. Neil is by far in a worse way than the other two. Poor bugger will probably go into the DTs. This is not a simple matter of sleeping it off. Then again, he suddenly thought, perhaps it is. He unlocked the door, then relocked it when he was in the hallway before hurrying downstairs and across to the pharmacy, where he selected a bottle of capsules from a dispensary shelf before hurrying back to the Majestic.

Yappy was sound asleep when Vance entered the room, took a bottle of rum along with three plastic cups from the dressing table, then went to the bathroom across the hall. Once in the bathroom, he shook the contents of one capsule into each glass before pouring a stiff nip of rum in on top. He took the rum bottle back to Yappy's room before unlocking the other one.

'Come on, you men,' he said loudly. 'Time for a fix. I'll give the fix, but you have to promise to drink a little water afterwards.' The three men eagerly reached for their drinks and gulped them down, followed by a mouthful or two of water.

'How about another one?' asked Neil and Faith. Vance smiled.

'Later, my friends.'

¶

Less than half an hour later they were sleeping like babies. Vance woke Yappy with a gentle shake of the shoulder.

'Safe to go in with the others to sleep now, mate. Lock yourself in before I leave, and I'll see you in the morning when I bring breakfast.'

'You're on,' agreed a still half-asleep Yappy as he got out of bed and accompanied Vance to where the other men slept. Vance waited until he heard Yappy turn the key in the door before deliberating on whether to go home to Delores and his, by now sleeping, children or wait until Louise finished work and go to the creek.

'Bugger it, it's too cold for the creek; I'll go home. Poor bloody Delores will be surprised to see me this early. Oh, well, there's a first time for everything. If she starts to carry on, I'll pretend I'm asleep.'

¶

Jake stayed with the girls until they kicked him out around two in the morning. As they heard his car zoom up Brolga Street, Lou commented, 'There may be more than just beer and skittle to Jake Carmichael, after all!'

TC agreed. 'Perhaps.'

Vance was at the Majestic around 7 am. Apart from Yappy, the men were still sleeping. He sent Yappy off to shower and shave, then one by one woke the other three.

'Where am I?' from a groggy Little Joe.

'You're in bed, mate. You are fine,' replied Vance.

Faith simply opened his eyes and looked at Vance before slowly sitting up and yawning. Neil opened his eyes, saw Vance through blurred vision, mumbled 'Bugger off,' turned over, and went back to sleep.

Yappy returned, looking dapper once again. After Faith and Little Joe showered and dressed, they headed for Con's to eat breakfast.

'What about Neil?' asked Faith.

'We'll bring some back for Neil,' replied Vance. 'Let him sleep; he's enjoying it.'

❡

Lou and TC were walking to the pharmacy when they saw Vance and the others go into the café, so they followed them.

It was the first time TC had worn one of the two pink Innoxa uniforms a cosmetic rep had given her months before. 'I'll wear this for luck, Lou,' she had said when Lou expressed surprise. Vance spotted them the moment they walked into Con's and smiled in somewhat disbelief.

'Well, look who is here, men. If it isn't Little Miss Pink Professional and her shadow.

'Little Flower, you look like a pink rose,' said Faith with a warm smile. 'Look at her, Yappy, pink bow in her hair, pink outfit, and little pink shoes. Don't you think she looks like a little flower, Yappy?' Yappy scrutinised TC from head to toe and agreed.

'Spot on, mate.'

'What about me, Vance?' asked Lou. 'After all, I am offering you my help today for free.'

'What do you mean, Lou?' asked Vance.

'It's mail day, Boss. Thought you might like some help. Looks as if you have your hands full, so if you care to hand over the shop keys, we will go and get started.' Vance stood up, extracted the keys from his pocket, and handed them to TC with a smile.

'Thank you. Thank you, too, young Lou.'

❡

After TC and Lou were gone, Yappy turned to Vance.

'What's the name of the little one in pink?'

'That's TC, Yappy. Why?'

'I know her old man. Great bloke. Gunny shearer and horse trainer. Word has it his missus made a mistake with the kid's name when she was born, so she's always been tagged TC. Bloody small world. Tell you what, Pill-Pusher, if the kid is half the person her old man is, she's a bloody good kid.'

'That she is, Yappy. Let's eat,' replied Vance.

Mail day at the Brolga Pharmacy was a frenzy, as usual.

'Don't know how the hell Vance will handle everything,' sighed Lou when a local delivery truck pulled up outside late morning and the truck driver started unloading what seemed to be a never-ending stream of boxes and cartons from the drug houses.

'Never mind, Lou. Let's keep at it. With a little luck, we will have everything unpacked and, on the shelves, before we collapse.'

¶

Just before siren time, TC slipped next door to the newsagency and purchased a few cards. She wrote one to Lisa Kasa, thanking her.

"Dear Mrs Kasa, Thank you! Everything was wonderful! The cake looked (and tasted) so lovely we were reluctant to cut it (we did, of course!). Probably, we will be living on pies and peas from the Café De Wheels in a few months' time. Thank you for a lovely memory. Lou and TC."

TC showed it to Lou for approval. Lou nodded as the siren sounded.

'I'll go buy us a couple of shakes,' she suggested as she glanced around. 'We can enjoy them on the move.' TC smiled.

'Look at is this way, Lou; we will have an hour without phone calls.'

'You spoke too soon,' replied Lou as the phone rang.

TC picked it up but did not get the chance to speak.

'Are you coming home?' It was Delores.

'Mrs Callahan, it's TC.'

'What are you doing there, TC? I thought you had finished up.'

'I came in to help the boss with mail day, Mrs Callahan.'

'I see. Is he there?'

'No. Sorry.'

'Where is he?'

'I don't know, Mrs Callahan. Last time I saw him, he was in a meeting.'

'Fine.' Delores hung up.

Some things really don't ever change, thought TC, as she began getting the new order together. The phone rang again.

'TC, you will tell him I called, won't you?'

'Of course, Mrs Callahan.'

'Good.' Delores hung up again.

Poor lady, thought TC, with a sigh. Lou returned from Con's with Jake in tow.

'Well, look at Miss Cutie Pink Pie,' laughed Jake. 'You look cute enough to eat, darling.' TC rolled her eyes.

'Don't start that again, Jake.'

'Where is Vance?'

'We don't know. He has not been here.'

'What time do you think you will get things finished here?' TC and Lou both shrugged.

'Probably ten or midnight, Jake. Depends on how many interruptions we get.'

'I get the message. I'm out of here. Be back later.'

Jake left, secure in the knowledge that he could call one of the nurses, make a date for nine, go to the creek, get his rocks off, and be back at the pharmacy to take the girls home when they finished working.

As usual, it did not enter Jake's head that he was a full-blown mongrel, especially where the nurses were concerned. His motto had always been, "If they want it, I'll give it to them. No problem."

§

Vance was rushing around trying to locate and organise one of the truckers to collect his camp equipment, which he had been assured was on the goods train. He was not quite sure which site he would give a try first. He intended to flip a coin when the okay for the third site came through.

'Just hold it at your depot until I decide, will you, mate? Apart from that, it will probably take a few more days or so to get my crew ready for hard work.'

'Yeah, heard about that. It's a bloody joke, mate—a drunk rescuing drunks! Hope it comes off for you, mate. Good bloody luck, that is all I can say, mate.'

'Thanks, mate. I suppose only time will tell.'

Vance then went to the local car dealer to buy a ute before going to check on Yappy and the others.

'They are better than I expected, Boss; even eaten a few chocolate bars and drank a fair bit of water.'

'Good, Yappy. Unless they bung on a turn, don't give them a drink until tonight when I come back.'

'Okay,' agreed Yappy seriously as he nodded his head.

Vance decided he had best go home to see Delores.

¶

'What is TC doing back at the shop, Vance?'

'She's helping out.'

'I thought she finished up?'

'She did. She's helping out because it's mail day and I have other things to do.'

'I thought she was leaving town?'

'Oh, for God's sake, and yours, leave it alone. I'm out of here.'

¶

Vance drove to Carmichael and Carmichael to see Jake. Jake was wrapping parcels for the mail drop.

'What's up, mate?' he asked Vance, who looked and was furious.

'Nothing I want to talk about, Jake. Got time for a few drinks?'

'Have to help the staff for about an hour, then they can finish the rest.' Vance looked at his watch.

'Meet you at the Empire in an hour, then,' he called before he walked out, got in his car, then drove to the creek where he silently meditated on anything and everything.

⸿

Vance could not recall having been to sit by the creek before in daylight; he knew for sure he had not been there alone. He couldn't help but notice how quiet and peaceful it was. Even pretty, he observed. The water, almost still with the huge gum trees overhanging and casting shadows that could be interpreted as a million images. He momentarily considered getting a rope and hanging himself from one of the trees. The thought was fleeting and soon went away. He noticed some magpies swooping down for a drink. How free those lucky birds are; wish I could be that free. What a dream of a life that would be. Become tired of location or circumstances, just spread your wings and fly away to wherever the breeze or instinct takes you.

Suddenly, he remembered he was supposed to meet Jake, glanced at his watch, switched on the ignition, reversed away from the creek, and was on his way.

'Poor, bloody Jake. He's probably been in the Empire waiting like a shag on a bloody rock, while I've been sitting by the creek commiserating on my lot in life.'

⸿

As Vance walked into the Empire heading for the bar, he heard Jake call him.

'In here, mate.'

Vance turned towards Jake's voice to see Jake sitting at a table in the ladies' lounge with the nurses from the hospital.

'Come join us,' suggested Jake. Vance shook his head before smiling.

'No thanks, Jake. Everyone in Brolga is aware of the fact that I already have more than enough woman woes. I'll see you later, Jake.' Vance turned, then walked out through the front door where he almost walked head-on into Bert Romeo.

'How're those drunks going?' asked Bert.

'Good, Bert. I'm on my way to see them after I pick up some food from Con's.'

'Good boy.' Approved Bert.

Vance decided he would repeat the night-before procedure except that he would give them the drink before they ate. The men were more likely to go to sleep earlier, which would enable them to have a less restless night then otherwise they would endure.

¶

'They all have the shakes, Boss,' proclaimed Yappy when Vance arrived. 'Get a look at Neil; he is the worst struck. They really need a drink. Seeing this is enough to turn a man off the bloody grog for life.' Vance laughed.

'I know exactly what you mean, Yappy.' Vance looked at Neil, who was sitting upright, staring into space with a glazed look in his eyes. Neil's entire body appeared to be shaking. Faith and Little Joe were both lying down. They were also shaking, but they looked as if they were enduring a severe attack of the shivers.

'I'll get you a drink,' announced Vance as he unlocked the door. He returned five minutes later with three drinks—a heavier one for Neil than for Faith and Little Joe.

'Here, Neil, mate. Drink this. I'll hold it for you. Just sip a little at a time.' Neil put his two shaking hands on the cup in an attempt to hold it himself.

'No, mate. I will hold it for you because you will spill it.'

Yappy was silently observing. He was thinking, *A man would assume the boss was talking to a small child if I was not sitting here watching. Vance has got a soft side to him. Looks as if he's a bloody good bloke.*

After Neil eventually finishing his drink, Vance convinced him to drink a little water and lie down.

Faith and Little Jo sat up for their drinks. They were pretty shaky but not so far gone that they would spill them. They also drank a little water.

'Do you need a break, Yappy?' asked Vance.

'No, Boss, I'll be fine. I'm in the middle of a good book, so after we eat, I'll settle down to that,' replied Yappy with enthusiasm.

'Good man, Yappy. Now, see if you can get Neil to eat something. Don't force him; just suggest. I think they'll be asleep in an hour or so. I'll just get some more rum. We are almost out. I'll go now, Yappy. I'll see you in the morning.'

¶

Vance dropped into the Empire and bought a couple of bottles of rum from Jack Romeo. Louise was working, so he arranged to pick her up when she knocked off at ten. He then drove to Neil's mother's house to fill her in on the men's progress and collect their now-clean clothes. Vance left Neil's mum, momentarily thought about going home, instantly decided against it, and soon after pulled his car in behind the pharmacy. As he had anticipated, Lou and TC were still there.

'Hello, girls, how was your day?'

They both replied, 'Busy.'

'The orders are all finished and ready to go. We started unpacking the new stock just a short while ago, Boss.'

'That stuff came at the right time.' Vance smiled. He opened the cash register and extracted some money.

'Lou, go to Con's and buy half a dozen Cokes, will you? Also pay him what I owe him.'

'Sure, Vance.' Lou was out the door in a flash.

TC stopped unpacking cartons and looked at Vance.

'You gave me too much money.' Vance laughed and shook his head.

'No, TC, I didn't pay you nearly enough. I didn't give you anything, TC, except perhaps a hard time.'

Lou returned. Vance poured himself a rum and Coke, lit a cigarette and sat at his desk thinking and watching TC and Lou through the dispensary's one-way mirror. Vance had a few more drinks and chain-smoked, waiting for ten o'clock to come, when he would pick up Louise.

When ten came around, he drove into the backyard of the Empire, picked up Louise, and, without a word, drove her home.

'It's over, Louise. Please don't say one word. It's over between you and me. Now, please, get out of my car.'

Louise was in so much shock that she did exactly what she was told. She watched the back of his car as he drove away, walked inside her house, and threw herself on her bed, where she lay crying uncontrollably until she was exhausted and fell asleep.

¶

Once again Vance thought of going home, then decided against it. He went to the pharmacy and resumed his seat behind his desk with a rum and Coke and a cigarette.

Jake knocked on the front door at half past ten. The girls let him in, and he joined Vance in the dispensary. Jake and Vance talked about the usual things they always discussed—houses, cards, etc., until TC and Lou had finished unpacking and stacking shelves.

TC asked Jake to put the empty cartons outside the back door while Lou swept and TC mopped the floors.

'Would you like a Coke?' asked Vance when the girls had finally finished. They both declined.

'Well, Boss, that's it!'

'Lou, did you give the Boss his change from Con?'

'Oh, damn, I forgot,' replied an embarrassed Lou as she reached into her skirt pocket and fished out Vance's change and a docket.

'Sorry, Vance, I promise that will not happen again.' She smiled. 'Not for a while anyway.' Lou yawned. 'I want to go home to bed, TC. I'm tired'.

'Me, too', agreed TC.

'I'll drive you home, ladies,' said Jake.

'No! You stay here and talk to the boss, Jake. We will walk ... I mean, run, home. You will want to hang around, and we are both tired.'

'Drive the girls home and then come back,' suggested Vance.

'Good idea,' agreed Jake.

¶

Jake was back within five minutes. They played poker until four in the morning when Jake was too tired to concentrate.

'I think we're about even, mate. Good time to quit.'

Vance agreed, so they went their separate ways—Jake went home, and Vance went to the Majestic, where he fell asleep in Yappy's bed in Yappy's room.

A few hours later, he was knocking on the door where the men were.

'You look bloody terrible, Boss. Looks like you slept in your bloody clothes.' Vance smiled at Yappy.

'I did, as a matter of fact, Yappy. Not only that, I slept in your bed. Let's repeat yesterday's procedure, then I have to go home and make myself respectable, after the mail truck picks up from the shop, that is.'

¶

Poor Delores was beside herself when Vance eventually went home to get cleaned up.

'Vance, where on earth have you been?! I've been worried sick!'

'Jake and I played cards,' he replied. 'Now I have to hurry.'

¶

TC was sitting on the Seat of Knowledge talking to Carmel when Vance arrived at the pharmacy. She said goodbye to Carmel and walked towards Vance, who was waiting at the door. Vance laughed.

'What? Are you going to be a slave again today, TC?'

'No. I came to say goodbye to the best boss in the world.' Vance looked around.

'Where is he?'

342

'Don't be silly. You know I'm referring to you.' Vance became serious. 'Come in, Butterball. God, I'm going to miss you.'

'No more than I'll miss you, Boss. I'm feeling sad about leaving all this,' she said as she threw wide her arms and cast her eyes around with a smile. 'It's just that I promised Lou. You told me once, if we make a promise, we keep it or die trying.'

'Wish I had not told you that one. I hope you remember everything I've told you, Butterball.' TC laughed.

'Yes, especially the "not to do".'

'Good girl.'

'Lou and I are leaving in the morning. Thanks to you I have much more money than Lou. She has a little less than three hundred pounds, and I have little over seven hundred pounds. I don't think it is fair that I have so much more than she because I'll be able to buy things that she can't afford and then I'll feel terrible.'

'For heaven's sake, TC, you've earned that money, and you earned it hard, so stop feeling guilty, otherwise I'll be forced to call you stupid again.' They both laughed.

'Boss I want to leave my bank book and another two hundred pounds here with you. That way I won't be tempted to go on a spending spree and I won't go broke.' Vance shook his head in disbelief.

'TC, I sometimes find it difficult to fathom the wisdom stored in that head of yours.'

TC handed Vance her bank savings book, two hundred pounds, a deposit slip, and a half dozen signed withdrawal forms.

'I'll deposit it on Monday,' said Vance with a smile. 'Now, Butterball, when you get settled, I expect you to let me know your address, where you work, and telephone numbers of both.'

TC nodded, 'I will, I promise,' as she felt tears welling in her eyes.

'Now get out of here, young lady, before I start to cry,' commanded Vance.

TC walked around his desk, patted him on the head, then leaned down and kissed him on the cheek before saying, 'Goodbye, Boss. Thank you for teaching me so much about so much. I'll keep in touch.'

Vance watched TC disappear through the door, stubbed out his cigarette in the ashtray, closed his eyes, and cupped his head in his hands before talking to himself.

'What a bloody tragedy. She's only a girl but she's the best, most principled person I have ever known. If she ever comes back, I'll have to remember to tell her.' The phone rang. Vance picked it up.

'Having a bet this afternoon, mate?'

'Yes, Jake, I'll meet you at the Empire around one after I've checked on the men.'

§

Lou and TC finished their packing apart from what they would wear to the movies with Jake and clothes for their train trip. Lou was over the moon.

'This time tomorrow, we'll be on the train,' she said as she fixed rollers in TC's freshly shampooed hair.

'Lou, we have to put covers over the furniture, roll up the mattresses on the verandah bunks, and put them inside, wash up Lisa Kasa's dishes, and make certain Jake takes his records with him tonight when he leaves.'

'You are such a worry wart, TC!'

'No, I'm not, Lou. I simply don't like leaving things to chance.'

'There you go. Your rollers are all in. Let's put our beauty masks on our ugly faces and start getting things done.'

§

Vance checked in with Yappy.

'I had to change their sheets, mate,' explained Yappy. 'Poor buggers have been sweating so much their sheets were wet. That housemaid, Sam, helped me. Neil is the only one I had to give a drink to. Faith and Little Jo are getting into the chocolate and water.'

'Good, Yappy, that's great,' replied Vance, 'Do you want me to put a bet on for you?'

'Yeah, Boss, I would. I'll give you ten quid. Make sure you put it on a winner for me.'

Vance laughed as he took the ten-pound note from Yappy. 'All right, mate. I'll be certain to put it on a winner.'

'Good on ya, Boss. Know you'll come through for me.'

Vance smiled. 'Don't think I have any choice, Yappy. See you later.'

After a couple of initial bad bets, both Vance and Jake ended up well in front by the time the last race in three states was run.

'Think we've been hit in the butt by a bloody rainbow, mate,' said Jake as they totalled up their winnings. Vance nodded in agreement.

'Yes, Jake, there are three things at which we excel—gambling, drinking grog, and womanising.'

'Prime pair of bastards, that's us.'

'Yes, that is us, my friend. Jess, get us one for the road, please. I have a date with two young ladies tonight, so I have to get going.' Jess rolled her eyes towards the ceiling.

'Smart, young mongrel! I'm also going to be crowned Queen of England,' she replied tongue-in-cheek as she collected their glasses. When she returned with their refills, she slammed them on the bar before collecting the exact amount of money from the change on the bar.

'Only two young ladies I know of in this God-forsaken hell hole are TC and Lou. I know they are too smart to be going on a date with the likes of you, Jake Carmichael.'

'You might be surprised, Jess, my darling,' replied Jake with a mischievous twinkle in his eyes and a cat-that-got-the-cream smile on his face.

'Young mongrel,' muttered Jess as she stormed off to the cash register.

Vance looked at Jake. 'Trust Jess to be spot-on, mate.'

Not too long later Vance arrived at the Majestic with food for the men.

'How did I go? Did you back me a winner, Boss?' asked Yappy the moment Vance walked through the door. Vance laughed.

'Yes, Yappy, I backed a winner for you. First, give me a chance to put this tray down.' Vance then counted out forty pounds and handed it to Yappy.

'Are you happy, Yappy?' asked Vance.

'Yes, Boss, I'm a very happy Yappy,' he smiled as he put the notes in his pocket.

'Oh, stop pissing in each other's pockets,' yelled Neil.

'Yeah,' added Faith. 'A man's fed up with Yappy this and Yappy that. Now it's bloody happy, bloody Yappy, as well. Enough to make a bloody man vomit.'

'I'm hungry. Quit your bullshit, all of you,' interrupted Little Joe. Vance and Yappy laughed.

'Looks like you men are getting well,' said Vance.

'I need a drink, Pill-Pusher,' coming from an aggressive Neil. 'You'd think a man is a bloody camel.'

※

Jake was at home, waiting to hear the train whistle as it crossed the bridge over the creek, thus heralding the arrival of the Flea.

Bloody Flea, he thought, as he got in his car. Tonight, you bring the film reels; tomorrow you'll take TC away.

The girls heard Jake's car hustle into the driveway, the car door slam, and Jake's footsteps on the steps. Jake feigned surprise when he saw the two girls.

'I must be in the wrong house. I'm accustomed to blue faces and rolled-up hair. Now I see before me two movie stars. Every male heart in the illustrious Brolga theatre will bleed with jealously when they observe me make my grand entrance with you two beauties.'

'Give it a break, please, Jake,' snapped Lou even though she knew she looked pretty good and enjoyed Jake's compliments.

'I agree,' added TC.

'All right, all right, I'm getting a beer,' said Jake, 'but you do look lovely.'

Lou was wearing a yellow, empire line dress with long, tapered sleeves and a scooped neckline. The colour complemented her long, auburn hair, which hung in curls around her face and down over her shoulders. Her high-heeled shoes were a camel colour to match the coat her mother had given her as a going-away present.

TC's dress was a pale-green, tapered sheath with long sleeves and a waistband with four tiny buttons. Her shoes were high-heeled, cream in colour, with a little matching purse. TC's blonde hair was pile up on top of her head with tiny blonde curls wisping from her neck, over her ears, and covering her forehead. Both of them were wearing nylon stockings for the very first time in their lives and, unusual for both of them, full make-up.

Jake saw the coat he had bought for TC. It was draped over a lounge chair. He looked at the coat and then at TC.

'Don't you like it?'

'Of course, Jake. It is a lovely coat. I'm wearing it tonight.'

'Well, get it on, then. Let's go,' said Jake before taking his last swig of beer.

¶

Jake pulled in opposite the picture show and made a grand deal of opening the car doors for the girls before purposely positioning himself between them to walk across the street. The girls stood back as Jake went to the little window to purchase tickets.

'Three please,' he said to the gentleman behind the window. The man looked at Jake and smiled.

'Three is a crowd, young Jake.' Jake winked at the man, then replied, 'Yes, I know.'

As they entered the theatre, TC was surprised to see Carmel at the door taking tickets.

'Finally, young lady, you have come to our picture show,' said Carmel with a smile.

'I didn't know you worked here, Carmel,' replied TC.

'I don't. We own it. I get to see free movies. I also get to throw my weight around if anyone plays up and breaks the rules.'

TC laughed, 'That's good, Carmel; if you have power, use it.'

Jake steered the girls into three vacant seats in the back row of the canvas-seat section. Jake always sat in the back row because he was so tall and didn't want anyone sitting behind him complaining because they couldn't see. Jake seated himself between Lou and TC. That way he avoided Lou sitting next to him and then TC next to Lou. He also knew he would be privy to every word they uttered should the need or opportunity to speak to each other arise.

At last, the lights dimmed and Tom and Jerry lit up the screen.

Thank heavens the lights have gone out. Feels as if everyone in the place has been looking at us, thought TC.

Bloody gossiping sticky beaks, thought Lou. I'll be happy, oh, so happy, to climb on the Flea tomorrow.

The first movie was Casablanca, featuring Humphrey Bogart and Lauren Bacall. It was an old movie made before Lou and TC were born. Still, they both had tears in their eyes when it ended. The lights came on and there was a human stampede towards the door. Some people were rushing to the pub to get a drink while most made a beeline for the café for refreshments.

The girls and Jake decided they didn't want anything, so they continued to sit and chat mostly about the movie they had just watched. Jake almost jumped out of his chair when he felt someone touch him on the back of the neck. He quickly looked around as did Lou and TC. Jake wished he could disappear. It was the nurse he had taken to the creek the night before. She put her head down, smiled and looked Jake directly in his eyes.

'Jake, darling, I see you are slumming it tonight,' as she looked at TC, then Lou.

Jake smiled at her before replying, 'No, I did that last night.'

'You are such a prick, Jake,' snarled the nurse before storming off.

'Sorry about that, ladies,' apologised Jake. The girls said nothing.

The second movie was a relatively new release called Rio Bravo, starring the Brolgaites' favourite movie star, John Wayne. Every time John Wayne, who played the part of sheriff, fought and, as always, won or shot a gunslinger, there were shouts from some movie patrons of 'Give it to him, Duke,' Good on ya, Duke,' or 'Kill 'em, Duke!' After John Wayne had killed all the bad guys, the movie ended. After the movies in Brolga, there was nowhere to go except home, the creek, or crash a party. Only the desperate for sexual satisfaction and heated cars hit the creek this time of the year. It was too cold. As one young Brolga lout who owned a ute said, 'Secure screwing at the creek in winter time, especially in the back of a ute. Freeze your bloody balls off.'

'Come on, ladies, I'll take you home. Perhaps we can give poor Old Slim one last whirl on the stairs.'

'Thank you for shouting us to the movies, Jake,' said TC.

'Yes, Jake,' added Lou. 'I really enjoyed the bit with the nurse. If my dad had heard her, he probably would have told her off.'

'Let it go, Lou,' suggested TC. 'I feel like some hot coffee and toast and vegemite.'

Lou and Jake chorused, 'Sounds great.'

Jake added, 'I'll have a beer on the side while I beat you ladies in a game of monopoly.'

¶

'Glad there's no money involved,' grumbled Jake after the second game was finished. Lou had one game to her credit as did TC. They heard TC's alarm sound at 5 am.

'Jake, go home, please,' said TC.

'Yes, the Flea leaves at seven,' said Lou.

'I'm not going home. Mum will make me go to mass. I don't want to. I want to drive you to the station.'

By six fifteen, Lou and TC were fully packed. Everything that needed covering was covered. Lisa Kasa's dishes, trays, etc. and Jake's records were in the trunk of his car. TC gave Jake an envelope containing money for electricity and telephone accounts, which he had agreed to pay when they came in, along with the keys to the house.

'Jake, would you give these to Jess and Sam?' as she handed three cards to him. The third one is for you; open it later.'

'Okay,' nodded Jake. 'Now let's get you ladies to the station and onto the Flea.'

¶

There was no conductor on the Flea. The station master punched the tickets to Curloo where ongoing passengers would have their tickets re-punched at the ticket window, then checked by the train conductor shortly after the train pulled out of Curloo. Jake lifted the girls' suitcases onto the metal luggage rack above the seats in the small passenger cabin. Both girls wore jeans and jumpers, flatties, and ponytails. They had large, thick, woollen brown shawls wrapped around them. The shawls were compliments of Lou's mother, who loved to knit and did so beautifully.

'Where are your coats?' asked Jake.

'We packed them because they would have been covered in coal dust by the time we got to Curloo,' replied TC.

'Good thinking,' replied Jake. 'Anyway, you both look pretty good in brown.' He smiled. 'Just thought of something,' he said, as he jumped down onto the platform and hurried towards his car. The departure whistle blew as Jake returned just in time to hand a cushion each to the girls who had their heads out a window of the carriage. 'Make it easier to sleep,' he yelled as the train began moving.

Both girls mouthed, 'Thank you,' blew him a kiss, put up the carriage window, and sat down as the train whistle blew again, signifying it was about to cross the rail bridge over the creek. At that same moment, Vance joined Jake on the station platform.

'I missed saying goodbye from the looks of things, Jake.'

'Yes, mate, I did, too, in a way. I feel as if I've got a hole in my gut.'

'Me, too, Jake; me, too. Think I need a drink. No, not "a" drink, a bloody thousand drinks.'

'Me, too,' replied Jake. 'I'm going to TC's house for a while. I've got beer there and records in my car.'

'I'll go see the men. They are almost right. Yappy can look after them today. I've got a couple of bottles of rum. The men won't be needing anymore. I'll meet you at TC's in a little while.'

'All right, mate. Don't worry about Coke; there's plenty there.'

¶

Once back at the house, Jake retrieved the records from the trunk of his car, grabbed a beer from the still-turned-on fridge, placed a "Poor Old Slim" record on the turn-table, lit the kero heater, and sat down on one of the lounge chairs to read TC' s card—

"Dear Jake,
Thank you for everything you have done for me, like bailing me out with the Romeos, lending me money, the beautiful overcoat, the suitcases, arranging with your mother for us to do our laundry at her house, for driving us here and all over the place, for buying us Coke and food, for arranging the lovely dinner and cake, for taking us to the movies, and most of all for making us laugh.
I know I shall miss you, just as Lou will. You have been a great friend.
Take care of yourself, Jake,
Thank you once again,
TC."

Jake read it three times before ripping it up in anger.

'Stupid little bitch,' he said out loud. 'I don't want your bloody thanks; I want to marry you.'

Jake was about to open another beer when Vance walked in.

'Too cold to drink beer, Jake. Have a rum and Coke, instead.'

'Bloody good idea,' agreed Jake. 'Let's get effing plastered.'

¶

By that time, Lou and TC were sound asleep en route to Curloo, each curled up in their brown shawls with a cushion under their heads. They failed to stir when the Flea pulled up at a settlers' camp and the only other passenger disembarked. They were oblivious to the break-neck speed at which the Flea was flying, which was just as well.

¶

Jake and Vance drank themselves to sleep by mid-afternoon as neither of them had slept the night before—Jake because he'd been playing monopoly with the girls, and Vance because he simply couldn't sleep. No matter how hard he tried, his mind couldn't switch off.

Vance woke up before Jake and immediately checked the level of the rum in the second bottle.

Only a third of a bottle left, he thought. I'd best go buy some more. He drove via the back street to the rear of the Empire, where the Sunday afternoon session was about to end.

When Jack Romeo spotted Vance standing at the door to the bottle room, he said, 'Tied a few on, have you, mate?'

'Sure have, Jack. Intend to tie a few more on. Give me two bottles of Bundy and some Coke.'

'You should go home to bed, mate. You will feel bloody terrible tomorrow.'

'Jack, here's your money. Mind your own so-and-so bloody business,' replied Vance.

¶

Soon after, he was back with Jake, who was sitting up while still half asleep.

'Oh, good, we've got more grog,' mumbled Jake. 'I have to go take a break and wash my face.'

'Me too,' agreed Vance.

They stood on either side of the landing and urinated through the gaps in the railings.

'Don't splash my car, mate,' muttered Jake. Vance laughed.

'Think I already have, Jake.'

'Oh, bugger it, I couldn't give a tinker's tit; I'm going to wash my face.'

Jake went to the kitchen sink, turned on the tap, and splashed water on his face, his clothes, and the floor before opening a cupboard door, finding a tea towel, and wiping up the mess on the floor, then dabbing at his clothes before wiping his face. Vance then washed his face and used the same tea towel to wipe it.

They didn't talk about much at all, as they had done during their earlier session; they sat listening to records, mostly Ray Charles, and took turns at fetching drinks. Each of them sat in silence, far away and deep in thought. Jake got up and staggered to the kitchen to get more drinks and noticed the time on his watch as he added Coke to the rum.

'I'd better call my mother. Tell her I'm not coming home tonight. Better tell her I'm playing cards. Can't tell her it's because a man is too bloody drunk to drive.'

'You are a lucky bastard, Jake. I have to go home, have to sort some things out. Let's drink this, then we'll have one for the road.' Vance didn't know this 'one for the road' would be the last drink of alcohol he would drink for the rest of his life.

Roadie finished, both Jake and Vance were drifting off to sleep. Vance shook himself awake, stood up, and, after repeating the previous face-washing procedure, staggered down the stairs to his car, slowly reversed out of the driveway, drove on the wrong side of the street to the corner, and took the back way home. Delores was sitting in their lounge room smoking when Vance stumbled in.

'You are drunk, Vance!'

'What else is new?'

'Where have you been?'

'That's my business.'

'It's all right for you, Vance. I am the one stuck here with the kids.'

'Well, Delores, get someone to mind them. You get someone to go to every other bloody thing. Every time you run away to your mother, you spend money like a woman possessed. It's a wonder you haven't sent us bankrupt.'

'You gamble, Vance'

'I also win!'

Delores went on and on and on.

'Vance, what on earth is wrong? What has made you act like this?'

'This has been the worst day of my life.'

'Why?' enquired Delores seriously.

Vance looked directly at Delores, then replied, 'TC left town this morning.'

Although Delores was elated, she didn't dare say so with Vance in his current condition. She simply nodded.

'Oh, I see. It's a miracle you didn't wake the kids. I'm going to bed.'

¶

When Vance woke up on the verandah bunk the next morning, he realised his right hand was in pain. He lay there wondering how he had hurt it. It was not until he heard his oldest son, Jonathon, ask his mother what had happened to the wall that Vance remembered what had happened.

'That's it! No more grog for me. I must have hit rock bottom when I start punching walls.' Vance showered and dressed before leaving to check on his crew. On his way out, he told Delores he was sorry and that no such thing would ever happen again.

'How can you be sure of that?' asked Delores.

'Because I won't be drinking again, Delores,' he replied sincerely and seriously.

¶

When Vance arrived at the Majestic, he was surprised to find the men, including Neil, showered, shaved, and dressed. They were ready and eager to go for breakfast at Con's.

Over breakfast, Vance asked the men if they were keen to go to work. They all nodded in agreement. Vance looked at Neil.

'Are you sure?'

'I'm sure,' replied Neil with a smile. 'Thanks, mate.'

It was arranged that the men would rest up in their room for a couple more days while Vance arranged to ship the gear for the camp out to the site. He also had mail and doctor day on Tuesday.

'So, looks as if we get moving on Wednesday if all goes to plan,' explained Vance before leaving them to collect the mail, open the pharmacy, and make a phone call to the truck depot holding the camping gear.

Vance opened the mail. He was happy to receive the third site approval from the Department of Mines.

'Lucky last.' He made up his mind there and then. 'This is the one we'll try first.'

Vance telephoned the truck depot. Everything was okay for Wednesday. The truck would leave at 5 am, so if Vance wanted anything else added to the load, he would have to get it to the truck depot by seven on Tuesday night. Vance then phoned Jake to make sure he was still in the land of the living.

'Come see me this afternoon, will you, Jake? Got a load of crap on my mind. Have to unload it on someone.' Jake agreed to see Vance at siren time. Vance called Delores to once again apologise. He then went to the Majestic to tell Yappy to make out a detailed grocery list and an order for the butcher. Vance kept himself busy until Jake arrived right on siren time.

'What's the problem, mate?' asked Jake as he sat down opposite Vance.

Vance looked at Jake and replied, while shaking his head, 'Everything. I was so angry with Delores last night I wanted to hit her. Instead, I put my fist through a wall. I told her it was the worst day of my life because TC had left town. Poor bloody Delores has never done a hard day's work in her life except when she goes shopping, that is. She can't seem to comprehend where the money comes from. Don't know how

I'm going to handle this joint without TC, especially now I'm taking on this opal thing.'

'Find someone else to run the place, Vance.' Vance sighed.

'Don't be ridiculous, Jake. TC knows the place backwards. I even made her practice my signature a thousand times or more. She signs my name so well that I can't tell the difference myself. I made a landmark decision this morning, Jake. I have quit the booze forever.'

'Cold turkey?' questioned Jake. 'Won't be easy, mate. Look at Neil, Faith, and Little Joe.'

'Jake, I have to be a better man, a better husband, and try to be some semblance of a father to my children. So far, I've been a losing bastard on all three counts.'

'Good luck, mate. I really mean it, including the opal deal. Guess I'll have to find a new drinking mate and visit you here.' They both laughed.

'After all, I'll still be me, Jake. I just won't have a permanent fixture of rum and Coke attached to my hand. I wonder where the girls are?'

'Who knows,' replied Jake with a shrug of his shoulders and a far-away expression on his face.

❡

Lou and TC were sitting on the Interstate Platform in Brisbane's Roma Street railway station, securing the accommodation section of the Sydney Herald newspaper. The train from Curloo had arrived in Brisbane an hour earlier. After collecting their cases, which they had checked through in Curloo, they took a shower and changed their clothes.

'Decision-making time!' said TC. Lou looked at TC.

'You decide.'

'Let's flip a coin like the boss and Jake do,' suggested TC. 'You call, Lou'.

'Heads we go to Sydney, tails we stay here,' said Lou seriously.

TC flicked a penny with her thumb. It spun in the air before falling onto the grey, concrete platform.

It landed heads up.

'Sydney, here we come,' said Lou.

'Looks like it, Lou.'

'Let's go find out when the next train to Sydney departs and buy tickets on it. Lord help us, I hope Sydney is ready for a couple of bush girls like us.'

'More importantly, are we bush girls ready for Sydney?'

'We'll handle it, TC,' replied Lou enthusiastically.

'I miss Brolga already, Lou,' said TC softly as they walked to the information window. 'Sure, it's a one-horse town, but at least everyone knows exactly where they stand. It's uncomplicated.'

'Don't put a damper on our adventure, TC. We'll be fine.'

In less than two weeks, Vance's crew had erected the camp and were ready to begin searching for opal in whatever direction Vance pointed them.

'I'll be glad when that bloody wood stove gets here,' said Yappy as he leaned over to extract the billy filled with boiling tea from the red-hot coals. 'This bloody camp oven is burning all my bloody hair off my head and arms. Just as bloody well it's cold, because if I were wearing shorts I'd have no hair on my legs as well. As it is I have to shove my trousers in the top of my bloody boots, otherwise my bloody trousers would catch on bloody fire.'

'Stop grumbling, Yappy,' said Neil. 'Otherwise, we will throw you in the bloody fire.'

'Yeah, Yappy. Not much of you, mate; wouldn't take you too long to be reduced to smouldering bones,' added Faith.

'Bloody bastards,' said Yappy while the other three laughed as they took turns dipping their mugs into the billy and helping themselves to iced Vo Vo and Monte Carlo biscuits from an enamel plate on the ground. The men were seated on upturned buckets around the fire, which was situated on the ground in the middle of a corrugated iron three-sided lean-to.

'Wish a bloody table and chairs would arrive, too,' said Faith.

The camp was situated on high ground a couple of hundred yards from a dry creek bed which was known to flood on the odd occasion there was heavy rain.

Neil, who had previously been employed as a loader operator with the Brolga Shire Council, had cleared and levelled the campsite while Faith and Little Joe cut down trees to clear the way. They also cleared an area of about twenty yards around the perimeter of the campsite itself. This was done as a precaution in case of sparks from the camp fires igniting a bush fire and snakes invading the camp undetected.

'Only the shower to finish. I'll get into that now,' said Faith as they all stood up after morning tea.

'Yeah, Little Joe and I will do a water run,' from Neil.

Vance had bought an old tray-backed truck from the Brolga car dealer. The men had secured a large water tank on the back of the truck and, with the permission of the property owner on which the mine was located, it was agreed the men could fill their tank when required from the closest windmill and dam, which were located about ten miles away from camp, through the creek bed, and over a rough bush track.

Yappy discarded the residual tea in the billy, collected the mugs, and wandered over to the shower as Faith was finishing off.

'Hope the bloody Queen doesn't decide to visit.'

'If this set-up is good enough for our poor bloody soldiers; it's good enough for the Queen,' replied Faith with a smile. 'Not only that, Yappy, it's good enough for us.'

The shower had a sloped, rough-concrete floor, which sloped towards the back of the tarpaulin-enclosed cubicle. Three sides were fixed to poles; the front side clipped when necessary. Above the shower cubicle there was a larger bucket hanging from a diagonally fixed chain across the top. Welded to the front of the bucket was an old-style toilet chain which, when pulled, tilted the bucket, causing the water to fall onto the person taking the shower. The idea was to pull the chain, get wet, lather the body, then pull the chain again to rinse off.

'Come on, Yappy,' said Faith while bearing a mischievous smile. 'Peel off and jump in here under the bucket; we'll give this bloody contraption a try.'

'Go to buggery, Faith! You peel off and jump under the bloody bucket yourself,' replied Yappy indignantly as he looked up at Faith, who stood almost a foot taller. 'I'm out of here before you lay any more crap on me,' added Yappy as he high tailed it towards the kitchen.

The kitchen was constructed of corrugated iron walls set in concrete footings. It was fifteen yards long by five yards wide. The iron roof was planted downwards towards the back so that, in the event of rain, the water would flow off the roof and downwards in the direction of the creek. There were two long windows on the front, one located either side of the door, and one smaller window at either end. The windows and door were rough, wooden-framed and with heavy gauze tacked on the inside to keep out the flies. Vance had arranged for Lou's father, Jordan, to knock up some rough corrugated-iron push-out windows and door for the exterior of the kitchen.

The kitchen floor was compacted red dirt. There were two long, wooden benches with a shelf underneath. On one bench, Yappy had neatly stacked the provisions, which took up both top and lower shelves. In the corner next to these shelves was a six-inch-high wooden platform on which was a bag of sugar, two bags of flour, a bag of potatoes, a bag of rice, and a bag of onions. The other bench was, as Yappy referred to it, his work bench, where he would prepare meals and do the dishwashing on the top. Underneath, he stored cutlery and cooking utensils, all neatly lined up and stacked. There was a large, old, but reliable, kero fridge in the corner.

Vance was going to fetch a wood stove and a collapsible table and chairs next time he visited the site.

Yappy looked at the hole in the roof waiting to accommodate the stove chimney and said under his breath, 'Hope you bloody well hurry up, Boss, so I can cook these poor bastards a decent feed and some fresh, baked-by-Yappy bread.'

The sleeping quarters were a tarpaulin-round-marquee with roll-up, roll-down panels between each set of side upright poles. There was a heavy, longer pole in the centre of the marquee to support the weight of the roof.

The men's bunks, along with a few spares, were placed at intervals inside the perimeter. Beside each bunk in use, there was an unturned rough-pine fruit case, which served as a storage spot for their folded clothes and a bedside table on which Neil, Faith and Little Joe had empty tobacco tins to serve as ashtrays and a battery-operated torch. Yappy was a non-smoker and was also the cook, which meant he had to be up at least an hour before the others to prepare breakfast. His fruit box-cum-bedside table sported his small alarm clock along with his torch. The floor in the sleeping quarters was hard red dirt just as was the floor of the kitchen.

The only form of lighting they had, apart from their torches, were carbide lamps, four of which were conveniently placed around the central weight-bearing pole.

There was a wooden bench alongside the shower. On the bench, there were two large round wash tubs turned upside down. A thin rope clothesline hooked up between the shower and the sleeping quarters.

As yet the bush was the toilet. When the warning signs of impending bowel movement came, the men took off for the bush with shovel in hand and eyes vigilantly looking out for snakes.

¶

Neil and Little Joe returned from the water run mid-afternoon. Faith was pegging his washing on the clothesline, and Yappy was placing a cast-iron pot filled with potatoes on the camp oven next to the billy filled with boiling water.

'Want a cuppa?' asked Yappy after Neil and Joe had gotten out of the truck.

'No, thanks, Yap. I'll take a beer if you've got one,' replied Neil with a smile.

'Wouldn't we bloody all,' added Faith.

Little Joe was a man of few words so, as usual, he said nothing. He simply smiled.

'How long have we been here, Yappy?' asked Faith.

'Twelve days, mate, must seem like a bloody one hundred and twelve when a man is craving a drink,' replied Yappy. 'Anyway, think of the money you'll have after three months dry.'

'Think of the bloody headache we'll have after we spend the money,' said Neil. 'In the meantime, Faith, my friend, I think I'll try out your shower. I must admit it's a pretty illustrious piece of equipment.'

They all laughed except Faith, who retorted, 'Why don't you try the bloody thing before you ridicule it!' as he threw his hands in the air and made a hasty retreat to the marquee, where he rolled a cigarette, then slumped on his bunk to sulk.

Bloody Neil, he thought. Why the hell did he have to mention the grog!

¶

Vance was in the pharmacy flat-out. It was doctor day. The phone, as usual, rarely stopped ringing. Vance knew he had to go to the site early next morning. He knew the men must be tired of stale bread and sitting on upturned buckets when they ate. He had to get the stove, collapsible tables and chairs, and what seemed like a million other things to them. Most of all he had to make the decision where they would make the first cut in the hill. How the hell did he know? He had read everything and anything he could regarding opal mining. He had sought but a couple of so-called experienced men who claimed they had given it a go, mining opal in the area. Vance had quickly reached the conclusion that they were bullshitting or, if they did indeed know anything, they were keeping it to themselves.

Only thing Vance was sure of was that some Chinese people had given it a "go" a long time ago. He knew this because he had made a point of taking a look at their diggings. Apparently they had tried to find the opal by the same methods successfully used by the mines in Coober Pedy in South Australia. This was obvious because of a series of tiny tunnels which had been chipped out of the hillsides. The size of the tunnels and the countless pick marks made it almost unbelievable that the poor souls could have survived in such confined spaces, picking away at the rock-hard red dirt which turned into red dust as it fell. Would have been dreadful, especially during the hot months. Rumour had it that many had perished, and it was no wonder. Vance decided he would have to try another method if he was to be successful. As far as Vance was concerned, he wanted to get going in his search for opal; the pharmacy was a bloody nuisance, even though he was very aware of the fact that he would need the pharmacy to finance the mining.

¶

Vance was surprised to see the Flying Doctor himself walk into the pharmacy that busy day. After the proverbial handshake, the doctor said, 'I thought I'd come and say hello to you as I won't be coming here on a regular basis much longer.'

'Why is that?' asked Vance with a shocked smile. 'Is Brolga going to be thrown into the too-hard basket?'

'Not at all,' replied the doctor. 'As soon as some appropriate accommodation can be organised, you'll have your own resident G.P. The Government has been trying forever to get some poor bugger to volunteer for Brolga. Seems they have finally got someone. God help him, that's all I can say.'

'Me, too,' agreed Vance. 'Thank you for letting me know.' The Flying Doctor once again shook Vance's hand, then left a few seconds before the siren sounded. Vance phoned Delores.

'I won't be home for lunch; got a million things to do.'

'Vance, I hope you are not going to the hotel,' replied Delores.

'No, Delores, I am not going to the hotel! I told you, I have a lot of things to do. It is doctor and mail day. Apart from that I have to think of a lot of other things besides lunch.' Vance hung up. This husband crap is not going to work, he thought, as he once again picked up the telephone to call the truckie who had carted the camp gear to the site.

'Yeah, mate, I have already loaded your fuel; picked it up from the fuel depot this morning. Also collected your stove, etc., from the railway station. Anything else? I'm leaving at five in the morning.'

'Good. The men will be happy. I'll see you at the site,' replied Vance. 'No, nothing else, mate.'

Vance went about getting the mail orders together. His mind wandered from his obligation to Delores and his children, then to Anna and Louise. Finally, he thought of TC and Lou and wondered why he had not heard from them.

Not like TC to go back on her on her word. Thought I taught her better than that. She'll call, he told himself. Probably getting settled in, wherever she is.

¶

Jake found he didn't enjoy drinking at the Empire too much anymore, now that Vance was off the booze. No one Jake wound up having a session with was as intelligent and witty as Vance. Jake decided he would go on the party route for a while. After all, he was Jake Carmichael. He was welcome anywhere in Brolga. Jake attended a half dozen or so parties, then realised he found them boring compared to the ones Vance used to throw. Of course, he continued to head off to the creek with whatever nurse was available, three or four times a week. He was even beginning to find that boring! Every time he drove past Auntie Flo's house, he remembered how happy he had felt sitting on the stairs with Lou and TC while Poor Old Slim burst forth from the airwaves of 4CL.

Overall, Jake felt miserable.

Thel Carmichael was surprised and concerned when Jake began spending more and more time at home.

'What's the matter with you, Jake?' she asked one night over dinner.

'Nothing, Mum. I suppose I'm just bored with this town,' replied Jake defensively.

'Have you heard from the girls, Jake?'

'No, Mum, I haven't. I'm going to bed.'

Thel Carmichael realised immediately what Jake's problem was.

He was missing the girls, particularly TC. 'Hope those girls contact someone soon.'

¶

Jordan and his wife, Carmel, were thinking the same. Jordan checked the post box every day in the hope of hearing from Lou.

'They'll be all right, luv,' Carmel would tell Jordan every day when he returned home from the pub and the post office empty-handed except for a half dozen bottles of beer.

¶

Lou and TC had not been in Sydney for very long when they decided it was not nearly as exciting as they had imagined. They had spent the first few days in a Salvation Army Girls Hostel in the city. People rushing everywhere on narrow footpaths that looked dirty and a million years old. They decided to find somewhere to live, then look for jobs close by.

Lou found immediate employment as a telephonist-receptionist in a small hotel on the North Shore. A few days later, TC was taken on as a stock sorter and marker in the upstairs stockroom of a famous doll shop, also on the North Shore. They shared a spacious bedroom in the home of a loving and caring, childless couple who lived only a short distance from where the girls worked. The son of the owners of the hotel where Lou worked was lead guitarist with a then-famous Australian rock and roll band. He was also friends with famous Australian rugby league players.

By the son's invitation, Lou and TC attended rock and roll shows and rugby league games. Both of them enjoyed the rock and roll music but loathed the football games. They were also invited to attend after-show and game parties. After accepting a few such invitations, both Lou and TC decided they would both have to become groupies or go back to Brolga, where life was so innocent. On several occasions, they were called 'bloody prudes' when the expressions of shock on their faces at what they observed were obvious. They decided to leave that scene.

'At least we will leave with respect from all,' they agreed.

'I'm calling the boss,' said TC.

'I want to go home to Brolga,' agreed Lou.

¶

'Where the hell have you been, Butterball?' questioned a relieved yet angry Vance.

'I don't like it here, Boss. I want to come back.'

'Have you got the fare?'

'Yes, I've been working.'

'Doing what??'

'Working in a doll shop.'

'That would be right,' he laughed. 'A "doll" in a doll shop. When are you coming home?'

'As soon as possible.'

'I'm angry with you, TC.'

'I know!'

'I have been worried about you. So has that rat, Jake. Get back here as soon as you can. I miss you and I need you to take care of things at the shop. By the way, we have found opal. Don't know if Delores will be happy to see you back but I bloody well sure will be.'

'Boss, please tell Lou's parents she is coming home.'

'Done. Be good girls.'

'That is the problem here, Boss. We are good girls.'

'Stay that way.'

'See you soon, Boss.'

'Keep in touch, Butterball.'

TC hung up as the coins she had inserted in the money machine of the phone box ran out.

¶

Jake walked in through the back door as Vance picked up the phone to call him.

'Good timing, Jake,' said Vance. 'The kid is coming back, Jake. Better call your Uncle and Aunt and get that house cleaned up. Get a message to Lou's parents when you see them at the pub. I'm a happy man, Jake.'

'I am too, mate,' replied Jake with a broad smile. 'Tired of those bloody nurses. Need a thousand nights or so sitting on those bloody stairs listening to Poor Old Slim. When are they coming back?'

'Soon,' replied Vance.

They both laughed as a song titled, Sweet Little Angel, blasted out from 4CL.

'How appropriate,' from Jake.

'That is correct, Jake, my friend. "Sweet as sugar" if we do the right thing; "poisonous as arsenic" if we cross her.'

'You sure have that right, mate,' laughed Jake as he left the pharmacy in a hurry to seek out Jordan and his wife, phone his aunt and uncle, and, most of all, tell his mother, who had told him what seemed a few million times that TC would come back to Brolga.

Delores was not at all impressed when Vance announced to her that TC was returning.

'I see,' was all she said.

Vance told Delores, 'Delores I'm off the booze, trying to keep the pharmacy going to finance the mining costs and your spending sprees. There's a permanent doctor coming, which means someone will have to be at the shop five-and-a-half days a week because the bastard will be writing bloody prescriptions which someone will have to be at the joint to fill. You have thrown in the towel on trying to learn how to cut the bit of opal we have found. You have never had to work for anything. All you are good at is spending money—which we have not got—having kids, playing bloody golf, and sucking up to the people you think are in the right social circle. TC is coming back! That is that!'

Delores nodded her head. 'All right, Vance. I think I'll go to Brisbane for a while. I have to make arrangements for Jonathon to go to school there.'

'As expected,' replied Vance. 'I'm going to the mine!'

So that was the way things were between Delores and Vance.

⁋

TC and Lou gave a one-week notice to their respective employers, said sad farewells with promises to keep in touch forever to their landlords, and caught a train to Brisbane, where, within a few hours, they happily boarded the train to Curloo, where they would connect with the Flying Flea to their much-missed and much-loved, end-of-the-line Brolga.

Jake was waiting to meet them. So were Lou's parents along with Jake's mother, Thel.

'Been meeting the last four Fleas,' complained Jake with a smile.

'Why didn't you call us?' from Lou's Dad, Jordan.

'Because you don't have a telephone, Dad,' laughed Lou as she hugged first her mother, then her father.

Thel Carmichael smiled at TC.

'Glad to see you back, luv,' she said as she gave TC a hug. Little Carla looked on.

'Mummy says Jake has missed you, TC.'

'About bloody time you came back,' smiled Jake, hoping nobody had heard Carla. 'I need some of Slim's music resounding through my ears. Vance and I have been waiting to hear from you.'

'We were too busy trying to get home as soon as possible,' replied Lou and TC in rehearsed unison.

The usual crowd on Flea-greeting evenings had disappeared to the movies or pubs or Seat of Knowledge. Thel Carmichael and Carla went home after saying, 'Happy to see you back.' Lou's parents were heading for the pub. 'Do you want to come and join us?' asked Jordan.

'Tired Dad, Mum, see you tomorrow,' replied Lou.

Jake was happy. Looked as if he was escorting the girls to Uncle Doug and Auntie Flo's house, which he had cleaned meticulously and put beer for himself and Coke for the girls in the fridge. He even had a Slim record for the stereogram, ready to go for old times' sake. Con Kasa appeared as Jake was placing the girls' luggage into the boot of his car.

'Great to see you young ladies back in our beautiful metropolis of Brolga,' he said with a smile. 'Jake, call by the café in twenty minutes; I will help Lisa make hamburgers for the three of you. These girls must be hungry. Who wouldn't be after a trip on the Flying Flea?' Con laughed as he walked away from the railway station. 'Glad to see you ladies back,' he said to TC and Lou over his shoulder.

'I'm no bloody lady,' came from Jake.

'Was not talking to you, mate,' laughed Con without looking back.

'Thanks, mate. See you in a little while,' said Jake.

¶

'Doesn't seem to be as much gravel as there was when we left,' said TC as Jake whirled into the driveway alongside his aunt and uncle's house.

'That's because I have been coming and going for a long time now. Every time I drive the car in, the bloody stuff flies all over the place. Check the mountain of stuff on the neighbour's side of the wire fence. Anyway, I'm dropping you off. Do whatever you want to do while I go and collect the food from Con and Lisa.'

'Jake, before you go, how about a hug for the both of us?' asked Lou with a smile. 'After those assholes we have seen in Sydney, you're great.'

TC nodded. 'Yes, Jake, you are not as bad as I thought.' Jake was elated.

'About bloody time a man got some recognition. From two lovely ladies, at that.' Jake leaned forward and hugged Lou. 'Nice to see you back, Lou.'

Then he turned to TC, who smiled as she said, 'I'll take a rain check, thank you, Jake. Nice to see you. Thank you for caring enough to meet the Flea four times.'

'That was before I got lucky and you ladies arrived on the fifth one!

Vance is in the bush. I'm going to Con's. See you soon,' said Jake as he dumped the girls' bags on the back landing, then opened the unlocked door to the fully-lit, clean house. 'Put Poor Old Slim on,' he said as he hurriedly got in his car and reversed at his usual break-neck speed onto the street.

TC and Lou hugged each other.

'Toss you for who gets first shower,' laughed Lou.

'You go first, Lou. I'm a bit frightened of snakes now that there is not much gravel left,' from TC.

'Thanks, TC. There is probably a colony of snakes under the house,' replied Lou with a sarcastic grin.

Lou went off to take a shower after quickly retrieving necessities from her bag. TC was about to play Slim's record on the radiogram when she heard Lou's scream emanating from the back stairs.

'Snakes! Two of them!'

TC ran for the landing. Sure enough there were two snakes on the concrete path to the bathroom from the stairs.

'A wonder your screaming didn't frighten them,' whispered TC as she observed the snakes lazing on the path.

'Bugger Jake and his car spreading the gravel,' whispered Lou as she timidly backed up the stairs. 'It is summer, so the snakes are up from the creek to get cool.'

'You were probably right, Lou, when you said there could be a family of them living under the house,' replied TC quietly.

Both girls were terrified of the snakes that gave the appearance of confidently owning the path as if they had territorial rights for life. The girls heard, with great relief, Jake's car turn into the driveway. They watched silently in amazement as one of the snakes slithered quickly away under Jake's car as it came to a halt. The second snake coiled with its head raised and eyes blazing. Its tongue was popping in and out of its open mouth defensively.

Jake jumped out of his car, hamburgers in hand, saw the coiled snake, dropped the food, and yelled, 'Holy shit, the bastard is ready to attack.' Jake frantically looked around and grabbed a shovel, which was leaning against the laundry door. 'You bastard, you are dead,' said Jake as he thrust the blade end of the shovel at the snake. The blade severed the snake's head from its body, which slithered for what seemed an eternity.

Lou and TC were silent, mouths open with both shock and amazement.

'Poisonous bloody things,' said Jake as he looked up at the girls.

'Another one went under your car, Jake,' said TC.

'Don't think I ran over the bastard,' said Jake. 'Probably coiled up underneath,' he said as he got into his car. 'Pick up the tucker. I'll be back soon. Have to drive like a lunatic and brake furiously to get rid of the bloody thing. Make the exhaust pipe so hot the bastard can't stand it and lets go; then I'll run over it a couple or three times.'

Jake blasted off in reverse. Lou collected the wrapped food from where Jake had dropped it where it now lay close by the brown snake's head.

'I'm not hungry now, Lou,' said TC.

'Me, neither,' replied Lou.

'I don't think either of us needs a shower tonight. Look at that poor snake's body there on the path with its head two feet away on the dirt,' said TC.

'I agree,' replied Lou as they happily and relievedly went inside.

TC firmly locked the door as Lou went to the radiogram to start Poor Old Slim's record.

Meanwhile, Jake did exactly as he said he would. He drove his car until the speedometer was off the clock, braked, and then repeated until he got the second snake. He was west of Brolga's cemetery and observing the squashed snake's body in the beam of his car headlights when along came Vance heading east into town. Vance pulled his car to a halt and jumped out.

'What on earth are you doing out here, Jake?' Jake told Vance the story. Vance was elated.

'See you at the girls' house, Jake. Stop looking at that bloody snake. Come on, Jake. Turn around. I'll follow you. Little bitch came back and didn't even tell me when she was coming.'

'She is here mate. See you at their house.'

¶

Half an hour later Lou and TC were dozing in chairs in Auntie Flo's lounge room when they were awakened by Vance's voice announcing, 'Here is dinner, girls.'

Both girls screamed in disbelief when, after groggily shaking themselves awake, they saw in front of them Jake holding the snake's head and Vance holding the rest of the dead snake's body wrapped around his throat.

'Are you drunk, Boss?' asked TC sleepily.

'No! Butterball, I am not drunk. Why didn't you call me?'

'Pity you girls can't light the wood stove. We could cook this bloody thing,' said Jake.

'Take the poor thing away,' said TC.

'Jake, you are an idiot,' added Lou.

'Seen enough of them in Sydney,' said TC. Lou nodded in agreement.

'Jake, I'll get a sugar bag from my ute and throw this snake's carcass in it,' said Vance seriously. 'I'll get rid of it somewhere.'

'Thank you, Boss,' said TC drowsily. Lou stood up to change the record.

'Put on Lou Armstrong, please, Lou,' said Vance from halfway down the stairs.

Vance was covered in red dust with the long side of his thinning hair off to one side. He wore red, dust-encrusted, suede-looking boots, jeans, an R. M. Williams shirt with one pocket tearing away from inserting and extracting his cigarette packet.

Jake as usual was dressed immaculately. Black, slim fitting trousers, polished black shoes, pale blue long-sleeved shirt with the sleeves partly rolled back, black leather belt to match his shoes. The belt had a gold buckle to match his gold watch band.

The girls were in jeans and blouses they had worn since showering and changing clothes at Brisbane Railway Station, which seemed a million years ago.

'Vance didn't even give us a hug,' said Lou.

'He had that poor snake flying around his neck, Lou. I'm glad he didn't,' replied TC with a look of disgust.

Jake and Vance came back laughing.

'Come here, Lou. Great to see you girls back in Brolga,' said Vance.

'Hope you both washed your hands,' said TC.

'Of course,' interjected Jake with a look of innocence on his face. Vance finished hugging Lou, then looked at TC.

'Come here, Butterball. I knew you would come back. I knew you would help me.' Vance hugged TC tightly. She kissed him on the cheek.

'I expect you to hug and kiss me on the cheek for the rest of my life, little one. It's so good to see you.'

'You, too, Boss,' replied a smiling TC. 'I didn't just come back to help you—I, we, came back for ourselves, as well.'

'Lot of mongrels in the Big Smoke,' said Lou.

'Thank God you are back, ladies,' said Jake. Louis Armstrong's voice could be heard in the background.

'You girls are too honest,' coming from Vance. 'Anyway, Butterball, I'm going to continue to think you came back to help me.'

'Of course, she bloody well did,' said Jake.

'It's fate, Boss,' smiled TC.

'You can say that again,' added Lou. 'Think you should both go home so TC and I can have a lick-and-a-promise bath in the kitchen,' said Lou.

'No!' from Vance. 'Jake, let's check the girls' bathroom for more stray snakes and sit on guard on the steps while they take their showers.'

'Bloody great idea, mate,' replied Jake. Jake desperately wanted to have a beer. He decided against it as he realised how difficult it must be for Vance to be in the company of drinkers, now that he was on the wagon. After all, what are mates for?

Lou opted for first shower while TC busied herself unpacking. Vance and Jake sat in silence for a few minutes, both deep in thought as to how relieved they were now that the girls were back safely in Brolga.

Vance suddenly broke the silence.

'Jake, get yourself a bloody beer, a Coke for me and one for TC.' He then looked over his shoulder and yelled towards TC's bedroom. 'TC, come out here now. You can do whatever you are fiddling with tomorrow.'

TC heard his command, rolled her eyes, and immediately strode to the back landing. 'Mr Callahan, I'm not back five minutes and already you are giving me orders,' snapped TC with one hand on her hip and the other hand pointing at Vance.

'Oh, stop it, young lady. Sit down here with Jake and me. Jake, she likes ice in her Coke. Have you forgotten?' Jake sighed, stood up, and went to put ice cubes in TC's Coke.

'Bloody women,' he muttered as he returned to the steps. 'How was the Big Smoke, TC?' asked Jake.

'We hated it, apart from the rock and roll shows. My job with the dolls was nice. Lou can tell you about hers.'

'Meet any nice young men?' queried Vance.

'No. We met lots of young men, but they thought we were prudes because we declined to get into their bed or back seat of their car or jump on a sofa or the floor with them. One rugby league player told us we are an endangered species and should return to the safety of the Queensland bush. Don't know what the hell he meant!'

Both Vance and Jake burst into gales of laughter.

'What is so funny?' asked TC.

'You,' replied Jake.

'Stay the way you are little one. It is so good to have you back.'

With that Lou opened the shower door and Vance stood up to go.

'Jake, you and Lou can keep an eye out for snakes while TC showers. I have to go back out to the mine tomorrow. TC, I'll bring the shop keys before I leave. Have tomorrow off and start work on Monday. The pharmacy is in a terrible mess; perhaps you will give TC a hand for a while, Lou?'

Lou nodded. 'Sure. Same deal as before?'

'Of course, Lou,' smiled Vance. 'See you kids later.'

'Is the pharmacy as dirty as you are, Vance?' asked Lou to Vance's retreating back.

'You'll see. Opal mining in Queensland is a dirty business,' he answered over his shoulder.

Dirty, all right, in more ways than just being covered in red dirt. Vance would realise that in the coming years.

The girls told Jake to go home immediately TC came out of the shower.

'Some gratitude I get for saving you from the snakes. Can I come back tomorrow?'

'Of course, Jake,' said Lou.

'As if we have any choice,' added TC as she closed and locked the back door. The girls went to bed immediately after.

¶

A knock on the front door woke them around eight the next morning. TC groggily staggered to open the door, thinking it must be Vance with the shop keys. She was wrong. She opened the door to a very serious Delores.

'Hello, TC. Vance asked me to give you these.' Actually Vance had not asked Delores to deliver the keys. Delores had insisted.

'Happy to be back, TC?'

'Yes, Mrs Callahan,' smiled TC as she took the keys from Delores.

'Good,' snapped Delores as she turned and walked down the stairs.

'Thank you, Mrs Callahan,' TC called out as Delores slammed the gate and walked to her car.

TC closed the door as she wondered why Mrs Callahan seemed to be in such a bad mood.

Little bitch, thought Delores, as she slammed her foot on the accelerator of her car and furiously sped off up Brolga Street to her home. Nobody has the right to look that cute, especially when they have been awakened from an obviously deep sleep.

Vance was sitting at the kitchen table talking to the boys when Delores burst into the house.

'Happy now?' asked Vance.

'Deliriously,' snapped Delores. 'Easy to see why you are happy she is back.'

Vance abruptly stood up and furiously pushed his chair across the room as the boys took off onto the verandah.

'Are you crazy, Delores? I am going opal mining. I can't be in two places at the same time. We need the income from the pharmacy to finance the mining. TC can run that place with her eyes closed. She works all hours like a bloody drover's dog for a pittance of a wage. Never puts her hand out for a cent of overtime. Wouldn't rob me to save her life. Wake up to yourself, Delores!'

'I'm going to Brisbane!' yelled Delores.

'Good! I'm going to the mine!' replied Vance as he stormed out.

¶

Vance drove to the pharmacy and phoned TC.

'Sorry about this morning, TC. Delores insisted on fetching the keys.'

'Mrs Callahan didn't seem too happy,' replied TC.

'Don't worry about it. I'm going to the mine now; probably be back late tomorrow night. See you Tuesday.'

¶

The men knew Vance was coming before they heard his car. As soon as Yappy spotted the cloud of red dust above the mulga trees, he lifted the billy onto the fire, then put out the mugs of tea, coffee, sugar, powdered milk, and the proverbial huge tin of Arnott's mixed biscuits.

The tiny camp area was enshrouded in red dust when Vance's ute screeched to a halt. The men knocked off for a smoko when they saw him arrive, then made their way to the camp for a cuppa and a yarn. They were always interested to hear the latest gossip about what was going on in Brolga.

'What are you doing back here?' asked Yappy as Vance jumped out of the ute and extracted his packet of cigarettes from the torn pocket of his shirt.

'Yes, Yappy, good to see you, too, mate,' answered Vance with a sarcastic smile.

'I didn't bloody well mean it that way, you smart bastard,' replied Yappy while shaking his head from side to side.

Neil, Faith, and Little Joe wandered along.

'You're back again, Boss. That was quick,' from Neil.

'Yappy, where the hell is the coffee?' asked Faith.

'It's ready, it's ready. Stop nagging a man,' replied Yappy.

They helped themselves to tea, coffee, and biscuits and sat down on the ground on the shady side of the shed-cum-kitchen.

'So, what does bring you back out here so soon?' enquired Faith.

Vance smiled. 'Tired of nagging; bloody women should sum that up, Faith.'

'They can be bitches, all right,' from Neil.

'Yeah, that's why none of us have one,' added Faith.

'That's not bloody true,' argued Yappy. 'It's because you're all bloody drunks. As for me, I don't like women since some bitch broke my bloody heart when I was young and stupid.'

As usual, Little Joe said nothing. He simply sat in silence with a slight smile on his face.

'What do you think, Little Joe?' asked Vance. Little Joe simply shook his head and sipped his coffee.

'Well, don't suppose you have any gossip, Boss, seeing as you left here only yesterday?' from Neil.

They all looked at him with interest.

'You'll be seeing a lot more of me out here.'

'How are you going to manage that?' asked Yappy.

'Well, men, your Little Flower has come back.'

The men all smiled.

'Fair dinkum,' from Neil.

'God, strike me pink,' from Faith.

'Knew the little bugger would come back to us,' from Yappy.

'God bless her,' very quietly from Little Joe.

'Well, men, now that I won't have to spend so much time in the bloody pharmacy, we can really get stuck into finding some real opal, hopefully with beautiful colour. Not like that stuff we've found so far. It is, as you know, pale blue. Won't be easy because we still don't know what we are doing. Lots of trial and error, but we will learn by our mistakes. Come on, let's go have another look at this hill.'

§

When they returned to camp for lunch a couple of hours later, Vance, Neil, Faith, and Little Joe were deep in discussion.

'You lot been bludging?' asked Yappy. 'Didn't hear the loader.'

'That's because Neil didn't start it,' smiled Vance.

'Why?' from Yappy.

'Oh, Yappy, be quiet for once. Where's lunch?' said Faith.

'Yes Yappy, you are worse than an old woman sometimes. You want to know every bloody thing,' added Neil.

'Get off my back, both of you, or you'll starve at dinnertime. I'll go on strike!' threatened Yappy.

§

Little Joe, Faith and Neil sat at the table and helped themselves to corned beef, canned beetroot, tomatoes, Yappy's freshly baked bread, and sweet mustard pickles.

'Speaking of dinner, Yappy, Jake and I offered TC and Lou some fresh meat for dinner last night. They were not hungry, so I brought it out for you men. Of course, it won't be quite as fresh now. Been in the back of the ute overnight and this morning. I'll go get it.'

He returned with the sugar bag and handed it to Yappy, who said, 'Might be all right, Vance; the sugar bag is nice and clean and doesn't feel too hot.'

'Should bake up well, Yappy,' said Vance with a smile.

Yappy reached into the bag, froze, and went white as a sheet. As the bag dropped onto the dirt floor, the dead snake's head flew out, along with half of the headless part of its body. Vance, Faith, Neil, and Little Joe laughed uncontrollably at Yappy's reaction.

'You smart bastard, Callahan. I quit! I mean it! I quit.'

'Oh, come on, Yappy. Even the two girls didn't carry on like you. Be a man.'

'Bet the girls didn't put their bloody hands in the bag and feel the bloody thing. I quit!' Vance forced himself to stop laughing. He could see Yappy was serious. Faith, Neil, and Little Joe continued in gales of laughter.

'Oh, come on, Yappy, mate. It's not as if the poor thing is alive,' said Vance.

'I don't care, Callahan! That was a lousy, bloody trick to pull on a man! I quit.' Vance turned to the other men and winked.

'Now, stop laughing, you men. I was out of line by pulling that trick on our cook.' He turned his attention back to Yappy. 'Come on, best bread maker in the universe. You can't quit! What would we do for laughs around here if we didn't have our happy Yappy chappy to ask questions and order us around?'

Yappy looked at Vance. 'Get the bloody thing out of here. Put it in the forty-four-gallon drum around the back. I'll burn it later.' Vance knelt down with a sigh of relief, picked up the snake, placed it in the bag, and took it out back to the drum. Vance washed his hands at the outside tub and returned to the kitchen for lunch. They ate in silence for a few minutes; then Yappy broke it with, 'Am I really the best bread maker in the universe?'

They all nodded. Little Joe surprised everyone, even himself, by saying, 'The boss said you are, Yappy, so you must be, mate.'

Yappy smiled and nodded. 'Okay.' He was happy.

Vance and the other three men went back to the cut and spent the rest of the day discussing, 'What if we do this? Or that?'

That night as they lay in their bunks, Vance decided they must be going in the wrong direction.

Right, he thought to himself, instead of cutting along the hill, we'll cut across it. Have to go back to where we found that pale-blue stuff. Stands to reason that must be the start of the opal level. Vance didn't sleep a wink that night. He had trouble keeping up with his racing mind. He had visions of huge piles of rocks with thick veins of blazing red opal running here, there, and everywhere throughout. Vance didn't have a clue what the next step would be. He would worry about that when the time came. Vance had never been too much into religion; however, something told him that this new direction had come to him via the Lord. He just knew it.

§

When Yappy's little alarm clock sounded, Vance already had the billy boiling on the open fire.

'Strike me pink,' said Yappy in surprise. 'Did you wet the bloody bed?'

Vance laughed, 'No, Yappy, I couldn't sleep. Too much on my mind.' Vance drank coffee after coffee and chain-smoked while Yappy beat eggs, thinly sliced a few onions, and sliced some bread. Before placing the little bucket containing the scrambled eggs on the open fire, Yappy called the men. By the time they had a wash and cleaned their teeth, breakfast was ready at exactly 5 am, Vance sat in silence observing Neil, Faith, and Little Joe. Their eyes were clear and bright. The three of them somehow appeared years younger.

'What's up, Boss?' asked Faith.

'Nothing wrong, mate. Just thinking how healthy you all look since you've been off the grog.'

'Take a look in the mirror,' came from Neil.

'Why the bloody hell did you have to mention grog?' snapped Faith.

'Sorry, mate,' replied Vance. 'Have to admit I miss my bottle or two a day myself.'

'Enough,' snapped Yappy. 'Time you lot went to work. We are here to find opal, not commiserate about how much you miss the bloody booze. Now get out of here and let me get on with that I have to do.'

Vance saluted to Yappy. 'See you at smoko, Yappy.' Vance explained to Neil, Faith, and Little Joe what he thought they should do.

'I think the opal level starts where we found that pale-blue stuff; think they call it "potch". I want to go through the hill, not alongside it. I just know the opal is running in that direction and starts at that level.'

'Bloody hell, mate,' said Neil. 'Look at the dirt we'll have to move. We'll need another machine.'

'Shame we can't blow it up,' mused Faith. Little Joe nodded. They stood in silence as each of them lit a cigarette and observed the hill.

After a few minutes Vance discarded his cigarette and said quietly, 'Right. That is exactly what we'll do. We'll blast the top of the bloody thing off.' The men were surprised to say the least.

Neil looked at Vance, 'You're fair dinkum, aren't you, mate?'

'Never been more serious, Neil. It's common sense. We'll blast a bit at a time until we are almost at the opal level.'

'Where will we get explosives, Boss?' enquired Faith.

'I have no idea. All I know is that we will get them. Now let us take a walk over this hill and make our plans.'

¶

Smoko time came and went. Yappy was furious because he had baked scones for them. Bugger them, he thought. They can eat the bloody things for lunch.

¶

They arrived back at camp a little before lunch time.

'I'm out of here, men,' from Vance before Yappy had a chance to launch into his now renowned interrogation and what they were doing. 'The men will fill you in, Yappy.' Vance was in his ute and gone in seconds.

Vance was half-way between the mine site and Brolga when he realised he had not filled his petrol tank. He checked the petrol gauge.

'I'm a bloody idiot,' he muttered to himself as he remembered removing the demijohn from the back of the ute early in the morning when he was waiting for Yappy to get out of bed. He recalled placing it on top of one of the fuel drums to remind him to top it up.

'Bloody thing was three-quarters full. Didn't even need topping up. No way I'll make it to town.' He continued mumbling to himself. Vance knew he was out of fuel, so he guided the ute off to the embankment beside the road. Without a second thought, he got out of the car and began walking briskly towards town. It didn't dawn on Vance to put up the car windows or take the key out of the ignition—nobody around here was going to pinch the bloody thing. Even if someone did, where the hell could they go?

¶

Vance had been walking for a little over an hour when the police sergeant and his new constable pulled up alongside him. The young constable was driving.

'What a relief,' said Vance as he opened the door of the police care and quickly jumped into the rear seat.

'You're a lucky man, Vance, in more ways than one. Lucky it's not the middle of summer; lucky some poor bloody jackeroo on one of the stations had to be served with a summons; and lucky that we chose today to serve it. What happened, Vance? Did your ute break down?' Vance felt embarrassed.

'No, mate, I ran out of fuel. I was in such a rush to get back to town that I forgot to fill up at the camp.' The sergeant laughed.

'What? Has one of the new barmaids at the Greeks' pub got you on a promise?' Vance laughed.

'Nothing like that this time, mate.'

'This young man here is my new recruit, Graham Sandler,' said the sergeant. 'Graham, meet Vance Callahan, better known around Brolga as the Pill Pusher.'

'I've heard a lot about you, Mr Callahan,' said Graham while looking at Vance via the rear vision mirror.

Vance laughed. 'Prefer not to go into that, thank you, young man. We shouldn't believe everything we hear. It might be true.' They all laughed. The sergeant and Vance chatted all the way into town. The young constable silently listened with great interest.

'Drop Vance off at the pharmacy, please, Graham. Then we will do a couple of laps of the main street just to let the locals know we are on duty and alert.'

¶

TC hurried to the front door of the pharmacy when she saw Vance getting out of the police car. Vance was thanking the sergeant and constable for giving him a lift when TC walked onto the footpath to say 'hello' to the sergeant.

'TC, when did you come back?'

Saturday night, thought the constable. I saw her and another girl get off the Flea.

'Saturday night, Sergeant,' replied TC.

'What did you think of the Big Smoke?'

'Lou and I didn't fit in.'

Vance winked at the Sergeant. 'You know why, don't you, mate?'

'I can imagine,' laughed the sergeant. 'Let's go, Constable.'

'Who is that girl, Sergeant?' asked Graham Sandler as he drove the police car down Brolga Street.

'Why do you ask?'

'I think I'm in love,' replied Graham.

'Don't waste your time, young fellow. Jake Carmichael has been after her since the minute she arrived in Brolga a year ago. So far, he's made no headway. Hope the young prick never does. She's too bloody good for the likes of him.'

¶

He's in a foul mood, thought TC, as they went to the dispensary.

'I need coffee, TC. Make some, will you, while I make some calls.'

'What happened, Mr Callahan? I thought you were not coming back until tomorrow.'

'Just make the bloody coffee. Where the hell is Lou? I thought she was supposed to be helping you clean up this joint.' TC ignored him as she filled the electric jug, then turned it on.

'I'm hungry,' snapped Vance. 'Go to Con's and get me something to eat.'

'Sure, Mr Callahan. Perhaps I'll have some rat poison sprinkled through the ingredients.' Vance didn't hear her—he was on the phone talking to Jake.

TC stormed into Con's café. 'He's hungry, Con. Make him a sandwich, will you, please? Whatever is the quickest, Con.'

'Okay, luv. Come out to the kitchen and talk to me while I fix it. Did Vance get arrested, TC?'

'I don't know, Con. All I know is that he's in a bad mood. Why? I haven't got a clue. I'm just the hired help, according to Mrs Callahan and Louise. Of course, they are correct.'

Con handed TC a plate on which was a huge ham and salad sandwich covered by a cloth napkin.

'Let me know if Vance is in trouble, luv.'

'Sure will, Con. Thank you.'

TC hurried across to the pharmacy. Vance was still on the phone. This time he was shouting at Delores.

'I'm not in the mood for this, Delores. If you want to go, then go!' Vance slammed down the telephone, then turned on TC, who was making his coffee.

'Did you have to go to Siberia for the sandwich? Took you long enough,' snapped Vance sarcastically.

TC had to control her tongue as she placed his coffee on the desk next to his sandwich. She really wanted to throw it at him but managed to remain relatively calm.

'There is your food and coffee, Mr Callahan. I'm going to get on with cleaning up this pig sty.'

'I asked you before, where is Lou?' snapped Vance as he picked up one half of his sandwich.

TC turned towards Vance and angrily replied, 'She has gone to buy some groceries for the house. Don't worry, she won't charge you for the time she is away. We have been here since six this morning and, in case you haven't noticed, have made quite a difference to the disgusting condition in which we found the place. It is our intention to get the shop finished before we go home tonight, start on the dispensary tomorrow, and be finished before mail and doctor day on Wednesday.'

Vance could tell TC was furious because she had gone into her bar-window mode of hands on hips.

'We are short of stock. Gaps everywhere. Have you placed an order? If not, do I have your permission to phone one through? When I worked at the doll shop, my boss always spoke to me with respect and appreciated extra work I did without being told. I also got paid for every minute I worked. She told me one day, always treat other people the way you would like to be treated yourself. You should try that, Mr Callahan. I have been back one day and already I'm your door mat.' With that, TC turned up the radio station 4CL and stormed off back to her cleaning.

Vance wasn't hungry anymore. He pushed his sandwich aside and lit a Craven A.

'Bloody hell, I'm a prick of a man. I need a drink.' Jake and Lou came through the back door.

'Hi, Vance,' said Lou as she looked at her watch. 'I've been gone for an hour and fourteen minutes. I'll deduct it from my total hours.' Lou picked up a feather duster and joined TC in the shop.

'Are you ready mate?' asked Jake. 'I picked up a couple of demis of petrol for you. Let's go.'

'Jake, I'm a real bastard of a man.'

'I know,' agreed Jake. 'So am I. Come on, let's go get your ute.'

'Jake, I need a drink,' pleaded Vance.

'Not now, mate. If you still need one when we get back to town, I'll have one with you. So, let's go.'

¶

Vance slept en route to collect his ute, even though Jake had the car radio blasting at a million or so decibels of sound. Jake woke him as he pulled up nose to nose with the ute.

'Come on, mate, wake up. Wash your face. We'll put some fuel in your car and get back to own.' Jake jumped out of his car, opened the boot, and took out a large bottle of water. Vance cupped his hands into which Jake poured water. Vance splashed it over his face.

'Again, please,' requested Vance. Jake pulled his neatly folded handkerchief from his pocket and handed it to Vance.

'What a pair we are,' said Jake.

'I know,' laughed Vance.

'Here, mate, you hold the funnel and I'll pour the fuel,' said Jake.

That done, without a word to each other, they were in their cars and on their way back to town. Jake decided he would follow Vance in case he fell asleep.

Poor bugger looks bloody terrible, thought Jake. I'll have to see if I can talk him into going home. Don't hold much hope, but I'll try.

¶

Vance pulled to a halt behind the pharmacy. Jake was right behind him. They got out of their cars and entered the dispensary.

'Vance, mate, you look buggered. Why don't you go home, get cleaned up, and have a sleep?'

'I thought you were my mate, Jake, not my bloody babysitter,' replied Vance, seriously. 'I told you I need a bloody drink. Are you coming?'

Jake threw his hands up in resignation. 'Sure.'

Vance looked at the clock on the wall. It was just after six-thirty. He noticed the front door of the shop was still open. He stormed past Lou and TC, who were both engrossed in cleaning stock and shelves. He slammed the door and bolted it. With that, he yelled at the girls.

'Haven't I got enough bloody problems? Do you pair of idiots want me to get robbed as well?' Both girls looked at him in shock as he hit open the button on the cash register, extracted half a dozen or so of notes, furiously pushed the cash register drawer closed, and snapped at Jake, who was waiting in shock in the dispensary.

'We're out of here, Jake. Let's go.' Jake really wanted to deck Vance.

'You didn't have to speak to the girls like that, Vance. You know very well no bastard around here is going to rob this joint.'

'Let it go, Jake. I need a drink.'

With Vance and Jake gone, the still-speechless girls both sighed and got on with their work.

¶

Louise was on duty at the Empire when Vance and Jake fronted up to the bar.

'Well, if it isn't the bloody Bobbsey twins,' said Louise as she began getting their drinks. 'Beer for you, Jake?' Jake nodded.

'Thanks, Louise.'

'What about you, luv?' Louise smiled at Vance. 'Double Bundy and Coke?'

'Make it a triple,' snapped Vance.

Louise returned with their drinks.

'Thought you had given up the grog to become a model husband and an opal miner,' said Louise with a smile. Vance pushed a ten-pound note across the bar to Louise.

'Now do your job. Take the money, bring the change, then piss off until we need a refill.'

'Yes, sir,' said Louise with a smile as she snatched the note and returned seconds later with change that she literally threw on the counter whilst uttering neurotically, 'Shithead.'

'Let's get drunk,' said Vance.

'You can, mate,' replied Jake. 'I think I'll pace myself.'

¶

The girls were busy cleaning in the pharmacy. They had made a pact that they would be finished by midnight. Con and Lisa were talking to Constable Graham Sandler, who had developed a routine of eating dinner in their café every night around seven.

'So, you didn't arrest Vance?' asked Con.

'No, Con. His car ran out of fuel a fair way from town. The sarge and I just happened to be out that way on police business. We gave him a lift.'

'That's good. I thought my friend might have been in some sort of trouble.'

From where Con was standing behind the counter he had a perfect view of the pharmacy.

'Vance is a lucky man that kid came back. Lou and she are over there cleaning up. Mark my words, Graham, they'll stay there until the job is done.'

'That's dedication, Con.'

❡

Within an hour Con had told the young constable everything he knew about TC and Lou. Graham asked a few questions. He simply listened with great interest.

'They went to Sydney for a while,' concluded Con. 'They came back last Saturday night. Jake Carmichael told me, off the record, that they returned to Brolga because they didn't fit in with the promiscuous ways of most young city girls. Got tired of rock and roll and rugby league stars making fun of them.'

'Very interesting, Con. Very interesting, indeed.'

With that Lisa emerged from the kitchen.

'You gossiping again, Con?' she asked with a smile.

'Just telling young Graham here about TC and Lou.'

'That's why I came out, Con. Those girls have been working over there all day. I want you to take them across a couple of thick-shakes. Take young Graham with you and introduce him. Obviously, you being you, he knows all about them, so he may as well meet them.'

A few minutes later Con and Graham were at the front door of the pharmacy. Con tried to slide the door open as he usually did. When it wouldn't open, he knocked loudly. Both girls were on ladders with their backs to the door, so they had not seen him. They turned, saw Con and Graham, quickly got down from the ladders, and rushed to the door, all smiles.

TC unbolted the door and slid it open.

'You locked me out, mate,' said Con in an exaggerated hurt voice.

'Not at all, Con,' smiled TC. 'The boss locked us in. I think he's gone crazy, Con. He told us we were trying to get him robbed by leaving the door open.'

'He's gone crazy, all right,' added Lou. 'In more ways than one.'

'Well, TC, if you did get robbed, I would find the thief and put him in jail,' from Graham, smiling.

TC shifted her attention to the young constable. Her heart started beating furiously.

'Who are you, beautiful?' asked Lou.

'Come in, Con. You, too, whatever your name is,' from TC.

'Don't forget to close the door,' from Lou.

'Most certainly not,' laughed Con. 'Wouldn't want to upset Vance.'

'My name is Graham Sandler. I'm a rookie police officer. Pleased to meet both of you.' He was looking directly down into TC's upturned face. 'I know your name is TC.'

'And I'm Lou. How come you aren't looking at me that way? I'm hurt,' Lou gave a fake sob. 'You sure are beautiful, Constable Sandler.'

Silently TC agreed with Lou. He was beautiful—around six feet tall, with thick, jet-black hair and short sideburns, perfectly shaped face, huge blue eyes with long black eyelashes, and a smile and a voice that would melt a million hearts. He was not too thin, no excess weight. Just perfect. TC averted her gaze.

'Lisa thought you girls might need a "pick-me-up" as you have been here working since day break.' Con placed the shakes on the counter.

'Come on, Graham, we will go so the girls can get on with their work.'

'Thank you, Con. Please thank Lisa. We'll pay you tomorrow.'

'Not this time, girls. This time is on us. We are so glad you are back. Tell Vance he owes me for the sandwich.'

'I will,' smiled TC.

'See you, TC,' came from Graham.

'What about me?' moaned Lou.

'Don't see as I have much choice in that, Lou. See you, too,' replied Graham.

§

By nine o'clock Vance was blind drunk. The triple Bundy and Cokes had hit home. Jake was bored beyond belief by Vance and Louise bouncing vicious one-liners against each other.

'Vance, mate, I've had enough. Let's go to Con's and have a feed and then I'll drive you home.'

'Sure, Jake. Good idea about the feed, but not too sure about the "going home" bit,' slurred Vance. 'Need a bottle to take with me,' he said as he handed Jake a twenty-pound note.

Jake bought the bottle from Jack Romeo, who said, 'He's on it again, eh?'

'Looks like it, Jack' replied Jake. 'Poor bugger.'

Jake escorted Vance to Con's café after putting the bottle of rum in Vance's car. Jake ordered steak and eggs. Vance decided he wasn't hungry. Con nodded and quietly told Jake that he would bring Vance a bowl of soup and some toast.

Jake ate his meal while chatting with Con. Vance had but a couple of mouthfuls of soup and a few nibbles at his toast before falling asleep while sitting upright on his chair. His head bobbed up and down occasionally.

'Our friend has had it,' laughed Con.

'He's got a lot on his mind, Con. I think he's frightened of failure with this opal thing. As it is, most of the town thinks he's a bloody fool for even trying. Imagine the crap he'll cop from the mongrels if he doesn't pull it off.'

'I know, mate. Let's hope our friend jams it to the lot of them.'

'I agree, Con, but our friend won't be jamming anything to anyone in his present condition. Help me get him across to the pharmacy. He can sleep it off in the dispensary. I think there's a pillow and blanket from ages ago.'

'No problem, mate,' replied Con.

§

The pubs were closed and the street deserted as Jake and Con slowly helped the still-almost-asleep, mumbling Vance across the road. The girls were just finishing up. The shop part of the pharmacy was sparkling clean and in order apart from the gaps.

Lou was surprised to see Vance in his present condition. TC was not.

'I thought this was going to happen.'

'How the hell did you know, TC?' came from Jake.

'I read it in his red book. He can't cope with the reality of his circumstances at the moment; so, he sought escape by swimming to the bottom of a bottle.'

Con looked at TC in amazement.

'You are only a baby, TC. How do you know such things?'

TC smiled. 'He made me read the red book, Con.'

'Yes, and she drove me almost crazy with boredom while she was reading it,' added Lou as she took the pillow from a shelf and placed it on the floor in the dispensary.

'There you go, mate,' said Jake as he and Con lowered Vance to the floor. TC handed Jake the rug and he placed it over Vance, who was now again sound asleep.

'He'll be all right. He'll sleep it off. I'll go fetch his car from outside the Empire and pull it around the back here. Then I'll get my car and drive you girls home if you like.'

'Thanks, Jake,' nodded the girls. Con and Jake left without another word.

'Look how vulnerable he is, Lou.'

'Now I understand why he was off the planet today,' replied Lou.

Both TC and Lou were deep in thought until Jake came through the back door carrying a bottle of Bundaberg rum, which he handed to TC.

'Hide this for an emergency, TC. No way I'm leaving it in his car. Come on, lock up. I'll take you ladies home.'

'You can't come in, Jake, because we are tired,' said TC.

'What else is new?' quipped Jake. 'On the other hand, there could still be a few snakes slithering around.'

'Lick-and-a-promise tonight, Jake.'

'Nice try, anyway, Jake,' from Lou.

'All right, ladies, a man knows when he is beaten.' Jake waited until the girls were inside the house before speeding off home to bed. Some things never bloody change, he thought, as he arrived home and slammed the car door, which woke his mother and Carla. He kissed his mother on the cheek, undressed, and threw himself on his bed to sulk.

¶

Vance was still asleep on the dispensary floor when TC and Lou arrived at seven-thirty next morning. They had decided to go later so he could have more sleep.

'Let's leave him there for a while,' suggested TC.

'Good idea. We can go have breakfast at Con's place. That way we won't need to worry about food later.'

¶

'He's still asleep, Con. Thought we would leave him rest for a little longer.'

'Con, I would like crispy bacon, scrambled eggs, grilled tomato, and toast,' said Lou.

'Sounds good, Con. I'll have the same as long as you don't pile up the plate like you do for everyone else.'

Lou looked at Con. 'Same goes for me, Con.'

Con elaborately wrote himself a note, making a point of underlining TINY SIZE SERVES. Fifteen minutes later, Con emerged from the kitchen with their food. The girls laughed and both jumped up and hugged Con when they saw their eggs and grilled tomato were in the shape of hearts. Lisa's voice came from behind them.

'Don't hug that old Greek, darlings; hug me. It was my idea.' Lou and TC then hugged Lisa. 'Go on enjoy it while it's warm,' smiled Lisa.

Vance stirred not long after the girls went to Con's. His vision was blurry as his eyes kept opening and closing. He eventually willed them to stay open.

'Where on earth am I?' he said to himself. He slowly looked around again and again until he realised he was on the floor in the dispensary. 'How the bloody hell did I get here? Second time this has happened. I'm crook. I need a drink ... No, you don't. That's what got you here in this condition,' he told himself. Looks as if I'm back to where I started. Weak bastard, I am. Perhaps I'll have to get Yappy to lock me up and wean me off the grog like we did to poor bloody Faith, Neil, and Little Joe.'

Vance reached for his cigarettes, then fumbled for his matches. He inhaled deeply while staring at the ceiling. Suddenly he remembered the drama he had staged yesterday. 'Can't blame the booze for that deal. Can't blame TC if she has quit again. Can't believe I acted like such a prick.' Vance finished his cigarette, then slowly stood up at the sink before splashing cold water on his face and running his wet fingers through his thinning hair. He opened the back door. Sure enough, the ute was there. Good old Jake, he thought.

¶

Vance steeled himself to face Delores, so he forced himself to walk into the house as if nothing was wrong.

'Vance where have you been?' demanded Delores.

'I ran out of fuel on the way back from camp.'

'That is a ridiculous excuse, Vance.'

'I told you I ran out of fuel.'

'Vance, I'm going to Brisbane.'

'So you've told me, Delores. At least a dozen times. Just go.'

'One of my friends from the ladies' golf club will travel down with the kids and me. She will come back to Brolga by train.'

'Sounds like a good idea. When are you leaving?'

'Tomorrow.'

'Good.'

'I'll need some money.'

'Of course. How much?'

'Not much.'

'That's good. We haven't got much.' Vance knew his idea of not much was totally different from Delores'. 'Delores, I asked you how much?'

'About three thousand pounds.'

'My God, Delores! The shelves at the shop have gaps as big as Texas! The twenty-thousand-pound overdraft is almost to the limit. I need to buy fuel and explosives for the mine; there's a foot-high pile of bills from the drug houses on the dispensary desk, not to mention wages for the men; and you think three thousand pounds is not much?! I'm going to take a shower and get out of here.'

'That's right, Vance, run away.'

Vance was at the bathroom door. He turned towards Delores.

'That is, indeed, a matter of the pot calling the kettle black!'

¶

Vance was a little surprised to find Lou and TC cleaning in the dispensary. The telephone rang as he walked in. He picked it up. It was Delores.

'Vance, I'll need that money tonight. We are leaving early in the morning.' Vance didn't say a word. He put the telephone back in its cradle. Vance sat down at his desk; he lit a Craven A and smoked while staring at the pile of bills in front of him. Lou broke the silence.

'Vance, you owe TC two bob for your sandwich yesterday. She paid Con out of her own money.' TC glared at Lou. Vance laughed as he put his hand in his pocket and pulled out some change. He put three shillings on the desk.

'There you are, TC. You get a shilling bonus for protecting my reputation with Con.'

'Thank you, Mr Callahan,' nodded TC.

'I'm going out. Lou, you keep cleaning shelves; remember to keep the bottles and boxes in alphabetical order. TC, you sort out these papers, make a list, then add up what we owe in total. I'm going to see Jake.' TC couldn't control her tongue. She looked into Vance's eyes.

'Please don't get drunk again today, Mr Callahan.' Vance smiled.

'Mind your own damned business, Little One. Now, get those bills sorted out.' He was gone.

⁋

Jake was outside his store talking to Bert Romeo when Vance pulled alongside. As he got out of his car to join them, Bert Romeo asked, 'How's your head? My brother told me you did a number on yourself last night.'

'Think of the money you made, Bert,' laughed Vance.

'See you boys later,' said Bert as he walked away towards the Majestic. It was opening time.

'Jake, I need to talk to you, mate,' said Vance.

'Too early for me today; think I'll lay off the booze for a while,' replied Jake. Jake was thinking that if Vance had to find another drinking partner, he might stay away from the pub and get on with his opal mining.

⁋

'Wasn't thinking of going to the Empire. I thought we might go sit down by the creek for a while. I just need someone I can talk to without worrying what I say will go any further.'

'Not a problem, mate. We'll take my car. It is cleaner.'

⁋

Time meant nothing as they sat there by the creek, parked in Vance's favourite spot. Vance talked and talked as Jake listened intently. Finally, Vance concluded. 'That's it, mate. Bottom line is the shop needs stock but I can't get any until I pay for what I have already sold. I know the opal is there; we just haven't found it yet. I need explosives but wouldn't have a clue as to how or where to acquire them. Delores is going to Brisbane and wants three thousand quid, which will totally max the overdraft. The whole bloody town is laughing at me. Truth is I haven't a bloody clue as to what we'll do with the opal when and if we find it. Apart from that, I've got a hangover from hell.'

'I see,' said Jake with his left elbow leaning on the steering wheel and his left hand cupping his forehead. 'Well, mate, let's get back to town so you can take a couple of aspirins.' They both laughed as Jake turned the ignition key, reversed from the creek bank, and sped off towards Brolga.

The knock-off siren sounded from the power house as Jake pulled up behind Vance's ute in front of Jake's shop.

Jake said, 'I'll call Mum and tell her I won't be home for lunch. I'll meet you at the pharmacy in a little while.' Jake immediately phoned TC. 'Are you and Lou going home for lunch?'

'No, Jake. We are busy as usual.'

'Do me a favour, TC. You and Lou get out of there for a while today. I want to talk to Vance.'

'All right, we'll go home. Call us when you've finished.' Vance entered via the back door as TC put down the phone. 'Come on, Lou, let's go home for lunch today. I need to hear some Elvis and Jerry Lee for an hour.' Lou looked at TC is surprise before answering.

'Sounds good to me. See you, Vance.'

'We'll be back in a while,' called TC. Vance watched them walk out. He observed TC close and lock the front door.

'No wonder the poor little buggers don't want to be around me after the way I treated them yesterday.'

Jake arrived as usual via the back door fifteen or so minutes later. He was juggling a napkin-covered plate in each hand and a large bottle of Coke under one arm.

'Eat this, mate, and I'll give you a Coke to go with it,' said Jake as he placed one plate in front of Vance, the other near the phone, and the bottle of Coke on the table.

'I'm not hungry,' replied Vance quietly.

'Well, I am, mate. Look at this. Con has outdone himself,' as he lifted the napkin covering Vance's food. 'Best bloody steak-and-egg burgers on earth. Con has even cut them in halves for us.' Vance looked at the food.

'I'm not hungry.'

'Do you want a Coke?' asked Jake.

'Only if there's rum in it,' replied Vance.

Jake went to the freezer, extracted a tray of ice cubes, squeezed a few into each of the two glasses before topping one glass up with Coke. Jake began eating his steak burger while Vance simply stared at his. Between mouthfuls, Jake said, 'Tell you what, mate. You eat half that burger and I'll pour you a rum and Coke.' Vance's eyes lit up.

'We haven't got any rum.'

'I know where there is some, trust me.'

Vance forced himself to pick up one half of the burger and began to eat it slowly. Jake had finished eating and refilled his glass with Coke. Vance pushed the last bite into his mouth and looked at Jake.

'Okay. Good man,' said Jake before walking to behind the dispensary and extracting the bottle of Bundy from where he had seen TC hide it the night before.

'No triples today, mate,' said Jake as he poured rum over ice and added a little Coke. 'I also want you to drink it slowly.' Vance nodded avidly as he picked up the glass.

'Are you trying to wean me off it?' asked Vance quietly.

'Something like that, mate. I'm not sure of what I'm doing. Just don't want to see you burn out, that's all.' Jake looked around the dispensary, then through the one-way mirror to the shop. 'The girls sure have done a great job of cleaning up the joint.'

'I know,' replied Vance nodding his head slowly. 'I abused them yesterday. Mostly TC.'

'She understands, Vance. Said she read it in some bloody red book.' Vance sighed and shrugged his shoulders.

'I forgot about that.' He pushed his empty glass towards Jake.

'Okay, you can have this one, then one more. That will have to do you until tonight when you eat dinner.'

'Thank you, Jake, you're a good mate.'

'The council has explosives,' said Jake. 'I know because a couple of years back a few of us used to go fishing. We called it fishing, but really we went to party, not watch bloody fishing lines. One day one of the boys who worked for the council came fishing, armed with a few sticks of jelly he had pinched from work. We got more fish than we could count that day. You should have seen them float to the surface every time the creek blew up. Some of the poor things even landed in the trees. Wonder the silly things didn't blow up, as well.' Jake poured Vance his third drink before discarding Vance's left-over food and collecting Con's plates and the bottle of rum.

'I have to go now, mate. Figure out how much money you need to keep going. If I've got it, it's yours.'

Vance replied quietly, 'I didn't unload my problems on you, Jake, so that you would lend me money.'

'I know that. I'm out of here.'

Jake drove to the girls' house to collect them, dropped them opposite the pharmacy, then went to have a chat with Con.

'How's our mate today, Jake?' enquired Con.

'He's okay, Con.'

'How about a game of poker tonight, mate?' asked Con.

'No, Con. Can't afford it. I'm saving my money.'

'What the hell for? You never have before,' came from a somewhat surprised Con.

'People change, Con. Perhaps I'm growing up at last.'

'Believe that when I see it, my young friend,' laughed Con.

Jake left and went to see how his business was going.

Vance was still at his desk when TC and Lou opened the front door. He looked at his watch.

'You are both almost half an hour late.'

'So, Vance,' said Lou, 'you just saved yourself one pound.'

'Don't start, Mr Callahan,' added TC in an acidic tone of voice. 'You got away with it yesterday. I suggest you don't push your luck. Now, if you have finished with your desk, I shall get on with my job of figuring out how much money we owe.'

Vance slowly stood up with a soft sigh. Lou had already resumed sweeping dust off pill jars.

¶

'Lou, stop what you are doing for a moment, will you? I want to apologise to both of you for the foul way I treated you yesterday.'

'Don't make a habit of it, Vance,' replied Lou with a smile.

TC simply nodded her head a couple of times before saying, 'We've had a few orders phoned through this morning for tomorrow's mail. A lot of things we haven't got. I told the customers our order from Brisbane was late, and we would send them next week. I hope it works out that way.' Vance nodded.

'It's the end of the month. Everyone will be paying their accounts. Add up how much will be coming in.'

'I already have. Two thousand, six hundred and seventy-two pounds, eight shillings, and six pence.'

'Don't forget the eight shillings and six pence,' interrupted Lou. Vance's mind was racing. 'That will almost cover Delores. Hope they all pay,' to himself.

'Write the cheques when you've finished adding. Date them all yesterday. I'll sign them later. Call your orders through to the drug houses; tell them I have been away and their cheques were posted this morning.'

'Now you are teaching her to lie for you,' coming from Lou.

'For heaven's sake, butt out, Lou,' snapped Vance. 'This is a matter of sink or swim.'

'Not as many accounts there as you think. A lot of them are account rendered. Everything will be all right,' said TC matter-of-factly.

Vance put down the phone, extracted a leaf from the cheque book, and hurriedly went to the bank across the street. Within minutes he came back, stormed through the dispensary and out the back door as he said, 'We've hit rock bottom, girls; the only way is up.'

❡

Delores and her friend were in the kitchen packing sandwiches when Vance got home.

'We are leaving this afternoon,' said Delores, matter-of-factly. 'With luck, we'll make Curloo before it gets too dark. Stay there in a motel tonight and leave for Brisbane early tomorrow morning.'

'How's opal mining going, Vance?' asked Delores' friend.

'Nowhere,' replied Vance. Vance handed Delores a small bank bag containing her money. 'Here you go. Drive safely; remember, you have the kids with you.' Delores nodded.

'See you later, ladies. Hope you have a nice trip.' With that, Vance got into his car and drove to the police station. Although Delores' golfing friend was in shock at the lack of warmth between Delores and Vance, she said nothing. It was none of her business.

❡

The sergeant was surprised to see Vance.

'Are you stalking me, Mr Callahan?'

'No, you're the wrong gender,' laughed Vance. 'I need to get hold of some explosives. I want to blow the capping off a hill.' The police sergeant thought for a minute or two.

'Think you'll need a permit, perhaps from the Mines Department. Also have a feeling the person doing the blasting is required to have some certificate of qualification. Not absolutely certain but think it goes something like that.'

'Neil and Faith said they know how to do it. Seen it done a hundred times or more. Neil said all we have to do is drill some holes, put in the explosives, wire them up, and push the plunger on the detonating device.' The sergeant laughed.

'If those drunken bastards are doing the detonating, I suggest you hide well in the clear.'

'They are okay, Sarge; they are different men, sober.'

'Aren't we all, mate,' replied the sergeant.

¶

Vance went immediately to the pharmacy and phoned the department in Brisbane. After what seemed like an eternity of explanations and questions, Vance abruptly put down the telephone on the tail of saying an abrupt, 'Thank you'. He looked around at the dispensary shelves. TC was at the desk writing cheques.

'Where is Lou?' questioned Vance.

'She went home. She finished a little while ago. Said she didn't see any point in sitting around here charging you money you can't afford for her to do nothing.'

'How much do we owe, TC?'

TC handed him a sheet of paper on which was a written list of to whom and how much.

'Quite a lot, Boss. A little over seven thousand two hundred pounds, but that includes everything—rent, butcher, grocery store, Mrs Callahan's charge accounts in Brisbane, and all the drug houses.' Vance sighed, then reached for a cigarette.

'Did you call in the stock orders?'

'Sure did. Only one place gave me a hard time. In the end, the man told me they would get the order together and send it as soon as they received their cheque. Talking of cheques, can you at least sign his so I can post it?' Vance nodded.

'Give me the lot, TC. I'll sign them all. You could sign them, anyway. Even I can't tell the difference between my own signature and your version of it.'

'You told me that's for an emergency. This is not an emergency,' replied TC. TC finished writing the last cheque. 'You sit down, Boss. I'll go buy some stamps.'

Vance looked at the neat stacks of cheque, envelope, cheque, envelope leaning against the side of the filing cabinet. He observed the neatly written amount for each cheque written on the top right-hand corner of each envelope where the stamp would eventually be fixed.

Bloody incredible, he thought. She forgot nothing while she was away.

The phone rang. It was Jake.

'Sort out your problems, mate?'

'Yes, Jake.'

'I know TC is not there; saw her go to the post office and spoke to Lou earlier on her way home. Thought I'd give you a call while the coast is clear.'

'Jake, I feel terrible,' replied Vance.

'Bullshit! You should feel relieved. How much?'

'Seven-and-a-half.'

'No problem. See you soon.' Jake was gone.

¶

TC returned from the post office.

'Stamp them and post them before you go home,' directed Vance as he stood up. 'Delores has gone to Brisbane.'

'I know. Jess told me when I passed by the Empire. She saw the station wagon go by and that it was loaded up.'

Vance laughed 'Nothing can beat the Brolga grapevine, TC.'

'We'll be busy tomorrow. About a dozen orders or more already have been phoned in,' replied TC.

'You and Lou can handle it. I have to go, see a guy on one of the seismic camps about twenty miles from the mine; then I'll go to the mine. Anyway, I'll see you in the morning. I have to pick up some supplies for the camp.' TC collected her small purse and started off to post the bundle of cheques. 'TC, don't lock the door. I was just being a mongrel the other day.'

'I know that,' replied TC as she left.

¶

Jake as usual arrived via the back door.

'Been hanging out for a drink,' said Vance with a sigh of relief when he spotted the rum bottle and Coke Jake was carrying.

'Hang on, mate. Business first,' said Jake as he extracted a wad of notes from two of his trouser pockets, then a third wad from his shirt pocket, all in twenty-pound notes.

'There's ten thousand quid there, mate. Would like you to count it?'

Vance looked at Jake enquiringly. Jake responded to the look.

'Better to have a little more than you need. While you are counting, I'll get us a drink.' Vance began counting the money then paused and looked at Jake.

'Thank you, mate. I won't forget this.' Jake nodded.

'Just keep counting it if you really want a drink.'

Jake was pouring their second drink when Vance asked, 'Do you know the American bloke who's in charge of the seismic exploration deal?'

'Yes, mate. Young, good-looking Yank; met him at the Empire a few times. Pretty good man; likes a laugh and enjoys a few drinks. Hear a couple of the nurses think he's pretty hot.'

'Probably his accent,' laughed Vance.

'Either that or he does more for them than I do when he takes them to the creek.' They both laughed.

'Better lift your act, mate,' said Vance with a smile before explaining to Jake what he had been told by the Department for Mines.

'Will take time to go through all the bureaucratic crap. Time is something I don't have. Got to find the opal now, not bloody next year. I'm going to go see the American tomorrow and ask him to lend his help and expertise.'

On the third drink Jake said, 'That's it, mate. I'm going home to bed. Hopefully, if I concentrate all night, I'll come up with a way to win over TC.'

'Don't like your chances, Jake,' laughed Vance.

Within a few minutes they were on their way home to bed.

How peaceful, thought Vance as he showered before bed. No one to nag me. Poor bloody Delores. Poor kids. Poor me.

§

Next morning Vance fuelled the ute, collected what was needed for the camp, and was on his way. He was halfway to camp when he realised he had forgotten to talk to TC.

Oh, stuff it, he thought. I'm a man on the go.

As Vance drove past the rough-track turn-off to his mine site, he briefly wondered what the men had been doing in his absence.

Shortly afterward, Vance saw the white post with blue arrow indicating the location of the seismic camp. Vance was surprised because the track leading to the camp was in far superior condition to the main road. Of course, it was red dirt but it had been compacted to a smooth, hard surface, on either side of which more dirt had obviously been moved in to achieve the present condition of the road. Ahead he could see the camp. There were four large caravans and a huge rectangular transportable building, which was raised off the ground. There were a few steps to and from the doorway entrance. A smooth concrete slate the length of the transportable and around six yards wide accommodated a row of garbage bins neatly lined up at one end, a couple of large tables with a beach umbrella protruding from the centre of each, and perhaps ten or twelve chairs.

Sure as buggery puts our camp to shame, thought Vance, as he braked and his ute pulled to a halt.

Three men, each holding a coffee cup, were standing on the concrete slab. They had been deep in conversation; now they turned to look at Vance as he left his car and approached them.

§

Vance was surprised by their immaculate presentation considering the 'in the middle of nowhere' location. They all wore blue jeans, brown leather boots with matching belts along with pale blue short-sleeved shirts with a company logo on the pocket. With right hand outstretched, Vance laughed.

'If I didn't know better, I would think I am on a movie set somewhere in Texas. I'm Vance Callahan.'

'I know,' replied the tallest, best-looking of the three, who reached forward and shook Vance's hand before introducing his two companions.

'I was hoping to have a word with the man in charge,' said Vance.

'You're looking at him,' replied the tall, young man as he removed his sunglasses. 'How is TC? Heard she's back.'

Bloody hell, just my luck, thought Vance as he recognised the young man as the one who had hung around the pharmacy and was with TC that day in the Bucks beer garden.

'Sorry about that, mate,' said Vance.

'Sure. Pigs might fly, too, pal. What can I do for you?' Vance explained his problem as the three Americans listened intently until he finished speaking.

After a brief silence, one of the Americans asked, 'So you are sure the opal is there? My mother loves opals.'

'I feel it. Guess you might call it a gut feeling.'

'We'll give it some thought. In the meantime, I suggest you clean the top of the hill,' said the young man in charge.

Vance nodded, then thanked him before shaking hands and climbing into his ute, then starting it up.

'See you tomorrow if you can guarantee me a date with TC,' laughed the young American.

'That is up to TC,' replied Vance with a smile before driving off.

'Not while you are guarding her every move,' mumbled the young man to himself as he watched Vance's departure.

¶

Vance was surprised when he pulled up to the mine camp. Usually, Yappy would run to greet him with question upon question. Vance smiled to himself as he thought, Hope the mad little bugger hasn't gone on strike. He could hear the sound of the loader working, so he decided to unload the supplies before joining the men. He was placing perishables in the kerosene refrigerator when he heard Yappy's voice behind him.

'About bloody time you got back, Vance.'

'Only been two days, Yappy,' replied Vance.

'Seems a bloody lot longer. I'm supposed to be the cook and camp caretaker, not a bloody labourer. Neil made me go up on the hill and help them.'

'Help them do what, Yappy?'

'Neil decided the bloody hill had to be cleared before we blast the top off.'

'Neil is right, Yappy. I'm happy it is started because that is exactly what needs to be done.'

'Started, my foot!' replied Yappy. 'It's half bloody finished! Neil has been knocking down that mulga faster than a bloody speeding bullet. All right for him; he's sitting in the machine. Faith, Little Joe, and myself are the bloody slaves. We have to clean up what he leaves behind and take it off.' Vance laughed.

'Never mind, Yappy. Throw some smoko together now. I promise I'll take your place on the hill for the rest of the day.'

'Yes, well, I am supposed to be the cook,' mumbled Yappy with relief.

Glad it's not a very big hill, thought Vance, a few hours later. No wonder poor little Yappy was buggered. Never mind. Better to keep up with Faith and Little Joe. Don't want them to think I'm a wimp. If I ever get rich, I'll have to remember to pay them more. Poor buggers sure earn it.

⁋

They worked until sundown, as usual. Vance didn't mention anything about the possibility of help from the Americans and avoided any questions regarding when and with what they were going to blow the hill.

Neil, Faith, Little Joe and even Yappy smiled to themselves when, after showering and eating the evening meal, Vance said, 'Goodnight,' then went directly to his bunk where he fell asleep instantly.

'Must be the bush air,' said Yappy with a wink and a smile.

'Must be,' nodded the others.

§

By mid-afternoon next day the surface, ends and the side of the hill were clear and clean apart from the odd rock formation jutting up or out here and there. The open-cut side of the hill they had been working on previously remained the same. They were now in the process of creating a twenty-yard clearing around the base of the hill that did not involve the open-cut section.

Vance looked at his watch for what seemed to him the millionth time while despondently thinking, Really thought the Yanks would help us. Never mind, we will just have to be patient and wait to go through the proper channels.

At knock-off time, Vance told the men he was going back to town.

'When you finish the clearing, Neil, I want you to service the machine. It's been working pretty hard. Faith, you and Little Joe do a water run, then throw together some semblance of a toilet in case we get some female guests. Yappy, as usual, you do whatever you wish as long as you feed the men well.' As an afterthought, he added, 'There's a slight possibility a young American might show up. If he does, show him around. I believe he's an engineer, so he should know what he's talking about.'

The four men nodded with interest as Vance sped off down the track.

'Wish he wouldn't take off the way he does. Throws up too much bloody dust,' whined Yappy.

'I'm going to take a shower,' came from Neil.

'I have some washing to do,' added Little Joe.

§

'Yappy, stop yapping,' laughed Neil as he began rolling a cigarette after perching himself on the side of his bunk, wishing deep inside himself that the bunk was a bar stool and in front of him was a bottomless glass of booze. Anything would do as long as it would eventually allow him to escape reality.

Unbeknown to Neil, Faith in the shower and Little Joe at the washing bench were thinking virtually the same thing. Oh, how they craved a drink, knowing full well that one drink would lead to countless more, which would eventually cause them to pass out when sweet oblivion would overcome them until they finally woke up and were forced to face their real worlds, when, if funds allowed, the cycle would begin again.

¶

Vance was fighting off his own demons regarding his need for a drink as he guided his speeding ute precariously over the dirt road in a hurry to reach the paved stretch, which would mean he was almost in town. Vance was unaware that he was engulfed by self-pity. His situation was, as far as he was concerned, everyone else's fault. He blamed Delores, the Mines Department, the young American engineer, the townsfolk for laughing at him, Louise, even TC and Lou for having gone away for a while.

It was a little after nine when Vance pulled to a halt outside the Empire. He looked around for Jake's car but it was nowhere to be seen.

'I stink,' he muttered as he left the ute and walked along the back verandah of the Empire.

Jack Romeo was talking to a tall, slender, well-dressed, young, blonde woman, who, at a rough guess, Vance estimated to be around twenty-five or twenty-six years of age. She glanced at Vance as he approached, couldn't believe her eyes, so she looked again, this time with disbelief. Never in her life could she recall seeing anyone so filthy, let alone in such dismay.

Vance was covered from the top of his head to the tip of his boots in thick, red dust. His usually blonde hair was off to one side and stiff with red dirt. She glimpsed the top of his cigarette box jutting out from his torn shirt pocket. She wished the revolting creature would stop smiling at her.

'You look well, boy,' smiled Jack Romeo.

'Wish I felt it,' replied Vance. It did not occur to him that Jack was being sarcastic.

The young woman was taken aback by Vance's voice and perfect enunciation as he continued looking her over and smiling. She was practically a double for his Anna. Same blonde hair pulled back and held with a clip; what he imagined to be perfect breasts hidden under her dress; tiny waist exaggerated by a wide and buckled belt above a slightly flared, knee-length skirt. Her dress was pale green. Anna's favourite colour was pale green. This woman wore flat, white shoes. Anna loved and wore white shoes almost all of the time.

'What do you want, boy?' asked Jack Romeo.

Vance wanted desperately to reply, What I'm looking at, Jack. Instead, he ordered a bottle of Bundy and a bottle of Coke.

'While you are at it, Jack, you could introduce me to this young lady.' Jack Romeo either didn't hear Vance's request or chose not to.

'My name is Claudia, and I wish you would stop looking at me with that stupid grin on your disgustingly dirty face.'

'Sorry, you remind me very much of a friend of mine. I haven't looked in a mirror since my last shave. That was a couple of days ago. I've just come back from the bush. I'll try to be clean next time we meet.'

'That is, if there is a next time,' replied Claudia.

'In Brolga, you have to be joking.'

'Thanks, Jack. I'll pay you tomorrow. Just came from the mine, so I have no money on me,' said Vance as he took the bottle of rum and the Coke which Jack Romeo handed him. Vance nodded at Claudia.

'See you later, Claudia,' before turning and heading towards his ute, which he noted was literally caked with red dust. If I look half as bad as you, no wonder Claudia told me I am disgustingly dirty, thought Vance, as he slammed the car door. As he drove off, he laughed to himself. 'We'll see, Miss Claudia, we'll see.'

Meanwhile Claudia was curious about Vance.

'Who is that man, Mr Romeo?'

'His name is Vance Callahan. Amongst other things, he's a married man. I strongly suggest you stay away from him. You meet Jess in the bar here at a quarter-to-ten in the morning. Don't be late.'

Claudia nodded. 'Thank you, Mr Romeo. Goodnight.'

Something strange about this one, thought Jack Romeo, while he watched Claudia's back as she walked towards the staff quarters. She was not expected to arrive until Saturday night on the Flea. Instead, she's hitched a ride with a commercial traveller from God knows where. 'It will come out in the end; everything does.'

When Vance got home, he immediately poured himself a drink, then lit a cigarette, which he inhaled deeply as he sat down by the telephone. Vance rattled his glass to hear the ice clink, then took a sip of his drink and another drag on his Craven A before sighing as he looked around the room thinking, At least one thing is good. I can come home to my own home and sit down in peace with a drink and a cigarette. I should call TC to find out how things are going. I imagine Delores has phoned and phoned and phoned. Stuff it! That can all wait until tomorrow. Everything can wait until tomorrow.

Vance decided to play a Ray Charles record. As he walked past the bedroom to the stereo, he caught a glimpse of himself in the wardrobe mirror and began to laugh. Bloody hell, he thought, no wonder that Claudia woman was looking at me as if I came from another planet.

As Ray Charles' voice and piano began to sound throughout the house, Vance slumped down at the kitchen table and poured himself another drink while telling himself that he didn't care what he looked like, that he didn't care about anyone or anything. He cared about nothing. The telephone rang a few times. Vance ignored it. He sat there in silence listening to Ray Charles, pouring drink after drink, and chain-smoking until he fell asleep slumped over the kitchen table.

¶

He had not bothered to shower, so he was still covered in red dirt when

Jake arrived early next morning. Without knocking, Jake opened the front door and walked through the house to the kitchen, where he found Vance, an almost-empty rum bottle, and an overflowing ash tray. Jake, immaculately attired, as usual, looked as his mate with sadness and compassion. These were rare feelings for Jake as he usually only thought of himself. Jake gently shook Vance's shoulders.

'Come on, mate. Come on, wake up. You're a bloody mess, mate.'

'Go away, Jake,' mumbled Vance without raising his head. 'Can't a man die in peace?'

'You aren't going yet, mate. You still have a lot to do while you are here.'

'Go away, Jake. I told you I want to die,' replied Vance with his head still down.

'That is effing bullshit, mate. Now, wake up! Stand up and take a shower. You smell and look as if you've been rolling around in a pigsty. I'll make you some coffee; then, if you still want to die, I'll go by the pharmacy and collect a couple of hundred sleeping pills for you. At least you'll die clean.'

Vance slowly raised his head and slowly rubbed his forehead in small circular motions with both hands. His gaze was focused on the overflowing ash tray. 'You are a bastard of a friend, Jake.'

'So are you,' replied Jake as he placed a cigarette between Vance's lips before extracting his cigarette lighter from a pocket and lighting up for Vance, who inhaled deeply.

'You really do look bloody awful, Vance. Now, please finish that fag, then get cleaned up. You have a lot to do.'

'Jake, you are also a bloody nagger,' replied Vance as he pushed back his chair and slowly stood up.

'Someone has to look after you, mate. You're not doing it yourself, so you are stuck with me at the moment,' replied Jake as he went about clearing the table. Vance stubbed out his cigarette in the now-clean ashtray, then made his way to the shower. After a few minutes, Vance called out loudly from the bathroom.

'Jake, mate, put a Louis Armstrong record on, will you? If you won't let me die, I may as well listen to the best while I'm alive.' Jake laughed and happily carried out Vance's request.

When Vance finally reappeared in the kitchen, he looked like a different man. He was clean-shaven, his hair combed, and to Jake it appeared that his friend had somehow shed numerous facial lines. Jake also noticed, as Vance stood with a towel wrapped around his waist, that facial lines were not the only thing Vance had lost. Vance was little more than skin and bone.

Jake tried to hide his shock by saying, 'Mate, love your patchwork tan. Your face and neck are brown from three inches above your elbow down. Suggest you either cut your shirt sleeves off at the shoulder or wear long-sleeved shirts.'

'Screw you, Jake. I'm going to get dressed.'

'The new doctor arrived in town the night before last. Suggest you wear some proper pill-pusher clothes today. TC told me he phoned the pharmacy every hour on the hour yesterday. He wants to meet you and talk to you.'

'Bugger it, I forgot about him. Give me another cigarette. What did TC tell him?'

'The usual. You were unavailable at the moment and could she take a message,' replied Jake with a smile.

'Forget the cigarette. I had better get dressed.'

'Most impressive, mate,' said Jake when Vance emerged from his bedroom wearing a long-sleeved white shirt, light-grey trousers, grey belt and shoes and even a grey tie. Jake looked at his watch.

'Let's go have Con cook us some breakfast. There is plenty of time before the shops open.'

§

'You look a bit agitated, mate,' said Jake as he sat with Vance in Con's Café waiting for their food.

'I'm a bit worried about having a permanent doctor here, Jake. Don't know if he will accept TC filling the prescriptions. With him here all of the time, you can bet there'll be scripts every day,' replied Vance. Jake thought for a few seconds before speaking.

'Everyone in town knows TC fills the prescriptions and runs the pharmacy, mate. Even the flying doctor and matron; all the hospital staff know. No one has a problem with it. As a matter of fact, I've heard it said more than a few times that a lot of people are happy it's TC who takes care of their medicine needs, especially when you're on the slops.' Vance laughed.

'Who can blame the poor buggers.'

'Exactly!' said Jake.

'That's not the point, Jake,' replied Vance. 'If this new doctor is the run-of-the-mill, fresh-out-of-med-school, know-it-all, arrogant young prick, he'll pull rank, probably report me to the pharmaceutical board, which will mean I'll have to close the pharmacy to go opal mining or keep the pharmacy open and forget opal mining. I cannot afford the opal mining without the income from the pharmacy, and I cannot pursue the mining if I have to be in the pharmacy all the bloody time.'

'I see,' said Jake nodding his head. 'Well, mate, we have to hope that the doctor is not a know-it-all, arrogant, young prick. You haven't even met him yet. See what happens'.

Con, who was usually chatty, sensed that his friends wanted privacy, so made himself scarce after serving their meals.

Vance and Jake ate their breakfast in silence. When finished, Vance looked at Jake. 'Thank you, Jake. You are right about the doctor. I have to keep an open mind. No point in burning any bridges before I come to them. Just that nothing is going according to plan. I feel defeated. Never thought I would hit this level of depression. Never thought of myself as a quitter.'

'You are not a quitter, Vance. Everything will be okay. You'll find your opal. Who knows, mate. Maybe you'll put Brolga on the map. Perhaps we'll become famous for something else other than being the end of the bloody line.'

They thanked Con and left.

'Good luck, mate,' said Jake as he got into his car, and Vance started off across the road to the pharmacy.

As Jake drove off, Sam and the new girl in town, Claudia, appeared on the footpath via the Empire's front door. Sam was on a day off. As was Sam's way, she had befriended Claudia on sight the night before. They were now en route to buy cigarettes from Con at his café.

'Who is that?' asked Claudia.

'That's Jake Carmichael, local hotshot, thinks he's God's gift to women, especially when he's hooning around in his flash bloody cars. I don't like him,' concluded Sam.

'Not him,' replied Claudia while shaking her head. 'I mean the one unlocking that door across the street,' as she pointed towards the pharmacy.

'Oh, him; that's the chemist, Vance Callahan, commonly referred to in town as the pill-pusher.'

'What is he like?' enquired Claudia with interest.

'He's all right. He's married with three kids. His wife leaves him every other week. She takes the kids, of course. So far, she always comes back. He's a drunk and loves women. A while back he supposedly quit the booze and rounded up some local down-and-outers to go work with him. He told them and everyone else he was going opal mining. As yet, don't think he's found any opal, and as far as I know he's still a bloody drunk. Watch out for him, Claudia; he loves women. Poor bastard is also the joke of the town.'

Claudia nodded as she continued to absorb every word Sam had spoken regarding Vance.

'Who's your new friend, Sam?' asked Con as the girls entered the café.

'This is Claudia, Con. Claudia, this is Con.'

'You are a good-looking young lady, Claudia,' smiled Con. 'Welcome to Brolga.'

'Claudia is interested in Vance. What do you think of her chances, Con?' laughed Sam.

'Claudia, please leave my friend alone. He already has enough problems,' smiled Con.

¶

Vance sat at his desk in the dispensary smoking a Craven A as TC placed a cup of coffee in front of him.

'Have you got a date, Vance?' asked Lou as she sat on a stool opposite the desk, pencil-sketching Vance.

'Yes, Lou, I think I'm going to meet the new doctor for the first time. Thought I should look the part for our first meeting. Vance looked at his watch. 'Lou, haven't you got something more constructive to do?' Lou glanced at the wall clock, then replied.

'I have exactly eleven minutes before I'm on the payroll. Hopefully by then I will have the masterpiece completed.' Still sketching, Lou continued, 'Think I'll call it, "Well Dressed Pharmacist of Brolga."

'What has been happening, TC?' asked Vance.

'Mrs Callahan has called many times. She would like you to phone her. The new doctor called half a dozen or so times yesterday. His name is Doctor Jackson Pierce. He sounds young. He'll call you again this morning.' Vance nodded. 'Thank heavens, you are back,' added TC. 'I think Dr Pierce is anxious to meet you.'

'That goes two ways, TC. What else has been happening?'

'A lot of cheques have come in for payment of accounts. We were very busy with mail day. We should receive a lot of stock today as the goods train arrived this morning.'

'Time to work,' said Lou as she got off the stool and plonked her sketch on the desk for Vance's approval. Vance picked up the sketch and smiled.

'Excellent, as usual, Lou. I mean it. I truly think you could make it big as an artist.'

'Sure!' replied Lou as she picked up a feather duster and exited the dispensary.

The telephone rang. TC picked it up, thinking it was Delores or the doctor. It was the Postmaster asking for Lou. After a brief conversation with the postmaster, Lou put the phone down.

'I start back at the exchange next Monday. I'll be able to keep up with all of Brolga's juiciest gossip again. Of course, I'll still help out here when needed. There is nothing better to do in Brolga. May as well keep busy working.' TC raised her eyebrows.

'Don't start, Lou; we've already experienced Sydney.'

'Don't remind me,' answered Lou as she swaggered away, waving the feather duster over her head. With that the delivery truck laden with cartons pulled up in front of the pharmacy.

At that moment, a slim man around thirty years of age entered through the front door. He was perhaps five-feet-eight with thick, curly, black, collar-length hair with short sideburns. He was wearing tight, blue jeans and a casual, yet expensive-looking, white shirt. His face was pretty, too soft to be handsome. Huge blue eyes and long black eye lashes. He appeared hesitant, not confident. TC smiled at him.

'Good morning.'

'Yes, good morning. I'm Jackson Pierce. I was hoping Vance Callahan is in today,' he replied in a soft, precise voice. Vance appeared from behind the dispensary partition wall.

'Come in,' said Vance as he and Jackson shook hands.

'TC, make us some coffee. How do you take yours, Doctor?'

'Please call me Jackson. Haven't had the Doctor title long enough to get used to it yet,' replied the young doctor before turning to TC. 'Black coffee, please.'

TC returned with the coffee.

'Do you need sugar, Doctor?' asked TC. He shook his head.

'No, thank you. Please call me Jackson.'

'Jackson,' interrupted Vance. 'This is TC. TC knows the pharmacy backwards. She virtually runs the place.'

'You look too young to be a pharmacist, TC,' remarked Jackson.

'I had best help the truck driver and Lou unload,' smiled TC as she left the dispensary.

Vance decided there and then to be straight with Jackson, to tell him the truth regarding himself and his situation. Jackson would soon find out via the gossip grapevine of Brolga, anyway, so Vance saw no point in beating around the bush.

'Jackson, TC is not a registered pharmacist. She does literally run the place and does a damned great job of it. She is young. She is also smart. Everyone around here knows she fills their prescriptions. So far, no complaints.'

Jackson sipped his coffee and listened in silence as Vance continued.

'Until recently, I spent most of my waking hours in the Empire bar drinking rum and Coke. I quit for a short time, but I'm now back fighting the demon. So far, the demon is winning. I have a wife and three kids. My wife leaves me periodically; so far, she eventually returns. She's a good woman. Lord knows, she has to be to put up with me. As far as other women are concerned, I love them. Can't help myself, especially when I'm full of rum.'

'All right if I help myself to another coffee?' interrupted Jackson with a slight smile.

'Stay there, Jackson. TC will get it,' replied Vance before calling TC, who immediately made another coffee for Jackson along with a refill for Vance before leaving them alone to continue their meeting.

'Please go on, Vance,' requested Jackson. 'I find your honesty refreshing and unexpected.' Vance smiled and nodded.

'A while back, I heard from a reliable source that there is opal in the hills west of here. I have researched extensively, and I am convinced beyond a doubt that what I heard is correct. Anyway, I applied for mining leases, rounded up a few town down-and-outers and weaned them dry, sold my other pharmacy, bought some new machinery and camping gear, and here we are today. The reason I have told you all of this is simply I cannot be at the mine and here at the same time. I need to be in a position to spend a lot of time at the mine, which means I won't be here to fill a few prescriptions every day. Apart from that, Jackson, I cannot afford to go opal mining without the income from the pharmacy. It's a "catch twenty-two" situation.'

§

'I understand, Vance,' replied Jackson after a couple of minutes in deep thought. 'Bottom line is you would like me to agree to allow TC to continue filling prescriptions in your absence? You are concerned I'll blow the whistle on you?' Vance shrugged as he lit a cigarette before replying.

'Something like that, Jackson.'

'Vance, I'm sure you understand this puts me in an extremely difficult situation,' said Jackson slowly and precisely. 'I'm the new kid on the block. It is not my intention to cause unnecessary problems. I have been well and truly warned regarding Brolgaites' parochial attitudes. Due to ethical reasons, I am unable to make an agreement with you regarding your problem. That does not mean I can't close my eyes to the issue. If everyone else is happy, what I don't know can't hurt me,' concluded Jackson with a smile.

Vance sat in relieved, surprised silence before speaking.

'Jackson, I don't know how to thank you for your trust and understanding. TC is not too enthralled about mixing ointments, by the way.'

'Who is?' replied Jackson with a smile. 'I'll try not to order any for my future patients. You had best find opal, Vance; otherwise, we had this conversation for nothing.'

'I will find it, Jackson,' replied Vance seriously. 'I have to, especially now.'

They talked until siren time, when Jackson left to inspect his accommodation and newly erected doctor's surgery and Vance went across to meet Jake at the Empire, where, for once, Vance did very little drinking and a lot more talking than usual. After finishing telling Jake about the new doctor and what a great, understanding man the doctor was, Jake laughed.

'Aren't you happy I didn't let you die, mate?'

'I'll drink to that, Jake' replied Vance as his lifted his glass of rum and Coke to his lips before adding, 'Let's go have lunch at Con's.'

'Great idea, mate. Miracles do happen—two feeds for you in one day. Let's go.'

'Feel as if a great weight has been lifted off my shoulders, Jake. First the kid came back; then you got me out of trouble financially; now the new doctor turns out to be a decent type of man. All I need now is to blow the top off that bloody hill.'

'It'll happen, mate,' said Jake encouragingly.

'I know, Jake,' replied Vance as they seated themselves at a table in Con's café.

'Want a game of cards later?' asked Con with a smile, when he served their meals a while later.

Both Jake and Vance shook their heads as they replied in unison, 'Sorry, Con, we are broke.'

'Lying bastards,' said Con. 'If you're broke you must have been losing a lot on the horses because you have been winning all my money.'

'That means the three of us are broke, mate,' laughed Jake, who in fact was not broke at all., He had another twelve or so thousand quid in his kitty but had decided to hang onto it in case Vance needed more financial help.

'All right, all right, my friends,' laughed Con as he walked towards his kitchen.

§

After finishing lunch with Jake, Vance had been back at the pharmacy only a few minutes when the doctor returned.

He's changed his mind, thought Vance.

'Vance,' said Jackson, 'I have written half a dozen fake prescriptions. I thought you and I might make ourselves scarce while TC fills them.'

'No problem,' replied Vance as Jackson handed the scripts to TC. 'Don't worry, TC; there are no mix-yourself ointments on these.'

'Thank you, Doctor Jackson,' replied TC as she looked through the scripts. 'See you in about twenty-five minutes.'

Jackson and Vance decided to sit on the Seat of Knowledge while waiting. Old Jess saw them through the Empire window.

'Well, I'll be buggered. He's on the bloody seat himself. Wonder where TC is, and who the hell is that bloke with Vance?' Jess moved to the Empire window and called to Vance.

'Where's the girl?'

'She's working, Jess,' replied Vance with a smile.

'Who are you?' demanded Jess of Jackson.

Caught unawares by Jess' directness, Jackson hesitated; so, Vance replied with a laugh, 'This is Doctor Jackson Pierce, Jess; he's come to Brolga to take care of sick people.'

'Lot of sick bastards here. Good luck, Doctor Jackson Pierce,' replied Jess as she turned away from the pub window, muttering to herself, 'God knows, you'll need it with all the mongrels we have here in Brolga.' To say the least, Jackson was taken aback by Jess' remarks.

'That's Jess,' smiled Vance. 'One might say Jess is a legend in Brolga. She's been here forever and knows everything about everyone. Jess has a bark worse than her bite. She's a kind-hearted soul deep down.'

'I see. Still, wouldn't want to get on her wrong side,' replied Jackson as he looked at his watch, and they both stood up, then walked back to the pharmacy, where TC had neatly lined up the filled prescriptions on the dispensary counter.

Jackson was impressed as he read the neatly typed directions on the labels before checking the contents of the assorted medication containers. After ten or so minutes, he turned to Vance.

'My eyes are closed, Vance,' then nodded, 'Well done, TC,' before excusing himself and leaving with confidence that there would be no stuff-ups as far as the Brolga pharmacy was concerned.

§

'Mrs Callahan phoned three times while you were out,' said TC. 'I think you should call her.'

'When I'm ready,' snapped Vance. TC was back in the shop with Lou within seconds.

Why the hell did I snap at her? thought Vance, as he observed TC silently handing bottles of baby oil to Lou, who was on the ladder. All she did was tell me Delores had called. Perhaps it's Delores I'm angry at. Perhaps I don't bloody well want to phone Delores. She's the one who left. Bugger her! I'll call her when and if I feel like it. Vance began drifting into deep thoughts of mostly what-ifs, then, before too late, snapped himself out of it. Bugger it, he thought, I'm on a roll, not going to let depression get a hold on me again. Not now, anyway. He glanced through the dispensary's one-way petition when he heard a vaguely familiar female voice asking TC if he was in.

'Just what I bloody-well need. Another bloody woman,' he mumbled to himself when he saw Claudia through the mirror. He reluctantly stood up from his desk and walked to the dispensary entrance.

'Come through, Claudia,' he said with a broad, fake smile on his face.

'So, you remember me? Must say you are much more presentable today than you were in your filthy, dust-encrusted, opal-mines uniform last night.'

'Yes, first impressions are obviously not important to some people,' replied Vance.

'Why do you say that?' questioned Claudia naively.

'Because, Claudia, if they were, you wouldn't be here.' They both laughed as Vance placed a cigarette between his lips. Claudia picked up his matches before looking directly into his eyes while she struck a match and held it to his cigarette.

Oh, shit, here we go again, thought Vance, as he inhaled deeply before deliberately blowing his inhaled smoke into her face.

Claudia didn't divert her gaze as the smoke surrounded her face; instead, she blew Vance a kiss.

I don't believe this, thought Vance, as Claudia placed her hands behind his neck and began softly rubbing them up and down. She may look like Anna but that is where it starts and finishes. This one is hot. She's too hot.

'Mr Callahan, Lou and I need to take some empty cartons through to the backyard,' interrupted TC from the dispensary doorway.

'Not now,' replied Vance without looking at TC. 'Go get the mail and take Lou with you.'

TC found it difficult to conceal her disgust as she replied, 'No, Mr Callahan, we'll leave the cartons there until tomorrow. We'll go home now.'

Vance was far too engrossed with Claudia to notice TC collect both her own purse and Lou's small bag. He also did not notice that TC had left her shop keys on the counter alongside the telephone. He heard the front door slam shortly after which he and Claudia were engaged in wild, abandoned, no-holds-barred, almost animalistic sex. Vance had countless women but never one like Claudia. She was sexually insatiable.

They were so engrossed with each other that they did not hear Jake come through the open back door, then leave silently after briefly observing their naked bodies as they writhed and rolled all over the floor. Jake laughed to himself as he got into his car out back of the pharmacy.

'Just as well Delores is out of town. Hate to think what would have happened if she had walked in on that deal.'

Jake drove down Brolga Street, expecting to see TC and Lou perched on the Seat of Knowledge. To his surprise, they were not there. Bet she's pulled the pin again, thought Jake, as he pulled up in front of his shop. Jake immediately went to his office and phoned the nurses' quarters. Ten minutes later he was driving towards the creek with a pretty, off-duty nurse beside him.

'This is a surprise, Jake. Didn't know you were an afternoon man. Thought you preferred the darkness of night,' she giggled.

'Anytime is the right time with a girl like you,' replied Jake. 'Can't wait to get your clothes off.'

'You don't have to wait too long, Jake. I'll take them off now,' purred the nurse in a soft, sexy voice as she removed her blouse and bra and unzipped her shorts out of which she wriggled until they lay discarded on the car floor.

Jake braked to an abrupt halt, then was out of the car in a flash as the nurse climbed over onto the back seat of his car.

'Hurry up, Jake, sweetie,' she said as she dangled her black bikini briefs in her hand.

'What the bloody hell do you think I'm doing?' replied Jake, as his trousers fell to his knees.

'Stick it in me, Jake, stick it in me,' moaned the nurse who was still dangling her briefs in one hand and softly fondling her breasts with the other. Her legs were wide open and welcoming.

Jake was so engrossed in observing his target as he fumbled with his underpants, trying to manoeuvre the front section over and past his erect penis that he lost his balance and fell backwards onto his bottom.

'Bloody hell,' he yelled in agony as he realised he had landed on a patch of bindi-eyes. The nurse sat up.

'What is wrong, Jake?' she asked before bursting into gabs of laughter when she saw Jake. He was sitting on the patch of bindi-eye, his trousers were wrinkled around his ankles, his underpants were on a downward angle at the sides and just above his crotch in the front. His face wore an expression of excruciating pain.

'Get your bloody clothes on, woman, and stop laughing. Can't you see a man is in bloody agony. I need you to help me get up. Feels as if I have a million burning darts stuck in my bare arse.'

The nurse, still giggling, quickly got herself dressed, put on her flattie shoes, and carefully helped Jake up from his vulnerable position on the ground. Once Jake was standing, he was motionless.

'Aren't you going to pull up your trousers, Jake?' asked the nurse quietly.

'How the bloody hell can I?' snapped Jake. 'I've got burrs in the back of my legs as well as in my arse.'

Eventually Jake lay face down across the back seat of his car as one by one the nurse removed the bindi-eye with a small pair of pliers from the tool box Jake had in the boot of his car. The car ash tray was the receptacle for the offending prickles.

'I'm itchy,' complained Jake. 'How long will this take? That is the bloody end of day-time sex for me. Bugger my mate for getting me turned on. There's a time and a place for everything, the nurse thought for a while, as she went about extracting bindi-eye after bindi-eye.

'Jake, it wasn't the time that was wrong. It was just the wrong place,' she said between fits of laughter. 'I really wanted you to stick it in me, Jake. I truly did.' Jake moaned.

'I haven't got anything to stick anywhere at the moment. I'm the poor bastard who got stuck.'

¶

Back in the dispensary, Vance and Claudia, now fully clothed, were standing beside the dispensary bench, reluctantly parting ways.

'You sure know how to turn me on,' said Claudia as she and Vance hugged each other tightly.

'Could say the same for you, Claudia,' murmured Vance as he kissed the top of her head. With that, the telephone beside them rang. 'Bugger it,' said Vance as he reached to pick it up.

'Think it rang a few times while we were busy,' whispered Claudia with a smile.

'Vance, I've been calling and calling. Why hasn't someone answered? Is the shop closed? If so, why? Where is TC? I thought you employed her so that the shop wouldn't be closed?' Delores went on and on. Vance said nothing. He simply placed the telephone back into its cradle, then lifted it up again before placing it on the counter.

'No one there?' asked Claudia.

'My wife,' replied Vance. 'I'll call her later'.

¶

Claudia left via the back door as she went off to prepare herself for her night shift at the Empire. Vance picked up the telephone to place it in its cradle. He spotted TC's shop keys, which were beside the cradle.

Oh, shit! he thought before sitting at his desk and lighting a cigarette. Vance, you sure are a crappy piece of work, he told himself.

¶

Vance was still sitting at his desk. He had been chain-smoking since Claudia had left. There was a knock on the open back door, followed by Jake's voice.

'Are you decent, mate? Is it okay if I come in?'

'Of course, you can come in, Jake. What are you on about? You have never knocked before.' Within seconds Jake was standing opposite Vance.

'I will always knock in future. Never know what I'll see if I come through that open back door unannounced.'

'What do you mean, Jake?' asked Vance curiously and surprised when Jake sat down and removed his shoes, then his trousers.

'I'm itchy, mate. Find me something to get rid of the bloody itch on my arse and legs, and I'll tell you why it is your fault I am in this condition.'

Vance went into the pharmacy and returned to the dispensary, where he handed Jake a bottle of methylated spirits.

'Rub this on your itchy parts. Might sting a little bit. Now tell me why it's my fault you have an itchy arse and legs.'

'It does bloody sting,' complained Jake as he rubbed the metho on his bottom and back of his legs.

'Well, I came through the back door, and there you were "at it" on the floor with some bird whom I've never seen before. Probably wouldn't recognise her if I ran into her again. All I saw was her back and her gorgeous arse,' continued Jake as he kept on rubbing. 'Anyway, I got out of here quickly. Thanks to you and her, I left here with a stiff prick.'

Vance could not control his laughter as Jake recounted his story while re-applying methylated spirits to his worst itchy parts.

'And here I bloody well am,' concluded Jake as he sat on a stool, picked up his trousers and examined them for tell-tale burrs.

'Give me a pair of tweezers,' demanded Jake. There are still a few of the bastards stuck in my pants,' that is, if you can stop effing laughing long enough to locate some.' Still laughing raucously, Vance went to find tweezers for Jake while trying hard to compose himself. Vance returned to the dispensary.

'Here, give me your trousers, Jake. The least I can do for you is pull a few burrs out of your dacks.'

'So you bloody well should,' replied a sulky Jake. 'Wish you had a bloody drink. A man feels like a bloody fool.' Vance burst once more into gales of laughter as he handed Jake his now burr-free trousers.

'Not as big a fool as you will feel when word of your escapade hits the local gossip grapevine, Jake.'

'Oh, shit,' moaned Jake as he pulled on his trousers, did up the zipper, and buckled his belt. 'I didn't think about that,' as he joined Vance in gales of laughter. 'Man may as well laugh at himself because every other bastard will be.'

'Take it from one who knows, Jake. In Brolga, if we do it, we wear it. Trick is just pretend we didn't do it,' laughed Vance.

'I really need a drink now,' said Jake. 'I don't feel like showing my face at the Empire. There's some booze at the girls' place. I put it there before they came back. Do you feel like going there?'

'Sure. I have to, anyway,' replied Vance as he jangled TC's shops keys in his hand. 'I have some fast talking to do. Apart from that, I definitely do not want to go to the Empire tonight.'

¶

As Vance and Jake departed via the back door of the pharmacy, the on-duty telephonist at Brolga telephone exchange was listening intently to a conversation between a nurse at the Brolga Hospital and a female friend in Brisbane. The telephonist held her hand firmly over her mouth to stifle her giggles until the call ended, then she immediately phoned Lou, who listened to the story with a smile on her face.

'Don't you think you think it's hilarious?' asked the telephonist.

'Serves Jake right. He should have chosen a better landing strip,' replied Lou.

'Think we'll have to call him "Jake Burry-Butt". I have to go now, Lou. Got calls lighting up the board,' said the laughing telephonist.

As Lou put down the telephone, she heard Jake's car pull into the driveway. TC emerged from the bathroom as Vance and Jake got out of Jake's car. TC had a pink towel wrapped around herself and another around her head to dry her wet, freshly shampooed hair. Lou stood on the landing.

'Put some clothes on, TC!' commanded Vance. TC said nothing. She was embarrassed by their presence.

'Bet you don't say that to your girlfriends, Vance,' quipped Lou.

'Like your little pink-bowed slippers, TC,' said Jake.

'You like TC's slippers, do you, Jake Burry-Butt?' snapped Lou before grinning sarcastically. Vance laughed as he looked towards Jake, who felt he had no option other than to laugh himself.

'News sure travels fast in Brolga,' smiled Lou as TC quickly brushed past en route to her bedroom.

'You two really take the cake. You rock up uninvited, then before even a "hello" you start on TC,' continued Lou as she sat down on the landing as if to bar their entrance into the house. Vance and Jake slumped down on the lower steps with their backs towards Lou.

'Anyway, TC and I have decided to return to Sydney,' lied Lou to their backs. 'Only difference between you two and those randy rock and rugby league stars is that you know we won't put up with it, so you don't pull any of your crap, as my dad calls it, on us. You just come to us when things go wrong for you and you need a place to hide out.' Vance looked over his shoulder at Lou.

'Are you really going back to Sydney?' Lou ignored him. Jake looked over his shoulder at Lou.

'Lou, Jake Burry-Butt needs a drink. Is it okay if I get one?'

'We threw your grog out,' lied Lou again with a smile.

'Lying little bugger,' said Jake as he immediately jumped to his feet, stepped over Lou, and made his way to the kitchen, where he sighed with relief to see the beer, rum, and Coke just as he had left it.

'I give up,' said Lou as Vance also stepped over her while heading towards Jake and the sound of tinkling ice cubes.

TC, dressed in blue jeans and a long-sleeved blouse, still with a towel wrapped around her head, came into the dining room carrying a small bag containing hair rollers along with a brush and comb.

'Will you roll my hair, Lou?' she called as she placed the bag on the dining room table.

'No problem,' replied Lou, who left the landing and joined TC, who was now seated at the table.

'Going somewhere, TC?' asked Jake. TC ignored him.

'I told you, Jake Burry-Butt, we are going back to Sydney,' said Lou as she ran the brush through TC's hair.

'Stop it, Lou! Stop calling me bloody Jake Burry-Butt,' snapped Jake furiously. 'I mean it, Lou! I'll have enough of that coming my way. Can't cough in this dead-end, shithouse town unless all bloody sundry knows about it.'

'What's wrong?' asked TC.

'Nothing!' replied Jake and Vance in unison.

'Tell you later, TC,' said Lou while pretending to whisper.

'You'd better bloody not tell her later,' said Jake furiously.

'Oh, shut up, Jake. Go get another drink, then phone Con and order in some food for dinner,' laughed Lou as she fastened the first roller in TC's hair.

'That means we can stay for a while?' asked Jake imitating a begging voice. TC rolled her eyes as Lou answered.

'Knowing you pair, we don't have a choice.' Jake and Vance sat down at the table.

'TC, you forgot your keys,' said Vance as he placed them on the table in front of TC. TC looked directly into Vance's eyes.

'No, Mr Callahan, I did not forget them. I left them there on purpose.'

'Don't tell me you have quit again, TC?' interjected Jake.

'Mind your own business, Jake,' said TC.

'Yes, Jake, mind your own business,' agreed Vance.

'Right, Jake. I have almost finished rolling TC's hair. Time to call Con,' said Lou.

'All right, all right. I'll phone and order. I'll pay for whatever you want, but I refuse to go into Con's café to pick it up.'

'Why?' asked Lou.

'Yes, why, Jake?' asked Vance with a smile.

'Because some of the bloody nurses might be there. That is why,' answered Jake seriously.

'You order and pay, Jake. I'll come with you and pick up the food while you wait outside,' said Lou.

'Deal,' replied Jake.

¶

The moment Jake and Lou left for Con's, Vance asked TC, 'Why did you leave your keys?' TC thought for a few seconds before answering.

'Because some things never change. I thought that you were happy that I came back. I thought you needed me to help you while you go opal mining. So far, all you seem to do is treat me like a door mat. You yelled at me the other day, then again the next. I do my best, but obviously my best is not good enough for you. I've done everything you've told me to do so far. No more! I made up my mind today that I am never going to sit on the Seat of Knowledge again while you entertain your girlfriends in the dispensary. Do you know how I feel when Mrs Callahan calls? I feel dreadful because I know you are either in the hotel or with one of your women. You disgusted me today when you couldn't make time to call your wife, then had all the time in the world for your new floozy when she showed up.'

'What if I don't bring women to the shop?' asked Vance.

'You don't bring them there. They simply show up. Whenever they appear, I have to quit whatever I am doing and disappear. Even if you do manage to quit the rum, even if you do manage to find opal, the procession of women will continue. No wonder Mrs Callahan leaves you repeatedly. I don't blame her. I feel so much pity for her, especially when she calls for you. I'm tired of making excuses for you. Lou is right—you are turning me into a liar. In reality you already have. Every time Mrs Callahan calls and I tell her I don't know where you are, it's a lie.'

Vance lit a cigarette before speaking.

'TC, you are right, of course. I'll never give up women. What if I tell them not to go near the pharmacy unless they want to buy something? Regarding Delores, I plan on being at the mine a lot of the time, so she won't be calling too often because she will know I'm out of town.' They heard Jake's car pull up in the driveway.

'Please think about it, TC. By the way, I am sorry for being a bastard to you sometimes,' concluded Vance before smiling broadly at Jake and Lou as they walked into the room. 'Something missing here tonight, Lou.'

'What's that, Vance?' asked Lou.

'Music. Put one of my Louis Armstrong records on, will you?'

'I'll do it, Boss,' said TC with a smile.

Thank God for that, thought Vance. She called me Boss; that means she's going to give me another chance.

¶

'Con said to give you this. He said an American man left it with him because the pharmacy was closed,' said Lou as she handed Vance an envelope, which he immediately opened, and then read the enclosed note.

Hello, Vance,

Your hill is done. Good men you have at you mine site. Amusing and hard-working. Left some gear there for further use. Your men know the ropes now. Don't forget, you owe me a date with TC and an opal for my mother.

Going on leave.

See you when I come back through Brolga.

Good Luck.

(Unable to read first name) Elliot (The Yank)

'What is it, mate?' enquired Jake as Vance reread the note.

'Well, I'll be buggered! The Americans have blown the hill for me,' replied Vance. 'What a day! Must have been hit by a rainbow. I'm going to be an opal miner!'

'Let's have a drink to celebrate,' suggested Jake.

'You have a drink for me, Jake. I have quit!' replied Vance matter-of-factly as he began eating his steak sandwich. 'Thank you for shouting dinner, Jake. This is my third meal today. I have not had three meals in one day for years.'

'Do you good. You are too thin,' said Lou.

'I agree, mate,' added Jake.

'Suppose you'll be going to the mine tomorrow?' asked TC.

'Sure will. The men will be wondering where the hell I am,' replied Vance. 'Don't know when I'll be back in town. Suppose it will be when Yappy needs supplies or something goes wrong,' replied Vance.

'Be positive, mate,' urged Jake. 'The ball is in your court. Go with it.'

§

'Drive me home, will you, Jake?' asked Vance when they had finished eating.

'I'll have to give the ute a hose-down by moonlight if I want to see through the windscreen in the morning.'

'I'll help you, mate,' offered Jake as they stood up to leave. Vance looked at Lou, then TC.

'Lou, help TC whenever you can? TC, thank you. When Delores calls, tell her I'm at the mine. You'll be telling her the truth.'

TC smiled, then said, 'Find opal, Boss. See you when you come back to town.' Both Lou and TC kissed Vance on the cheek.

'Where's mine?' asked Jake. Both girls ignored him.

'Please don't come back here tonight, Jake,' said TC.

'We are going to listen to Elvis, then go to bed to dream about him,' added Lou. Vance laughed at the expression on Jake's face as they went down the back stairs.

'Bloody Elvis. The bastard's on every woman's brain. A real man hasn't got a look-in,' mumbled Jake.

Vance asked Jake to stop outside the Empire so he could arrange with the garage owner to get fuel early next morning. The garage owner was sitting alone in his far corner of the bar when Vance approached him.

'Want a drink?' asked the garage owner.

'No, thanks, mate. I'm off it at the moment.'

'Heard that one before,' the man replied.

'I want to get an early start tomorrow morning, so I was hoping to get my ute and a couple of demijohns filled up with fuel,' said Vance.

'Sure, help yourself, Vance,' replied the garage owner as he removed a couple of keys from a bunch he had produced from his pocket. 'Just promise to bring them back to me before the pub closes.'

'Thanks, mate. See you soon,' said Vance as he took the keys and hurried out of the bar. 'Let's get out if here, Jake,' said Vance as he got into Jake's car and slammed the door.

'You look bloody awful, mate. Did you see a ghost?' asked Jake.

'Close, Jake,' replied Vance. 'Louise is on duty with Claudia. I know they saw me. How could they help it? I pretended not to see them.'

'Who the hell is Claudia?' enquired Jake.

'Claudia, my friend, is the naked body you saw on the dispensary floor with me.'

'Bloody hell, Vance! Talk about grease bloody lightning,' exclaimed Jake as he slammed his foot on the accelerator. 'A new woman with a beautiful body comes to Brolga, and you are at her before I so much as know she's here.'

'She's too old for you, Jake. Now, be a good boy and help me get my car fuelled.'

§

The new police constable, Graham Sandler, was driving the police car down the opposite side of Brolga Street when he saw and heard Jake take off in the other direction.

Wish I was on patrol in the city, he thought. I could book that smart-aleck mongrel. Can't touch him here in Brolga because, as the Sarge says, 'Leave the locals alone! Merge in with them! Only play policeman when and if necessary. Trouble is usually caused by people passing through. Shearers between sheds, drovers at the end of a contract, or fettlers on leave are the troublemakers. These people have been alienated from alcohol while working. Consequently, when they find themselves between jobs or on leave in a small town like Brolga, most of them welcome the fact that there is very little to do except get drunk.

'The Greeks love it. They pick up their pay. When they hit the bars, they are like brothers, laughing, patting each other on the shoulder, reliving good times which occurred wherever they have been. By the time the pubs close, their blurred minds are focused on every negative experience they have shared during the past weeks or months while living under each other's toes, so to say. This is when they start bear-rolling. And this is when we step in.'

All right for the sarge to tell me all that. I'm bored witless waiting for anything to happen here in Brolga, thought Graham, as he pulled up in front of the Majestic.

'No one here,' said Bert Romeo, who had just locked the doors to the bar. 'No one at the Brick, either. It's a quiet night.'

'All right. Good night, Mr Romeo. I'll go to the Empire,' replied Graham as he got back into his police car.

'Always something going on there, young fellow,' said Bert Romeo as he waved to the young constable. Constable Sandler pulled the police vehicle to a halt as Vance got out of his ute, which was parked directly ahead. Louise was abruptly watching for Vance to return with the garage-owner's keys. She began screaming at Vance the moment he appeared in the doorway to the bar.

'You bastard, Callahan. You have to have every effing woman who comes here to work with me? I hate you! Do you understand? I hate you!'

Vance, ignoring Louise, quickly handed the keys to the garage-owner, said 'Thank you, mate,' then left. Vance was in such a great hurry to leave that he almost knocked Graham off-balance as they passed each other on the small verandah.

'That's right, run!' continued Louise. 'I can't catch you to knock you out, you bastard, so I'll do the next best thing.' With that, she picked up a tray of used beer glasses and hurled it with all her might at Claudia while screaming, 'Wear this, Claudia Clap-infected.'

Jack Romeo was in the smoking room with shock written all over his face. The bar patrons were silent as glass after glass smashed to the floor. Claudia, whose head was dizzy, muttered, 'You effing bitch. I don't have the clap,' then fell to the floor.

Louise screamed, 'You mob of bastards can all go get f****d! Hope the effing clap-riddled bitch goes to hell,' as she ran out of the bar, then through the front door of the Empire, and down the street.

Jack Romeo stepped out of the smoking room and walked towards the young constable, who was on the other side of the bar.

'Sorry, Constable. Sometimes strange things happen here in Brolga.'

'I understand, Mr Romeo. Is that lady on the floor all right?'

'Does she really have the clap?' came a voice from the background.

'Everyone, please leave,' commanded Graham with a voice filled with as much authority as he could muster.

Con Kara and Bert Romeo came bustling in.

'Heard what happened. Can I help?' said Con.

'Has your new girl really got the clap?' asked Bert in a high-pitched voice unusual to him.

'Con, mate, you can help by getting out of here,' said Jack. 'But close and lock the doors, as usual. I do not know if this girl has the clap or not! All I know is that she is lying on the floor.'

'Think we had best get her to the hospital!' said Graham, who was now kneeling beside Claudia, touching her forehead. 'She's had one hell of a whack on the head from the front and probably a worse one on the back of her head when she hit the floor.'

'Please be quiet, all of you. I need to go to bed! I do not have any disease,' murmured Claudia. 'My head hurts!'

'We'll take you to hospital, anyway,' said Graham. 'Come on, let's get you to the car.'

'Take a long, bloody hike, Constable. I told you I want to go to bed,' said Claudia, this time in a loud, controlling tone of voice.

'Sounds as if you are telling me to rack off, Claudia,' said Graham.

'Spot on, Constable. Now you and my Greek employers have my permission to help me to my sleeping quarters.'

Jack went ahead to alert Jess, who took control once Bert and the constable arrived with Claudia.

'At last Brolga has a permanent doctor,' said Jess as she helped Claudia onto her bed. 'Would you like me to call him?'

'Maybe tomorrow. Thank you, Jess,' said Claudia feebly.

¶

Back in the office of the Empire, 'Do you think Claudia will want to press charges against Louise?' asked Constable Graham.

'Accidents happen, Constable,' replied Jack Romeo.

'Yes, Constable, accidents happen,' added Bert Romeo with a smile.

'I see. It's late. I understand. I think it's time for me to go to bed myself. Brolga is that sort of place. Goodnight, gentlemen.'

No wonder they call this joint the end of the line! thought Graham, as he walked out of the Empire. It is! That is why!

§

Of course, from their vantage point on the Seat of Knowledge, the town elders had witnessed the entire scenario.

'Some bloody things in Brolga never change,' said Jock to his mates as they dispersed in the direction of their homes. 'Great gossip for tomorrow!'

§

As Constable Graham Sandler drove to his quarters, Vance was trying to sleep but couldn't. He knew he was going to find opal. He was too excited to sleep.

§

Jake was rubbing metho on his itches for what seemed the millionth time in a few hours.

Screw women, he thought, if you land your arse in a patch of bindi–eyes.

§

Louise was contemplating suicide as she chain-smoked and considered the repercussions of the night's events when her husband returned to Brolga and heard about everything.

⁋

Delores was attempting to sleep in her mother's house in Brisbane. 'I wonder what Vance is doing? I hope he calls me soon.'

⁋

Doctor Jackson Pierce was wide awake, thinking, *I'm so damned lonely. What on earth have I gotten myself into?*

⁋

Lou was dreaming about meeting Elvis Presley somewhere in Memphis. TC was tossing and turning because hair rollers were digging into her head.

⁋

Neil, Faith, Little Joe, and Yappy were all having trouble sleeping. They were excited. That day, the loader blades had pushed out a few rocks. The blade had chipped a portion of the edge on one of them. The chip exposed veins of pink and blue colour. The men were all anxious for Vance to arrive at the camp. They knew this was the beginning of Vance's destiny.